CAUGHT IN A RUNDOWN

A Novel Introducing
Jewel Averick and Dee Sweet

LISA SAXTON

SCRIBNER

SCRIBNER
1230 Avenue of the Americas
New York, NY 10020

SCRIBNER and design are
trademarks of Simon & Schuster Inc.

Designed by Colin Joh
Set in New Caledonia

Manufactured in the United States of America

1 3 5 7 9 10 8 6 4 2

Library of Congress Cataloging-in-Publication Data
Saxton, Lisa.
Caught in a rundown : a novel introducing Jewel Averick and Dee Sweet /
Lisa Saxton.
p.   cm.
I. Title.
PS3569.A927C3   1997
813'.54—dc21   97-15592
CIP

ISBN 0-684-82967-3

This book is dedicated to:
(1) My parents, Yvonne Brookes-Saxton and Pete Saxton, and
(2) Anyone who buys it.

ACKNOWLEDGMENTS

I'd like to thank God for blessing me with the following (not to mention answering my persistent and somewhat self-serving prayers):

- A mom who insisted I had talent ever since she saw me dancing to the washing machine.
- A dad who taught me there's more to baseball than cute guys. Here's to a base-clearing triple!
- Four of the best and funniest friends: Thornette Johnson, Amy Ulness, Maria Buttaccio, and Sharon Moore.
- The West Coast Saxtons: David, Myrsalena, and Madelyn.
- An editor who gave me a chance: Susanne Kirk and her assistant, Elizabeth Barden.
- Friends who encouraged and/or supported this effort: J. Branhan, F. Cosby, J. Crispens, L. Davage, J. Hammonds, R. Harper, P. Johnson, L. Klepacki, W. Means, P. O'Meally, G. Roberts, M. Slezak, J. Ulness, C. Weston, E. Young, and J. Zoeller.
- And Jerry Bauer, photographer extraordinaire!

CONTENTS

CAUGHT
IN A
RUNDOWN

1ST INNING:
Reached on an Error

Jewel Averick stared at the old baseball glove that sat on her coffee table. *I'd like to kick the crap out of him.*

Held together with what looked like thin strips of rawhide and bubble gum, the leather eyesore rested delicately in a clear plastic case. She clenched her fist and slammed the case. *How dare he pay fifteen thousand dollars for this piece of garbage?*

The glove was not the real focus of Jewel's wrath. Russell Averick, star center fielder for the D.C. Diamonds, baseball zealot and avid memorabilia collector, was the true object of her frustration. Jewel calculated that this latest artifact was the zillionth glove in her husband's collection.

"Fifteen thousand!" she shouted into the vaulted ceiling of her four-thousand-square-foot Chevy Chase, Maryland, house. *That jerk could have bought something for me! But no! He had to spend it on this!* She kicked the plastic box, sending it off the table and seven feet across the living room. *I mean, whoever heard of Two-Mile McLemore? I've heard of Hank Aaron and Josh Gibson, but I've never heard of any black slugger named Two-Mile McLemore.* Jewel stomped into the den and slammed the newest addition to Russell's collection next to all the others that regally sat in a specially designed glass showcase. Taking in the countless bats, gloves, balls, shoes, jerseys, and caps, she wondered how anyone could be as selfish as her husband.

Legend has it Two-Mile McLemore only played one year with the Negro Leagues as a barnstormer in the late 1930s, primarily with a team called the D.C. Diamonds, a name the major leagues adopted when Washington was awarded a new team in the early eighties. Two-Mile was said to have hit a ball so hard and far . . . it traveled two miles. Many historians attribute his existence to the fanciful imagination of children and aging story-tellers—something along the lines of John Henry. There are a few, however, who believe Two-Mile actually walked the earth and was quite a force on the baseball diamond. Trouble is, they've never been able to prove his existence. It seems Two-Mile vanished. Disappeared. No records, no family, no trace.

"What the hell do you mean, you didn't get it?!"

Anthony Graves stared at the tips of his burgundy kid-leather shoes before daring to look at Duke "Quiet" Crammer's heavily bagged, bloodshot, and angry eyes. Anthony Graves knew he'd screwed up and prayed he'd right the situation . . . quickly. "I went to the wrong Hilton. I thought the auction was at the Washington Hilton. And by the time I got to the Capital Hilton, the glove had been sold."

"You stupid-ass moron! I'm too old for this shit. You two have disappointed me." Duke Crammer turned his stare on the bowed towhead of a hulking figure standing next to Graves. "Mr. Snow, what have you to say for yourself?"

Mr. Snow shrugged his shoulders. "I do what Anthony tells me, boss."

"You can't think for yourself?"

"No, boss."

Duke Crammer cursed, while Graves and Mr. Snow glanced apprehensively at each other.

"So, it was auctioned off? I don't suppose you idiots know who has it?" said Crammer.

"Russell Averick, the Diamonds' center fielder, bought it."

Duke Crammer raised his bushy gray eyebrows. "Is that right? That's one damn good ballplayer . . . a lot like Willie Mays.

Kid can do everything—you know, in a way, he kind of reminds me of Two-Mile McLemore. Now that's what they call irony." He paused, perhaps mentally comparing the players. "How much did Averick put out for that glove?"

"Fifteen big ones."

The old man let out a long whistle. "Well, do what you have to. I want that glove. And I want it now."

"Not to worry, boss," said a suddenly grinning Graves. "I've got a plan."

Crammer sighed. "I hope it involves bringing me Two-Mile McLemore's glove in the next twenty-four hours. I've waited a long time for this, and I'm not going to let some shithead ballplayer keep me from it . . . again—especially not a spoiled, overpaid one."

"Oh, Averick isn't going to be a problem, because I'm going to get his wife to give it to me."

Duke "Quiet" Crammer worked his craggy facial features into something close to a thoughtful smile. "Now, that's using your head, you half-wit."

Jewel jumped at the chiming sound of her doorbell. In the two and a half years Russell had been with the Diamonds, she could count on both hands how often family and friends had paid a visit. Actually, she could count on one hand how many friends she possessed; fact is, she really didn't have any. So who was at her door? Last time she checked, Russell had a key.

"Cindy, could you get that?" Of course, she could just as easily have answered the door herself, but she figured that's what Jacinta O'Hara was paid to do.

Contrary to her name, Jacinta O'Hara was neither of Spanish nor Irish descent. She was named after a flamenco dancer for whom her father had had a great infatuation, and she married a man named O'Hara. When Jewel had inquired about the olive-skinned, Asian-eyed, kinky-headed woman's origins, Mrs. O'Hara listed every country but Spain and Ireland.

Jewel knew Jacinta didn't like her, but being the housekeeper of a rich and famous baseball player made Jacinta somewhat of a celebrity in her Northeast D.C. circles. Now Jacinta cautiously opened the door.

"May I please speak with Mr. Russell Averick?" It was a strange voice, almost too high to be masculine.

"I'm afraid he ain't home right now."

"Is Mrs. Averick home?"

Jacinta gave the man the once-over. "Who's calling?"

Soon Jacinta trooped back into the den, where Jewel had been observing the proceedings. A man named Anthony Graves wanted to talk to Jewel about the glove Russell had bought at the auction.

If she hadn't been so ticked off about the glove in question, Jewel might not have been the least bit interested in seeing what this man wanted. But she was curious. *Has Russell been duped?* she wondered. *Is it a fake?* She practically ran to the front door.

The man was white, about her height, and looked to be in his early forties, judging by the graying temples and the lines on his face. He had little black eyes and no lips to speak of. Aside from his temples, his hair was dark brown and sort of greasy-looking. He wore worn jeans and a black jacket and tie over a burgundy shirt that matched his burgundy shoes.

"I'll get right to the point, ma'am. I'm here to see if you and your husband would be willing to part with Two-Mile McLemore's baseball glove," he began, showing some surprisingly white teeth behind his nonexistent lips.

"Part with?" She shook her head, knowing she should appear reluctant. "I'm afraid not, Mr. Graves. Russell is unnaturally attached to the thing."

Graves looked sorrowful. "My son will be so disappointed."

"Your son?"

"You see, Mrs. Averick, my twelve-year-old son, Anthony, Junior, is in the hospital with a rare blood disease, and his one

wish is to own any item belonging to Two-Mile McLemore, on account of there's a lot of people who say he didn't really exist."

"Yes, I've heard that." She hadn't, but felt like playing along with this man, who she instinctively knew was lying.

"I got to the Hilton too late, and the glove was already sold. But, I'll be honest with you, Mrs. Averick, I'm a desperate man. And I'm willing to give you twenty thousand dollars for it . . . for my kid."

Jewel jerked forward so quickly, her forehead banged into the screen door.

Graves lowered his eyes. "It's my life savings. But there's no sacrifice too great for my little boy."

"I understand, Mr. Graves," she mumbled, running everything through her head. "Now it's my turn to be honest with you; my husband has stepped out, so I'm not in a position to help you at this time."

"Are you sure, Mrs. Averick? I don't know how I'll be able to face my boy without that glove. And I know your husband is a kind man."

"Did you approach Russell about your son after the auction?"

"I tried, but he was hounded by autograph seekers and I think he tiptoed out a back door or something to get away from them."

That had to be a fib, thought Jewel. Russell wouldn't leave any such function without taking care of his fans. He loved the attention. Clearly, the man on the other side of the screen door just wanted to get his hands on Two-Mile's glove and was trying to run some corny con with a dying-child story. She thought about threatening to call the cops and shutting the door on his face. But then she thought of Russell hugging Two-Mile McLemore's glove instead of her . . . *Dammit, Russ! Why can't I ever come first?*

Jewel, too, donned a woeful expression. "Had he known about your son, Mr. Graves, I'm certain my husband would have wanted Anthony, Junior, to have Two-Mile's glove. *I* want him to have it!"

Graves flashed his pearlies. "That's very kind of you, Mrs. Averick."

Kindness has nothing to do with it, Mr. Slick. "Do you have the money now?"

"Yes, I brought cash." Graves allowed a little laugh. "Of course, I'm not in the habit of carrying that kind of money around, but I figured you wouldn't take a check."

Jewel smiled. *You figured correctly.* "I appreciate that, Mr. Graves. There are a lot of shysters out here, you know," she said, letting her voice drop with contrived disillusionment. "Still, it's not wise to carry that much money on you."

"Like I said, I'm a desperate man, ma'am."

So it appears. Jewel shifted her weight forward so her nose pressed against the screen. "I hope you don't think me too callous, Mr. Graves, but I'm sure you can understand my position when I ask to see the money . . . ."

Graves held up his hand, indicating Jewel need not say another word. He then reached inside his jacket pocket and extracted a wad of bills.

"Wait here!" She could hardly contain her delight as she made a beeline for the den.

Scanning the gloves in Russell's collection, she whispered the vital information on each one's accompanying engraved copper plate. "We've got a Ted 'Double Duty' Radcliffe . . . Leon Day . . . Leroy 'Satchel' Paige . . . James 'Cool Papa' Bell . . . William 'Judy' Johnson . . . Max Manning . . . James 'Cool Papa' Bell . . . Hello? Two Bells? I'm sure Russ doesn't need two."

As she delicately extracted and switched Bell's and Two-Mile's decades-old gloves from their protective cases, Jewel ran the name around in her head. *Cool Papa Bell? Is that the man Russ said could run fairly quickly?* Since she was pretty certain this Bell man existed—unlike the Two-Mile character—and since Russell had two of Bell's beastly gloves . . . *where's the real harm?* she reasoned, as only she could.

"I believe this will make your son happy, Mr. Graves," she announced, opening the door and thrusting the glove at his chest. When he reached for it, she snatched it back and eyed the cash. "Ah, ah, ah."

"Yes, of course." An all-too-eager Graves handed over the bills. But Jewel didn't pass along the glove. Instead, she shut the screen door and locked it again. "HEY!" cried the man with no money or glove.

"Just making sure it's all here, Mr. Graves," she explained as her quick hands counted two hundred C-notes faster than any high-tech bank machine. "It all seems to be in order. As promised, here's the glove for your son. I hope it helps in some way." *Maybe Russ won't even know it's gone,* she said silently, before reopening the door and handing Cool Papa Bell's glove to Graves.

Anthony Graves looked at it lovingly. "Thank you, Mrs. Averick, you're a kind woman. My best to your husband." He hustled back to his car.

When he had driven the black Buick out of sight, he looked into his rearview mirror. "I got it, Snow," he announced to the big man who was cramped from hiding in the backseat.

Snow groaned and snapped body parts as he straightened his giant six-foot-five, two-hundred-eighty-pound body. "That's great, Anthony. I knew you'd get it from her. Was she suspicious?"

"Are you kidding? She was like putty in my hands. I'm telling you, Snow, chicks always fall for that sick-kid crap. Women can be so stupid."

Jewel smiled to herself and waved the wad of bills under her nose as she closed the door. "Sucker. Men can be so stupid."

Jacinta O'Hara closed the living room curtains after watching the Buick drive off. She'd stayed out of sight, but heard the entire conversation between Mr. Graves and Jewel. A slow grin played across her face as she contemplated what Russell Averick's next wife would be like.

19

❀   ❀   ❀

Not again. Dear God, please tell me he's not at it again.

Dee Sweet felt an old familiar pain in the deepest recesses of her heart as she hung up the phone with a shaking hand. She collapsed in a nearby chair and closed her eyes, trying to shut out the images running through her head: images of her husband, Mark, throwing back drinks with a lusty, star-struck blonde; images of his whispering in the woman's ear; images of infidelity.

The images had been planted gleefully by Lucille Winship, a fellow Diamond wife and notorious gossip. It seemed Lucille had spotted Mark out on the town after yesterday's game.

Dee didn't go to the Sunday-afternoon game. She'd been to so many over the years, she believed she was beginning to suffer from baseball burnout. Instead, she'd stayed home and played with their three little children. She'd wanted to ask Lucille for more details, but her pride refused to let her. Sighing, Deanna Duffy Sweet did what she'd done for most of her thirty years; she turned the other cheek.

Lucille had called to ask what Dee was planning to do for that evening's dreaded charity talent show, featuring Diamond wives as well as other local sports-associated personalities. Lucille was co-chairing the show, and she knew very well that Dee was going to play the guitar while Jewel Averick played the piano and the manager's wife, Yvonne Sager, sang. So when Lucille let slip that she'd seen Mark cuddling some young thing in the corner of a Georgetown joint, it didn't take a Mensa member to figure out the reason for her call.

A six-year-old voice calling out from the playroom temporarily diverted Dee's attention. She went to check on her daughter Jessica. The redheaded moppet informed her that she no longer cared to referee her little brother, four-year-old Eric, and her two-year-old sister, Nina.

"What? Are these two outlaws giving you trouble, honey? I'll take care of them," said Dee, play-wrestling with her three darlings until they were giggling uncontrollably.

"Hey, hey, keep it down in here!" ordered an amused masculine voice from the doorway. Dee pried a chubby hand off her eyes and twisted around, with Eric clinging to her back, to focus on her husband.

"So you're finally up. Must have been some night." She hoped the edginess she felt stayed out of her voice. He nodded as his children joyously attacked him.

Dee fell back on the floor and looked at Mark's bloodshot eyes as he played. She'd been married to him for nine years, but she'd known him all her life, having grown up with him in a small Ohio town. The years had taken their toll on Mark. While he still was physically fit, standing a shade under six feet, his face was that of a man ten years his senior. The piercing blue eyes of the twenty-one-year-old she had married had paled with the rigors of living—and, more precisely, living it up. His once thick black hair had receded, leaving only a thinning peninsula on the top of his head.

"So, Duffy, what are you up to today?" he asked when they finally adjourned to the kitchen.

Dee wanted to ask him what he'd been up to last night after the game. He hadn't come home until one in the morning and he'd reeked of booze. She had sniffed for perfume when he tumbled heavily into bed, but detected none. She *wanted* to ask, but didn't. "I have to go over to the Sagers' to practice for tonight's talent show."

"Is that tonight?"

She nodded.

"Man, I forgot about that. You're playing, right?"

Another nod.

"Oh, Duffy, I hope you understand, but I won't be able to

21

come tonight . . . you know I wrenched my knee yesterday and need to stay off it all day. But McKnight is going to tape the show, so I'll eventually be able to watch you."

Dee took a deep breath and avoided eye contact. "There wasn't anything wrong with your knee last night; I hear you were out carousing."

The statement hung between them.

"Is that why you're upset? If you had come to the game, you'd have been *carousing,* as you put it, with me. But you don't want to be bothered coming out to support me anymore, now do you?"

This time Dee looked Mark square in the eye, preparing to tell him how much his behavior hurt. But she'd said all that years ago. "Since you'll be here, I guess there's no sense calling the sitter for tonight."

Mark Sweet, the D.C. Diamonds' second baseman, shrugged an indifferent shoulder in agreement. She knew their conversation had come to an uncomfortable end. Mark had never been good at communicating with her. Silently cursing him, she wished, yet again, that things were different between them. But Mark had traveled so far off the path, she wondered if they'd ever find their way back to the road of wedded bliss.

Jewel was scared. It had taken Russell all of thirty seconds to detect there was something amiss with his baseball shrine.

Exhibiting a practiced casualness, she had told him she'd put Two-Mile's glove with the others. She then strolled to the kitchen and listened to his frantic search efforts.

"JEWEL!"

She jumped, which effectively stopped her nervous knuckle-gnawing. For the first time in her life, she just might have stepped over the line. Instead of feeling vindicated, she was straight-up frightened. Why had she dismissed Cindy for the rest of the day? From the sound of Russell's voice, she needed that bountiful buffer. Her heart flip-flopped as it suddenly became clear that her brash action had been terribly ill-advised. Nevertheless, she marched purposefully into the den. *What's done is done, and there's no turning back. He'll just have to get over it.* "What is it, Russ?" she asked, giving a valiant impression of innocence.

"My Cool Papa Bell glove is missing. And someone put Two-Mile's glove in the case. *And* there's no sign of Two-Mile's case." His voice was dangerously low. "Cool Papa Bell's glove is gone. The fastest man to ever play the game. The glove he used when he played with the legendary Pittsburgh Crawfords of the thirties. And it's just up and disappeared!"

Jewel tried to ignore her husband's bug-eyed glare and the visible quake of his large frame. She sashayed over to the collection. "Well, here's a Cool Papa Bell glove," she said, pointing to the remaining one.

"There were two." Russell studied her face.

From his heartbroken expression, Jewel realized she hadn't camouflaged her guilt.

Sighing heavily, he asked, "What'd you do with it?"

Jewel Averick took the deepest breath of her thirty-two years. "Now, I don't want you getting bent out of shape. Promise you'll listen to the whole story?"

Russell sat down in his favorite chair and refocused his gaze on her. She knew she looked great in her jeans and white tank top. But, for the first time since he'd laid eyes on her, she had a feeling he wasn't the least bit impressed. "Go ahead, I'm listening."

"What about the getting-upset part?"

"Tell the damn story, Jewel."

She told the damn story, hoping she hit just the right note of heroism, then paused to gauge Russ's reaction. He just stared at her, his mouth agape.

There was an unbearable silence before Russell stood and walked slowly to his wife. She backed up a step or two. "You believed this man?"

"Sure, why not?" she lied.

"And you considered yourself performing an act of kindness?"

"Y-y-y-yes." It wasn't like her to stammer, but Russell's manner was so forbidding, she was sure he'd explode in the next minute. She didn't have to wait that long.

"I'M GOING TO WRING YOUR FRIGGIN' NECK!!"

Jewel squawked and moved to the other side of the room. "Russell! What's the matter?! Why are you acting like this?"

"YOU never performed a selfless act in your life! I don't believe you believed him! I believe you went behind my back and sold it to someone, to pay me back for buying Two-Mile's glove!"

"THAT'S NOT TRUE! I'D NEVER DO THAT!" she cried, denying the accuracy of his statement before returning her voice to a calming tenor. "Listen, Russ, it's true . . . some man named Anthony Graves came here and wanted to buy Two-Mile's glove. I gave him Bell's because you had two, so he could fulfill his kid's dying wish! And since he *thinks* it's Two-Mile's, I don't see the harm."

"YOU NEVER SEE THE HARM! YOU NEVER SEE ANYTHING BUT HOW THINGS AFFECT YOU!"

"Please stop yelling, Russ! It was just a stupid old glove."

Jewel could have sworn she saw his heart stop beating through his tight T-shirt. He was breathing so hard, she thought he might be having some kind of heart attack.

"How could I have ever thought of you as anything other than a spoiled brat? You don't give a damn about me, my things, or my feelings. All you care about is yourself. I've heard how the truth hurts—well, I'm in a lot of pain right now, baby. A whole helluva lot."

Jewel took tentative steps to stand by her husband and lightly touch his arm. "Please, Russell, don't . . ."

He shrank away from her touch. "Just tell me something, Jewel. Did you take this guy's money?"

She was about to shake her head, but one look at Russell's face showed he already knew the answer. Wringing the skin off her

24

hands, she studied the floor and uttered an almost inaudible affirmation.

Russell said nothing and began to walk out of the room, which he seemed to find confining. "I'm outta here."

If she hadn't opened her mouth, if she had just let him go, perhaps things would have been okay, but she demanded to know where he was going. She was in a panic. She'd never seen Russell so angry and distressed. However, the prideful Jewel Elizabeth Howard Averick had trouble with apologies, so she said what came naturally. "Don't go, Russ. Look, if it's the money that's got you so upset, you can have it."

He had the door open, but her statement stopped him as he turned a disbelieving eye on her and slammed it shut. "You just don't get it, do you, Jewel?"

"Get what?"

"The money isn't the issue here. It's the fact that you gave away something you knew was very important to me with no regard for my feelings. You saw dollar signs and cheated this man and screwed me for a lousy twenty grand we don't even need!"

She shifted her weight and poked out her bottom lip. "I don't know what you want me to say."

He shook his head in a defeated manner. "I don't expect you to say anything."

"So you're just going to leave it at that? You're going to walk out of here mad . . . for the *second* time today?"

"I'm going to go before I say something I'll regret."

Not usually one for physical confrontations, especially with someone twice her size, Jewel felt the need to force Russell into saying what he felt. If he had a serious problem with her, she wanted to know it. Goaded by an unknown spirit, she shoved Russell's broad shoulders, catching him off guard and sending him back a step. "No, don't go! Say it!" She shoved him again.

"Don't push me, Jewel."

She shoved him a third time. Russell grabbed his wife by her upper arms. "Okay, here it is," he said, his face only half an inch from hers. "I'm asking myself what in God's name I ever saw in you. I'm asking myself why I put up with your shit year after year."

He ignored her pained expression and the atypical tears that began to moisten her eyes. "You are nothing but a selfish, self-centered, greedy bitch! And right now, I'm ashamed to call you my wife. You're spoiled rotten and I don't know why I ever married you! You only married me because of the money I was making!" He suddenly let her go, sending her stumbling back half a dozen steps.

No one had ever dared talk to her like that. And although thoroughly stung, Jewel wasn't about to take the assault standing up. "Well, since you brought it up, ask yourself exactly why you married me in the first place, Russell!" His face contorted; she knew she'd struck a nerve. "God knows we hardly get to spend any time together. And when we do get a chance, like today, you have some damn sanitary sock to buy or you have to make a personal appearance."

Russell frowned as if trying to see an image clearly. "So *that's* what this is about? You sold the glove because you were mad I didn't go to the shore with you today?!"

She stuck out her chin, but said nothing.

"Are you that vengeful?" He was incredulous. "You're a real piece of work, Jewel. I cancel one thing with you—"

"One?! Ha!"

"You are so selfish—"

"And *you* care more about that stupid glove than me!"

Russell narrowed his eyes and stared at her before quietly admitting, "You know, sweetheart, at this moment, you're absolutely right."

Jewel gasped as her heart lurched erratically. But she was a fighter and refused to let that be the last word. "If that's the case, Russ, then tell me, *please,* why on earth did you marry me?!"

He was silent.

"What's the matter? Can't you face the truth about yourself? Can't you admit you married me because of how I look?"

"That's not—"

"DON'T you stand there and try to deny it! You only married me because I'd look good on your arm. I'm sure you said, 'I'm rich, I can get any girl I want.' You think I didn't hear all that malicious talk? 'He only married that bitch because she's light-skinned and long-haired . . .' Are they right, Russell?!" Jewel halted her raving to see him lower his shaking head. "You see, I *know* who and what I am; you're the one who hasn't been honest with yourself. Go ahead, tell me I'm wrong. I dare you."

"No, Jewel, that's what you want to think to excuse your behavior. You think you can treat people like shit and then claim they deserve it because they're shallow."

"Then why did you marry me and not your precious Carla Hunter, huh? You dumped her fast enough when I showed a little interest. Why don't you admit it: You got rid of her because she wasn't pretty enough for you!"

"THAT'S NOT TRUE!" He rushed over to close the gap between them. "AND YOU KNOW IT!"

"Do I?"

Russell didn't answer. He couldn't answer. He flew out of the house faster than he'd ever run from first to third on a single. Hot on his trail, Jewel yelled after him at the front door, "RUN-NING FROM THE TRUTH, RUSS?!"

Jewel stomped into the den and grabbed the cursed case containing the damned Two-Mile McLemore glove and slammed it to the floor. The protective case shattered in two, with the bottom falling a good three feet from where the top landed. She picked up the glove with an emotion she'd never felt before and slammed it hard once, twice, three times against the wall between jerseys that once belonged to Bob Gibson and Mickey Mantle.

She flinched as the glove broke open between the index and middle fingers. An old piece of yellowing paper escaped from the hole and fluttered to the floor. With vision blurred by tears, Jewel bent to pick up the mysterious scrap. This was the exact moment when she identified her newfound feelings.

As she delicately unfolded the paper, she acknowledged how cruel it was to realize you truly love someone just when you send him screaming out of your life.

#1
*TO FIND D.C.'S STAR DIAMOND, JUST FOLLOW
   THESE CLUES.
THEY'LL TAKE YOU ON A JOURNEY WHERE YOU
   MAY WIN OR LOSE.
YOU'VE MANAGED TO FIND CLUE #1 THAT I
   STUFFED IN MY OLD GLOVE,
NOW YOU MUST TRAVEL TO THE CITY OF BROTH-
   ERLY LOVE.
ONCE YOU ARE IN THE BIG TOWN GO TO WHERE
   TWO STEPHENS MEET.
IT'S CLOSE TO WHERE WE PLAYED BALL—YOU'RE
   LOOKING FOR A STREET.
HERE ASK AROUND FOR THOSE WHO KNOW A
   MAN NAMED HARRY B.
IF HE'S STILL KICKING HE'LL GIVE YOU THE NEXT
   CLUE IN YOUR SEARCH FOR ME.*

Mystified, Jewel sniffed and wiped her eyes for a better view of the neatly printed words. She read the note again. She was halfway through a third reading of the cryptic note when Dee Sweet called.

"Are you still coming over to Yvonne's to practice for the talent show tonight, Jewel?"

"Talent show?"

Dee sighed. "The charity talent show . . . you're playing the piano for Yvonne's solo. Remember?"

"It's tonight?"

"Yes. Isn't Russell going?"

"No, I don't think so," Jewel murmured. Russell was "going," all right—but away from her, not to any stupid talent show. "Ahh . . . listen, Dee, I'm afraid I won't be able to come tonight. I hope you understand." She could tell Dee didn't understand, but she didn't really care.

Exactly thirty seconds passed, then Jewel's phone rang again.

"Jewel Averick, this is Yvonne Sager. What's this I hear—you're not coming?"

Yvonne Sager was the wife of the Diamonds' manager, Pete Sager. Jewel knew she wouldn't be as easily disposed of as Dee Sweet. Yvonne viewed herself as sort of a den mother, having at least twenty years on all the other wives. She was always there to listen and give advice. And Jewel actually admired Yvonne Sager, because she didn't take any stuff from anyone and was impressed with . . . well, nothing. She was as unaffected and down-to-earth as they came. In fact, it was Yvonne who had insisted Jewel participate in the talent show, chiding her for not giving back to the community.

"That's right, Yvonne. I can't make it." Jewel took a deep breath and prayed that would be the end of it.

She prayed in vain.

"Are you sick?"

"Um . . . no." Jewel rolled her eyes to the ceiling.

"Other plans?"

"Um . . . no, not really." *Damn! Is she sending some kind of truth serum through the telephone?*

"Well, young lady, you said you'd play the piano and I expect you here in fifteen minutes. It's already going on five o'clock. We have to be at the theater at seven."

"But—"

"Jewel Averick, you gave your word. So there's really no room for 'buts' in this situation. See you in fifteen minutes." Yvonne hung up.

If Russell hadn't accused her of selfishness, Jewel might have ignored Yvonne's order, but she felt she had to prove she wasn't as bad as he claimed.

She looked at the note still clutched in her hand. This time her eyes caught sight of something they'd clearly overlooked during the first three passes. In the bottom right-hand corner was a very faint script that looked like capital letters. Holding the paper up under a light, they looked suspiciously like "T.M.M." *Two-Mile McLemore! Holy shit!* Two-Mile McLemore!

Jewel threw a black blazer over her tank top and bolted out of the house. Looking up and down the street, she willed Russell to come home. But after a minute of standing there looking silly, she realized he wouldn't be coming home anytime soon. She slowly walked back inside, wishing she could share her discovery with him.

Her house, while always quiet, had never felt so cold. She actually wrapped her arms around her chest to stop the shiver that racked her body. Looking around at her perfectly decorated dining and living rooms, she saw no life. The only room that radiated any warmth was the den . . . Russell's favorite room; his sanctuary.

And she had violated it. She'd taken away a piece of his comfort zone. Walking into the den, Jewel picked up the torn and tattered Two-Mile glove and gingerly placed it in the showcase. Then she did something that many had thought impossible . . . Jewel Elizabeth Howard Averick empathized with someone else's feelings. She knew she'd messed up, big time.

"I'll make it up to you, Russ, I swear," she whispered, folding Two-Mile's note and putting it inside her jacket pocket.

She hustled to gather her purse and keys. If she was going to figure out Two-Mile's riddle, she'd need help. And Yvonne Sager was a damn good place to start.

2 ND INNING:
Stepping into the Batter's Box

"Do you think she'll come?" Dee asked, gratefully accepting the soda pop Yvonne Sager offered.

"With that one, you never know. But from the sounds of it, I doubt it," said the gracious hostess, letting a most skeptical look play across her smooth chocolate-colored face. "I've seen many a prima donna in my thirty years as a major league baseball wife, but none can compare with Jewel Averick. If there was ever a child who needed to be spanked, it was Jewel."

Yvonne gazed at the young woman who nervously patted her guitar. "You, Deanna Sweet, on the other hand, are the exact opposite."

Dee recognized the sympathetic look on Yvonne's pleasant countenance. She knew most of the Diamond wives thought she was a wimp for putting up with Mark's escapades. But what could she do? Where could she go? After all, she had the kids to think about. She felt helpless. She felt trapped.

Most observers might say that Mark Sweet was lucky to have such a patient and forgiving wife. Having been drafted by the Diamonds when he was only eighteen, Mark had become one of the team's bona fide superstars and fan favorites. Unfortunately, he had also become a bit of a favorite with the ladies: as meticulous as he was on the field, he was as sloppy off. By the time Dee Sweet reached the tender age of twenty-five, she'd officially entered the category of "long-suffering." It was Yvonne Sager who had finally insisted her husband, Pete, have a talk with his young star about getting his act together, especially in this day of AIDS. It seemed to take. Or, at the very least, Mark Sweet had learned the art of discretion during the past four years.

"Dee, is something wrong?" Yvonne asked. "I've raised four daughters and I recognize the signs."

A demanding knock on the front door prevented a response. It was Jewel. "Listen, Yvonne, I have something very important to show you."

"Hello to you, too?" Yvonne fastened on to Jewel's arm and steered her into the living room.

Jewel frowned, seeing Dee. "Oh, hey, Dee. You're still here?"

Dee tried to keep her eyes from rolling at Jewel's salutation.

"Have a seat at the piano, Jewel. The sheet music is there."

"Okay, okay. In a minute. But I have to ask you if you've ever heard of Two-Mile McLemore?"

Yvonne's eyes sparkled. "Absolutely! I heard Russell bought a glove that supposedly belonged to him. He must be very excited about that."

"Did this guy really exist?"

"For everyone who's sworn he did, just as many have told me he's nothing more than a myth. It's kind of fascinating, actually."

"Well, get ready to be further fascinated. I think I have proof that he did exist."

"What's that? The glove?"

Jewel reached into her jacket pocket and carefully pulled out her discovery. "Nope, something that was hidden *inside* the glove." Yvonne tentatively took the note and scanned its contents. "Look closely at the initials at the bottom. See? It looks like T.M.M."

"How about that . . . I think you're right. It's some kind of riddle. Take a look at this," she said, turning to Dee.

While Dee read the note, Yvonne related all she knew about Two-Mile McLemore, which, sadly, was next to nothing. "Besides the home runs, the stories say he was adventurous and loved to play games. Perhaps he *did* write this, hoping to create some kind of scavenger hunt."

"That's what I was thinking!" said Jewel. "In Philadelphia, right?! What do you think he wants us to hunt?"

"Looks like he wants you to find him," said Dee, handing the note back to Jewel. "I wonder if he's still living. That note looks pretty old."

Jewel closed her eyes. "What would Russell think of me if I unearthed his precious Two-Mile? He'd have to look at me differently."

Dee and Yvonne stared at her with curiosity.

"Ah . . . what I mean is . . . I'm going to figure this out and find Two-Mile McLemore."

"That's wonderful, Jewel. I'd be happy to help you in any way," offered Yvonne. "I'm sure Pete would be able to help as well. And Gibby is a Negro Leagues scholar. He'd wet his pants for a chance to help find Two-Mile."

Somehow Yvonne's comments about involving her husband, Pete, and their youngest son, Gibson, seemed to douse Jewel's enthusiasm. Dee gazed at Jewel, attempting to read her mind. No doubt, if everyone got involved, then Jewel wouldn't get the credit. She'd be pushed to the background. And if there was an empirical truth about Jewel Averick, it was that she didn't like being pushed . . . by anyone . . . anywhere. She obviously wanted to keep her discovery to herself.

"Listen, Yvonne," said Jewel. "I'd appreciate any information you can provide, but I don't want anybody else to know about this note. At least, not now." She turned and looked at Dee Sweet. "Can we make a pact that it will go no further than the three of us?" Dee and Yvonne muttered their assurances. "Thanks. You see, I'm trying to do this for Russell and *I* want to be the one to find out if Two-Mile really existed; I don't want anyone else to beat me to it."

Dee tried not to let her doubt show on her face, but Jewel Averick doing something for someone other than Jewel Averick was highly unlikely.

"Do we have to start the hunt right away, or can we practice at least once before we go and make fools of ourselves?" Yvonne laughed, pushing Jewel toward the upright piano.

"Ahhh, why do we have to form this stupid jug band?" said Jewel, grudgingly plopping down behind the ivories and scanning the sheet music for "Stormy Weather" and "September Song."

"I've been waiting my whole life to croon these tunes," giggled the latter-day Lena Horne before offering to get Jewel something to drink.

Jewel was left alone with Dee, who was strumming a mellifluous moody tune. "That's pretty; what is it?" asked Jewel.

Dee's head shot up in surprise. Her face reddened. "Oh . . . nothing . . . I really don't know."

"Well, don't let me stop you."

"No, I think we'd better run through Yvonne's songs."

"Suit yourself." Jewel shrugged, but before turning back to the piano, she stared at Dee Sweet.

It was the first time in their slight acquaintanceship that she had actually looked at the woman—really looked at her. Had Dee's dark brown eyes always expressed such sadness? Did she always avoid eye contact with a shy lowering of the head? Was she embarrassed by her lovely guitar playing, or was she just naturally flushed? Not one to pay a lot of attention to the physical attributes of other women, Jewel discovered that Deanna Sweet was attractive in a plain, understated way. Her short auburn hair clung to her scalp like an old-fashioned ruffled bathing cap, setting off her oval face and fine features to perfection. Jewel wondered how Dee's nose, which appeared dead-set on being straight as an arrow, could turn up so drastically at its tip. And although Dee was about Jewel's height, she looked more voluptuous in her tan, unfitted suit. That's what comes from having a host of kids, she thought.

As Yvonne Sager returned with a pitcher of water, Jewel noticed that Yvonne's fifty-something svelte figure showed little sign of her six children. She guesstimated the elegant black tank dress the older woman wore was a size ten. There was a certain glowing charm about Yvonne Sager that Jewel had recognized and liked immediately. Her beautiful skin was flawless, and she wore her gray-streaked black hair in a very short style similar to Dee's, causing Jewel to reconsider her own flowing mane.

"So, are we ready?" Yvonne asked.

Dee was thankful for Yvonne's return. She had felt awkward under Jewel's assessing stare. She resented the woman's blatant appraisal, knowing she didn't measure up to Jewel's level of beauty—her light brown skin, sharply carved features, almond-shaped hazel eyes, and her curvy size-six figure. Dee was jealous of Jewel. Jealous of her looks, her moxie, and her seemingly faithful husband.

Yvonne took a deep breath to fill her lungs with air, as she began a rocky rendition of "Stormy Weather." "Was that as bad as I think?"

"Not at all," said Dee quietly.

Jewel snorted. "We're likely to get booed off the stage."

The women practiced poorly for the next half hour before deciding their performance wasn't likely to get any better. They were almost ready to leave for the show when Dee decided to check on her children. "Oh, Yvonne, may I use your phone? I just remembered I washed Mr. Wuv-voo today and he's still in the dryer. If Nina doesn't have her security blanket, Mark will never be able to get her to bed."

"Certainly, dear," Yvonne said, pointing to the nearest phone.

But Mark didn't answer. Marianne, the baby-sitter from next door, answered the phone, sending a surge of familiar pain through Dee's gut.

"Hi, Dee!" bubbled the seventeen-year-old Marianne. "I'm so glad you called. I can't find Mr. Wuv-voo for Nina. She's been screaming her head off for it."

"Umm . . . yes . . . that's why I called. He's in the dryer. If not there, check the laundry basket; it may be buried in that pile of clean clothes I never folded." Dee paused. "Mark isn't home?"

"No, he called me about a half hour ago and left as soon as I came over. Said he'd be back around ten or so."

Dee felt sick. *So much for his wrenched knee. He couldn't come out to see me in the talent show, but he had it in him to run the streets!* "Did he say where he was going?"

"No."

Before she had even hung up, she was crying.

"My Lord, dear, what's the matter? Are the kids okay?" asked Yvonne, wrapping her arms around Dee's heaving shoulders.

Shaking her head, Dee let out a foghornlike sound that actually caused Jewel to jump. "They're fine."

"Well, what is it, honey?" Yvonne led Dee back to the sofa and pushed her down gently, while Jewel huffed, crossed her arms, and rolled her eyes. Dee knew other people's problems never held much interest for Jewel.

"I'm . . . I'm . . . okay," Dee choked out. "I'll . . . b-b-be . . . f-fine."

"Are we going to this dumb-ass talent show or not?" Jewel demanded.

"Jewel! For heaven's sake!" snapped Yvonne. "Have some compassion. Can't you see Dee's in pain here?"

"You mean, can't you see she's upset because her husband isn't where he's supposed to be?"

Dee knew Yvonne had come to the same conclusion when the older woman squeezed her shoulder harder. "Do you want to talk about it?"

"She doesn't need to talk. She needs a good stiff drink!" said Jewel, clapping her hands.

It was Yvonne's immediate and forceful opinion that Dee needed no such thing.

"Sure she does; don't you?"

Dee frantically moved her sobbing head up and down in agreement.

"See, Yvonne, I know affairs of the heart."

Yvonne twisted her face in disbelief. "Please, spare me the fiction." And in a comforting voice only Dee could hear, she said, "Affairs of the heart, my eye . . . rumor has it Miss Jewel doesn't have a heart."

Dee stopped sobbing and giggled.

"Stop talking about me, Yvonne. That's rude," said Jewel. "Okay, well, *I* want a drink, how's that? I'm feeling like I need a shot or two to get me through this nonsense tonight. A little hooch sharpens my piano playing."

Yvonne waved a sanctioning hand toward the wet bar.

"Got any cranberry juice?"

"In the fridge."

Jewel proceeded to whip up a tumblerful of vodka and cranberry juice for herself and one for Dee. Yvonne declined to participate. Upon hearing Dee bravely attempt to hiccup an end to her tears, Jewel added a trifle more vodka to Dee's drink. "That ought to do the trick."

It did more than the trick—it did the whole damn show. Truth is, the concoction loosened Dee's tension in the most delightful way.

"May I borrow a thermos?" asked Jewel. "I'd like to take along some cranberry juice."

"What for?"

"Because I like it! And they might not have any at this shindig."

"Oh, all right. But hurry up," Yvonne said, removing a thermos from under the bar.

Jewel surreptitiously emptied the vodka bottle in the thermos, adding a drop or two of cranberry juice.

It would be a night to remember.

By the time the trio of modern-day vaudevillians was ready to take the stage, Dee Sweet was tanked to the back teeth.

Yvonne was concerned. "Dee, dear, are you going to be all right to perform?" While the younger woman was steady on her feet, she possessed a frighteningly vapid expression and the most ridiculous grin. She looked like some crazed circus clown who'd just received her walking papers.

"Sewer, Von, I'm fine." Dee threw her head back so far, it seemed to bounce off her shoulder blades. She just stared at the ceiling with her mouth agape.

Jewel, too, was feeling no pain, having had a swig or two or three of "cranberry juice." But, to her delight, Dee had polished off most of the thermos's contents.

"It's not funny, Jewel," snapped Yvonne.

"Of course it is. At least she's not crying. You should thank me for making her happy."

"I should hit you for making her soused."

"Well, if you had let us go on when we were scheduled to, she'd be in much better shape."

Yvonne had requested the last spot on the program, hoping to sober up Dee with some strong coffee. Unfortunately, Dee had refused the java—loudly. Not wanting to create a scene, Yvonne had hustled her back to her seat. And, for the most part, Dee and Jewel behaved themselves, clapping and whistling ferociously at the appropriate times.

"And now," barked Lucille Winship in her naturally nasal tones, "Mrs. Yvonne Sager, Mrs. Jewel Averick, and Mrs. Mark Sweet will perform for us."

Through her alcohol-filled mind, Dee caught the slight Lucille delivered, calling her 'Mrs. Mark' rather than 'Deanna,' as if her very existence was only justified because she was Mark Sweet's wife. Normally, she would have moped, but she had folks to entertain.

Jewel warmed up the crowd with a raucous, foot-tapping boogie-woogie number that left the audience clapping thunderously. Taking a deep breath, Yvonne cast a glance at Dee, who sat on a stool adjacent to the piano. Although precariously rocking back and forth, Dee seemed capable of plucking the strings. So, after Jewel chirped, "And a one . . . two . . . three," the ladies sailed smoothly through "Stormy Weather" and "September Song."

Yvonne rose to the occasion with a clear, rich voice that won the crowd's approval. Taking a deep breath, she grinned, bowed, curtsied, and then threw her arms out to acknowledge Jewel's and Dee's surprisingly adroit accompaniment.

Jewel stood, bowed, and headed off the stage, followed by a waving Yvonne. Dee, however, chose to totter to center stage and peer out into the audience. "Where's that Lucille Winnn-siiip?" she slurred, teetering forward.

Yvonne was nervous; Jewel was larklike happy. When Yvonne made a step to retrieve Dee, Jewel restrained her. "No, Yvonne, let her have her moment."

"She might say something stupid!"

"If we're lucky."

"Oh, Jewel, really," said Yvonne, pulling away from the younger woman's grip. But she was too late to stop Dee.

Nothing could have stopped Dee. She was determined to seek out Lucille as she stepped closer to the edge of the stage. "Where are you, L-u-u-lu-u . . . oh, there you are . . . right in font. Lu-lu? . . . that reminds me of a s-song. It goes . . . wait . . . how does it go?"

Yvonne joined Dee onstage and gently tugged on her arm. "I think we're through here, dear."

"NO!" bellowed Dee, jerking away so hard she almost fell off the stage, causing a collective gasp to fill the theater. "No, Von, I wanna sing 'bout Lu-lu. It goes to the tune of 'Good Night Lad-dies,' I sink."

Yvonne took tentative steps toward her young friend, trying, once again, to coerce her off the stage. But Dee had already started belting out her little melody. "Lu-lu had a boyfend . . . his name was Diamond Dick . . . she never got a diamond, but sure got plenty of BANG, BANG, Lu-lu . . . BANG, BANG AWAY!"

Dee Sweet's bawdy ballad was cut off as Yvonne—this time joined by a smirking Jewel—tackled the surprisingly strong Dee and semi-dragged her off the stage. Perhaps the whole thing wouldn't have caused such a stunned silence if Dee hadn't com-plemented each loud "BANG" with a pronounced pelvic thrust.

Followed by a mixture of disapproving and mirthful murmurs, Yvonne and Jewel hustled the slobbering Dee off the stage and out of the side-exit door, which put them in a narrow, floral-carpeted hallway. "Quick, this way," said Yvonne, spotting an out-of-the-way ladies' lounge.

"Wassa matter, Von? I wasn't through," giggled Dee just before Yvonne pushed her head down in a shell-shaped sink and splashed freezing water on her bright red face. "Hey!! Thas' cold!" she protested, jerking out of her captor's grasp and stum-bling blindly for a towel.

"Here ya go," offered Jewel, thrusting the rough brown paper in the sloshed woman's hands.

Whimpering, Dee Sweet wiped her dripping face. Then, as if remembering something of utmost importance, she abruptly stopped her frenzied movements and fixed Yvonne with a sur-prisingly reverent look. "You were wonderful!"

"You were better," said Jewel.

Yvonne grabbed Dee around her shoulders and steered her toward the lounge's exit. "Come on, dear. We better get you home."

"What 'bout my gui-[hiccup]-tar?"

Jewel reached for the instrument and handed it to her. "You guys go on."

"Aren't you coming?" Yvonne asked.

"I'm right behind you. I just want to use the facilities."

"Okay, we'll be in the car. I hope there's a rear exit to this place."

"Oh, hold your head up, Yvonne. If it wasn't for us, this thing would have been a joke."

"*Because of us* this thing—as you call it—*was* a joke."

"Oh yeah, like Meg Thibideaux's interpretive dance routine was artistic genius. She got more applause when she tripped over that carelessly placed cable."

Rolling her eyes with the practiced skill that comes with raising six children, Yvonne pushed Dee out of the lounge.

Jewel washed her hands, touched up her makeup, shook her hair out, and winked at her reflection in the mirror, as she silently congratulated herself for making the evening less of a bore.

Of course, the fact that she purposefully got Dee Sweet drunk and caused her great embarrassment never crossed her mind. The important thing was—Jewel got what she wanted.

Emerging from the ladies' room, Jewel hadn't taken two steps down the narrow corridor before a man materialized from nowhere, grabbed her arm, and roughly cornered her against the elegant green-and-gold wallpaper.

"Hey! What are you doing?" she shouted, before focusing her startled gaze on Anthony Graves. She cast an anxious eye past him only to discover she was alone with the obviously agitated man. "Mr. Graves! You really shouldn't sneak up on people like that. What are you doing here anyway?" she asked, trying to reestablish a normal heartbeat.

"Sorry I frightened you, ma'am."

Jewel knew Graves didn't have lips, but now his eyes, too, disappeared behind a most menacingly squinty glare. "Mrs. Averick, I'm afraid there's been a mistake."

Jewel swallowed a nervous lump that had gathered in her throat. "Mistake?"

"Yes. It seems that wasn't Two-Mile McLemore's glove you sold me this afternoon."

"It wasn't?"

Anthony Graves opened his mouth, then closed it.

"Well, I don't know what to tell you, Mr. Graves. The case it was in said 'Two-Mile McLemore.'" Jewel succeeded in wrenching herself from his uncomfortable grip. "And besides, I'm sure your *son* won't know the difference." She raised an eyebrow for two-can-play-this-game emphasis. "Now, if you'll excuse me, my friends are waiting, and I'm sure they're wondering what's keeping me."

Graves grabbed both her upper arms and forced her back against the wall. "Look, lady, I'm not playing games. You either give me Two-Mile McLemore's glove, or else . . ."

The man was so close, Jewel not only felt his hot breath on her face, but a few drops of spittle as well—which, needless to say, did not go over well with Mrs. Russell Averick, who most certainly didn't take kindly to threats. She vowed then and there that this man *was not* going to get the glove. Any apprehension she had felt earlier evaporated as she straightened and practically put her nose on his. "Look, Mr. Graves, or whoever you are, I'm telling you that's Two-Mile's glove. And if you don't step aside this instant, I'm going to scream down the joint."

He didn't step aside. Instead, he issued a sharp little shake to the slender Averick frame. "I *paid* for Two-Mile's glove!" His hiss was low and husky, with unconcealed frustration.

Certain she had the upper hand—not to mention a riddle that was apparently more valuable than she'd ever imagined—Jewel smiled slyly. "You paid for Two-Mile's glove and that's exactly what you got . . . you can't prove it isn't." (She didn't know this for a fact, but threw it out there anyway.) "But, to show you I'm willing to bend, I'll be happy to send you your money back, if you'll just give me your address . . ."

Graves immediately released her and took a tentative step backward. "Uh . . . that won't be necessary, Mrs. Averick. I just want you to give me the right glove, or—"

"I know, I know . . . 'or else.' Or else what, Mr. Graves?"

"Don't mess with me, lady. I'm going to get that glove one way or another."

"And I'm sure my husband and the police will be most interested to hear that."

Now it was Graves's turn to sport a sly smile. "Hear what?"

Jewel let out an exaggerated sigh. "I'm tiring of you, Mr. Graves. For the last time, you have Two-Mile's glove. What makes you think you don't?"

"Ohhh . . . Jewely . . . there you are!" Dee Sweet, still several sheets to the wind, sang out just shy of a shout. "We bin lookin' faw ya." Dee turned a cheery eye on Graves. "Oh, hello, Misser."

Jewel tried to hide her glee behind a skillfully manicured hand. The sight of the normally docile Deanna Sweet so out of control was too scrumptious. However, what came tumbling out of Dee's sweet mouth next effectively wiped the smirk off her face. "Hey! I bin thinkin' 'bout za riddle you found in old Two-My's mitt. I think I know—"

"DEE!!" Jewel cried in a shrill pitch, shoving Graves out of the way. "We should be leaving now!"

Anthony Graves let her go. He'd found out what he needed to know, thanks to Averick's drunken buddy. "Yes, you run along, Mrs. Averick . . . I'll be in touch."

It hurts to think. Deanna Sweet was content to lie very, *very* still underneath the comforting covers of her king-size bed. For half an hour, she'd stared at the ceiling, listening to the far-off laughter of her children, which, she thought thankfully, indicated she hadn't died. She could tell it was well past noon by the summer light streaming through her west-facing window. *Okay, this is good . . . if I don't move from this spot, the pain in my head will eventually go away. Of course, that could take weeks, but I'm willing to tough it out. I'll have Mark call Mom to come and look after the kids.*

She was just snuggling deeper into the bedding and closing her eyes when a husky "Well, well, well . . ." sounded above her aching head. "If it isn't the life of the party." Her body tilted ever so slightly from the weight of her husband sitting down on her side of the bed.

On any other occasion she might have withered under Mark's disapproving look. But, though she had blocked out much of the previous night's exploits, one reality remained indelible: Mark had said he'd be home, but he had sneaked out after she'd left. She rolled over to give him the best of her back and avoid further eye contact. "So you heard?" she mumbled into her down-filled pillow.

"I heard, the neighbors heard, and after reading this story"— Mark paused to make a production of rattling the newspaper—"the whole country's heard. I won't bore you with the details—after all, you were there—but let me just read you this: '. . . however, it was an allegedly inebriated Dee Sweet, wife of Diamonds shortstop Mark Sweet, who literally stopped the show with a salty ditty about the questionable mating habits of a woman named Lu-Lu . . .' Need I go on?"

Mark waited for an explanation, but Dee murmured something about yellow journalism and defamation of character, which brought a wry smile to his face. Sitting quietly next to her, he tentatively placed his hand on the spread where it draped her hip, and gently shook her. "Duffy?"

Her barely audible "Sorry" infuriated him. Mark jumped up from the bed and began to pace. "Don't apologize to me, Duffy.

Apologize to Mrs. Jensen next door. Last night, when Yvonne and Jewel Averick poured you on the front porch, you called her a 'gawking nebshit'!"

"NO!" Dee bolted upright and immediately regretted her action as her head began to throb. "I didn't!"

"Oh, I'm afraid you did. And while you're at it, apologize to your kids for waking them from their dreams and insisting on telling them how you *won* a talent competition. I mean, seeing their mother rocked with the right stuff and cussing up a storm, who knows what kind of therapy they'll need?"

"Mark! Stop it!" Dee hid her red face behind shaking hands. *What have I done? What did I say?* "Is there anything else?"

"That about covers it. That is unless you want to review the video of your performance. Andy McKnight was kind enough to rush it over here at the crack of dawn."

Dee fell back against the pillows and moaned, while her husband let out a dramatic sigh. "I'll be the laughingstock of the clubhouse."

You don't need my help for that. And if I was still liquored up, I'm sure I'd say it out loud.

Mark slammed the newspaper on the bed. "What happened, Duf? Why would you get ripped for a charity event?"

Ashamed and humiliated as snippets of the talent show came back, Dee started to get teary-eyed. Then she remembered what had led her to drink excessively. "And just where were *you* last night?"

Dee could tell by the way he looked to the ceiling and twisted his mouth that he was ready to tell a lie.

"Don't bother denying it," she snapped. "I called here last night and Marianne answered the phone."

"What? Were you checking up on me?"

Dee threw the covers aside and crawled across the bed to where her husband stood seething. "No, Mark, I wasn't checking up on you!"

He shook his head in disbelief. "You just can't trust me, can you?"

"I trusted you once and look where that got me."

"I've told you time and time again, all that's behind me."

"Yeah, right." Dee stood up and wrapped her arms around her underwear-clad body. "Then where were you? Why'd you tell me you had to stay home because of your knee?"

This time he didn't look toward the ceiling; he only stared at her as if deciding whether to blab a first-class lie or one of the simpler, third-class variety. "It's a surprise."

"What? Really, Mark, you're pathetic!"

He grabbed her as she tried to fly by him into the bathroom. "What does it matter, Duffy? If you want to believe I was out screwing other women . . . fine . . . we'll have it your way. I was out screwing other women." He released her arm and tried not to notice the hurt flash across her face. "There, happy now?"

For years, Mark Sweet had endured base runner after base runner barreling into him as he tried to complete a double play. But nothing had prepared him for the force of the open-hand blow Dee delivered to his cheek as they stood in their sun-drenched bedroom that afternoon. Any pain the slap may have caused was immediately superseded by her hysterical "I HATE YOU! I MEAN IT! I HATE YOU!" just before she slammed the bathroom door in his face.

"He wants us to go to Philly, right?" Jewel anxiously watched Gibson "Gibby" Sager as he painstakingly read and reread each word of Two-Mile's clue. The fifteen-year-old's tongue poked out from the corner of his mouth and he clapped his knees together at a twenty-beat-per-second pace.

"I think this may be too much for Gibby," said a grinning Yvonne Sager, who leaned across the table to pat her son's shoulder. From the moment she'd taken him aside and whispered about the note, he'd oscillated between a state of catatonic shock

47

and hysterical hyperactivity. Jewel had grudgingly let the young-ster in on the secret when it became clear they needed his expert help to solve the clue. She and Yvonne just weren't cutting it.

As a stripling in the throes of adolescent change, Gibby was only slightly on the wrong side of pudgy, having thinned out con-siderably from his "fat kid" younger days. Nevertheless, there was heartthrob potential, as evidenced by his edible-looking cocoa-colored skin, curly black hair, sparkling eyes, winning smile—and a deep dimple in his left cheek.

Jewel couldn't believe how much Gibby had grown during the two years she'd known him. She used to tower over the kid; now he had at least an inch on her.

Gibson Sager was the envy of all his high school chums for obvious reasons: (1) he was the son of a major league manager; (2) he was able to rub elbows with superstars; (3) his family had more money than most; and (4) girls feigned amorous interest due to numbers one through three.

Still, Gibby was far from content. He was neither athletically nor academically inclined—two things his father demanded from his sons. Gibby struggled for Cs in school, and if he was permitted to play on any team, it was because of his father.

Conversely, Gibby's nineteen-year-old brother, Dave Sager, was busy making Pops proud, dazzling the college world with his 89-miles-per-hour fastball and his knowledge of the physics involved with trying to hit it. Dave was certainly a hard act to fol-low, and Gibby gave up trying when he was twelve.

But there was one thing he never gave up on, he never stopped begging for. And that was to be a batboy for the D.C. Diamonds. Gibby was a fervid fan of the game, much like his favorite player, Russell Averick. His father, however, informed his youngest that unless he brought his grades up to Bs, he wouldn't be able to don the uniform—a fact that tore at the youngster's heart every time he had to pay attention while some boring teacher droned on about impossible mathematics or how to diagram a damn sentence. He wanted to learn about baseball only in order to reach his goal of becoming a premier sportscaster. His mother was sure he'd fulfill that dream and told him so regularly. His father agreed, but never said a word.

"So, Gibson? What's it mean?" asked Jewel, slowly pulling the note away from the teenager's clutches. She was afraid he'd drool on it.

Gibby looked at Jewel and his fifteen-year-old hormones began to course. "I don't know, Mrs. Averick. It could be a hoax."

"You're right; it may not have been written by Two-Mile McLemore, but I still want to find out who wrote this and why. So, what's it mean, kid?"

Gibby wrenched his gaze off Jewel and returned it to the clue. "Well, the Negro Leagues' Philadelphia team in the late thirties was the Philadelphia Stars; so he's probably telling us to go where the Stars played baseball."

Jewel and Yvonne exchanged excited looks. "And where was that, Gibby?"

"I don't know, but I can find out easily enough. I'll just go upstairs and look through my books."

Gibby disappeared up the stairs just as the Sager doorbell rang. It was Dee Sweet and her three children.

"Where's Gibby, Mrs. Sager?" asked Jessica Sweet as she and her younger siblings began jumping up and down with zealous anticipation. They loved climbing all over Gibby, who happily let them.

"Upstairs in his room, sweetie . . ." She'd barely gotten the sentence out before three sets of sturdy legs ran over her and up the stairs.

Accompanied by the overhead sound of one teenager being ambushed by a trio of Sweets, Yvonne led Dee back toward the kitchen.

"I wanted to thank you for taking care of me last night," Dee said, "and apologize for any embarrassment I may have caused. I don't know what came over me."

"Alcohol will uninhibit the best of us, Dee." Yvonne paused. "You know, if I were you, the next time I saw Jewel Averick, I'd punch her right in the nose."

"I should." Dee allowed a tiny laugh, then immediately regretted it as she walked into the kitchen and came face-to-face with Jewel. She'd seen Jewel's Lexus parked in Yvonne's driveway, but assumed it was still there from last night.

"Take your best shot, Sweet," offered Jewel, smiling graciously.

"Sorry, Jewel."

"Don't apologize." *Will someone please give this girl a backbone.*

Dee sat down wearily. She'd wanted to talk to Yvonne about Mark, but she certainly couldn't do it with Jewel Averick hanging around. The day was going from bad to worse. "What brings you here, Jewel?"

"I came over to let Gibby look at Two-Mile's clue."

"Oh! What did he say?"

"He's figuring it out now." Jewel looked at Dee. "Last night, you said you figured out the clue. Do you remember?"

Dee reddened. "I said a lot of things I don't remember."

"Well, here, look at it again; maybe it'll come to you." Jewel slid the old piece of paper to Dee, who, after several seconds, shrugged and suggested it had something to do with Philadelphia.

"No kidding. You're no help."

Jewel saw Dee's clenched fist and was afraid the woman might actually deliver the punch Yvonne had recommended.

Gibby came tearing into the kitchen with Jessica on his back, Nina on his hip, and Eric clinging to his leg. "I've got it! I've got it!" he cried.

"Gibson! You figured it out?!"

"Sort of. According to a couple of my books, the Stars played in a stadium called Penmar Park off of Girard Street in Philadelphia."

"That's wonderful, honey!" said Yvonne.

"And what about the two Stephens?" asked Jewel.

Gibby shrugged. "Beats me. But, according to the riddle, all we need to do is find where on Girard Street they played. There's still other books I have to go through; don't worry, I'll figure it out."

Jewel slapped her thighs. "Okay, then. Tomorrow I'm off to Philadelphia."

"WHAT?!" came a chorus of adult voices, followed by mimicking juvenile ones.

"Can't you people hear? I said I'm going to Philadelphia and ask around for Harry B."

"Can I go, too?" begged Gibby.

Jewel smiled at the young man and was going to say yes, but something in her hesitated as she remembered Anthony Graves. She hadn't told anyone about Graves's threats. To Gibby, the hunt might look like an innocent little adventure, but she knew there was more to it than that. She couldn't take a kid. Then, again, he knew all about this baseball crap and she could use a navigator of sorts. Still, what would Russell say if something happened to his "little buddy," Gibby? He'd never forgive her.

"I'm afraid you can't go, Gibson."

"What?! Why not? Can't I go, Mom?"

"Sure, sweetie, if Jewel says it's okay."

"Please, Mrs. Averick . . . ?" whined the kid.

"No."

"Thanks for nothing . . . see if I help you again."

Realizing she needed Gibson on her side, Jewel asked to speak with him privately. He led her to the family room, where he petulantly turned on the ball game. Jewel quickly scanned the tube, anxious to catch a glimpse of her husband, whom she hadn't seen since he stormed out of the house. The Diamonds were batting, but number 42 was not at the plate, so she returned her attention to the young man pouting on the black leather sofa. "Listen, Gibson, I'm not trying to be mean," she began honestly. "I just don't think I should be taking a kid along at this time. But I still need your help. Clue number one certainly indicated there will be more."

"Why should I help you?"

"Because I'm asking you to." When he remained noticeably unmoved, she added, "Isn't there anything—other than going to Philadelphia—I can do to make it up to you?"

Gibby's eyes caught fire and a broad grin spread across his face. "I've been waiting to hear those words for two years."

"Within reason," Jewel amended.

"Could you somehow get my dad to let me be a batboy? You're his best player's wife; I'm sure you could." Gibby did a little knee-lifting dance.

"That's it? You want to be a batboy?" Jewel was incredulous. "Your father's the manager and he won't let you be the stupid batboy? Haven't you ever asked Russ to help you?"

"Many, many times, but Dad won't budge."

"What makes you think he'll budge for me?"

" 'Cause I heard you always get your way."

Jewel appreciated the kid's honesty, but it burned the open wound Russell had left on her conscience.

"So you'll help me?"

"Of course I'll help you. If you want to be the batboy, you'll be the batboy."

"Promise?"

"Yeah, yeah, yeah . . . whatever . . . I promise."

"How are you going to do it?"

"Just leave that to me." Jewel had no idea and no intention of worrying about Gibson and his batboy hopes. She had more pressing matters at hand. "All you have to do is figure out where in Philadelphia I'm going, and you'll be the next great Diamond batboy."

"Just keep the kids away from me and I'll have your answer before you leave," said the joyous man-child, heading for his bedroom.

Two seconds later Dee Sweet popped into the family room with her kids. "We're leaving, Jewel. I wanted to say good-bye."

"Daddy! Daddy! Daddy!" hollered Nina, running over to plaster her face on the mammoth TV. Against her will, Dee peeked at the screen and discovered that Mark wasn't on the screen. But every time Nina saw a baseball player on the tube, she assumed it was her father.

"Come on, kids. It's time to go."

"No, Mommy, look . . . Daddy's up now," announced Jessica, running over to plop down in front of the set. The six-year-old was correct. Dee tried to hang on to Eric's hand, but he bolted to join his sisters on the floor.

"Strike out!" said Dee just before Mark Sweet's well-hit ball sailed on a beautiful arc into the upper deck of the Diamonds' stadium. Led by Jessica, the kids went wild. Dee watched Mark slowly circle the bases and then head toward the dugout, where his teammates gathered to high-five and butt-pat him to death. The camera zoomed in on Mark's face—he looked ecstatic, his joy was apparent, not a care in the world.

Dee succumbed to her misery. "Oh, why couldn't he have struck out?" she sniffed, focusing her red eyes on Jewel. "I would have taken it as a sign that our fight somehow affected him."

"Fight?" Jewel took a step away from Dee, certain the white woman was about to wig out.

"Who am I kidding? Even if he had struck out, it would have been because he simply missed the stupid ball."

Jewel was heading out of the room to corral Yvonne, who she assumed would be much better equipped to handle the hysterical Dee Sweet. But Dee's strident wail stopped her. "Lucille Winship was right; I *am* Mrs. Mark Sweet. When I was Dee Duffy I was more independent. I've become the pathetic marionette to Mark's master puppeteering. If I'm happy, it's because Mark makes me so. If I'm unhappy, it's because Mark makes me so. If I'm mad, it's because Mark makes me mad . . ."

"Look, Dee, I really don't—"

"Well, dammit, no more! I'm going to do something for me— something Mark has nothing to do with!"

"Good for you. I suggest a full body wax."

Wiping away her runaway tears, Dee fixed Jewel with a determined stare. "If you're really going to go to Philly tomorrow, I'd like to join you."

"Pardon me?"

"I said I'd like to go with you to find Two-Mile."

Jewel had turned toward the television, where she was soaking in the sight of Russell's fine body in the batter's box. *I know you don't think I care, but I'm glad you're alive and well. Hit a homer for me, Russ.* He promptly struck out.

"Did you hear what I said? I want to go with you."

"No way."

"I want to go."

"Why?"

"Because I'm interested, and I want to solve this thing, too."

"No way."

"Why not?"

" 'Cause you'll mess everything up. Look at you now; you're a basket case. And don't get me started on what happened last night."

Dee was confused. "What'd I do last night?"

"Nothing."

"Look, Jewel, I know you don't want word of your find to get around. Either I go with you, or I'll tell everyone, starting with the town crier, Lucille Winship."

"You wouldn't dare."

"Don't try me, Jewel. At this point, I'd like to make someone sorry. It can either be you or somebody else. You decide."

The two women stared at each other, while the game blared behind them. Finally, Jewel said, "Okay," through clenched teeth. "But we'll take your car. Heaven knows where we'll end up and I don't want anyone to mess with mine."

"Fine, we'll take the Volvo. It's Mark's car."

Gibby reappeared and announced that one of his books said Penmar was located on Girard and Forty-fourth. "And, get this: This other book said Penmar was near the *Stephen* Smith Home for Aged and Infirmed Colored People!"

"That's one Stephen!" cried Jewel.

Dee walked to a set of librarylike encyclopedias on a nearby bookshelf. She pulled out a volume and quickly began to flip the pages, as Jewel and Gibby filled in Yvonne, who had joined them in the family room.

"AHA!" Dee slapped the book closed. "Apparently, Girard was the name of a prominent Philadelphian in the old days. And guess what his first name was—"

"NOT STEPHEN?!" shouted Jewel.

Dee smiled and nodded, before they all began to prance around in a circle.

It was Jewel who finally broke away to demand everyone's attention. "Okay, look, people. I can't say how important it is to me that we don't tell *anyone* about this. Not Pete. Not Mark. Not anyone. If word gets around that we're tracking down this Two-Mile character, we'll be the last to find him." Everyone nodded in agreement. "So, I want everybody to swear they're not going to say a word to anyone. I mean it—cross your heart, hope to die, stick a needle in your eye, and all that . . ."

"Really, Jewel, there's no need for theatrics; we're not children," said Yvonne.

All adult eyes turned to the three Sweet children, who were

playing leapfrog and giggling uncontrollably, oblivious to the concerned adult expressions. Dee could only shrug. "I'll try my best to keep them quiet. But I think we're safe; I'm taking them to my mother's in Annapolis tonight, since I'm going out of town tomorrow."

"You're going out of town?" asked a clueless Yvonne.

"Yes; I'm going with Jewel."

Yvonne looked from one to the other. "You two?"

The women nodded reluctantly.

"And not Gibby—after he helped you solve the clue?"

Sporting a broad grin, Gibson threw Jewel a mischievous wink. "That's okay, Mom. Mrs. Averick is going to reward me in another way."

"I'm not touching that one," remarked a dubious Yvonne.

"Well, I better be moving out if I'm going to get the kids packed and off to Mom's," said Dee, looking more animated than she'd been in years.

Jewel followed her out. As she watched Dee strap Nina in a car seat and make sure her other two kids were buckled up for safety, something made her want to tell Dee the truth, or something very close to the truth.

"Dee . . . there's something you should know . . ."

"What should I know?"

"There's a man who's also after Two-Mile's clue and, therefore, I guess after the same thing we're after."

"What man?"

"I don't know, some character named Anthony Graves. You probably don't recall meeting him last night, but he showed up at the theater after that so-called talent show. He threatened me for the clue."

"Threatened you? Are you scared of him?"

Jewel took a deep breath and answered truthfully, "No, not

really. I just thought you should know, in case you wanted to back down . . . I mean, with your kids and everything . . ." Jewel's voice trailed off as she bowed her head and kicked at a nonexistent pebble.

After a tense, extended silence, Dee firmly said, "You know, Jewel, if you hadn't used the words 'back down,' I probably would have begged out of this little outing. But I've done enough backing down. I told you I was in the mood to make someone sorry. If he's smart, Anthony Graves won't mess with us."

Jewel focused her gaze on Dee Sweet. Everything about her seemed different. Her tone was confident, her posture was ramrod straight, and her attitude was bad. She certainly did not resemble the woman who was determined to live up to her last name.

Anthony Graves chomped nervously on his bottom lip before clearing his throat. "The Averick woman found the clue, Duke." He attempted to sound matter-of-fact and self-assured. "And it appears she doesn't want to cooperate with us."

Duke "Quiet" Crammer ran his chilling stare over the man sitting across from him, realizing that if Anthony Graves weren't his third cousin, he would have dismissed him long ago. But these days, even bad help was hard to come by. And at the present time, Graves and Mr. Snow were all the trustworthy help he had. "Well, you're going to have to get her to cooperate."

"I realize that, Duke. And I have a plan."

Duke Crammer let out a harsh sound that may have been a disbelieving guffaw of some sort. "And just what if she's shown the clue around town, huh? She could have the whole city looking. Damn, my bad luck! Why'd I have to be strapped with you two idiots?"

"There's no need to get upset, boss," said Mr. Snow, who'd been doing his best quiet hulking bit next to his pal Graves, "because Anthony said she ain't told no one, 'cept for maybe Mark Sweet's wife."

"And just how do you know this, Einstein?"

"Well, for one, there ain't been nothing in the news about it, and two, judging by the stunt she pulled on us . . ." Graves began.

Mr. Snow coughed conspicuously.

". . . pulled on *me,* I think we're dealing with a very bored and greedy lady. Sweet's wife acted as if it was a game between the two of them. A gut feeling tells me they're going to go for it."

"You better be right."

"All we have to do is watch Averick, and she'll lead us right to the spot."

"Well, then, can I ask you a question, Anthony?"

"Sure, Duke, anything."

"What are you doing here?"

3RD INNING:
Caught in a Rundown

He stood silent in the dark, waiting to pounce on his prey like the most patient puma. He heard the key in the door; his body tensed. She entered the house.

"WHERE THE HELL HAVE YOU BEEN?! IT'S DAMN NEAR ONE O'CLOCK! AND WHERE ARE THE KIDS?!"

Dee Sweet didn't flinch; she was prepared for such an attack. Apparently, she couldn't ask Mark about his comings and goings, but he had every right to know about hers. "I took the kids to Mom's," she said, not bothering to look at him as she turned on a light. "How'd ya do today?"

"Never mind that!" he bellowed before lowering his voice to claim, "Two for three . . . a walk and a three-run dinger. But forget that! Why'd you take the kids to your mother's? I come home, there's no family! . . . There's no note! Nothing! You scared the shit out of me."

"I took them to Mom's because I'm going to Philadelphia tomorrow. I'm not sure how long I'll be gone and didn't think it would be fair to ask Marianne to sit indefinitely." Dee started up the stairs, then turned. "Unless, of course, you'd like to take the day off . . ."

"Yeah, right! Very funny. Why are you going to Philly?"

"I'm going with Jewel Averick."

Dee hadn't seen such a disbelieving look on Mark's face since the time she told him she was pregnant with their third child. "What? Since when have you two become chummy?"

"Who said we were chummy?"

Mark followed his wife up the stairs. "Okay, Duffy, do you care to tell me why you're going to Philly with a woman who's not your friend?"

"Can't."

"Why not?"

" 'Cause I can't."

"God! Talking to you is like talking to Eric . . . only he makes more sense."

Dee sauntered into the bathroom and once again shut the door in her husband's flustered face. This time, however, he charged in after her. "Duffy! You better tell me what's going on."

Dee sighed before briefly explaining how Jewel had found Two-Mile McLemore's clue and that they were simply going to Philadelphia to begin the hunt.

If she hadn't been brushing her teeth at the time, Mark might have understood her. As it was, he caught not one word.

"What'd you say?"

She spit out the toothpaste. "I can't repeat it. I've already got to stick a needle in my eye. And if you think that's pleasant, think again, buster."

"What the hell are you talking about?" He leaned in to smell her minty-fresh breath. "Have you been drinking again?"

Dee suddenly tired of the game and desperately wanted to go to bed. "Oh, for heaven's sake, Mark. I'm only going on a day trip. What's the big deal?"

"The big deal is you won't tell me why you're going, and why you've relocated our kids."

An impish grin spread across Dee's face. "It's a surprise."

As she reached for her washcloth, Mark grabbed her wrist. "So this is about last night, is it? Well, fine, Duf, do what you like. I couldn't care less." He left her alone to stare at her reflection in the mirror. For the first time in years, she liked what she saw.

✲　✲　✲

Dee Sweet was an on-time kind of person. Jewel Averick was black and ran on CP (colored people's) time. Therefore, as Dee sat patiently waiting in Jewel's living room, she found herself being "entertained" by Jacinta O'Hara.

"So you and Jewel's heading for Philadelphia today?" asked the corpulent housekeeper as she handed the rare guest a glass of fresh-squeezed orange juice. Dee smiled brightly but said nothing. Jacinta sat down next to her on the billowy sofa. "What you ladies going to do?"

"Jewel didn't tell you?" When the amiable Mrs. O'Hara shook her head, Dee shrugged. "I'm just going along for the ride. I suspect Jewel will be shopping for something."

Jacinta seemed to take this at face value before looking around to make sure they were indeed alone. "You know, Russell ain't been home in two days."

"No?" Dee wouldn't have thought much of that, but Jacinta's gossipy tone indicated it was a juicy tidbit.

"Yes . . . 'parently, they had a huge fight over that baseball glove and he stormed out. Hasn't called or nothin'."

"Really?" Now Dee was genuinely interested.

"It's true. I was here when Jewel tricked that man into thinking he bought Two-Mile's glove. And—"

"Whoa, whoa, whoa—back up a sec, Mrs. O'Hara." Dee took a sizable gulp of OJ. "What do you mean, 'tricked that man'? What man? When did this happen?"

Jacinta blurted out the story in exactly three and a half seconds. "This all happened two days ago, right after Russell brought home the old glove for his collection. As usual, Jewel thought he'd spent too much and told him so. Russell ran out of here in a snit. And right after he left, a man showed up wanting to buy the glove. Jewel sold it to him behind Russell's back— only, she deliberately sold him the wrong glove."

Dee choked on her drink. "You're kidding. Do you remember this man's name?"

"Andrew Hayes . . . Anthony Gray . . . or . . ."

"Anthony Graves?"

"Yeah! That's him . . . I remember . . . said his name was Anthony Graves!"

Dee grabbed a firm decorative pillow off the sofa.

Jewel grabbed a fancy designer purse off her dresser.

Dee vaulted off the couch and headed for the living room's exit.

Jewel hopped down the stairs and headed for the living room's entrance.

Dee rounded the corner.

Jewel rounded the corner.

POW!

Jewel Averick stumbled back two steps and wondered when her cushions had learned the art of self-levitation, because one had just plowed right into her face. Pulling herself together, she focused on Dee, who stood with the errant pillow in her clutches. "What? Why'd you do that?" Jewel attempted to grab the mascara-seeking pillow but she was too slow. Dee popped her in the face again.

"STOP THAT! What's the matter with you?!"

"You weren't exactly honest with me about Anthony Graves."

"What are you talking about? And look at that lipstick on my cushion!"

"You neglected to mention that you gypped Graves out of Two-Mile's glove. No wonder the man threatened you."

Jewel's eyes immediately sought out her big-mouth house-keeper, who was standing behind Dee. Jacinta tried to affect an innocent expression. "It slipped out," she confessed with a one-shoulder shrug.

This time when Jewel attempted to retrieve the pillow, she succeeded. "Here, Cindy, have this cleaned; it's got makeup all over it." Jacinta knew she'd been dismissed and gladly left the room. But, as usual, she didn't go far, hovering just out of sight.

"So?" Dee demanded.

"So?" echoed Jewel. "What are you saying? You don't want to go now?"

"Well . . . I don't know. I mean . . . no . . . I guess I want to go. But I want the whole story. I want the truth."

Jewel stared at Dee Sweet for several seconds. "Okay, okay, here's the deal . . ." She then proceeded to relate every single detail of her two encounters with Anthony Graves. "Close your mouth, Sweet, you look like an asthmatic fish."

"I can't believe you did that! You are way, *way* too much. If I was Russell, I'd have killed you. And I'm sure Graves has every intention of killing you."

"Gee, thanks. You're a real comfort."

Although Jewel was aiming for sarcasm, Dee detected the despondent, almost desperate, tenor in her voice. She knew Jewel was afraid. But her anxiety had nothing to do with Graves. Her fear was for Russell.

They stood in an awkward silence, before Dee said, "It'll be okay."

"I hope you're right. I *have* to make it up to Russell. And this Two-Mile mystery is a perfect way."

"Well, from what you've told me about Graves, I think we're on to something big. You were right to keep it quiet." Dee paused to look at Jewel's cream-colored silk safari blouse, khakis, and classy Joan & David–type flats. "However, you were wrong to put on those shoes. You should have on tennis shoes."

Jewel, in turn, checked out Dee's very complicated looking sneakers (that appeared to have everything but a CD player), her figure-flattering jeans, leather fanny pack, and loose-fitting peach-colored polo shirt. "Do you think I should change?"

Dee groaned. "I've waited an hour already. You're fine; just put on tennis shoes and let's get this thing started."

✻　✻　✻

"Good God, what the heck did you pack?" Jewel couldn't believe the size of Dee's "overnight" bag that fought with a slew of tools in her Volvo's trunk. "And what's with the tools? Don't you have a garage?"

"Mark does all our auto work. He prides himself on never having been inside a repair shop."

"He's that good a mechanic?"

"Not hardly. When he's road-tripping, I sneak the car over to Al's Auto to undo Mark's damage."

Jewel flicked Dee's navy-blue nylon bag. "Wha'cha got in there, anyway?"

Dee shrugged as she went to open the passenger door for Jewel. "I dunno. Change of clothes, toiletries, a towel, another pair of sneakers, blow dryer, couple of cameras, and some sandwiches in case we get hungry . . . in fact, I better bring them up front."

"We're going to Philly, not Nova Scotia."

"I know . . . I know . . . what can I say? When you're the mother of three, it's hard to go anywhere without a lot of stuff . . . force of habit. Besides, I like to be prepared."

As the women drove out of the driveway, Jewel inquired as to the makeup of the sandwiches Dee had packed. "Ham and cheese."

"Oh, that's so fattening."

"Who cares?" Dee sang gleefully. "Let's forget the stupid rules. I'm here to have fun. We can be responsible tomorrow."

Jewel and Dee bickered all the way to the outskirts of Philly. Dee fumed after Jewel (the trip's designated navigator) left the maps and sandwiches on top of the car as Dee pulled out of the gas station. *She did that shit on purpose.*

Jewel incessantly made it loud and clear she didn't appreciate Dee's "deliberately heavy foot." *She's paying me back for those damn sandwiches.*

But, just before they paid the toll for the Ben Franklin Bridge, a calm seemed to settle over them.

"It's nice being able to cross a bridge without someone freaking out beside you," said Dee.

"Pardon me?" Jewel turned away from gazing at the Delaware River to notice Dee's white-knuckled grip on the steering wheel that belied her words. "Something wrong?"

"Huh . . . oh, no. It's just that Mark is . . ." Dee stopped herself, not sure if she wanted to divulge her husband's private pain— especially to the caustic Jewel Averick.

"Mark's what?"

"It's nothing."

"Yes, it is. Tell me." To Jewel, it was obvious Dee was bursting to reveal a secret. "Mark's afraid of bridges?"

Dee took her eyes off the road and gave her passenger a wry look. "Yeah, he is."

"Really? He-won't-go-over-them afraid, or just-gets-a-little-tense afraid?"

" 'A little tense' is putting it mildly; he gets totally spastic."

"Why?"

"He's hydrophobic."

"Get out!"

"I'm serious. When he was five, his family was involved in a boating accident while they were on some camping trip. To this day, he absolutely refuses to talk about it. But his brothers told me their mom drowned trying to save Mark."

Dee was expecting, "Oh, how horrible! That must be terribly traumatic for a child. I can understand his fear." But Jewel just sat back in her seat and stared straight ahead as Philadelphia loomed larger. "That's interesting" was her only initial comment. Finally, as they bumped through a pothole into Philly, she continued. "So how hydrophobic is he? Does he take baths?"

"No way."

"Showers?"

Dee allowed a mirthless laugh to escape. "Really, really quick ones."

"I take it you all don't have a pool? Turn right here."

"Are you kidding? I've begged and begged, but he gets hysterical at the thought. You know what the truly sad part about all of this is, Jewel? I'm a swimmer. I mean, I *love* to swim."

"Follow that car . . . Yeah, I remember Russ mentioning that you were an NAACP champ or something like that."

"Uh . . . that's NCAA. NAACP would be for you, I believe."

"Whatever. Get in your right lane. And I don't care what people say, this colored person can't swim. I sink like a rock. It's actually quite distressing."

"Well, *I* can swim. I love to swim. I snorkel and scuba-dive, too."

Something in Dee's voice caused Jewel once again to look at her companion in order to really *see* her. Was that passion and excitement she saw?

"In college," continued the suddenly gregarious Dee, "I was on the swim team and set two NCAA records; they've since been shattered, but I set them."

"Make a right here on Broad Street."

"I also played softball, hockey, and tennis." It wasn't like Dee to go on about herself. In fact, she *never* went on about herself. But she couldn't seem to stop. Besides, she was sure Jewel wasn't listening.

She was wrong. Jewel heard every word, even the unspoken ones. "So it seems Mark's not the only athlete in the Sweet family."

"Hell no! *I* was the star before he was . . . in high school . . . in college. Then, after we married, he started spraying line drives all over the place to the beat of a three-hundred hitter, and the rest, as they say, is history."

"I bet you were the prom queen, weren't you, Sweet?"

"Yeah! How'd you know? Actually, I went to eight proms in high school. Mom was always lending me out to some geek or another."

The picture was painted perfectly for Jewel. *Dee Sweet used to be the shit and then was pushed into the background when her husband made it to the big leagues. While Mark was creating a larger-than-life identity, Dee lost hers completely.*

"Tomorrow, we'll call a pool place and make arrangements for them to install one in your backyard."

Jewel's statement was so matter-of-fact, Dee was sure she misunderstood. "Excuse me?"

"You're going to get that pool."

"Jewel! I can't do that!"

"Why? Isn't your backyard big enough?"

"Sure, it's plenty big, but—"

"But what?"

"But Mark! Didn't you hear me? I said he's hydrophobic."

"That's his problem, not yours. He doesn't have to swim in it if he doesn't want to."

"I can't."

"Why not? Do you or don't you want your own pool?"

Dee sighed. "More than anything."

"Well, I honestly don't see the problem."

"That's the difference between you and me, Jewel. I think of people's feelings. You don't. If you did, we wouldn't be here right now." Dee didn't mean to bite like that, but deep down she wished she had a little more of Jewel's attitude. Maybe then she wouldn't have to schlep to the Y every time she wanted to swim laps.

Jewel huffed and twisted away to look out the window. She didn't have long to pout, though. "Oh, oh, turn here, turn here! This is Girard Street!"

Girard Street meant tough driving for Dee, with its hazardous trolley tracks, double-parked cars, flagrant pedestrians holding important conversations in the street, and kids darting out of nowhere to retrieve rogue toys.

Jewel sat quietly soaking up the beautiful summer day and Girard Street, with its brick row houses and active black residents, including ten-year-old boys standing in the middle of intersections hawking newspapers. At one such intersection a low rider pulled up beside the Volvo with the music blasting so loud, Jewel felt each thump in her heart. "TURN THAT DOWN! YOU MAY WANT TO GO DEAF, BUT I DON'T!" she screamed through her closed window with the most pleasant smile plastered on her face. The young man obviously didn't understand a word she said, but appreciated the smile and returned it, gesturing that she and Dee should pull over to continue the conversation.

"JEWEL! What are you doing?" cried Dee, slamming down on the accelerator two seconds before the light turned green. "This doesn't exactly look like a nice neighborhood, you know."

"You're only saying that because there're too many black folks around for your taste," Jewel said, looking in the side-view mirror at the low rider as it caught up and tailed them.

"No. No . . . that's not it." Dee's face turned an interesting shade of pink. "I'm just saying you shouldn't be yelling at people you don't know."

"Well, we're going to have to get out of this car and ask a lot of people we don't know about Harry B. And my guess is most of them will be black. You have a problem with that?"

"Of course not!" Dee turned to look at Jewel, who appeared relaxed and downright carefree. "You don't have any qualms about this neighborhood?" she asked softly.

"No more than any other neighborhood. I've got a news flash for you, Dee Sweet: shit happens everywhere."

Dee didn't buy the cavalier attitude, at least not from Jewel. "You didn't grow up in this atmosphere; you were privileged."

"So, what's that got to do with anything?"

Dee didn't have an answer; truth was, she didn't fully understand the point she attempted to make. "I don't know."

"Look, there's a whole bunch of white people going to the zoo. Does that make you more comfortable?" said Jewel, pointing to the zoological park's entrance, which was crawling with happy families of all colors.

"Oh, I'm sorry I said anything," snapped Dee. "Let's drop it."

"Fine."

Staring at the excited tots skipping along and clenching animal-shaped balloons in one hand and cotton candy in the other, Dee thought of her three dropped off at Grandma's. "If I'd known we'd be this close to the zoo . . . What street is this? Thirty-fourth? . . . I'd have brought the kids."

"Yeah, you probably would have had a good time. But you wouldn't have had it with me. I'm here to find Two-Mile's next clue, not entertain your brats."

"They're not brats!"

"I call all kids brats."

"Not mine."

"Fine. Yours are angels."

The women kept a strained silence as they looked for Forty-fourth Street. They didn't find it, but couldn't miss the Stephen Smith Home for the elderly that dominated the corner of Girard and Belmont. Dee executed a neat U-turn and parked her car next to a historical landmark sign. "Well, Dee Sweet," Jewel began, after taking a deep breath. "This is where the two Stephens meet. Are you ready?"

No. "You bet."

Jewel ignored the landmark sign, but Dee stopped and read it out loud: "Stephen Smith . . . 1795–1873 . . . An abolitionist, Smith bought his freedom and was one of America's wealthiest Blacks with his coal, lumber and real estate ventures. He was the major benefactor of the Stephen Smith Home located here."

Dee turned to Jewel, who was looking around in a most disinterested manner. "Isn't that interesting, Jewel?"

"Yes, it is. Blacks with money is always a fascinating subject." Jewel made a show of yawning and checking out her fingernails.

"I think blacks . . . I mean *people* with money who give back to the needy are extremely admirable. But, of course, you wouldn't know anything about that."

Jewel flinched. Once again, Dee's surprisingly biting tongue had hit home. But she recovered quickly. "It's already two o'clock. We'd better start asking around for Harry B."

The women asked until they were hoarse. They asked old people. They asked young people. They asked as they walked up Girard Street. They asked as they walked down Girard Street. They asked as they traipsed through Fairmount Park. They asked as they stopped off in a sketchy-looking joint for a famous cheese steak. At one point, Jewel even asked a man—who could barely speak the King's English—in French.

They actually did get to talk to two Harrys, but neither of the middle-aged men knew anything about Two-Mile. They also received roughly a dozen marriage proposals—and just as many not-so-old-fashioned offers. One particularly persistent suitor helped them in their search for about an hour, but even he tired of the challenge.

Near dusk, Jewel and Dee realized they had found nothing. "Damn!" Jewel slammed her fist down on the Volvo's hood.

Dee opened the passenger-side door. That's when she noticed the black sedan slowly drive by, with a big blond man behind the wheel. She'd seen him earlier in the day.

"Jewel?"

Jewel straightened. "Hmm?"

"What does Anthony Graves look like again?"

"I don't know. My height. Dark hair. Tan skin. No lips. I mean, none whatsoever. The man has no lips. Why?"

"It's nothing. I just saw a man drive by. He seemed very interested in us. Thought I saw him earlier in the day. But this guy is blond."

"I hate to tell you, but men have been driving by and staring at us all day."

"Yeah, I guess you're right," Dee mumbled, before clapping her hands like a tenth-grade cheerleader, hoping to pep up Jewel. "Well, we gave it a shot. Are you ready to go?"

"Yeah, but I've got to go to the bathroom. I mean, I *really* have to go."

"Well, there's no place to go around here."

Jewel turned and took in the large building that was established in 1865. She smiled. "There's always the Stephen Smith Home for the Aged."

"We can't use this place as a public rest room."

"Who can't? Come on."

In the reception area two young men, who were stuffing chicken sandwiches in their mouths while arguing about the results of a boxing match, seemed pleased to see the attractive women saunter into the building. Jewel quickly availed herself of an employee rest room, while the men asked Dee what had brought them there. She let out a tired laugh. "Harry B."

"Oh, yeah, Mr. Burrell. He always gets the pretty visitors. He's in room two-fourteen," said one of the men with the name "Kenny" stitched above his pocket.

Dee gasped.

"Are you okay, miss?" Kenny asked.

"Harry B. is here?!"

"Yes, ma'am. You came to see him, remember?" said the other man, whose name was Rawley.

Dee pulled herself together and resisted the urge to do a jig. *Christ! Why didn't we come here first?* When Jewel returned, Dee tugged on her sleeve. "He's here! He's here!"

Jewel frowned. "Who? Harry B? You're kidding?"

Dee grinned. "Room two-fourteen."

Jewel swung around to Kenny and Rawley. "Which way?"

The men pointed. The women charged down the just-waxed floors and up a flight of stairs, and barged into the room marked "214," surprising Harry Burrell, who was just tuning in a Phillies game.

Harry Burrell didn't seem offended. "Well, hello!"

They said nothing.

"I hope you girls are here for my sponge bath."

"Are you Harry B.?" gasped Jewel.

"That's me, young lady. And you are?"

"Jewel Averick. And this is Dee Sweet."

Both women gawked at the elusive Harry B., who sat in a wheelchair. He was, in a word, adorable. Even though he was probably over eighty, he still sported a full head of shocking white hair, which contrasted with his dark-chocolate skin that was as smooth as any twenty-year-old's. Age had taken away most of his body fat, but he sat straight up in the chair with the air of a king. His unusually large hands grasped theirs in appropriately strong handshakes. But it was Harry's eyes that were captivating. They were round and bright, without the hazy cataracts that often plague senior citizens.

"What can I do for you, ladies?"

Jewel and Dee exchanged confused looks. "Well," began Jewel finally. "This may sound crazy, but I think Two-Mile McLemore sent us."

Harry B.'s eyes stretched over his entire face, then narrowed to slits before flying open again. "Two-Mile McLemore," he began slowly, releasing each syllable at two-second intervals, "sent *you* two?"

Jewel fished in her purse and extracted her precious piece of paper. "I found this in an old glove my husband bought at an auction. It was supposed to have belonged to Two-Mile."

Harry turned off the television with the remote before reading the note. "Well, I'll be."

"Do you know what that means? Can you help us, Mr. B.?" asked Dee.

Harry didn't respond at first. He refolded the paper and handed it back to Jewel. "Two-Mile," he said in a hushed, awe-filled tone, looking to the ceiling as if calling an image to mind. "He was somethin' else."

"Did he exist, Mr. B.? Did you know him?" Dee asked, pulling a hard plastic cafeteria-type chair next to Harry's.

Jewel didn't want to get comfortable. She wanted the next clue, period. If Harry didn't have it, they were wasting their time.

"Oh, Two-Mile existed all right. He was 'round six feet five, a gigantic man with massive shoulders 'n' arms, and only 'bout ten hairs on his head. Course you couldn't tell how bald he was 'cause he wore a ball cap most times. You shoulda seen old Two-Mile swagger to the plate. People would stop talkin' and yellin' and just watch 'im. Man swung a fifty-two-ounce bat—"

"No!" Dee said, her eyes wide with wonder.

"I kid you not, young lady. Had his bats special made just for him. They was coal-black. Anyhow, no one wanted to pitch to Two-Mile. I mean, no one. Once when the bases was loaded, a Stars pitcher walked 'im on purpose just so he wouldn't give up the grand slam."

"No!" It was Dee again.

"I kid you not, young lady."

Jewel didn't mean to, didn't even know why it came out, but she found herself asking, "He was that good?"

"Better."

"My husband is fascinated with him."

"Jewel's husband is Russell Averick," Dee said happily.

The old man recognized the name. "Russell Averick of the Diamonds?" Jewel nodded. Harry whistled. "Is that right?! Well, how do ya like that? You know, the National Negro League's team was called the D.C. Diamonds. Of course, even the year

Two-Mile played, they weren't very good. 'Bout the only team that wasn't."

"Nothing's changed," Dee said dryly.

" 'Cept now they let you white people play with us."

The room was quiet before all three laughed.

"Did you play, Mr. B.?" Jewel asked, wondering where her newfound interest was coming from.

"No, dear, I did not. But I attended just about every game that was played over there by the railroad tracks. Those were the days. Why, I remember when Two-Mile and Boojum got into it. Two-Mile's temper was just as notorious as Boojum's."

"Excuse me? Boojum?" asked Jewel.

"Boojum Wilson. Don't tell me you've never heard of him? He was simply one of the best. He was a player/manager here with the Stars. Man hit damn near four hundred his whole career. But Boojum was a fighter. And one time he and Two-Mile had a disagreement and—"

"Boojum?" Jewel interrupted again. "Two-Mile? Boojum? Cool Papa? Why couldn't people just use their given names?"

"That's part of the game, dear," explained Harry B., as Jewel sat in the other "guest" chair and pulled it closer to form a tight little triangle. "Why, the Negro Leagues was filled with men called Hooks, Steel Arm, Smoky, Ping, Jelly, Pud, Popsicle, Groundhog, Showboat, Big Train, Foots, Bubbles, Goo Goo, Boots, Bullet, Suitcase, Moocha, Highpockets, Bad News, Double Duty—"

"I've heard of him!" cried Jewel. "I mean, Russell has a glove that once belonged to Double Duty Radcliffe."

"Old Double Duty would pitch one game and catch the next. Course, I didn't see him play much. I tell you, the Stars had to play in some crazy conditions. Sometimes the black smoke from the trains would cover the field and make playin' impossible. But the great Gene Benson could catch anything, even in the smoke. He was doin' those basket catches long before Willie Mays and your Russell Averick," Harry said. "So you say you're Averick's wife, young lady?"

"Yes. And she's Mark Sweet's wife."

"Is that right? Well, I'll be." Harry smiled at them before a blank look settled on his kindly face. "And what brings you here again?"

"Two-Mile's clue, Mr. B." Dee reached over to pat the man's huge hand.

"Ohhh, right. Two-Mile was always up to somethin'. He was always lookin' for excitement. He coulda been the best there was. But I guess he stuck his neck where it didn't belong, 'cause he disappeared in August of '39 and I ain't seen him since."

"How'd you know him, Mr. B.?" asked Dee.

"We met in an old waterin' hole after a game during that summer and he got drunk and rowdy. Things got ugly, and windows and furniture and a policeman's nose started getting broke. Well, I hustled old Two-Mile out a back door, just as the rest of the police showed up, and let him hole up in my place. Next morning he thanked me, said he'd never forget what I did for 'im and left."

"And you never saw him again?"

"Nope. But years later, in the fifties, a kid come by my house with a package, claiming it was from Two-Mile. So I opened it and there was five thousand dollars *cash* and a locked box."

Now Jewel was excited. "No, sir!"

"Yes, ma'am. I kid you not. Anyhow, there was a typewritten letter that said someone will come looking for the box and I was to give it to 'im. Said it was part of a game he set up. That was one thing about Two-Mile—he loved all kinds of games, loved playing with people."

"In clue number one, he said we're searching for him," Jewel noted. "Is that what we're doing, Mr. B.?"

"Could be, dear. But I've heard that an amateur filmed a game in Pittsburgh where Two-Mile hit a home run that still hasn't come down. He mentioned the film in his letter, sayin' it has to be found to prove he actually played. Could be he got ahold of it and made up this game to have someone find it."

"Who would go through all that trouble?" Dee asked.

"Two-Mile McLemore, that's who. Like I said, he loved a good game. And it looks like you two are the players . . . imagine that . . . after all these years. And two pretty little girls at that!"

"Do you still have the box, Mr. B.?" Jewel asked.

A slow smile spread across the old man's face. " 'Deed I do."

"Did you ever open it?"

"Nope. Letter said not to."

"So?!" Jewel was incredulous. "That shouldn't stop you. There could be another five grand in there!"

Harry giggled quietly, shaking his head. "To tell you the truth, young lady, I was so happy about the money I *did* get, I figured I should respect his little request. So I put the box in my chest, and over the years, when no one came lookin', I forgot about it—that is, until now."

"You're a better man than me, Mr. B." Jewel took a deep breath and asked for the box.

Harry Burrell pointed to an old black chest. "Open it; it's buried under that burlap on the bottom of the right-hand side."

Both women reached for the box—a splintery wooden number, about five inches square, secured with a tiny padlock. There was a slight tug-of-war, before Dee relinquished the box to the more determined Jewel.

"Well, Mr. B., thank you very much for this," said Jewel.

"Let me get a picture of Mr. Burrell before we go. I want to keep it as a memento of our visit here and our day in Philadelphia. I left my camera in the car. I won't be a minute."

"You know, young lady," said Harry, when Jewel sat down again, clutching the box. "Your husband reminds me of Oscar Charleston . . ."

"Who?"

"Why, Oscar Charleston . . . just one of the best ballplayers ever lived."

Much to her surprise, Jewel found herself listening to the old man with interest.

Anthony Graves was thankful for the cover of darkness as he and Mr. Snow slashed the tires of Deanna Sweet's car.

"They been in there awhile, Anthony," observed Mr. Snow. "Do you think they found something?"

Graves pocketed his knife and squinted into the darkness. "There's only one way to find out, Mr. Snow. Shall we go in?"

Kenny and Rawley weren't as pleased to see the two white men stroll into the Stephen Smith as they had been to see Jewel and Dee, but they were just as curious. "Can I help you?" asked Kenny.

"As a matter of fact, you can," began Graves, giving Kenny his oily smile. "We're here to pick up two women who came in a little while ago. I'm their driver and they have another appointment in fifteen minutes across town. If I don't keep Mrs. Averick on a tight schedule, she'll miss all her engagements. Ballplayers' wives have such a busy charity-work calendar, you know."

"Ballplayers' wives?" Rawley frowned, standing up to get a better look at the men. "Averick? Is that fine lady Russell Averick's woman?"

Graves nodded. "As I said, the ladies have to be at a banquet in fifteen minutes. If you'll be so kind as to tell me where they are."

"They're visiting Mr. Burrell in room two-fourteen; I'll go get them," said Rawley.

"Ah, that won't be necessary. Which way?"

Graves and Mr. Snow hustled down the hallway, passing the employee rest room a split second before Dee Sweet exited the lavatory. She continued down the hall in the opposite direction of the men.

Like ships passing in the night.

Jewel was so caught up with the stories of the old Negro Leagues, when Mr. Burrell looked up and said, "Hey! Hey! Hey!" she beamed. "I know that one! Willie Mays, the 'Say Hey Kid.' I met him! . . ."

A hand slammed down over Jewel's mouth, which halted her reminiscing and almost, more traumatically, her heartbeat. Panicked, she attempted to swivel around to see who was holding her. It was Anthony Graves!

Harry Burrell yelled, "Hey! Hey! Hey!"

"Shut him up, Snow!" said Graves in his high, iron-toned voice.

Suddenly covered with sweat, Jewel stared wide-eyed as Mr. Snow extracted a most intimidating-looking gun from his breast pocket and took a dead aim on Harry B.

With the gun a foot from his face, Harry Burrell judiciously chose to swallow his objections.

"Now that we have everyone's attention," said Graves, as he brought his head down to Jewel's ear, rubbing his face in her hair, "I want Two-Mile's clue. And I want it now!" To emphasize his point, he snapped Jewel's head back painfully, his hand still squeezing the hell out of the lower half of her face. Jewel attempted to talk, but naturally it sounded like muffled mumbo jumbo.

"Okay, lady, I'm going to remove my hand. If you so much as raise your voice one decibel, Snow is going to put a bullet through your pal here. Understand?" Jewel nodded her head. Graves slowly peeled back his hand and then remembered Averick's other "pal," who was nowhere in sight. "Where's Sweet?"

Jewel took a deep breath and tried to compose herself. She was scared, but she was more outraged than anything else. She turned and gave Graves a look that, if possible, would most certainly have killed him.

"How the hell should I know?" Jewel wasn't trying to throw off the two goons; in her jangled state she couldn't exactly remember where Dee went. "How dare you come barging in here like this?" It was a supreme effort to keep her voice at a normal level—but she had to think of Mr. Burrell, who was looking worse with each passing second. His breathing had become irregular and very loud. She'd have to get rid of Graves in a hurry. "Look, you big jerk. What in God's name do you want?"

"I want Two-Mile's notes."

"I told you I don't know what you're talking about."

"Fine," said Graves. "Have it your way. Snow . . ."

Mr. Snow cocked his gun and moved it five inches closer to Mr. Burrell. Jewel had no choice. "Okay! Okay! Here . . . take it, you jackass!" She slammed the box into Graves's gut. "Now go, so I can call the cops!"

Graves and Mr. Snow slowly backed up toward the door, the gun still leveled on Jewel and Mr. Burrell. "You're not callin' any cops, Averick, not if you want to live to see tomorrow."

Jewel sucked most of the air from the room into her lungs. "Are you threatening me?"

"Yes, ma'am, I am. Remember, I know where you live," he said, smirking. "Now, I trust I won't have any more problems from you. If you try to follow us, I'll put a bullet right through that pretty puss of yours."

The men then vanished from the room. Jewel lunged over to grab hold of Mr. Burrell, who had slumped down in his chair. "Are you okay, Mr. B.?" she cried, giving his limp body a little shake. "Mr. B.!"

The old man lifted his giant paw and placed it over Jewel's hand, which was clutching his T-shirt. He patted it twice before raising his head and looking her in the eye. "I told you, Two-

Mile was one for excitement." Jewel almost wept at the sight of the smile that bravely made its way across Harry B.'s beautiful face. "I'm all right, child. Don't worry about me. Just do me a favor—"

"Anything. What is it, Mr. B.?"

"Don't let those SOBs get away with this."

Jewel held on to Harry's hand. "Believe me, if it's in my power, I won't."

Dee was just about to shut the trunk after digging for her camera when the sight of two figures made her momentarily freeze: the blond man she'd seen a couple of times that day and another man—a man who was about Jewel's height, tan skin, dark hair. He was too far away to make out whether he had lips, but she knew he was Anthony Graves.

And he was carrying her box . . . er, Jewel's box . . . That scummy man was carrying their box!

This man wasn't just going to waltz in and take what she and Jewel had worked so hard to unearth. *No fucking way.*

She slowly raised the trunk hood with one hand and blindly fished around through Mark's tools with the other. She felt something that just might work, and watched the men walk to the Buick that was parked five cars in front of hers. She sent up a quick prayer, bent over at the waist, and then, without making a sound, ran up behind Graves just as he was opening the Buick's passenger-side door. Dee's hand shook as she shoved one end of the little tool in Graves's back. He became Popsicle-stiff. "I don't think that box belongs to you," she said in a low voice with a darkly threatening tone she hadn't thought she was capable of delivering.

Graves attempted to twist around, but Dee jammed Mark's Craftsman brake-spring washer tool in his back. "DON'T turn around, or so help me, I'll shoot you right here. Just hand over the box."

Dee's heart was pounding quadruple time. *Did those words*

come out of my mouth? I don't believe it! But she had no time to analyze her newfound ballsiness. She couldn't afford to think.

By this time, the dim Mr. Snow, who had been sitting patiently behind the wheel, popped out of the car to stare at his accomplice over the hood. "What's up, Antho——" he began before noticing Dee.

"Don't move, blondie," Dee ordered, "or I'll shoot him!" Mr. Snow did as he was told and Dee poked Graves again with the auto tool. "Now give me that box!" Filled with adrenaline that came with this new form of Russian roulette, Dee reached around Graves and grabbed the box, just as Jewel came running out of the building.

It took Jewel approximately one second to size up the situation as she came to a skidding, hopping, bouncing halt by the Buick.

"GET HIS KEYS! GET HIS KEYS!" yelled Dee, rushing her words.

Jewel frowned and wondered what she was babbling about.

"Get . . . his . . . keys . . . Jewel."

"Oh, sure thing." Jewel ran around to Snow and grabbed the keys out of the ignition. She also reached inside his jacket and yanked out his gun. The two women shared bad-girl stares, then silently acknowledged that it was definitely time to "git."

Jewel aimed the gun at Graves while Dee backed up and ran toward her car, clutching the box in one hand and pulling out her keys from the fanny pack with the other. She had barely settled behind the wheel when Jewel flew past the Volvo. Dee looked in the rearview mirror, but because her trunk was up, she couldn't see where Jewel had gone. *What the hell is she doing?* A moment later, the trunk was slammed shut and Jewel was fumbling with the door handle.

"GET IN THE CAR! GET IN THE CAR! . . . What are you doing?" Dee cried, as Jewel pushed Dee's humongous overnight sack into the car before falling heavily into the passenger seat and rolling down her window.

Aggressively using the bumpers of the cars in front of and behind her, Dee gunned the Volvo out of its tight parking space. Something was wrong. The horrible noise of the flat tires was undeniable, but she persevered as the two hoods bore down on them, with Graves wielding a gun. Jewel struggled to her knees, clutching Dee's bag, and leaned her entire torso out the window. Before Dee could even guess what Jewel was up to, Graves and Snow were reeling from the 30-miles-per-hour whack of the massive bag hitting their heads.

"Did you see that, Sweet? I knocked the gun right out of Graves's hand!" Her gleeful expression was soon replaced with a scowl. "What's up with the car?"

"I think those assholes slashed my tires."

"Well, keep driving, sis."

"I don't think I'll be able to."

"Just till we put some distance between—"

Whatever Jewel was going to say went unsaid as the Volvo hit some sort of large, misplaced item in the road, swerved frighteningly out of control, careened up on the sidewalk, and finally crashed into a shrub-covered fence.

The adventurers sat paralyzed, breathing heavily.

"You okay?" asked Dee.

"Yeah. You?"

"I think so. Did I kill anyone?"

"No. Just your car."

"You sure?"

"Positive."

"I can't move."

"Neither can I."

They sat for another second until a bullet shattered a backseat window, causing them to scream and bolt from the car to see Graves and Snow tearing down the street toward them. The sound of a gunshot had also stirred up the neighborhood.

Dee pulled herself together first. "Come on!" she ordered, reaching back inside the car to grab Two-Mile's mystery box and shove it in the blue bag recently used so creatively by Jewel. Then, with feline agility, she was on top of the car in two gigantic leaps. Clutching her purse, Jewel watched with stunned amazement, before the sight of Graves and Snow, only a half block away, galvanized her to do the same. Dee threw the bag over the leafy fence. "Come on, climb over!" she instructed, as she grabbed on to the twelve-foot fence and pulled herself up and over. Not known for any great athletic ability, Jewel proved to be just as nimble as Dee. She immediately dropped down on the other side, while Dee hung suspended for a moment trying to figure out just what kind of landing she wanted to make.

From the splashing sound Jewel created below, Dee knew it was going to be a rather wet landing. She let go of the fence and alighted on a slimy incline, before tumbling into refreshingly cool water.

Gripped with maniacal excitement, Jewel acted as if the four feet of water she had fallen into was the fabled twenty thousand leagues.

"Jewel! Calm down! Stand up. Stand up! You're all right."

Dee's orders had no effect on Jewel, but the blinding glare of a high-beam headlight and a masculine voice shouting at them worked magic. "HEY, YOU TWO! WHAT ARE YOU PLAYING AT? GET THE HELL OUT OF THAT HIPPO POOL!"

Jewel froze.

Once again, Dee's mind operated faster than Jewel's as she registered the "hippo pool" remark and instantly made a dramatic, if not awkward, bid to swim to land. Jewel, on the other hand, was petrified. The sight of a lumbering, grunting hippopotamus snapping his mammoth jaws a foot away prompted her to faint in an inglorious heap into the curious animal's water.

✽   ✽   ✽

In the zoo's security office, a soaking Dee Sweet took stock of her bizarre and thoroughly ignominious situation. Hating the feeling of her clammy wet jeans, she sat quietly on a stiff wooden chair in the corner of the mint-green-colored room and proceeded to shiver.

Had she, in the last twenty minutes, threatened two henchmen with a *pretend* gun? . . . just missed getting shot by a *real* gun? . . . hopped a fence and landed squarely in a hippo pool? . . . and saved Jewel Averick from drowning and getting squashed by a friendly, yet amorous, hippo named Horace?

The first three points she could actually believe and accept. It was the last that had her questioning her sanity. Why had she bothered to save Jewel? Not only did Jewel take a whack at the security guard as soon as she came to, she vociferously demanded to know why the zoological park "allowed wild animals to roam around unchecked."

Dee was certain the unruly and decidedly unapologetic nature of Jewel's histrionics would land them in jail before the night was through.

How was she going to explain this to Mark? That thought caused her back to stiffen and her chin to thrust toward the heavens as she wrung out the bottom of her polo shirt. Why should she explain anything? He had his life . . . his fun; why couldn't she have hers? Although this hadn't exactly been "fun," more like nerve-racking chaos. Still, a pleasing tingle ran down Dee's spine. She reached in her blue bag—which miraculously got snagged in a tree branch and was spared the bath—and felt around for Two-Mile's box. She also looked at her feet, only one of which still sported a sneaker; Horace had claimed its mate as a consolation prize.

Despite the fact that she had coughed up a considerable amount of water, Jewel's mouth proved to be particularly water-resistant. Her clothes, however, had definitely seen better days. There were at least five tears in her delicate safari blouse and khakis. And some highly tenacious leaves clung to her hair, which hung in her face like an old English sheepdog's.

"You can't hold me here!" she yelled, attempting to force her way past the frustrated security guard. She didn't succeed. As a matter of fact, the guard, a burly, middle-aged man, led her to, and unceremoniously pushed her into, a chair next to Dee.

Jewel was just about to protest her shabby treatment when two policemen arrived, followed by another man in plainclothes, one of the zoo's directors, who demanded to know what the women wanted with his hippos. "You're not some animal-rights nuts, are you? That's all we need . . . hippos roaming the streets of Philadelphia."

"Pah-lease," said Jewel.

"I eat meat," mumbled Dee.

"Well, then, exactly what were you up to?" asked a young freckle-faced, redheaded officer.

"We were running from—" began Jewel before abruptly stopping.

Jewel turned to look at Dee, who offered an it's-your-call shrug of the shoulders. Jewel, in turn, began to chew on her bottom lip. "Ummm . . . no one, really . . . we . . . ah . . . thought these two men were after our purses, but it turns out they were chasing a . . . dog."

"A dog, ma'am?" asked the skeptical officer.

"It was a big dog." Dee spread her hands so far apart, the mythical creature could only have been a llama.

The other policeman, a good-looking, brown-skinned pup, was the next to join in the conversation. "You know, ladies, it's funny . . . Before we got this call, we were checking out a Volvo that some careless clown ran up on the sidewalk, not two blocks from here. Eyewitnesses say two women—one black, one white—hopped out and over the fence." He paused here to let the women squirm a bit, which they did. "Would either of you happen to own that car?" When he received only guilty looks as a response, he asked to see their identifications and tried to keep from staring at their clinging wet tops. Jewel's unexpected plunge had made her blouse completely see-through, and an ill-placed rip rendered it particularly interesting.

The women reluctantly produced their soggy driver's licenses.

The policeman frowned as the zoo's director peered over his shoulder to see who had interrupted his quiet evening. "Averick? Sweet? You wouldn't happen to be related to the ball-playing Averick and Sweet, would you?"

The women exchanged unsure stares again, before Dee sighed and uttered a defeated "They're our husbands."

That single statement brought a general masculine uproar of excitement and intrigue, and the hasty, but superficial, administration of Breathalyzers. Soon the zoo had been guaranteed a promotional visit from Mark Sweet and Russell Averick (and a sizable donation); officers Fine Brother and Cute Freckles were promised autographed bats and jerseys; Frank, the security guard, insisted on a picture for posterity (much to the chagrin of the uncomfortably damp subjects); Jewel was allowed to phone an old acquaintance to come get them; Dee was permitted to change clothes in a cramped can; and both women were able to walk away without so much as a moving-violation charge.

4th inning: Doctoring the Ball

Xavier Lawrence wasn't surprised to hear from Jewel Averick. He was absolutely shocked.

And although Jewel had pressed upon him the urgency of the situation—there seemed to be some kind of trouble at the city zoo—he stared into space motionless for a full ten minutes. He was stunned. *She actually called me? She needs me? She wants me! It took a while, but I knew she'd come around.*

Of course, he admitted to himself, as he stepped under the rhythmic streams of water in his shower, she obviously wasn't pining for him, just in a jam. But it was a start. It was a start.

As Xavier dressed, he remembered the first time he met Jewel Howard. They both had been freshmen at Princeton. She was a long, beautiful swan; he was a panting eager puppy, who would do anything for her—and did. Jewel Howard, he recalled, was as self-absorbed as they came. When others tired of her demanding conceit, he managed to overlook it and remained her only friend.

Actually, Jewel and Xavier were boyfriend and girlfriend during the last two years of school—a fact that confounded all who knew them. Most figured Jewel was using Xavier to get through school and that, once she'd secured the diploma, she would drop him like a bad habit. In reality, however, Xavier was the one who often was buoyed by Jewel's academic prowess, which was based more on sheer arrogance than a brilliant mind.

Nonetheless, it was an odd pairing. And that was simply

because Xavier Lawrence was what some would call a first-class Poindexter.

Eleven years later, he still was dressing the part. For Operation Get Jewel, Xavier chose a robin's-egg-blue short-sleeve shirt (a wee bit too tight), a navy-blue cardigan vest (even tighter), and brown trousers (about an inch too short and showing off his ecru-colored socks. But, in all fairness to Mr. Lawrence, his pants would have been the proper length if his bottom didn't take up a good deal of material intended for his legs.). On his feet? Black wing tips.

Although he was three inches shy of six feet and thirty pounds above "ideal" weight, Xavier was cute in his own way. He was one of those blacks who fell right in between dark and light skin, and was the owner of the most beautiful set of eyes given to man. His eyelashes practically curled up to touch his inch-high perfectly symmetrical dark brown Afro. He also possessed a dazzling set of white teeth behind his full lips. And across his unusual Roman nose were eleven defiant freckles. Slapping on a dab of aftershave and patting five hairs in place, Xavier Lawrence checked himself out in the mirror and liked what he saw. *Jewel, sweetie, your baby is coming to get you.*

#2

DIRECTLY BEHIND THE DISH AT THE DIAMONDS' PLAYGROUND SIT HIGH IN THE SUN. THE DIAL WILL GIVE YOU THE NUMBERS YOU NEED AT EXACTLY THREE O'CLOCK, TWO AND ONE.

After making short work of the little padlock on Two-Mile's box with a hammer and pliers, Jewel, Dee, and Xavier took turns reading clue number two.

"Well," said Jewel, flopping down on a stool in Xavier's kitchen and resting heavily on the counter, "it's a lot shorter than the first one."

"This is the dial—see, it's a little sundial." Xavier pointed to a small gnomon in the middle of a circle of what looked like random numbers on a piece of wood. He carefully lifted this panel to reveal a small vault within the box guarded by a combination lock. "There it is," he announced in a hushed tone, as Jewel straightened on her stool and leaned across the counter for a better look, and Dee put down the second clue to gaze at what Jewel's friend had unearthed.

Deanna Sweet still couldn't quite believe that Jewel had blurted the entire Two-Mile story to Xavier on their way from the zoo to his town house in King of Prussia. Wasn't it Jewel Averick who had sworn her, Yvonne, and Gibby to secrecy? Then, after one glance at this geeky-looking character, Jewel spills her guts about the whole affair.

Dee quickly chimed in, "So, we must have to go to a Diamonds' day game and sit behind home plate. The sundial will point to the numbers in the combination."

"But it's not the same stadium Two-Mile played in," Jewel pointed out.

"That's true. But remember, the field is in the same position, they just built a better stadium around it."

Jewel allowed a happy smile to spread across her face. "Then it looks like we're going to the ballpark."

The sandman was on vacation.

For the fifty-eighth time in as many minutes, Jewel forced her eyes shut and willed her overworked mind to drift off to dreamland. It was no use; she was as awake as an overstimulated child on Christmas Eve.

In all her thirty-two years, she couldn't recall a day that had taken such a toll on her emotions. As if the Harry B.–Anthony Graves–zoo fiasco weren't enough, she was struggling with the disappointment of having called home every hour on the hour until well past midnight, only to discover Russell hadn't returned.

Pride prevented her from leaving a message on the machine. *Two can play that game.*

She also was dealing with the added turmoil of seeing her ex-flame, Xavier Lawrence.

"Zavie" hadn't changed, perhaps a few pounds heavier, she thought as she lay in his guest room's queen-size bed and stared blindly at the ceiling. When he picked them up from the zoo, he had been calm and comforting, focusing his masculine gaze on her with a kindness she hadn't seen in months. *Russell only stares at me with disdain anymore.* There was a lot of murky water under the bridge between Xavier and Jewel, but as soon as she felt his gentle touch on her arm as he guided her to his car, she knew there was still an undeniable spark. What else could explain the way she blatantly broke her own rule and blabbed about Two-Mile's scavenger hunt? *What if things had been different between us? What if . . .*

Jewel pushed the disturbing thought out of her mind as she heard Dee Sweet complete a fretful toss and turn on the floor next to the bed. Both women had started off on the bed, but after fifteen minutes Dee had declared she couldn't sleep with anybody and dragged herself and half the bedding to the floor. "No wonder you're having marital problems," cracked Jewel, as she snatched back the quilt Dee had taken overboard.

Now, an hour later, Jewel listened to Dee pound her pillow. It was clear she wasn't the only one having trouble catching some shut-eye. "Sweet?"

"Hmm?"

"You awake?"

"Yes."

Jewel rolled over and hung her head over the side of the bed. "This was some day, huh?"

Dee groaned as she sat up and wrapped her arms around her bent knees. "I can't believe it . . . definitely one for the grandkiddies."

"I *can't* believe you held up Graves with a damn car tool! That took guts," Jewel whispered with a huge smile on her face. "Why have you been faking all these years?"

Dee turned confused eyes on Jewel. "What are you talking about?"

"You know, pretending like you're this Milquetoast doormat, when you're really this fearless wild thing?"

"I haven't been a doormat!" The words didn't even ring true to Dee's ears. But they hung in the air for several strained seconds.

It was Jewel who broke the silence. "You probably shouldn't have married someone named Sweet; people tend to resemble their last name, you know. In grade school, I had a teacher named Mr. Gross; and he was pretty gross—used to pick his nose with wild abandon. Nope, sis, you should have married a Mr. Badass, because, after today, it's clear you're not so sweet."

Dee sat silently and tried to understand her bold behavior. She tried to be appalled, to say it was a fluke, to realize her body had been taken over by the spirit of some deceased soldier of fortune. She tried to rationalize her brazenness, to no avail, because the truth was lodged in her mind like a jujube in the back teeth. She had wanted to do it! She had been excited to do it! It felt good!

Faced with such a startling and unnerving realization, the human paradox known as Deanna Duffy Sweet burst out crying.

"What is it?" Jewel was genuinely concerned.

Dee shook her head as her body convulsed with each sob. "I don't know."

Jewel tentatively reached out to pat Dee's shaking shoulder. "It's delayed shock."

"No. You don't understand. I wanted to challenge Graves and Snow. I didn't think about my kids. I didn't think about Mark or my family, I just wanted to piss off those guys." Verbalizing her angst only made things worse, and Dee began to wail. "I'm sick . . . I need help!"

"There, there, Sweet. You'll be fine . . . Honestly, you white people act so goofy sometimes."

"What?"

"I said you white people act goofy sometimes, actually more than sometimes."

This time Dee's response was more chuckle than sob. "You're something else, Jewel Averick. Here I'm thinking, *She's not so cold,* and you come out with something really sensitive like that."

"It's the truth."

"If I said that about black people, you'd pitch a fit."

"That's the truth, too. But it wouldn't be the truth about us."

"Why is it that blacks can talk about whites any way they want and it's okay, but a white person can't say a thing about blacks?" asked Dee, this time wiping the remaining tears with her middle fingers.

"Hey, listen, there aren't many perks to being black in this country; why question the few we have?"

Dee was all cried out and permitted a little laugh to escape. "I don't know about you, Jewel. You're just bad news. First, you purposely get me drunk and let me make a fool of myself. Then you get me caught up in this Two-Mile rundown and nearly killed . . ."

"You wanted to come."

Dee took a deep breath and exhaled. "Yeah, I did."

Jewel's "Why?" was hardly audible, but the single-word question was so heavy and multi-layered, Dee realized Jewel already had an answer. "Why don't you tell me."

Jewel adjusted the pillow under her arms before speaking. "I think you had a happy childhood, a storybook high school life, and a prominent college career. You were pretty and athletic and you had the handsome jock-next-door for a boyfriend—high school sweethearts who everyone knew would get married. I think you found yourself playing second fiddle to Mark when he made it to the majors and started carrying around a celebrity status that made your school days seem amateurish, to say the least. And now you think Mark may be fooling around again, and instead of dealing with your fears and confronting your husband, you've run away on an adventure. I think you came with me today because you're looking to recapture some semblance of your carefree days. You're looking for excitement; you're looking to jump-start your life. You are, in a sense, Ms. Badass trying to shed boring old Mrs. Sweet."

Dee sniffed hard and smiled softly. "I don't know, Jewel, it's like I know I should be happy. Everyone tells me how lucky I am to have Mark and the kids and the money, the house, blah, blah, blah. And with my head I know they're right. But right here, inside me, I just don't feel it. The scary thing is I felt it today when we were running from Graves and hopping over fences into goddamn hippo pools!" She paused to chuckle. "Don't get me wrong, I love my kids more than anything and I'm happy I'll be able to raise them in a comfortable environment, but I—I—"

"You want the happiness—dare I say, the glory—you had before Mark hit it big?"

"Yeah, kind of. Does that make me a selfish or bad person?"

"That makes you human and a lot like me."

"God! Don't say that. I'm depressed enough." The women sat in silence with their own thoughts until the quiet became uncomfortable. "Talk about me! How 'bout you knocking Graves and Snow with my bag! By the way, what'd you do with blondie's gun?"

Jewel shrugged. "I think the police found it in the street. They were questioning me about that while you were changing your clothes—and on that subject, I'm not too big to admit you were right about being prepared. Next time, you can bring the whole damn closet, I won't say a word. Anyway, I said I didn't know anything about the gun."

"They believe you?"

"Not a word. But, with any luck, those troublemakers will wind up behind bars where they belong—sooner, rather than later, I'm hoping."

"I'll second that. It makes you think—wherever Two-Mile is taking us, those two Cro-Magnons want to get there first." Dee stopped as a shiver racked her frame. "I can't believe they shot at us."

"I'm sure if I hadn't just gone to the bathroom, I would have wet my pants."

The room was filled with another long silence.

"Why'd you tell Xavier about the hunt, especially after we had to cross our hearts and everything?" Dee asked.

Jewel rolled back on the bed to avoid meeting Dee's inquisitive stare. She closed her eyes and pretended the sandman had finally come round her way. But Mrs. Sweet wasn't buying it. Dee struggled to her knees, leaned on the bed as if she were saying her nightly prayers, and gave Jewel a shove. "Come on, tell me, Jewel."

Jewel shrugged in the red-and-white-striped pajama top Xavier had lent her. "I don't know. He asked; I told him. So what?"

"So what? Mark asked; I didn't tell him. Mrs. O'Hara asked; you didn't tell her. What's up with Xavier? How do you know this guy anyway?"

Jewel couldn't believe it, but she actually felt the warmth of blood rush to her face. She was never comfortable talking about her relationships with men . . . to anyone, let alone Deanna Sweet, yet she found herself saying, "I met him in college. We went together for—"

"WHAT? YOU AND XAVIER? I DON'T BELIEVE IT!"

"Keep your voice down! . . . *Yes.* Me and Xavier. Why's that so hard to believe?"

"You've got to be kidding me. I don't believe you."

"Stop saying that, Sweet." Jewel was truly baffled by Dee's

shock. "Zavie and I were very close; he was my boyfriend for something like three years."

"I just can't picture you two together."

"If you say that one more time, I swear I'm going to belt you with this pillow."

"I'm sorry, Jewel, but I can't believe—" As promised, Dee was cut off with the wicked whip of a feather sack to her head. She returned the blow with her own pillow.

"Why? What's wrong with Zavie?"

Dee thought how typical it was for Jewel to assume there was something wrong with Xavier and not herself. "I don't know . . . he's sort of a geek, isn't he?"

Jewel rose to an elbow and eyed her roommate with curiosity. "You think Zavie's a geek?"

"Well . . . don't you?"

"No. And I'll thank you not to call him that again."

"Were you guys serious?"

"Pretty serious."

"Marriage-serious?"

"We talked about it. But there was an obstacle I couldn't hurdle, so I broke it off with him." Jewel's words were stiff and her hands unconsciously clutched fistfuls of sheets.

Although it was obvious her questions were agitating Jewel, Dee couldn't stop. "What obstacle?" There was no answer. "Jewel?" Still nothing. It wasn't like Dee to pry, but she was convinced Jewel couldn't be serious. "Is Xavier rich?"

"His family is fairly well-off. His father wanted him to join the family shoe-manufacturing business. But Zavie wouldn't have it, so his dad said, 'Fine. Don't expect any of my money to support you.' "

"What's Xavier do for a living?"

"Some kind of social work, but it's not very high-paying, that's for sure."

Finally an answer to the conundrum, thought Dee as she sat back down. Jewel had latched on to the shoemaker's kid, then dumped him when Xavier fell out with his father—and, more importantly, his father's fortune. Certainly not a proper spousal candidate for Jewel.

Dee could tell she'd somehow hit a sore spot and brought the conversation back to the more pressing matter. "So, are we going to do this clue-number-two thingy?"

"*I'm* going to; if you want to tag along, that's fine."

Dee ignored Jewel's tone. "What if Graves and Snow are still out there?"

Jewel peeked over the bed's edge again and stared down at Dee. "From here on in, we're going to have to be very careful and make sure those jerks aren't following us. But I'm going to see it to an end; one way or another."

"And I'll be with you every step of the way."

While Xavier whipped up a scrumptious breakfast, Jewel and Dee took turns talking to Harry Burrell on the phone. Jewel had been concerned about the old man and wanted to thank him again for his help—and to her surprise, she apologized for the harrowing hassle. They would have gone to see him in person, but decided that, with Graves and Snow lurking about, it would be safer for Harry if they kept their distance. Dee, however, promised they'd visit again when the whole Two-Mile mystery was solved.

Next on the agenda was a trip to the mall. Jewel claimed she couldn't be seen in ripped threads and insisted on replacing the old with new. It was one-thirty when they hit the mall's exit. Then it was on to the garage to pick up Dee's sick Volvo. Even with new tires, the car was a wreck.

So, too, were Jewel's nerves after saying good-bye to Xavier.

Mr. Lawrence had bid farewell to Dee, shaking her hand as

she sat behind the steering wheel. He then pulled an obviously disconcerted Jewel off to the side for a private farewell. "Well, Zavie, thanks again for taking care of us. I don't know what we would have done without you."

Xavier chuckled, grabbed her hand, and gently yanked her into an informal hug. "You know damn well you would have stayed in the swankiest hotel in Philly." He ended the embrace to look at her face. "Tell me something, Jewely-girl. Why *did* you call me? You certainly didn't really need my help."

Jewel opened her mouth, but no words came out. She didn't have an answer, or at least not one she was capable of articulating. Xavier placed his hands on the sides of her face and forced her to meet his gaze. "I miss you, Jewel Howard. I don't want you popping in and out of my life when it suits you; when you need a favor."

"I'm not trying to pop in and out of your life, Zavie."

"Good . . ." Xavier leaned in and softly kissed the corner of Jewel's mouth, "because I certainly don't want to lose you again."

Jewel swallowed hard right before Xavier proceeded to kiss her like old times . . . briefly. "No, Zavie!" she gasped, taking a step back on shaky legs. She shook her head in an attempt to clear her mind, which was so bogged down with sentimental yearnings she couldn't think straight. "You . . . me . . . we're in the past."

"And the future," he said, reaching out to reclaim her hand. Jewel tried to pull out of his grasp, but he held firm. "Averick can't make you happy; he can never understand you like I do. And you know that. We're so much alike; we want the same things."

Staring into Xavier's eyes, Jewel held her breath. She was unconsciously immobile as he leaned in to kiss her again. Then he withdrew and released her, literally leaving her off balance and confused. "I love you, Jewel Howard," he whispered before turning to walk to his car.

Jewel didn't move. She stood where Xavier had left her in a state of stupefaction. She didn't snap out of it until Dee rolled up in the bucket of bolts that used to be a fine automobile and honked. "Hey, Jewel, you ready to go?"

"Huh?"

"Come on, get in; we're not going to get home until after five as it is." A zombielike Jewel fell into the car. "You okay?"

"Huh?"

"I saw that, you know." Jewel didn't respond, just kept staring out the window.

"Did you forget for a minute that you were married?"

The bitter tone in Dee's voice was unmistakable and caused Jewel to look at the auburn-haired, pixie-faced woman sitting stiffly next to her. "What's a kiss between friends?"

"I just can't believe how people carry on as if marriage vows are merely suggestions."

Jewel resurrected her bored voice. "Look, Sweet, it was a kiss, that's all."

"Yeah, right."

"Grow up."

"Shut up."

The ride back to D.C. was a very long one. With flashers blinking the entire way, Dee averaged five miles per hour under the minimum speed. There was little, if any, conversation—each woman was lost in her private thoughts. In fact, they were so oblivious, neither noticed when the front bumper went AWOL somewhere in Delaware.

Russell was hoping to talk with Jewel that Thursday afternoon and was disappointed when she wasn't home.

"Hello, Russell," said Jacinta O'Hara as she emerged from the basement with a basketful of clean underwear. "I didn't hear you come in."

"How's it going, Mrs. O.? Jewel's not here?"

Jacinta shook her head.

"Ahh . . . has she been upset? I mean . . . since I ran out."

"To tell you the truth, Russell, Jewel hasn't skipped a beat. She's been bopping around here, singing and whatnot, as if you hadn't left. With all due respect, that girl is a cold one sometimes. Matter of fact, she's gone off to Philadelphia on a shopping spree . . . course, she has that twenty thousand to play with. Who knows when she'll return."

Russell felt as if he'd been struck in the ribs with a fastball. He recovered quickly to spew an oath, snatch some clean "draws" out of the basket, and head for the great outdoors in his Ferrari.

A drained Jewel stumbled into her house at five-fifteen, just in time to catch Jacinta preparing to head for home.

"How was Philly?"

"Fine." Jewel hated to ask, but she had to know. "Cindy, did Russell come home?"

"Yes." Jacinta continued to pack her satchel. She always helped herself to whatever food items she desired. Today, it was a jumbo jar of spaghetti sauce, a box of pasta, and an unopened container of Parmesan cheese. When Jewel had mentioned Cindy's bold pilfering to Russell, he'd shrugged and said, "Let her have the stuff; she's got kids to feed—we don't."

"You missed that loaf of Italian bread, Cindy," Jewel said sarcastically.

"Oh, right. Thank you." Jacinta moved to retrieve the bread, oblivious of Jewel's behind-the-back eye-rolling action.

"Did . . . ah . . . did . . . Russell ask about me at all? Did he want to know where I was?"

Jacinta turned slowly. "Didn't say a word."

"Nothing?"

"Nope. Just came in, dropped off some dirty clothes, picked

up some clean underwear, and left. I don't even think he realized you wasn't home last night. I mean, how would he know?"

Jewel collapsed into a colorfully cushioned wrought-iron chair, feeling as if Jacinta had kicked her in the tum-tum.

"You okay? You look sick." Throwing her bag of goodies on the breakfast table, Jacinta took a seat across from her employer.

Before she could tell herself "not in front of the help," Jewel broke down. "Oh, Cindy, I think I really blew it this time. Russ'll never forgive me. He hates me!"

Jacinta reached over and patted Jewel's shoulder. "I'm sure everything will be fine. Russell always forgives you." She stood up and took her bag from the table. "Now, if you'll excuse me, if I don't leave this minute, I'll miss my bus."

Jacinta had just completed her three-block walk to the bus stop when a white Lincoln Town Car pulled over to the curb beside her. She watched with no little amount of interest as the opaquely tinted passenger window was rolled down halfway, revealing an elderly white man with curly gray hair and a pair of bloodshot eyes that had so many bags under them, she thought it was one of those Hush Puppies basset dogs.

"Excuse me, ma'am," he began in a halting voice. "I was wondering if I might have a word with you?"

Jacinta took a step back and looked to her left and right, trying to recall what she had learned in the self-defense class she had taken some twenty years ago. "Me?"

"Are you Jacinta O'Hara?"

"Who wants to know?"

"A friend of Mrs. Averick's."

"Jewel don't have no friends." Jacinta instantly forgot her reservations and walked closer to the Lincoln. "Now, who are you and what do you want? And make it quick, my bus is coming."

❖ ❖ ❖

Dee Sweet was one tired woman. She could muster only a short call to her mother's to check on her children before she collapsed into bed.

True to her maternal oath, Margaret Duffy had asked her daughter if everything was okay.

"Oh, sure, Mom," answered Dee as she switched the receiver from her left shoulder to the right in order to undress while she talked. "I've just got a situation here and I need you to look after the kids for another week or two."

"A week? Or two? Nothing like a little notice, Deanna! You've never been away from your children that long." The frown in Mrs. Duffy's voice came through loud and clear. "Is it Mark?"

Dee transmitted a satisfied sigh-laugh through the much-ballyhooed fiber optics. "No, Mom. I'm happy to say this has nothing to do with Mark. It's about me."

"Are you ill?"

"I'm fine. There's nothing to worry about, I swear. In fact, I haven't felt this good in a long time. I'm sorry about dumping them on you like this, but I think it's best they're with you. Now, put them on the phone so I can go to bed."

Dee registered five hours of sleep before she was awakened by a terribly inquisitive husband, who demanded to know why his car looked as if it had lost a demolition derby.

Dee turned her head so that only half her mouth was smothered by the pillow and proceeded to mumble an explanation in a half-comatose state. "Had an accident in Philly."

"Are you okay?"

"Fine."

"Was anybody hurt?"

"A hippo was frightened, that's about it."

"WHAT?" Mark waited for a response. He received not a peep. "Duffy?" He jostled her exposed shoulder a bit. "Duffy?" He soon realized it was no use; she was sound asleep. Dead to the world.

As Mark Sweet undressed, he kept a curious eye on his wife, who apparently had taken on yet another personality. And while he was truly thankful she hadn't been hurt or worse, he was secretly happy the car was wrecked. The Volvo would require many hours of his "expert" auto attention. He snuggled under the covers wearing a silly grin.

She hadn't allowed pets; she wasn't ready for children; she hadn't bothered to socialize with her neighbors; her husband no longer cared for her company; and Friday was Jacinta's day off. Therefore, Jewel was left to groan at Kathie Lee's shtick and chuckle halfheartedly through an "I Love Lucy" episode. Clicking off the tube, she was overcome with a feeling she recognized as loneliness.

There's a cure for that, she thought before running upstairs and rummaging through a nightstand drawer to find the official D.C. Diamonds directory. Her hands quickly paged to the S-section, where the only entry was "Sweet."

Normally, Dee would have been shocked to receive a call from Jewel Averick, but being shot at, swimming with gargantuan animals, and engaging in late-night pillow fights has a way of bonding people faster than the craziest glue. "Hey, Jewel, what's going on?" Even though Mark was still sleeping upstairs, Dee spoke quietly; she didn't want to take the chance of his sneaking up on her and overhearing her conversation.

"Nothing, really. I, ah . . . I was wondering what you were up to today?"

"Oh, God! Please, not another outing. I can't take it!"

"No, nothing like that. Besides, the next day game isn't until tomorrow."

"I know. Truthfully, I can't wait to continue Two-Mile's hunt. Does that make me sick?"

"Sort of. But I feel the same way. I was thinking we could go shopping?"

"That sounds like fun." *I'd rather get my wisdom teeth yanked.* "But I'm heading to the gym. Would you like to come?"

"You mean sweat on purpose?" *I'd rather pluck my nose hairs . . . with pliers.*

Dee laughed. "Yes, sweat on purpose. Come on, it'll do you good."

"Thanks, Sweet, but I think I'll pass."

Dee detected the sad note in Jewel's voice and wondered whether she should acquiesce and go shopping. No. She straightened her back. *Remember, it's all about what I want.* "Well, then, I'll talk to you later. We have to make arrangements for tomorrow's game."

"Yeah, I'll call you. Bye, Sweet."

After they hung up, Jewel and Dee stared at their respective phones for several seconds, not sure they had said what they wanted to say.

To her surprise, Jewel soon found herself in Russell's "Hall of Fame" den and immersed in a book detailing the history of the Negro Leagues. Hours later, after reading about the likes of Rube Foster and Monte Irvin (whom she found quite attractive), she closed the book, looked up at Russell's collection with new appreciation, and felt rotten for having sold off a piece of it.

"Jewel?! Where have you been? I've been trying to get you for two days now. Didn't your housekeeper tell you I called? You should have called. Come in. Sit down. Tell me, did you find anything in Philly? Gibby has been driving me crazy. It's all I can do to keep him quiet; I'm so afraid he might slip up in front of Pete. By the way, the entire Diamond organization—dare I say, the entire league—is still buzzing about Dee's performance at the talent show. Good thing she got out of town. The scrutiny might have been too much for her. She's got such a delicate constitution. Pete tells me Mark has taken quite a bit of ribbing in the clubhouse . . . What? Why are you looking at me like that?"

"You missed one pink roller right on top." Jewel helpfully reached up and extracted a tiny sponge curler from Yvonne Sager's graying mane.

"Forget the roller," snapped Yvonne with a swipe of her hand. "Tell me! What'd you find?"

"*If* you can control your blathering for a minute, I'll fill you in. Honestly, Yvonne, I had no idea you had such a rapid-fire mouth."

"Sorry, I get like that when I'm excited."

"Well, here's to keeping you calm, and here's what went down . . ."

Jewel related her version of the Philadelphia story—everything from losing the maps and sandwiches to spending the night with an old friend—everything except the part about Graves and Snow temporarily absconding with the box, wrecking the car, being shot at, and the zoo imbroglio.

"It was that simple?" asked an astonished Yvonne.

"Yep, really no problem. The next step is getting the combination to open Two-Mile's box."

Yvonne slapped her thighs and shook her head. "Well, Jewel, it looks like you're on your way. I can't believe Two-Mile actually existed."

Jewel's response was cut off by Pete Sager, who smiled at her as he came into the room. His raspy voice was worn thin from years of screaming at umpires. "What a pleasant surprise."

"Hello, Mr. Sager." Jewel's greeting conveyed an uncharacteristic diffident respect. Pete Sager struck a formidable figure. At six feet four inches, the fifty-five-year-old bronzed-skinned, broad-shouldered, bald-headed man was a fine example of middle-aged magnificence. There was no stoop, hump, slouch, bump, nor an ounce of fat in his 220-pound frame. He commanded attention and respect. And he generally got it.

"Please, call me Pete. I've been telling you that for two years now. Say, Jewel, is Russell with you? I was hoping to talk to him."

The simple question hit Jewel right in the gut. "Umm . . . no. I think he's already headed for the stadium."

Pete Sager ran a strong hand over his shiny head and frowned. "That's too bad. I suppose I'll have to catch up with him there. So, what brings you here, young lady?"

Gibson Sager's entrance into the living room, as his father's before, prevented Jewel from answering. "Mrs. Averick! You're here!" he exclaimed before plopping down next to Jewel on the sofa. "So, what'd ya find out?"

In a louder than normal voice, Jewel diverted the conversation. "Good Lord, Gibson, I believe you've grown two inches in two days." In case the kid didn't get the message, she gave him a meaningful your-dad-is-in-the-room head jerk, plus a sly "love" tap to his sneakered foot with hers—and, for good measure, a pinch on his forearm.

Gibby roger wilcoed.

Wearing a Kansas City Monarchs jersey, the youngster reclined on the sofa and said not another word, creating a terribly awkward silence. Yvonne began to inspect the ceiling and whistle a tune. Finally, she clapped her hands. "Pete, would you do me a favor and either turn down the air conditioner or get my blue sweater? I'm freezing."

"Can't you conjure up one of your hot flashes?"

"Get the sweater, honey." Yvonne attempted a cheery tone, but fell frightfully short.

As soon as Pete's backside had disappeared, Gibson took a cue from his mother. "Oh, Mom! I forgot. There's a phone call for you."

"What? Why didn't you say something? I didn't hear the phone ring!"

"Better go quick 'fore she hangs up."

Yvonne's skeptical facial expression said that ninety-nine percent of her didn't believe the child—not for a second. But apparently, the one stubborn percent that did forced her to jump off the sofa and head for the nearest phone.

"What are you up to, kid?" asked Jewel.

"Now's your chance to talk to Dad about me being a batboy."

"For heaven's sake, Gib—"

"You promised. Pleeeeease."

"Oh, for crying out loud—okay. But I don't know how—"

Both adult Sagers reappeared. Gibson winked at Jewel before leaping off the sofa and dragging his mother back out of the room with a hasty explanation that Mrs. Averick had to talk to his father in private.

"What is it, young lady?" asked Pete, sitting next to Jewel as she squirmed on the couch. She stammered a bit. "Is it Russell?" he asked. "I was going to talk to him today about his slump."

"His slump?"

"Yeah, you must know the poor kid is zero for his last fifteen at bats, two for his last thirty-one. Is it any wonder we've lost our last five games? I'm considering resting him, but we need his bat . . . desperately."

Jewel frowned and nibbled on her bottom lip as everything fell into place. She sighed dramatically, and made doelike eye contact with Pete. "I know, Mr. Sager—ah, Pete . . . he's having a really tough time with his *bat* at home, too, if you know what I mean."

Jewel's inference wasn't lost on the worldly Pete Sager, who opened his mouth, rolled his head back, then brought it slowly back down in a show of understanding. "Oooohhh."

"Terribly traumatic for a man like Russell, I'm afraid. I mean, not being able to step up to the plate, let alone hit a home run."

"I bet."

"Of course, you probably never—"

Pete coughed, sniffed, and hitched his pants up in a comically macho manner. "No, never. Never."

"I can help him, you know."

"You can?"

"Sure, this happened once before, when he was with the Yankees."

"What can you do?" Pete lowered his voice and averted his eyes. "I'm sorry. That's probably personal. But I'm extremely anxious to get him hitting again."

Thankful she was wearing shorts, Jewel allowed a husky note to enter her voice as she crossed her legs slowly and wiggled her hips in the soft cushions. "That's quite all right, Pete. I can . . . what is it you say? . . . groove one for him."

The manager of the D.C. Diamonds was momentarily bedazzled.

"But . . ." continued Jewel.

"But?"

"I'm just so angry at Russell right now, I don't think I can do it."

"YOU HAVE TO! Excuse me, I mean . . . please, won't you reconsider. I'm sure he's sorry about whatever he's done. In fact, he's kind of been moping around the clubhouse lately."

"Well, Pete, I'm willing to snap his bat back, so to speak, if you do me an awfully big favor?"

"You want me to talk to him?"

"NO! Ahh, what I mean to say is that talking to him won't be necessary. I'm sure it would only embarrass him to no end. You *cannot* talk to him about this."

"Okay, then what can I do for you?"

"First, you have to give me your word you'll do it."

"You can't expect me to do that, dear."

Jewel sighed, before letting a delicious edge enter her voice as she looked Pete square in his eyes. "Fine, then you'll be the one responsible for Russell's average diving below the Cardoza line."

"That's Mendoza."

"Whatever." Jewel clicked her teeth and waved a weary hand. "I can help you. All I'm asking you to do is a very special thing for a person who did something very special for me."

Pete's head was spinning as an uneasy sensation crept through his rock-solid body. He had a feeling he was about to meet the real Jewel Averick—the one everybody ragged on. He swallowed hard. "What is it, Jewel?"

"Do I have your word?"

"Will it be detrimental to anyone?" he asked. "I know all about the Dee Sweet talent-show debacle."

"Of course not. It's really no big deal. You're going to laugh when you hear what it is."

"Okay, you have my word."

"Let Gibson be a batboy."

Pete Sager didn't laugh. He exploded. "ARE YOU KIDDING?! ABSOLUTELY NOT!" He quickly stifled his outrage. "He knows my conditions."

"You gave your word."

"You tricked me."

"I did no such thing. This is called swapping horses."

Pete took a full minute to assess the situation and massage his temples. "Russell is honestly having a problem at the . . . ah . . . plate?"

"That is the absolute truth." *Didn't you just tell me he was two for his last thirty-one at bats?*

"Oh, all right. Gibby is fifteen now anyway. But if Russ doesn't snap out of his slump, Gibby is out. And you'll be the one who'll have to explain why."

"Deal." Jewel extended her hand. Pete stared at the woman before shaking it. He sent up a silent prayer for Russell Averick; being married to such a beautifully bewitching conniver surely must be a strange mixture of heaven and hell.

5TH INNING:
Rookie of the Year

It was the middle of June, but it felt like August, due to the infamous humidity in the swampland known as Washington, D.C. To her horror, Jewel felt a bead of sweat forming at her hairline as she walked with Yvonne, Gibby, and Dee from the underground player/VIP garage to the stadium clubhouse. She would have wiped the rogue drop of perspiration from her brow, but she was too busy keeping both hands on Two-Mile's box and both eyes on the alert for Lipless Graves and Snow.

It was Saturday, 11 A.M., two hours before game time. Jewel was nervous and hopeful and fearful that she would run into Russell. *Will he look pleasantly surprised and give me a quick kiss like nothing's wrong? Will he ignore me? Will he yell and humiliate me in front of Yvonne and Dee?* Jewel's stomach lurched at the possibilities. She would have called off the clubhouse visit, but Gibby insisted she be there in case his father had a sudden change of heart.

To his son's relief, Pete Sager immediately told Gibby to "suit up" while shoving a white uniform with broad black-and-red stripes into the eager child's hands.

The ladies waited outside in the lounge area to avoid Diamonds in the buff. Fifteen minutes later, "Gibson the Batboy" emerged with a grin not quite as wide as it should have been.

"Oh, Gibby! You look adorable! My baby!" Yvonne squealed, throwing loving arms around her offspring.

"Mooommm, chill," moaned the teenager, enduring his mother's jubilant kisses and hugs.

"That uniform's not very slimming, is it, Gibson?" said Jewel as she walked around the newest batboy, eyeing him as if he were an interesting museum piece.

"I think you look perfect," said Dee, snapping a picture of her three compatriots.

"You and that damn camera. That's the umpteenth picture you've snapped in the last half hour. I've got so many spots in front of my eyes, I could be declared legally blind."

"Too bad you're not legally mute, Jewel," said Yvonne, still straightening her son's uniform and picking off wayward strands of thread. "What's the matter, Gibby? You don't seem happy."

"I'm fine, Mom. I better go now."

Yvonne bussed her blushing baby boy one more time and turned to Jewel and Dee. "Well, ladies, I know you also have work to do. I trust all three of you will be on your best behavior." After hugging the younger women for luck, Mother Sager headed off to the luxury suites reserved for Diamond families and friends.

"Well, Gibby," Dee said, extending her hand, "good luck and don't get in the way of any screaming line drives headed for Mark—I'm kidding."

Gibby appeared to have missed the joke as he kicked the floor peevishly and mumbled unintelligibly. Jewel recognized the signs of malcontentedness. She'd perfected them. "What's up, kid?"

"Dad won't give me a number."

Jewel reached out and twisted the young man's shoulder so his back faced her. "So what? You've got a 'BB,' only players get numbers, right?"

"*Dad* has a number, the *coaches* have numbers—and they're not players."

"But, Gibby," said Dee, "batboys always wear 'BB' on their backs."

"Well, I don't want to. I want a number." If one listened to him with closed eyes, he sounded exactly like a four-year-old.

"Oh, for heaven's sake, Gibson," said Jewel. "Why do you let little things upset you? You wanted to be a batboy and couldn't get around your father without my help. Now, you want a number—Lord only knows why—and I can see I'm going to have to lend a hand again."

"HOW?" demanded both Gibby and Dee, the former with zeal, the latter with dread.

"Just hand over that jersey; I'll be through with it in two minutes flat." While Gibby stripped, Jewel reached in her just-purchased fanny pack and pulled out what looked like an X-Acto knife.

"What are you doing with that?" Dee asked as Jewel popped off the blade's protective cap.

"After the other day, I thought I should have a weapon. This was the only thing I could lay my hands on that would fit in this fanny pack and still leave room for my makeup."

"So what are you going to do?" Dee made sure she swayed her roomy backpack in front of Jewel. Once again, it appeared she was way ahead in the category of preparation.

"Watch . . . and learn." Using a nearby coffee table as an operating slab, Jewel proceeded to make several precision cuts to the jersey's letters, transforming the lowly "BB" into a lofty 33. "There now!" she trumpeted, placing the four extracted swatches into one of Gibby's hands and the altered jersey in the other. "I believe that should retract your poked-out lip."

Gibson Sager was ecstatic, jumping around like the liveliest puppy in a batch of beagles. Jewel and Dee chuckled as the happy stripling leaped into the clubhouse just as Russell Averick walked out of it.

The laughter died in Jewel's voice, replaced by breathless anticipation. Here she was, face-to-face with her husband, after an uncertain five days.

Russell stopped short, staring at Jewel.

"Hello, Russ," said Dee, struggling under the tense silence, as the Avericks stared each other down.

Russell turned and threw Dee one of his best pearly-white specials. "Deanna, it's nice to see you. How are you doing?"

"I'm fine; how've you been, Russ?"

"Great, just great." He swiveled back to Jewel and let all the warmth drain from his voice. "Jewel, how are you?"

His wife straightened her back and threw up her chin. "Fine."

"What brings you here?"

"Came to see the game."

"Is that right? What's the occasion?"

"Pete finally let Gibson be a batboy and I came down here to wish him luck."

Russell released a coldly skeptical laugh. "Yeah, right. Tell me another. Why are you really here?"

She bristled. "That *is* why I'm here."

"Come off it, Jewel. You wouldn't do anything of the kind. Whatever the reason you're here, I can guarantee it has nothing to do with Gibby."

The contempt in his voice and the validity of his words aroused Jewel's pride, which kept her from blurting out she was there for him—in an attempt to track down his damnable hero. Two of Russell's teammates chose that moment to pass through the lounge, halting any comment she might have made. When the beefcakes had departed, silence returned, until Russell finally murmured, "If you're not here to see me, then you'll have to excuse me; I've got a game to play." He paused and lowered his voice. "*Are* you here to see me? . . . Silly question. Of course not. You claim you're here to see Gibby. And I think we all know that's bullshit. You couldn't care less about the kid. I'm betting on another reason—one that would benefit you."

Jewel took a deep breath to alleviate the pain in her chest. "You're right, Russ. Of course I'm not here to see you. How could watching you strike out all over the place *possibly* benefit me?"

Russell Averick had no answer. He stormed past Jewel into

the clubhouse, but not before warning Dee about her choice of company and spitting out an unflattering oath toward his spouse.

Dee felt her own face flush as she stared at Jewel, who seemed unmoved. "Don't you think you should tell him about—"

Jewel threw up her hand to silence Dee. "I don't want to talk about it. Besides, we have a job to do. It'll be one o'clock before we know it and we want to be in position."

As they headed out the clubhouse lounge, Dee noticed that Jewel's hand shook when she reached for the doorknob. That almost imperceptible sign of fragility somehow made Dee feel better about Jewel Averick as a person—as a human being.

"What are we going to do?" Dee whispered as she and Jewel stopped at the first row of the upper deck. There wasn't a free seat available, and the occupants of the two seats directly behind home plate, or "the dish," were formidable-looking rowdies who belonged to a group of backward-baseball-cap-wearing, tattoo-sporting, torn-off-sleeve-adorning, beer-chugging, burping, brawny, and generally obnoxious men.

Jewel squinted at the stadium clock. It was twelve forty-five. "We have to be in position soon, so I guess we'll go sit down."

"Where?"

"Come on." Jewel began to "excuse me" and "pardon me, sir" her way down the front row, all to the delight of the "gentlemen" who whooped, whistled, and hollered their approval at being imposed upon by such an attractive maiden. Dee didn't follow.

"There's no seats here, but you can sit on my lap," offered a sinewy, unshaven character parked in the seat Jewel desired. She wondered how anyone could wear so many earrings and still radiate unquestionable masculinity.

"No, thank you. But I *would* like to watch the game from your seat. And my friend would like to sit there." Jewel pointed to the burping bumpkin next to the earring man.

"Is that so? Did ya'll hear that? The ladies want our seats."

After a generally lusty and lighthearted comment period, this crew of missing links settled down enough to let Jewel continue. "Would you be so kind as to find another seat?"

The man was no longer amused. "Look, sister, why don't you go find another one. These are ours. So get out of the way; the game's about to start." Jewel considered taking his advice. But she was on a mission and held her ground. "Look, mister, how'd you like to sit in the Diamonds' private suite? Rub elbows with friends and family of the team?" Jewel motioned for Dee to join her. "Give them our suite passes," she ordered, when a red-faced Deanna arrived at her side.

"What?"

"You heard me. We're gonna trade seats with these two gentlemen."

"But I don't—"

"Just do it, Dee Sweet."

Dee Sweet did it.

"Are you bullshitting me, lady?" asked he of many earrings.

"Absolutely not. You tell them Jewel Averick gave you the tickets. And if they have any questions, send them up here."

The men thought about it as they took in the casual, yet elegant look of the women in crisp jeans and even crisper T-shirts who were blocking their view. The rocks on their fingers certainly indicated no little amount of wealth. Finally, the men gulped a swig of beer, ran their arms across their mouths, sniffed, belched, and uttered, "Naaaaa... Sorry, girls. We like it here... with our boys."

"Go on, man. We'd rather look at these honeys than your ugly asses," shouted a crew member, giving the women a lascivious once-over.

"We should go," recommended Dee, tugging at Jewel's fanny pack.

Jewel ignored her and reached in one of the front pockets on her tight jeans. "Look, pal, I've tried to be nice, but I can see that won't work. Here—" She slammed two hundred-dollar bills in his hand. "Buy all the beer and junk you can stomach and go enjoy the game from a luxury box. They'll serve you hard liquor . . . free."

Five seconds later, Jewel and Dee were adjusting their rears in the upper deck's gray metal seats and signaling for the peanut man.

At twelve fifty-nine Jewel pulled Two-Mile's sundial panel from the little box and placed it on her lap among a smattering of peanut shells.

"Shouldn't you hold it up?" Dee suggested as she yanked a pen and tiny notebook from her big backpack, ready to write down the magic numbers.

"I don't know."

"What if it's not facing the right way?"

"Well, then I'll get a number this way, and then turn it around and get another set of numbers, just in case."

And so she did. At precisely one o'clock, the shadow of the sundial fell on 14. Jewel quickly turned around the panel and discovered the shadow again fell on 14. "Guess it doesn't matter. Two-Mile has us covered. Clever man." Jewel smiled, putting the dial back in the box, and beginning the countdown to two o'clock.

"D'ya want a beer, Sweet?"

"Are you kidding? After the other day?"

"What? A white person that doesn't want a beer? Thought that was your beverage of choice." Jewel chuckled.

"So we're goofy and beer-mongers, huh? What about malt liquor? Why is it all those commercials have blacks in them?"

Jewel shrugged. "Beats me. Never tried the stuff. Must have missed that in the 'How to Be a Negro' handbook."

"I remember one time in college, I got really shitfaced off Moosehead beer and started singing—or rather, screaming—patriotic songs in a local hot-dog hangout."

"You? Nooooo!"

Both ladies laughed as they stood to let one of their new acquaintances named Richie shuffle by. Dee leaned in and whispered, "Say, do you always carry big cash with you? I can't believe you gave those guys two hundred dollars."

"Money has a way of unsticking the stickiest situations, Sweet. And if our little game continues along these lines, you'd be smart to bring a few extra pesos yourself."

"I wonder how Lucille Winship is enjoying our two friends in the suite." Dee bugged her eyes and gulped air dramatically. "Oh . . . oh . . . oh . . . there must be a mistake . . . oh . . . oh . . . oh . . . these two men are so pedestrian . . ."

Jewel chuckled at Dee's performance but sobered when Russell's name was announced. She watched intently as number 42, chosen in honor of his idol, Jackie Robinson, strolled to the plate. "God, if he doesn't get a hit, Pete and Gibson Sager will never speak to me again."

"What's that?"

"Long story."

"Hey, Jewel," shouted a new buddy, Clyde, from three seats away. "Your old man needs a hit. He ain't been earnin' all that money they give 'im."

"Now, now, Clyde," answered Mrs. Averick calmly, "if he wasn't earning all that money, I wouldn't have been able to treat you and your pals to a dozen hot dogs, and, more importantly, two rounds of beer in the span of twenty minutes. You drink like a fish, son. I pity your liver."

Russell promptly drew a walk. "Oh well, at least he didn't make an out," said his wife.

For the next forty-five minutes, Jewel and Dee chatted and joked amiably with the crew. But at two o'clock, it was down to business. The second number was 30. An hour later, they happily noted the third number, 19, and the fact that their husbands had two hits each.

"Let's see what we have," said Jewel, placing the box on her lap and working the tiny vault's combination. She tried 14-left, 30-right, and 19-left. Nothing happened. She was about to try right-left-right when a man the crew called Bully leaned so far over to see what Jewel was doing he impeded her work. She cleared her throat. "Do you mind moving your macrocephalic head, Bully? Can't you see I'm operating here?"

The insult was lost on Bully. "What do you think's in there?"

"Don't know. That's what I'm trying to find out."

"Hope it's good. You girls have gone through a lot of trouble to get that combination."

"And a lot of money," Jewel cracked, eyeing the souvenir D.C. Diamonds teddy bear sitting incongruously on Bully's broad lap. She had bought the bear and other goodies in an attempt to prove she wasn't as selfish or greedy as her husband asserted.

Jewel tried 14-right, 30-left, and 19-right. The safe didn't crack.

"Wait!" cried Dee. "Try 19-30-14. Remember, the note said three o'clock, two, and one; not one, two, three!"

Jewel grinned stupidly as the little lock gave away under her agile fingers. "Sweet, you're a genius." Bully's head got in the way again. "If you don't back off—"

"What is it? What is it?"

"Calm down and I'll tell you." Jewel's heart sank as she opened the safe and saw only another yellowing note. "It's just a piece of paper, fellas. Nothing special. All this for nothing. No jewels, no money—Aunt Trudy is quite the prankster."

"What's it say?"

Jewel quickly opened the paper and wasn't surprised to see "#3" at the top; it was another clue. She refolded the note without reading it and shoved it in her pocket.

"Well . . . ?" Bully prompted.

"It says, 'The joke's on you.' "

"Man, your aunt has a strange sense of humor. Oh well, cheer up, Jewel," he said, boldly patting her thigh. "We had fun, didn't we? At least your old man got two hits today. You must bring him luck."

Jewel allowed herself a small smile at the irony of Bully's words. "I'd like to think so, Bully. I'd like to think so." She handed Dee Two-Mile's box. "Ready to go?"

They had only moved past three crew members when they saw Anthony Graves waiting for them at the end of the row. His grin was downright evil. Both women froze, their hearts pole-vaulting.

Dee spun around to push Jewel in the opposite direction. "Go! Go! The other way! Move it!"

Mr. Snow was waiting on the other side, blocking that alternative. Dee's stomach contracted. "Oh, crap!"

"I thought you were supposed to be looking out for them!"

"Me? What about you?"

"Okay, okay, let's think of something."

They stood still for five seconds until a beer vendor piercingly hawked his wares. "I've got it," Jewel whispered. "Follow me, and be prepared to run like hell. We'll head for the clubhouse, not outside. We don't want to be sitting ducks. Got it?"

"What are you going—" Dee began, but Jewel was already heading back toward Anthony Graves. She followed as Jewel re-excused herself down the aisle, grabbing two half-empty cups of beer from Bully and Clyde. "Sorry, fellas, but I need these," she muttered. When she was three feet from Graves, Jewel gave him a saccharine smile. Then she tossed the beer in his face, stunning him long enough for her to lunge and push him down on his skinny buttocks. Her cry of "RUN!" was not necessary, as Dee already was taking the cement stairs three at a time and bolting for a tunnel-like exit.

Jewel hightailed it, too, with Anthony Graves on her trail, and Mr. Snow hot on his, followed by a bewildered security guard. It was a strange parade that grew longer with each yard as strangers took up the chase. Shouting for a clear path, Dee led the pack of pursuers, taking them on a trek down winding ramps. She flew through hapless vendors, unguarded fans, and innocent children—many of whom were unceremoniously knocked out of the way by her backpack.

When she reached the field level, she headed back into the stands. Anthony Graves came to a complete stop and then was jolted another five feet forward, as the unobservant Mr. Snow plowed into his back. Next, a wheezing security guard stopped and gasped, "What's the problem?"

"You saw it, didn't you?" yelled Graves, throwing a hand out toward Dee and Jewel. "That woman threw a beer in my face and pushed me down for no goddamn reason. Who the hell does she think she is?"

"Okay, okay, calm down, sir. Did you provoke her in any way?"

"No!"

The young security guard, who looked fresh out of pre-K, adopted a condescending tone. "Well, there's no real harm done. They've probably just had a little too much to drink. We'll reprimand them for you. How's that, sir?" Graves thanked the young guard, who pretended to take up the chase again.

Dee and Jewel continued their Flo Jo at her best routine through the lower reserved boxes and on toward the field. Dee leaped onto the top of the Diamonds' dugout with a loud thud—two thuds as Jewel joined her.

They simultaneously jumped off the dugout, landing right in front of some surprisingly skittish bench jockeys, who were, to say the least, startled by the sight of two women flying onto the field and into the dugout and down the clubhouse runway.

"Wasn't that Sweet's wife?" asked one young Diamond.

Mark Sweet clearly saw the disturbance from his vantage point at second base. Russell Averick also witnessed the two female figures—suspiciously wearing the same clothes as Jewel and Dee—

leap off, and then into, the dugout. Both men blinked, as if trying to shake off a bizarre mirage.

Pete Sager knew *exactly* who had interrupted his game and charged down the runway after the two culprits.

Gibby Sager sat in front of Russell Averick's locker and pondered why his father had taken such an exception to his modest uniform modification. Gibby's musings were interrupted as Jewel and Dee shot into the locker room.

"Gibson!" cried Jewel.

"Mrs. Averick! Dad won't let me—"

"Got no time for that, kid. Need you to block this door! Hurry! We're in trouble." Jewel's words were rushed, as were her steps past Gibby, who immediately ran over to slam shut the heavy steel door that separated the dugout runway from the locker room. In doing so, the young man came close to going down in history as the person who broke the highly paid noses of Russell Averick and Mark Sweet—not to mention his own father's.

Bolting the lock, Gibby blocked out the angry protests on the door's other side. He then grinned and ran to follow the women.

Dee and Jewel sprinted to the VIP garage. "OPEN THE DOOR!! OPEN THE DOOR!!" Dee yelled to Mike, the guard who operated the garage doors from his little console booth. "QUICK . . . OPEN THE DOOR!!"

Mike slammed his hand down on a big green button, and within seconds the two large doors started to roll up, revealing the feet, calves, knees, thighs, hips, torsos, shoulders, and heads of Anthony Graves and Mr. Snow.

"CLOSE THE DOOR!! CLOSE THE DOOR!!" Dee ran to Mike's booth and pounded the hell out of his red button. But it was too late. The doors could only respond to one command at a time, and with the mixed signals they received, decided to jam in the three-quarters-open position. Graves and Mr. Snow already were comfortably inside and pointing their guns at anything moving.

"Noooo!" Jewel feverishly dug around for the keys in her fanny pack and jabbed her finger on the not-properly-encased X-Acto knife. "OOUUCCHH!"

Two months from retirement, Mike quickly shot his hands in the air, accidentally knocking Dee in the face, before fainting dead away.

Graves aimed his gun at Jewel. "Get over there with them! And keep your hands where I can see them! I've had just about all I can take from the two of you, and I don't want any more fuckin' trouble!"

"Yeah," added Mr. Snow, "younz is startin' to make Anthony crabby."

Graves rolled his eyes. "I'll handle this," he said under his breath. "Okay, now there won't be any trouble and no one will get hurt if you just hand over whatever you got from Two-Mile, starting with that box you shoved in your bag, Sweet."

Dee looked at Jewel, who slightly raised her eyebrows, before handing over the box. "Very good. Now we're getting somewhere. Okay, Averick, hand over that piece of paper you put in your pocket. And NO funny stuff, d'ya hear?"

A loud noise sounded from behind one of the cars. "Who's there?" demanded Graves, before ordering Mr. Snow to check it out.

"Check 'em all," said Graves, ". . . and hurry." He turned his gun back to Jewel. "Give me that paper—NOW!"

Jewel dug in her pocket and with great reluctance handed over the third clue. Feeling the sting of tears behind her eyes, she wished she had taken the time to read it.

Graves quickly perused the note's contents. "Let's go, Mr. Snow. We're done here."

There was no response from Mr. Snow. Keeping his gaze and gun leveled on his three hostages, Graves summoned his associate again. Nothing. "Snow! Come on, let's go!"

Walking backward, Graves retraced Mr. Snow's steps, looking

between each car. "Snow? What the—" said Graves, before disappearing behind a minivan that belonged to one of the Diamonds' trainers. Jewel and Dee knew that was the exact spot where Mr. Snow had disappeared from view.

Unlike the Bermuda Triangle, the mystery was solved as Gibby, wearing the widest one-dimpled grin in the history of such grins and twirling a Louisville Slugger over his head like a nunchaku, popped out from behind the minivan. "Got 'em!" he said as Jewel and Dee ran to him. There, lying in a heap, was the dazed and confused duo of bad guys.

Dee quickly grabbed the guns and pointed them at the men's limp bodies. Jewel retrieved Two-Mile's third clue from Graves's clutches, snatched a fistful of the villain's hair, and jerked his woozy head so that his ear was near her mouth. She whispered, "When you are hauled into jail, I strongly suggest you don't mention any of this Two-Mile stuff, unless you want the whole world searching for him. You just tell them you were trying to rob us, 'cause that's what we're going to say—you hear?" Graves moved his mouth and moaned a bit. Jewel shook his head. "You hear me, Graves?" He slowly nodded of his own accord. "Good."

The women ditched the pistols in a nearby garbage can, ran over to the Lexus, hopped in, with Jewel behind the wheel, and gunned the engine for a quick departure just as their husbands and an excited entourage arrived. Even with the car windows up, Pete Sager's "GIBSON!!" made them jump. Jewel slammed on the brakes. Dee didn't even have to ask. She popped her head out the window. "Come on, Gibby!" The batboy's face lit up as he powered his husky legs to the car and hopped in the backseat. Jewel burned rubber, just as the garage doors unstuck and started to descend.

#3
*CONGRATULATIONS! YOU'VE FOUND MY NEXT
CLUE BY WADING THROUGH MY JIVE.*

I HOPE YOU LIKED MY MAN HARRY B. IF HE WAS
   STILL ALIVE.
NOW, TO CONTINUE ON YOUR QUEST, YOU MUST
   PRESS ON WITH THIS RIDDLE,
YOU DON'T REALLY HAVE TO B.E.G., BUT YOU
   HAVE TO GO TO BIDDLE.
GO TO CLARE CHRISTIE'S HOUSE NUMBER 16311,
   PLUS THREE.
BE NICE AND TELL HER WHAT YOU WANT, AND
   SHE'LL BRING YOU RIGHT TO ME!

Jewel, Dee, and Gibby stared at the clue as they munched on Big Macs and fries at the McDonald's on New York Avenue, miles, and several income brackets, away from their Chevy Chase and Potomac digs—the last place, they resolved, anybody would look for them.

"Gibby, I still can't believe what you did. You're amazing."

Gibby, it seemed, had first thought the women were heading back toward the stands, but soon realized they must have gone to their car. When he arrived at the garage, Graves and Snow were wielding guns and Mike, the guard, had already been shot (or so Gibby thought). He tiptoed out of the garage to get help but tripped over a carelessly placed bat and formed a plan of action. Bending over, he stealthily retraced his steps, ran to the minivan for cover, and banged it with the bat. Soon Mr. Snow showed up. WHACK! Then Graves. WHACK! WHACK! "Simple as that," he said, with such cool bravado it was hard to believe he was only fifteen years old.

Gibby gobbled the last bite of his Big Mac. "What's really amazing is I know exactly what this clue means."

"You do?" cried the women, shoving the fries they couldn't eat onto Gibby's tray, figuring the junk food must stir his incredible gray matter.

"Sure, this one was easier than the first. Okay, basically, he didn't know if Harry B. was still alive. But, if he was, he hoped you liked him . . ."

"Ahh, Gibby," said Jewel.

"Huh?"

"We figured that much out."

"Oh, right. Well, here where he's saying you don't have to beg . . ."

"Yeah?"

"I'm sure that stands for the Baltimore Elite Giants. They played at Bugle Field, which was near Biddle Street."

"Biddle!"

The women leaned over and planted tandem kisses on Gibby's smooth chocolaty cheeks. He grinned giddily. "All the women want me! Got me some salt-and-pepper action!" Suddenly, as if realizing what he'd said, the youngster shrank down and looked sheepishly embarrassed. "Sorry."

Dee and Jewel just laughed and patted his fidgeting hands, which were making a nervous hash out of his fries. "My dad is going to kill me."

"Oh, don't worry about that, kiddo. I'll talk with your mom and dad and tell them that you saved us, and that you should be lauded, not punished."

"What about running away from him?"

"Tell him you weren't thinking clearly, you know—suffering from some kind of post-heroic stress, and just wanted to get away from those awful, bad, mean men in a hurry."

Gibson brightened. "Yeah, he'll buy that."

Dee looked at her watch. "The game is long over, we should be getting Gibby home. Even though we called, I'm sure Yvonne wants to see that he's safe and sound."

Yvonne was indeed happy to see her son and very proud of him. "Honestly," she said, hugging him close, "there are so many creeps out there. You just never know when you'll be a target for crime. So, they were after your jewelry and money?"

Dee and Jewel nodded.

"A lot of people are mugged in parking garages. How lucky you girls were to have my baby save you."

"You can say that again," said Jewel.

"Of course, if you weren't acting so silly, running on the field like that, this might never have happened. What in the world were you thinking?"

For once, it was Dee who came in first with a fib. "It was a stupid thing, Yvonne. We were up there drinking beer after beer and soon we started reliving old college pranks, and the next minute, you know, we dared each other to run on the field and through the dugout."

"Yeah, Sweet was going to take off her top, but thank God I talked her out of that bit of foolishness," said Jewel.

"That's two times liquor has gotten you girls in trouble. If I ever see either of you with a drink, so help me, I'll thrash you."

Pete Sager, when he arrived, was less sanguine about the interruption in play and the near forfeiture of the game. But even he managed to overlook the door-slamming-and-locking and running-away-from-the-scene misdemeanors when he learned of his son's heroics. Pete even forgave Jewel's jersey joke and said that for the next day's game, Gibby could wear number 99.

"Where to now?" Jewel asked, after they had visited the police station to press charges against "the lipless devil and albino giant."

"I don't really want to go home and hear Mark's mouth," said Dee. "But I guess I have no choice."

"You can come to my house."

"Thanks. As much as I hate to, I'd better go home."

Mark wasn't there. A sickening sensation settled in her innards as she pondered his whereabouts. Then he called.

"So you made it home?" he said. "I tried to catch up with you at the Sagers', but you and Jewel had already left."

"Is that right?"

"They explained everything to me. I'm glad you're okay. But I'm telling you, Duffy—and I'm serious when I say this—Jewel Averick is a bad apple. She's got you acting like a wild teenager. If you continue to hang out with her, you're going to end up in jail."

"Where are you now, Mark?"

There was a slight pause. "I'm at the stadium. Mac is working on my knee."

So it's the knee again, is it? "When will you be home?"

"Give me another hour or so."

"Sure, whatever," she said evenly. "Oh, and Mark?"

"Yeah?"

"Monday, I'm calling to see about having a pool installed in the backyard." She slammed down the receiver.

Mark hung up with a shaky hand. He turned to the attractive woman next to him and gave her an equally shaky smile. "We'd better hurry up, she's talking about getting a pool."

Things weren't much better in the Averick household.

Jewel entered her home with excited anticipation, happy to see both the Jeep and the Ferrari in the garage. Russell was in the den with all the trophies of former great players surrounding him. Sitting in his favorite old recliner, his chin resting on his clasped hands, he stared at his memorabilia case. Jewel was sure he heard her entrance, yet he didn't turn to acknowledge her presence. She softly walked over to stand in front of him. "Russ?"

He didn't answer. She stooped down to meet his gaze and placed a delicate hand on his knee. "Russ? Are you all right?" He didn't say a word, but his jaw jerked out of its socket. "You're mad at me because of today, aren't you? Well, I can explain all that. You see, Dee Sweet and I had a little too—"

"Don't bother, Jewel," he said. His voice was husky, as if he hadn't used it in a while. "I heard the story. You're just lucky Gibby was there to save you. Of course, he was the butthole who locked us out of the clubhouse."

She brightened. "So you're not upset?"

He closed his eyes and took a deep breath before opening them again and leveling a tired gaze on his wife. Jewel gulped at the intense sadness in his eyes. "Why should I be upset? You've obviously got everything under control. I'm just sorry you dragged Dee Sweet into whatever game you're playing these days."

"I didn't drag—"

"While I was gone," he interrupted, "did you happen to take a trip to Philly?"

Jewel was immediately wary. Something about the added tautness in his voice put her on guard. She pulled her hand off his knee, stood up, and took a step away from him—out of striking distance. Russell had never laid a hand on her and deep down she knew he never would. Nevertheless, better safe than sorry, she thought. "I might have . . . why?"

Did Harry B. track me down? Did the zoo call? The police?

"Xavier Lawrence called."

Shocked, Jewel sucked in a good deal of air. She kept quiet, trying to read Russell's face. He remained inscrutable, except for an occasional uncontrollable jaw jerk.

"The message is still on the machine."

Jewel hesitated, before tearing to the kitchen, where she banged on the answering machine's "play" button. "Hello, Jewel?" came Xavier's voice. "It's Xavier. Just wanted to repeat how happy I was to see you again. You can use this place as a bed-and-breakfast any day. Talk to you soon. Bye."

Jewel gasped and her eyes absolutely bugged at Xavier's delib-

erately provocative message. *Damn him! He probably was hoping Russell heard. I'm going to kill him! I'm going to . . .* Russell
had quietly followed her and was standing directly behind her.
As she turned, she rammed into his rigid frame, bouncing off
him as she would a trampoline. She let out a tiny squeal mixed
with surprise, guilt, and defensiveness.

"Russ . . . let me explain. Please. It's not what you think."

Russell spat out an icy laugh. "No. Don't say a word. I honestly don't want to hear it. I'm tired of listening to all your wild
stories and putting up with your scheming." He paused to throw
up his hands, and released the most dejected sound. He was in
pain. And it hurt Jewel to know she'd caused it.

Jewel had never seen her husband look older. Still a young
man, he suddenly resembled a world-weary middle-ager. "You
asked me the other day to think why I married you. And I have."

Jewel held her breath, sure she didn't want to hear whatever
was coming next. "Look, Russell, you're upset right now. You
don't want to say anything you might regret. Really, Xavier was
trying to make you jealous, can't you see that?"

"Jealous of what? He can have you! . . . Should I give a damn
about a woman who sells my belongings behind my back?"

"One time, Russ—"

"One time? You must be kidding. How about the time I
refused to go to a card signing because I didn't want to charge the
kids, and you went in my place! Do you know how humiliating it
was to have to track down all those people you ripped off?"

*Do you know how hard it was to forge your name on five hun-
dred damn baseball cards?* "I've already apologized for that.
Besides, the kids were happy—at least *I* didn't let them down
like you did."

"What about the time you deliberately screwed up our return
flight from Hawaii so we'd miss my brother's wedding—all so
you could spend a few more days in Maui?"

The same brother who tries to grab my ass every time he's alone with me? "That *wasn't* deliberate."

"The hell it wasn't. And what about a wife who won't go to her husband's awards banquets because she claims she's too damn sick?"

"Twice! That only happened twice. You win so many things, I can't possibly be healthy all the time. I was as sick as a dog."

"With what? A goddamn hangnail?"

Jewel blew a fuse. "OKAY, OKAY!! What do you want me to say? I'm a horrible person? I'm sorry? Is that what you want from me? Okay, Russ, I'm sorry. I'm sorry you find life with me so damn trying! . . ." Jewel's temper suddenly dissipated. "But most of all, I'm sorry you feel that way, because . . . I . . . ah . . . really like being your wife. It's just, sometimes, I wish we could spend more—"

Russell cut her off with a disbelieving snort.

"It's true," she continued. "I love you, Russ."

His head shot up to focus his shocked gaze on her. She could tell he wanted to believe her. "Don't say that, Jewel. It's just another lie to suit your current needs."

"You don't believe me?"

"Why should I? You've never said those precious three words to me before. You're only trying to throw me off."

"It's the truth! I do love you!" She reached out to hug him, but he stepped away from her touch.

"Then why won't you have my children?"

The soft words were whispered, but they literally rocked Jewel on her feet, as if he'd punched her. She shook her head with confusion and dismay. So that's it, she thought. She'd known for some time Russell wanted a baby, but she'd had no idea how much. She'd always told him she wasn't ready. And that was the truth. But now it was clear that, had she been ready and willing, their relationship might not have come to this critical crossroads.

✿   ✿   ✿

The ladies didn't head off to Charm City until Monday, because Dee wanted to spend Sunday with her children.

"So you're going to Baltimore with Deanna Sweet?" said Jacinta O'Hara as she gathered up the sheets from the Avericks' bed.

"Have you been listening to my phone conversations again, Cindy?" said Jewel, forcing her feet into a new high-tech pair of sneakers.

"What am I supposed to do—pretend like I don't hear you?"

Jewel rolled her eyes and strapped on the fanny pack.

"I don't know what you's up to, but a man who was very interested in Two-Mile McLemore offered me money to give him Two-Mile's glove—the one that Russell bought."

Jacinta talked so casually, Jewel at first thought she didn't hear her correctly. "Pardon me?"

"Yep, offered me a thousand bucks for it. But I know how upset Russell got when you tried that, so I turned him down."

"When was this?"

"Last week."

"That damn Graves," said Jewel.

"What was that?"

"Nothing."

"Why don't you tell me what you's up to?"

"What makes you think I'm up to something?"

"You's *always* up to something. Come on, Jewel, tell me—I might be able to help."

"Sorry, no can do, Mrs. O." Jewel threw her "majordoma" a crooked smile and hopped down the stairs and out of the house.

Jacinta stood at the window and watched Jewel roll her Lexus out of the driveway. When the car was out of sight, she stepped back and did a belly flop onto Russell and Jewel's oversized bed. She rolled over, reached in her apron pocket, and pulled out Two-Mile's third clue. Sometimes it paid to pick up after people. But removing personal items from her employer's fanny pack while said employer takes a bath was probably above and beyond the call of duty.

"I'm so glad the guys are on a road trip," said Dee, gazing at the beautiful Camden Yards as she and Jewel motored into Baltimore.

"How long have you been married?"

"Nine years," Dee said.

"That seems like a lifetime."

"Don't I know it. How in the world do people manage to stay married for more than that—like fifty-five fucking years?"

"Well, if you're still fucking after fifty-five years, that's worth hanging on to."

Both women paused, looked at each other, and then burst out laughing. They had been edgy and tense since they left D.C., each not knowing what to expect on this latest trip and, more distressingly, not knowing how their marriages could possibly stand the test of time. The introduction of foul language released the tension.

"But seriously, I think marriage can only last if there's a lot of turning the cheek and forgiving," said Jewel as she followed the flow of traffic past the Baltimore tourist trap known as the Inner Harbor.

"Think it's like twenty bucks to get into that aquarium these days," said Dee, pointing to the geometrical glass structure.

"For fish? I'd rather watch a 'Flipper' marathon."

"I used to love that show! I had a crush on Sandy, then later it was the kid who played Peter Brady."

Jewel smiled. "That was my favorite show. My mom hated the theme song and used to fly out of nowhere as soon as the first note sounded to turn down the volume. But I hummed it anyway."

"Who didn't want to be a part of the Bradys?"

"Me; they weren't black. I was so glad when Cosby developed

a black Brady Bunch, God bless him. 'Good Times' just wasn't cutting it."

Jewel turned onto Calvert and continued the journey along the narrow street, thankful for the huge street signs that periodically told her she was on the right track.

"It's funny . . ."

"What?"

"Well, don't get me wrong, but I'm assuming you were raised with a good deal of whites."

"Hah! That's an understatement."

"And yet you're not a . . . well, I had one black friend in college and she . . . she wasn't into being black at all. I honestly forgot that Debbie *was* black sometimes. She hung out with us, dated white guys—you know."

"Yeah, I know. My mom made sure I knew I was black. When we had show-and-tell in school, other kids would bring in a new toy or their goddamn smelly dog, but my mom made me stand up in front of all those white kids and talk about Martin Luther King and Rosa Parks."

"Really?"

"Absolutely. And she'd drive me miles out of the way so I could belong to organizations with black kids," said Jewel, silently acknowledging that she irritated the hell out of the black kids just as she did with the whites. "One time my brother dressed up as a baseball player for Halloween and Mom instructed him to say he was Jackie Robinson, not just a baseball player."

"Except for the fact that she obviously spoiled you to death, she sounds like a wonderful woman."

"I think I'll keep her," said Jewel with a soft smile, before turning to Dee. "What about you? Growing up being the only white kid in a black community must have presented some awkward moments."

Dee frowned and swung her head around to stare at Jewel, before laughing.

"We should be coming to Biddle shortly."

Like Girard Street in Philadelphia, Dee discovered Biddle to be a lower-middle-class neighborhood that might have seen better days, but was percolating with activity. There seemed to be a little store on every corner. Kids were bustling about playing with jump ropes and an assortment of balls, and men were taking great care washing their cars. Jewel came within a foot of hitting a man who ran into the middle of the street to shout at a neighbor. He had poorly processed hair and his oversized stomach was straining against the buttons of his shirt. "Kind of sad—all that man has to work with is a comb and a loud voice," said Jewel, before cracking up, while Dee scooted down in her seat, afraid the target of Jewel's comment might have somehow overheard.

Heading toward the railroad tracks, Dee said, "Gibby said the Giants played down here on Edison Highway. So number 16311 should be near here."

Jewel began eyeing the rows of neat, well-kept houses and soon pulled up in front of 16311. They hopped out, added three, crossed the street, and soon were knocking on the door of 16314.

A teenage girl, no more than thirteen, answered the door. She was brown-skinned and bright-eyed, with two thick plaits twisted on top of her head. "Yes," she said with a drawl that should have put her much farther south of the Mason-Dixon line.

"Hello," said Jewel, not sure exactly how pleasant she should appear. She didn't want to come off as a Jehovah's Witness or a renegade Avon Lady. "I'm wondering if someone by the name of Christie Clare lives here?"

"Clare Christie," corrected Dee, giving the youngster a toothy grin.

"Who are you?" asked the girl.

Jewel and Dee were so excited, they didn't answer her right away. "Who is it, Tracey?" The male adult voice, calling out from somewhere in the home, caused them to stop bouncing up and down in excitement and turn to the matter at hand.

"I dunno, some women are here to see Aunt Clare." The girl was joined by a round-faced, pleasant-looking middle-aged man with thick glasses and an old-fashioned crew cut. He wore light blue polyester shorts, dark brown socks, and sandals. "Can I help you, ladies?" he asked.

"We were hoping to speak with Clare Christie."

"And you are?"

"I'm Jewel Averick and this is Dee Sweet." Predictably, while ringing a tiny sports bell, the names meant nothing to the man, so Jewel rushed on, "And we're here because we think Two-Mile McLemore sent us."

"Beg pardon?" said the man, frowning so that all his features converged on the tip of his nose.

"We're here to see Ms. Christie about Two-Mile McLemore," echoed Dee.

"Come in," he said, opening the door and unconsciously pushing the kid to the side and out of the way. "AUNT CLARE . . . ," he bellowed.

The living room was packed with people. "Well, what do you know," whispered Jewel out of the corner of her mouth, "wall-to-wall Negroes."

She wasn't kidding. There were at least a dozen folks of all ages, shapes, and sizes sitting and meandering about. Dee instinctively retreated to stand behind Jewel, who was swatting at a toddler who had pounced on her leg.

"Hello," she said, throwing a hand out to the group. They issued a collective mumble of uncertainty. All eyes then turned to an elderly woman, who entered the room with the aid of a cane. She was short and slender, with a lighter-brown complexion similar to Jewel's and long gray hair pulled back in a ponytail. Her face was slightly wrinkled, and she wore glasses that made her eyes look like tennis balls. She sported a long tan tank dress with a snazzy matching crocheted jacket. And her lips brought new meaning to the term "shocking pink."

"What is it, Reggie?" she demanded in a crackly but stern voice.

"These ladies came to see you. They say Two-Mile McLemore sent them."

Clare Christie became so unsteady on her feet, one twenty-something young man had to help her into a nearby wing chair. When she had composed herself, she croaked out, "That's impossible."

Jewel walked over to stand in front of the woman. "I tend to agree with you, Ms. Christie, but nevertheless, we believe either Two-Mile has sent us here—or someone is playing a hoax."

Reggie ordered two of the younger members of the tribe to remove themselves from a love seat so the guests could sit down.

Clare cleared her throat. "I live alone in this house fifty weeks out of the year, and then every June, for my birthday, my family here visits for two weeks from Georgia—like Baltimore is Barbados. They're waiting for me to kick the bucket. Don't know why, haven't left them a cent. Anyway, I believe you've met my nephew, Reggie, and that's my niece, Gloria . . ." She waved a hand at the bubbling beanpole of a woman sitting on the sofa. "Every year their families expand. I can't keep up." She then instructed her family to state their names for Jewel and Dee. After these rather lengthy introductions, Clare continued, "And now I've got two young women coming here with news from my past. I don't know if I can take all the excitement." She focused her tennis-ball gaze on Jewel. "Now, tell me, dear, how do you know about Two-Mile?"

Jewel reached in her fanny pack to retrieve the clue and was alarmed to find it unretrievable. She turned a panicked eye to Dee. "It's not here."

"What do you mean, 'It's not here'?"

"I don't have it!"

"What are you looking for, dear?" asked Clare Christie.

Jewel took a deep breath, then related the whole story, starting with the glove and ending with Biddle.

The room was silent as all turned to stare at Clare, who sat back in her chair, sighed heavily, and closed her eyes behind the extra-thick spectacles. Finally, she said, "That boy was always one for crazy adventures and games. But I'm afraid I can't take you to see him."

"You can't?" said Jewel, filled with despair.

"I can, but I don't think it's what you girls had in mind," said the old woman quietly. "You see, he's dead."

"Noooo!" cried Jewel, louder and more dramatically than even she believed she could. Until that moment, she hadn't realized finding Two-Mile meant so much to her.

Dee reached over to squeeze Jewel's hand. "How did you know Two-Mile, Ms. Christie?"

"I met him through a mutual friend back in the thirties. He grew up in Baltimore, too. He had just played a double-header with the Stars right down the street at Bugle Field. And there was a little get-together at my friend's. Two-Mile and I hit it off and began a short-lived courtship."

"Weren't you going to marry him, Aunt Clare?" asked Reggie.

She sighed. "Well, we only knew each other for a few months, but I was sure he was the one for me."

"What happened?" Dee asked.

"In late August 1939, one of his fellow barnstormers showed up on my doorstep and told me Two-Mile had been run over by a car in Washington and was dead."

Jewel moaned a little; Dee squeezed her hand harder. "I'm so sorry, Ms. Christie. That must have been a very sad time."

"They brought his body back to Baltimore for his burial. You should have seen that service. Most of the Giants showed up, including their star pitchers known back then as 'The Big Three.' Bill Byrd, Andrew 'Pullman' Porter, and Jonas Gaines."

"We heard that Two-Mile was really something on the diamond," said Dee.

"Oh, he was something, all right. He could hit that baseball. It just soared and soared and soared. He was powerfully built, short and stocky with no legs to speak of, but barreled-chested, with huge broad shoulders. I remember one time he brought Biz Mackey to meet me—"

"The rapper?" asked Jewel, finally pulling herself together enough to speak.

Tracey and another youngster giggled at Jewel's confused statement. "Heavens no," said Clare. "Biz Mackey. The famous catcher. He taught Roy Campanella everything about being a catcher. Campy played for the Elite Giants, you know. I could tell he had talent. But I had no idea he'd make it all the way to that Brooklyn team." The elderly lady exhaled wistfully. "Those were some good times."

The same active toddler who had blitzed Jewel leaped onto Dee's lap, forcing her to slam back against the love seat—which, in turn, slid backward and hit the wall with a thud. "That's right, Sweet, break up the furniture," said Jewel.

Wrestling the baby into a sitting position, Dee inquired, "Does this chair always slide black like that?"

The room was silent as one and all took in what she had said. "Not when you're in it," said a young man with an impish grin.

Everyone howled, including Jewel. "Honestly, Deanna," she said, feigning disgust, "I can't take you anywhere. You'll have to excuse her, she's not used to bunches of black folks." Dee turned the color of Clare's lips, but laughed along with the rest.

When the giggles subsided, Jewel and Dee realized they had come to the end of the road. "Ms. Christie, the note said you would take us to see Two-Mile, but I guess that's impossible . . ." began Dee.

"I can take you to his final resting place, dear. I know that's not what you wanted, but I'm sure it will help you feel better about your trip."

Jewel and Dee looked at each other. "Want to?" asked Dee.

"Sure, why not. Then we'll be through."

The women followed Clare Christie and her nephew to a colossal cemetery not far from her house on Biddle Street.

"Cemeteries give me the creeps," Dee said in a hushed tone as they drove along the winding roads and rolling knolls of the graveyard, which was filled with everything from simple foot-high crosses to Parthenon-like monuments. Reggie pulled over at the base of a sizable hill. Clare pointed to a particularly pretty sycamore. "He's underneath that tree. I'd join you, but I'm afraid I'll have trouble with this hill," she said, tapping her cane a few times.

"That's fine, Ms. Christie," said Dee. "We appreciate you doing this."

"Do you want us to wait?" asked Reggie, whose stomach growled loudly. He obviously was missing some kind of meal and was anxious to get to it.

"No, that's okay, we'll be able to find our way out easily enough," said Jewel.

"Well, again, I'm sorry I couldn't have been more help, ladies. Good luck to you." Clare Christie graciously extended her slender hand, then she and her nephew drove away.

All the way to the tree, Dee politely excused herself to every grave she stepped on.

"Here he is." Jewel pointed to the large rectangular grave marker set flush to the ground. At the top was a baseball sitting between crossed bats. "His name was Robert." Jewel felt strangely sad for a man she had only first heard of a week ago.

CAUGHT IN A RUNDOWN

Robert "Two-Mile" McLemore

1910–1939

Here lies #4
In the valleys, in the hills,
On playgrounds, or in mills.
Like no other, he could hit a ball,
Finding eternity over the wall.
As his legend echoes on earth,
He now plays with spiritual rebirth
Behind where the ivy twines,
D.C.'s brightest star still shines.

Subdued, the women made their way back to downtown Baltimore.

"I'm hungry," said Dee.

"Yeah, me, too. I can't believe it's already six. Do you want to stop at Phillip's? I could go for some seafood."

Half an hour later, the two raised their wine-filled glasses inside the Inner Harbor's noted restaurant. "Here's to a battle well fought," said Dee.

Jewel clinked her glass and promptly downed the spirits, glad she had ordered a bottle of the stuff. "Here, here." They sighed and sat quietly, speaking only when it was time to order dinner. Jewel gulped down another glass of wine before slamming the delicate stemware down on the table. "Damn! I wanted this."

"I know." Dee was sympathetic, recognizing that Jewel had had much more riding on Two-Mile's hunt than she did.

"Do you think Two-Mile really left those clues?"

Dee shrugged as she poured herself another glass of wine. "Who knows? But those riddles mean a hell of a lot to old Lipless Graves and Snow. Whatever we were supposed to find was of great value; whether it was Two-Mile himself, concrete proof that he existed, or something else."

"I can't believe we went through all this trouble. Man, if he wasn't already dead, I'd strangle that Two-Mile character."

Dee shook her head and laughed. "I'd pay money to see you go toe-to-toe with that giant. What did Harry B. say? He was like six feet five?"

Jewel frowned. "That's right, he did."

"Wassa matter?" After a glass and a half of wine on an empty stomach, Dee's speech was already beginning to suffer. Jewel reached over and prevented her from taking another swig.

"Hold off on the hooch, Sweet, I want to keep your brain clear for a second. Didn't Clare tell us Two-Mile was short and stocky?"

Now it was Dee's turn to frown. "She sure did."

They were still pondering what that meant when their meals came. The best they could come up with was this: Either one of the two senior citizens was mistaken, or there were two players by the name of Two-Mile McLemore.

"Hold up!" blurted Jewel, spitting out a sizable chunk of crab-meat. "Clare said he died in 1939. And Harry said he received the money from Two-Mile in the fifties! Something is definitely wrong, Sweet. Something's just not right!"

"What are you thinking?"

"I have no friggin' idea." Jewel's enthusiasm deflated with the truth of her words. "I can't believe I risked life and limb to find proof of Russell's hero and all I can tell him is, 'Russ, he may have existed; then again, he may not have. He could have been one, two, or ten men. And did you know the short and stocky one's name was Robert and he wore number four?' Jeez, he probably knows that crap already."

Dee smiled and was about to agree, when two of Jewel's words stuck in the colander of her mind—too big to sift through. "Jewel!"

"What?"

"You said, 'number four'!"

"So?"

"Number four . . . as in clue number four."

The women stared wide-eyed at each other. " 'Here lies number four'!"

They bolted out of their chairs. "You pay for dinner, I'll go get the car," ordered Jewel.

"Okay . . . hey . . . hey . . . ?"

"Ah, come on, Sweet, we've got no time for you to pretend like you can't afford it. Besides, if we don't move now, we'll be crawling around a cemetery in the dark."

"CHECK, PLEASE!"

"This is the third time you've driven by that headless angel," snapped Dee, frustrated that she and Jewel couldn't quite recall the location of Two-Mile's grave. They'd been driving in circles; everything looked the same.

"Where the hell is that tree?" Jewel whined, rapping the steering wheel. "It's got to be around here somewhere. I remember passing that entire Williams Family back there . . . didn't they have lovely tombstones?"

"I'm not here to critique graves, Jewel. Hurry up and find it; it's getting dark."

Jewel drove on a little farther, then parked at the base of a hill. "I think this is the place."

They climbed to the top of the hill, with Dee tiptoeing and asking to be pardoned to nervous excess. "God, this place gives me the willies."

"Why? You think a zombie in this bone orchard is going to reach up and snatch you to hell?"

"Don't say that! What's the matter with you?"

"I'll tell you what's the matter. This isn't the spot."

"It's not?" Dee questioned, looking down for Two-Mile's marker.

"Nope. That is." Jewel spoke in a choked monotone that made Dee immediately look at her.

"What is it?"

Jewel pulled her behind an obelisk memorial. "Look over there, to your right, across the road, on the hill."

Dee did and gasped at the sight of two very familiar figures standing by a large sycamore. "Oh my God. How'd Graves and Snow get here?"

Jewel stuck her head around the monument to peek. "I don't know, but there's something terribly wrong with our penal system. They must have made bail."

"Look, they're writing down something."

"Shit! Do you think they've figured it out, too?"

The women stared at each other soberly. "That means," said Dee slowly, "we're now on equal footing. We don't have an advantage. If they solve clue number four before we do, we'll never find Two-Mile—or whatever."

They watched Graves and Snow totter down the hill, hop in a blue Jetta, and drive away.

Then it was their turn.

A man in his mid-thirties watched as Jewel Averick and Deanna Sweet left the cemetery just before its tall iron entrance gate swung shut for the night. A smile played on the man's lips as he crossed the street to a pay phone.

"Hey, it's me," he said, gripping the receiver between his broad shoulder and caramel-colored cheek. "Yeah, those idiots were here. But it seems they've got some lovely competition . . ."

6TH INNING:
Stealing Signs

If a person could literally knit his brows, Gibson Sager would be creating an impressive cardigan. The child was thinking so hard, Jewel could smell his cerebral noodles burning. Truth was, the aroma came from Yvonne's unsuccessful attempt to whip up a homemade pizza.

Jewel and Dee flanked the teenager as he pored over his baseball books. "Are you getting anything, Gibson?" asked Jewel.

He groaned. Like Jewel, he was struggling with the realization that Two-Mile McLemore was no longer "among us." "I don't know what he's talking about. Do you think Lipless and the abominable snowman figured it out by now?"

"I sure hope not. If they did, we're sunk," said Jewel.

Carrying her charred pizza, Yvonne sauntered into the living room to announce break time. "Honestly, people, you've been staring at that clue for two straight hours. Give it a rest. You're not going to have any fun with Two-Mile's game if you stress yourselves out over it. What's the urgency?"

Three pairs of knowing eyes focused on the blackened disk Yvonne plopped on the table.

"Gibby, go get plates and napkins. Deanna, get that pitcher of lemonade out of the refrigerator. Jewel, get some glasses, preferably the ones with the yellow tulips."

"Do you know which glasses she's talking about, Gibson?" Jewel asked.

"Yeah."

"Get them for me, will you?"

"Jewel! Get up from this table and stretch your legs, right now!" said Yvonne, before picking up the piece of paper with Dee's hastily scribbled words.

In the valleys, in the hills, on playgrounds, or in mills.
Like no other, he could hit a ball, finding eternity over
the wall.
As his legend echoes on earth, he now plays with spiritual
rebirth
Behind where the ivy twines, D.C.'s brightest star still
shines.

A wickedly self-satisfied smile danced across Yvonne's face as the trio returned. She waited until everyone was seated. "If yunz hadn't banished me to the kitchen—and I think you now know what a mistake that was—I would have saved you a lot of trouble."

The other three dropped their pizza bricks to stare at Yvonne. "What are you talking about, Mom?" asked Gibson.

"Well, so far, Two-Mile has sent you to the home of the Philadelphia Stars, the D.C. Diamonds, and the Baltimore Elite Gents—"

"Giants."

"That's what I said. Anyway, it only stands to reason that this clue also points to a 1930s Negro Leagues town. Don't you think?"

"You're right, Mom!" Gibby began flipping through one of his books. "Now we just have to figure out which one."

"*We* don't have to figure out anything, because *I* already did," said Yvonne.

"Tell us!" said Jewel.

"He wants you to go to Pittsburgh."

"What? How do you know?"

"I grew up there—I should know! Where else are you going to

find hills and valleys and mills—as in steel mills—in the Negro Leagues? They had the Pittsburgh Crawfords—"

"Cool Papa Bell," Gibby said in a reverently hushed tone. Jewel groaned at the name.

"—and the Homestead Grays," Yvonne finished.

"Josh Gibson." The boy actually blessed himself here.

"Yvonne!" cried Dee Sweet, extending her arm to squeeze the newly crowned heroine's hand. "You're brilliant! Isn't she, Jewel?"

Jewel Averick didn't smile or show any visible sign of appreciation. She only stared at Yvonne Sager for several seconds before finally reaching out to place her hand on Dee's, which still covered Yvonne's. "I can honestly say, if it was my style, I'd kiss the hell out of you right now."

The four then began to do an enthusiastic, if uncoordinated, version of big-league high-fiving. It was Dee who sobered first. "Even if it is Pittsburgh, we still don't know what to do when we get there."

Yvonne grinned. "Sure you do, you see—"

"I know! I know! Let me tell them!" Gibby pleaded.

"Be my guest, son."

Gibby Sager stood and puffed out his chest. "When they tore down Forbes Field in Pittsburgh back in the early seventies, they left the outfield wall as a memorial. Get it? Wall? '. . . finding eternity over the *wall*'? And the last time we visited Nana and Pop-Pop in Pittsburgh, Dad took me to the wall. And you know what?"

"What?!" demanded Jewel and Dee.

"It was covered with ivy!"

Jewel grinned at Dee. "Shall we take to the friendly skies?"

"Sounds like a plan. I'll call the airlines."

Feeling uncharacteristically generous—not to mention, terribly forgetful about Graves and Mr. Snow—Jewel turned to the Sagers. "You two want to come?"

Both instantly said, "Yes!" and then quickly added, "No!"

"What? Why not?"

"I forgot, my daughter, Gwen, is visiting from New Jersey tomorrow. I wish you could meet her. She's a lot of fun. Anyway, she's a newlywed and I haven't seen her since the wedding. Her husband owns a restaurant and I was looking forward—"

"Fine! What about you, Gibson?" asked Jewel, throwing up a hand to halt Yvonne's meandering speech.

"I'd love to, but I told Dad I'd meet the team in Philly on Thursday. Remember, I'm a batboy now—a workingman. I can't just drop my responsibilities to traipse around the country on a whim."

Not about to argue with a fifteen-year-old brandishing a bloated sense of self-importance, Jewel turned to Dee. "Okay, then make it two tickets for the first thing smoking to The Burgh."

Two and a half hours later, at about 3 P.M. on that sunny Tuesday afternoon, Jewel and Dee swerved violently in the backseat of a Pittsburgh cab as it sped through the Fort Pitt Tunnel (lovingly referred to as "The Tubes" by locals). They were on their way to Oakland, home of the University of Pittsburgh, the Carnegie Museum of Art and Natural History—and the outfield wall of old Forbes Field.

As Jewel paid the taxi driver, Dee looked at the towering Gothic eyesore known as the Cathedral of Learning, which dominated the collegiate atmosphere of Oakland. "Man, is that building gruesome, or what? I remember thinking the same thing every time we came here for a swim meet."

Jewel followed Dee's line of vision. "Is that the Forbes Field wall?"

"No! It's Pitt's Cathedral of Learning."

"Then who cares about it? Where's that doggone wall?"

"The cabbie said it's over there." Dee pointed to a rather rinky-dink ball field swarming with young women playing softball. A wooden sign on the fence declared that Jewel and Dee had stumbled upon "Mazeroski Field."

"Thought the name was Forbes?" said Jewel, squinting at, and scanning, the outskirts of Schenley Park. The Carnegie, and the Heinz Chapel. "I don't see any memorial wall," she said, her back not two feet from a twelve-foot brick palisade.

"Neither do I; but it's got to be around here somewhere," Dee said, resting against the wall of bricks.

Then, like that unforgettable cast of characters searching for the Big W in *It's a Mad, Mad, Mad, Mad World*, Jewel and Dee stared at each other, took a step away from their brick support, and turned slowly.

"Sweet! This must be it!"

"Well, it's not much of a memorial. Look, it's got graffiti on it."

They walked around to the other side of the wall, where they were instantly more impressed. "Now *that* looks like a ball-yard fence!" said Dee, taking in the sight of sunshine dancing off vivid red bricks, gorgeous green ivy, and the bright white of freshly painted "436FT" and "457FT" markers.

Dee handed Jewel her camera. "Here, take my picture; I'm going to stand by the flagpole."

Jewel backed up on the perfectly manicured grass, tripping over a pale, chunky coed who was sunning herself. "Oh, excuse me . . . say, since you're here, would you do me a favor? Would you mind taking a picture of that woman over there?" After brushing Jewel's sneaker print off her freckled leg, the girl obliged. It turned into quite the photo session because Dee insisted upon a picture from various parts of the famed angled wall that seemed to stretch out indefinitely as it disappeared behind ivy, shrubs, and trees. Jewel just sat at a picnic table and watched with boredom until Dee was finished.

"Well, Jewel, shall we start looking behind where the ivy twines?"

The two women took their time, starting at one end of the

wall, and checked brick by brick, leaf by leaf. They found miffed insects, but no clue. "This is such bullshit, I can't believe we're doing it," said Jewel.

"Fine time to say that. Don't tell me you want to quit."

"No, no. We're here; we might as well continue. Come on, Sweet, let's check again by the '436' sign."

They bent down at the base of the wall and began to peer underneath the ivy, when an object of some sort hit above them high on the wall. A small rock landed on Dee's head. "Ouch! What the hell . . . ! Where did that come from?"

Jewel Averick pointed to an area at the wall's eight-foot point. She stared at where she thought the stone had landed, blinked twice, then a third time, as she eyed what distinctly looked like the word "go" written on the brick in a rare leafless section. "Dee! Check it out! I see writing! See? Right there! Do you see the word 'go'? It looks like it's been painted on."

Rubbing her head where the rock had hit her, Dee squinted and barely made out the tiny letters. "You might be right! But how are we going to get up there?" She stopped her fancy footwork. "Here, let me climb on your shoulders."

Jewel's mouth opened in disbelief. "You must be joking."

"Okay, okay." Dee stooped down and bent at the waist. "You can climb on me," she said, quietly adding, "you wuss."

"What was that?"

"Nothing, hop up."

"Stand still, Sweet!"

"Get your damn knee off my nose!"

"Wait! Wait, here it is!" Jewel pulled back the leaves around "go" and found the word was actually "good." Upon further inspection, she revealed "good game." Then Dee collapsed, sending them both sprawling to the grassy ground.

"Excuse me," came a light feminine voice from above the women as they tried to regain their equilibrium and footing. It was the sunbathing coed, beaming down on them with a sympathetic smile. "Why don't you pull over the picnic table and stand on it?"

Jewel and Dee traded embarrassed looks before returning the younger woman's smile. "Thank you," said Dee. "Would you mind helping us drag it over here?"

"No problem. What are you doing anyway?"

Jewel briefly explained about a scavenger hunt set up by her aunt as they carried the table to the "436" sign.

Even with the additional footage the picnic table provided, Jewel discovered the beginning of the writing was still pretty high on the wall. But with some awkward jumps, she managed to relay each word of clue number five to Dee, who jotted it on her notepad.

The caramel-skinned man—who'd been standing inconspicuously behind the nearby "The Joseph M. Katz Graduate School of Business" sign—opened and closed his massive hand around another rock, before letting it drop to the ground at his feet. He didn't need it. The first one had done its job.

And it was a good thing. Graves and Mr. Snow had been at the wall early that morning. The ladies could not afford to fall behind.

#5

WELL DONE! YOU'RE ROUNDING SECOND, MY
    FRIEND, YOU'RE HALFWAY HOME.
THE GOAL IS WITHIN YOUR GRASP; IF YOU FOL-
    LOW THIS POEM
GO TO THE HILL ON OLD WYLIE AVE. WHERE
    HARV FAIRFEATHER RUNS HIS STORES.
HE, LIKE ME, LOVES A GOOD GAME . . . BEAT HIM
    AND CLUE #6 IS YOURS.

Anthony Graves took a deep breath as he entered Harv's Place on Wylie Avenue in the Hill District, a famous—if not somewhat notorious—neighborhood wedged between Oakland and downtown Pittsburgh.

Graves, along with the ever-present Mr. Snow, took in the little corner store with its two aisles of groceries and deli counter. While its chalkboard menu of sandwiches and grilled items was standard fare, the spelling left much to be desired (e.g., "pistrami Rubin").

Graves pushed past a tall woman, stepped up to the counter, and asked a young black man if he could find Harv Fairfeather in the vicinity.

"Maybe—depends," said the man, eyeing Graves and Mr. Snow.

"On what?"

"On who you are and what yunz want?"

"Tell him Anthony Graves is here . . . tell 'em Two-Mile sent me."

"Wait here. Lou! Watch the register!" The man disappeared and was replaced by Lou, a snarling mutt distressingly heavy on the pit-bull side. After ten minutes, he returned and instructed the white men to follow him. He led them to the back of the store and through an old, creaky wooden door, up a couple of flights of even creakier stairs, and into a smoke-filled and extremely warm room, which was lit only by the sun streaming in through six symmetrical windows. As Graves stepped inside to get a better look at the half dozen men who were lounging around, he could only make out their torsos and legs. The faces remained in shadows. He clearly saw, however, that this large, attic-type room sported two pool tables and a couple of card tables with daily Racing Forms scattered over them.

He didn't get far into the room before both he and Mr. Snow were frisked from behind and relieved of their pieces.

"Tsk, tsk, tsk, gentlemen. Is that any way to visit new acquaintances?" asked a voice with a distinctive whistle from the other side of the room.

"Fairfeather?" demanded Graves, taking another step forward.

The voice belonged to an elderly man who materialized from the shadows. He had straight, long gray hair pulled back in a ponytail. Judging by his brownish-red tones, slightly slanted eyes, and high cheekbones, Graves guessed Fairfeather, although black, was most definitely of partly American Indian blood. And by the wrinkles on his face and hands, one of which gripped a richly carved cane, the man had to be in his eighties. He wore a bright yellow shirt and a colorful southwestern print vest, along with jeans and moccasins. While the funky clothes detracted from his slightly hunched body, his buckteeth were so pronounced that Graves actually stared. "He looks like a goddamn beaver at Woodstock," he mumbled under his breath.

"I'm Harv Fairfeather. Who are you?"

"My name is Anthony Graves and this is Mr. Snow. We're here because Two-Mile McLemore said you would have something for us?" Graves checked out the other men in the room while he spoke. They were all black and, for the most part, they were all wearing black (with an occasional hint of brown and/or blue). There was also an abundance of patent-leather shoes. The men appeared to range in age from thirty to fifty; Fairfeather definitely was the elder statesman. Most were bigger and stronger-looking than Graves, but none compared in size to Mr. Snow. The men were giving him squinty-eyed glints of curiosity that would have made most men uncomfortable. *Uncomfortable* was having to go back to Duke Crammer without the next clue, Graves decided, and so he continued talking. "So, if you don't mind, we'd like the clue so you can get back to whatever it is you were doing."

"Did yunz hear that?" whistled Harv Fairfeather in his crackly old voice. "He wants me to just *give* him the clue." The gathered groupies began a halfhearted round of laughter. "Come now, gentlemen," he continued, "if I'm not mistaken, you have to beat me at a game to get it."

Graves and Snow walked farther into the room to stand within four feet of Fairfeather. "What kind of game?"

The old man waved his cane around the room, missing Mr. Snow's head by inches. "Pick one. Darts? Pool? Poker? Or perhaps you have another . . ."

Graves frowned and smirked. "And if I win?"

"You get the clue."

"And if I lose?"

"You don't get the clue—and, of course, you lose all that money."

"How's that?"

"Come on, boy. Don't be stupid. You don't expect me to wager something while you don't. Where's the fun in that?"

"And just how much am I to wager?"

"We like to start with a G-note."

"What? You're crazy." Graves's temper was starting to rise. He wasn't about to put up with this farting half-breed's shit. He'd had enough of that with Averick and Sweet. "I don't have that kind of money on me."

"Ain't you Crammer's man?"

"What if I am?"

"Then you got that kind of money on you."

"I don't!"

"Well, then you better get it, if you want to play for my clue."

The room was silent as everyone stood still and waited. Finally, Graves turned to give Mr. Snow a knowing look, which the blond giant read and understood. He then turned back to Fairfeather. "Are you sure that's the only way?" The old man nodded. "Well . . . I'm afraid there's going to be a change in your rules, Bucky."

"Hey! Who you callin' Bucky?—You sissy-voiced weasel . . ." began an indignant crony, making an attempt to step in Graves's face. He didn't get far, as Mr. Snow grabbed him around his throat, yanked him upright, and snatched the man's pistol out of his pants, tossing it to Graves.

"Now you know what kind of game *we* play," said Graves in his much-practiced sinister tone, putting the barrel of the gun on Fairfeather's forehead. "Perhaps you'll change your mind and just give me the goddamn clue."

While the chief and his men were momentarily paralyzed, Mr. Snow pranced over to the man who'd frisked him and retrieved their guns. Unfortunately, Fairfeather's warriors decided to put up a fight. The skirmish lasted thirty seconds, ending with one Fairfeather friend hopping around after a bullet found his patent-leathered foot and the others moaning and holding various body parts that Mr. Snow had attacked.

Panting hard and wiping blood from his nose and lip, Graves thought he'd try again, aiming the gun at Fairfeather, who'd just stood to the side and watched the frenzied battle of brawn and stupidity. "Now, do I get that clue, Bucky, or am I going to have to shoot it out of you?!"

"Wait here, I'll get it," Fairfeather said with a deep, whistling sigh. He walked over to a corner file cabinet, extracted an old-looking piece of paper, and handed it to Graves. "Here. This is it. Now get the hell out of here so I can get my man to the hospital. You damn near shot off his foot. Totally unnecessary. We just wanted a simple game of cards."

Graves looked at the clue before stuffing it in his pocket. "Well, Bucky, wanting things can hurt you sometimes."

Russell Averick *wanted* to believe his wife. Her words echoed in his head. *I love you, Russ . . . It's true. I love you, Russ . . . It's true. I love you . . .*

"Here's to Russ Averick, who's broken out of his slump and is poised to carry us to our first pennant." Pete Sager raised his half-filled wineglass and banged it against Russ's water-filled one.

The manager then turned to Will Black, a D.C. Diamonds radio broadcaster, who'd joined them for dinner at their Chicago hotel after a day game against the Cubs.

"He's right, Ave," said Will, "the team goes as you go. We were all praying for a speedy end to your slump. What snapped you out of it? It looked like you were holding your bat too low."

Apparently, the white wine Pete was drinking had the same effect as straight whiskey, because he let out a meaningful—and embarrassingly girlish—giggle.

"What's so funny?" asked an obviously confused Russell.

Made giddy from a six-game winning streak, the middle-aged manager chuckled some more. "Nothing, really."

"What is it? You laughing at my slump?"

"Course not," snapped Pete, who didn't seem capable of turning down the corners of his mouth to save his soul. Therefore, he took a swig of vino to give his mouth something to do.

Russ frowned, but returned his attention to Will Black. "I wasn't getting the bat head out in front."

Pete Sager promptly spit his drink across the table in a burst of laughter.

"What the hell is so funny, Pete?" asked Russell, wiping the wayward wine from his face.

Catching a tear before it ran down his face, Pete whimpered, "Nothing. Besides, I promised Jewel I wouldn't say anything."

Russell immediately stopped breathing as a wary uneasiness stole through him. "What . . . does . . . Jewel . . . have to do with this?"

The mirth that had consumed Pete Sager vanished like a competent magician's dove. He took a gigantic gulp of his drink. "Now, Russ, there's no need to get upset."

"I *am* upset. So tell me!"

"I'm certain you don't want to discuss this in public, do you?"

Both men turned to Will Black, who looked from one to the

other before judiciously deciding to leave while the bill was left unpaid.

When he was gone, Russ leaned over and whispered, "Now tell me what the hell Jewel said."

"Okay, okay. But first, let me say it's nothing to be ashamed of, and it happens to everybody at some point in time—not me, of course . . . but I'm sure it will . . ."

"What?"

"Jewel told me why you were slumping . . ."

Russell's frown developed into a genuine jaw-jerking scowl as Pete related Jewel's cock-and-bull story. Trying to hide resurfacing amusement, the tactless manager of men reached over and punched Russell's shoulder in comforting camaraderie. "I'm just glad you two were able to work things out."

Russell took three deep calming breaths before he choked out, "Did you repeat that bullshit to anyone else?"

Pete squirmed. "I may have mentioned it to Tory LaChance." LaChance was the team trainer.

"WHAT? That means the whole goddamn team knows!"

"Simmer down, you know he's got that Hippocratic oath—he didn't tell anybody."

"Hippo-shit oath! He's not a doctor, and half the time, he's not much of a trainer. You know LaChance's got a big-ass mouth! How many times have you had to switch signs in the middle of a ball game because of him?"

"Look, Russ—"

"No! You look! Whatever Jewel told you is a lie. That's all she does . . . is lie. And you're a damn fool to believe *anything* that comes out of her mouth!" Russell was so agitated, he rose to leave without pushing back his chair; he knocked it over as he strode away, leaving Pete Sager with the check and a guilty conscience.

✿   ✿   ✿

Mark Sweet was chugging his last drop of beer at the bar when his peripheral vision caught sight of Russell Averick striding toward him. Quickly swallowing, Mark reached out and stopped his teammate as he attempted to fly by. "Hey, Russ, got a minute?"

Lost in his wounded-male-pride thoughts, Russell was barely conscious of the hand that slowed his roll. "Huh?"

"You okay, man? You looked warped."

"Huh?"

Mark chuckled. "Russell Averick? Hellooo?"

"What is it, Sweet?" snapped Russell.

"I've been meaning to talk to you about our wives."

"What about them?" Russell remained unfocused as the blood continued to rush to his head.

"I don't know about Jewel, but Dee is acting crazy lately." Mark chomped on his bottom lip and paused as a worried look skipped across his face. "I'm getting a funny feeling they're in some kind of trouble . . . or at least doing something they shouldn't be doing."

Russell let out an ill-natured howl. "Oh, so you're beginning to think jumping onto the field and *coincidentally* running into gun-toting losers isn't quite right?"

"Well, yeah. And mysterious out-of-town trips, a cracked-up car . . . They're up to something, and I was hoping you could tell me what."

"Ha! That's a good one." It wasn't like Russell to be so sarcastically cold, but he couldn't seem to help himself. "I have no idea; nor do I give a fuck."

"Russ . . ."

"No, I mean it, man. If I were you, I'd take Dee aside and tell her to leave Jewel alone, 'cause whatever it is, the shit will hit the fan and I'm sure you don't want your wife covered in it."

Mark could see Russell was in no mood to discuss the matter and decided to change the subject. He had barely begun to talk about his new batting stance when a group of Diamond teammates surrounded them. "Sweet. Averick. Come on, we're going to dump the rookie in the pool to celebrate his first big-league hit," said the mustached and slightly overweight Sam Haversham.

Happy for the distraction, Russell followed the crew out to the pool. Mark didn't budge from the bar. For nine years, he'd successfully avoided hotel pools and was about to retire to his room, when his inner voice stopped him. *This is silly. You can do it. You can do it. Just walk out to the pool. Nothing bad is going to happen. Nothing bad is going to happen. You can do it. You can do it.* Silently repeating his mantra, he took a deep breath and began a hesitant, if not zombielike, walk to the pool.

By the time he got there, his teammates were whooping and hollering as the fully clad rookie outfielder, Gary Something-or-Other, splashed around in the pool. Showing poise and the confidence that comes with making the majors' minimum salary of more than a hundred grand, young Gary swam over to a bathing beauty and struck up a conversation.

Mark was twenty-five feet from the water's edge, but his legs refused to go closer. Just seeing the glistening blue water caused his heart rate to soar. And he found himself gulping for breath. *Calm down. This is fine. Nothing bad is going to happen. You're safe.*

McKnight, Mark's soon-to-be ex-buddy on the team, was tanked as usual and spotted him standing off, away from the splash party. "Sweetums!" he wailed. "Come on over, bud."

Mark was so nervous, he couldn't even remember how to shake his head, which was unfortunate, because McKnight and a couple of the rowdiest Diamonds ran over, picked him up, and began to carry him to the gigantic swimming pool.

Russell Averick had never heard a grown man produce such wild from-the-gut cries. Mark Sweet managed to bring new meaning to the words "freak out." His teammates thought he was clowning, putting on a show, but Russell's clear mind recognized utter terror; Sweet *sincerely* didn't want to take a dip. He writhed and bellowed like a madman as they carried him closer to the water, which prompted Russell to confront the unruly rabble and end Mark's torture. "Knock it off, McKnight! Put him down. He's not playing!"

Drunk or sober, nobody would dare mess with Russell Averick, the most respected Diamond. Within an instant, Mark was placed on his feet—sort of. His first attempt at walking was unsteady. His left leg missed the tiled deck and slipped into the pool, prompting a whole new wave of agonizing panic to grip him. "Oh God, oh God," he whimpered, making a supreme effort to hold down the bile in his throat and block out the images of his still young mother going under, and under, and under . . . as someone pulled him farther and farther away . . . his little hand outstretched for her . . . ugly, cruel, overwhelming water enveloping him . . . enveloping her.

The Diamond culprits stared in disbelief as Mark withdrew his leg from the water and collapsed prostrate on the deck. After a moment or two, McKnight reached down and touched his shoulder. "Sorry, man. I didn't know; can't you swim?"

"Is everything all right here?" asked a hotel employee who heard the commotion.

Russell answered, "Yeah, we're fine." He turned to his gawking teammates. "Okay, okay, show's over. Leave him alone. I'll take care of him. Go ahead . . . go away . . . and try to stay out of trouble." He jerked his head and made faces to indicate Mark would probably be less humiliated if they weren't hovering. After a slight hesitation, the band departed.

Not certain of what he should say, Russell stooped down and patted Mark's back, which was soaked with sweat. "You okay, Sweet? Can you move?" There was no response, just the wrenching sound of labored breathing and quiet sobbing. "Sweet?" Nothing. Leaning over so that his mouth was close to Mark's ear, he whispered, "I know you're upset, but you've got to get up. You want everyone to think you're a weak punk?"

Mark Sweet certainly didn't want that. He pulled it together fast and struggled to his feet with Russell's aid. He made it back into the hotel, leaning heavily on Russell, who gently reminded him to put one foot in front of the other. "Try to smile; let everyone know you're okay," Russell suggested out of the corner of his mouth. Mark wasn't very convincing.

Luckily, they got an empty elevator. And as soon as the doors shut, a trembling Mark immediately sank to the floor. "I think I'm going to throw up."

"I take it you're afraid of water."

Mark wiped the back of his hand across his mouth. "Hydrophobic."

"All this time, nobody knew?"

Mark shook his head and stood as the elevator reached their floor. Walking out on much stronger legs, he said, "Only Pete. Guess I couldn't keep it a secret forever. Now I'll be the butt of clubhouse jokes."

"Nah, I don't think so. We're all afraid of something. Look how long it took Jazz Johnson to get used to flying." Mark stopped at his door and rested his shoulder and forehead against it. Russell stopped as well and asked quietly, "Do you know why you're hydrophobic?"

Mark exhaled an unsteady breath. While he appreciated everything Russell had done and said, he wasn't about to delve into his personal problem. Shrugging, he said, "What's it matter? It's just something I have to deal with."

"You're right, it's none of my business . . . Okay, then, if you're sure you're all right, I'll be moving on. You can bet word has gotten to Pete and LaChance; they'll be by to check on you."

Mark slammed his hand down on Russell's shoulder and squeezed it. "Thanks, buddy. Who knows what would have happened if you weren't there. You're a good man."

As Russell continued down the corridor to his room, he had the satisfied feeling that comes from helping a person in need.

He thrived on being there for others. As the eldest of seven, the instinct came naturally to him. He had always been there for his younger siblings and his friends. Perhaps, he thought, hesitating before he inserted his card key, that's why his marriage felt so empty. Jewel never needed him. She'd never once asked him to do so much as kill a spider. She did it herself. She did everything herself, whether he approved or not. When he withdrew his affection, she simply went to Philly and picked up with Xavier Lawrence.

He'd told Mark, "We're all afraid of something," but he knew one person who wasn't. One person who didn't cower or quiver or quake. The one person who was fearless. The one person he had married. The one person who didn't need him.

Jewel looked around Harv Fairfeather's "play room" to give her eyes something to do rather than stare at his incredible buckteeth. Surrounded by rough-looking men, she wasn't the least bit intimidated. She was, however, hot; the place was an inferno.

Dee Sweet, on the other hand, was giving off tangible waves of tension and unease. "Let's get out of here," she whispered, grabbing Jewel's arm and pulling her toward the door. "These men are in no mood."

Indeed, while he was most impressed with the pulchritude of the two young women who had wandered into his lair, Fairfeather was still pissed off about his earlier visitors and had jumped on the pair upon their arrival. "I don't want any crap from you!" he said with that whistling sound of his. "We either play this thing by Two-Mile's rules or we don't play. Am I making myself clear?"

"Crystal," said Jewel, resisting the urge to chuckle at the man's inadvertent whistling.

"Crammer's men gave me a hard time, and they're going to be sorry they did."

"Excuse me?" Jewel frowned, wiping perspiration from her

forehead and taking a step closer to Fairfeather. "Who's Crammer? What men?"

"Duke 'Quiet' Crammer sent two of his boys here for the clue.
And they were extremely ill-mannered."

"They weren't Anthony Graves and a big man named Snow?"

"That's them."

Jewel and Dee exchanged dour stares. "How long ago was
that, Mr. Fairfeather?"

"This morning."

"And they got the clue?"

He nodded.

"We're through, Sweet," whispered Jewel.

"I have another copy of the clue," said Fairfeather.

"You do?"

"Absolutely."

"Then we have a chance?!"

"If you beat me . . . ah . . . so to speak."

"Oh, right," murmured Jewel, rolling her eyes. "What's all this
nonsense about beating you? What do we have to beat you at?"

Fairfeather pointed his mahogany cane to the pool table.
"Pocket billiards . . . of course, you'd have to beat Fats . . ."

Jewel looked at the remarkably slim man in his forties with a
goatee and beret—she could almost hear Dave Brubeck in the
background.

"There's also poker," said Fairfeather.

"Pool! Poker! You must be joking."

"I stopped joking when things got ugly this morning. Those
are your options. Pick one and let's get started. Don't pick one?
. . . It was nice meeting you, ladies."

Dee had remained silent through all of this and suddenly
stepped forward. "It's okay, Jewel. I can play pool."

Jewel's "What?" was the kind that first comes with a good deal
of disbelieving hot air. "Are you serious?"

"Absolutely. Not only can I play, I can beat Fats." Although she was sweating in the renovated attic's heat, Dee spoke with such self-assurance, there weren't many in the room who doubted her.

A slow smile crept across Jewel's face as she turned back to Harv Fairfeather. "Well, mister, it looks like you've got yourself a game of pool."

"Terrific," said the old man. "Now, you'll need to wager a grand against my Two-Mile clue."

"Come again?"

"You heard me, young lady."

"No way!"

"Then there's no deal."

The combatants stared each other down for several seconds before Jewel gave in. "I only have a check."

"That's fine; you said you're Russell Averick's wife, didn't you? Besides, if you bounce one on me, I'm sure the press would love to hear how you and Mrs. Sweet spent an evening of gambling in Pittsburgh's Hill District with the rather infamous Harv Fairfeather."

"Don't worry, Jewel. You won't be writing any checks," said Dee. "In fact, why don't we make this more interesting, Mr. Fairfeather? Why don't you put up Two-Mile's clue, and five hundred dollars. And we'll up ours to fifteen hundred."

Fairfeather squinted as he watched Dee casually run her fingers along his pool cues, checking each one for balance. She certainly looked like a pro. "Ahh . . . no, no deal."

"Well, then," she said, twirling one stick like a baton, "why don't you tell us everything you know about this Crammer person instead?"

"Instead of what?"

"Instead of me taking your five hundred dollars."

Dee was so smooth, Jewel could tell the old man actually felt he was getting a bargain.

"Duke 'Quiet' Crammer," began Fairfeather, "was a small-time racketeer based in Washington in the thirties and forties. He was a two-bit operator always looking for the big score . . . always looking for his ship to come in—actually, somebody else's ship; he'd just steal from it. I met the man once, maybe twice— what else can I say?"

"What's his connection to Two-Mile McLemore?"

Fairfeather shrugged. "Don't know. Years ago, I got a note from Two-Mile saying I should keep this clue of his and someday somebody—probably Crammer—would come looking for it."

"Was this in the fifties?"

"Yeah . . . I believe it was."

Jewel and Dee transferred glances again, silently noting that his story matched Harry B.'s. "What's your connection with Two-Mile?" asked Jewel.

"I met him when I was playing for Gus Greenlee's Crawfords. We hit it off right away. He called me Chief Fairball because I always got my hits right down the left field line. Two-Mile was somethin' of a force. Biggest swing I ever saw. Josh Gibson, who played for the Grays and the Craws, was as good as they got . . . 'cept for maybe Two-Mile." Harv Fairfeather's posture and facial features softened as he reminisced. "You girls ever heard of Gibson?"

They nodded.

". . . man died too soon. Only thirty-five years old. He wanted to play in the big leagues real bad; he was crushed when they picked Robinson . . . They called Josh 'the Black Babe Ruth.' Horseshit. He was better than anybody's Babe Ruth. He hit damn near a thousand home runs—one cleared Yankee Stadium.

"Gus's field couldn't keep him in the park either. You girls should have been in The Hill back then. Gus Greenlee was a black man who knew what he wanted. He built his stadium right down the street on Wylie for his Crawfords. One time he had Jesse Owens race a horse. Jesse won."

Harv Fairfeather inhaled briefly before continuing his reverie. "Back in 1932, when he opened his stadium, the Craws had the great Satchel Paige, Josh Gibson, Oscar Charleston, Cool Papa Bell, and Judy Johnson . . . can you imagine that? All on the same team!

"Gus also ran the Crawford Bar and Grille, which was the hot spot in the old days."

Jewel and Dee feigned interest for a bit. Then, when he stopped to inhale, Jewel said, "So, can we get that clue now, or not?"

Harv Fairfeather wasn't biting. "You know the deal. Win, you get my clue. Lose, I get your money."

Jewel turned to Dee . . . who turned to Fats . . . who threw away his toothpick, grabbed a cue, and issued a quiet, "Rack 'em up."

Jewel Averick could not believe what transpired next. Simply put, Deanna Sweet was a particularly pathetic pool player. Absolutely putrid. Her striped balls flew off the table so often, Jewel had to duck—twice!

"Well, that was interesting," Dee said in a slightly bored voice, taking a deep breath as Harv Fairfeather held out his hand for a check. "Not so fast. How about if we play best out of three— double or nothing?"

"WHAT?!" cried Jewel.

"That's right," continued Dee in even tones. "Mr. Fairfeather, this time, if I win we'll get the clue and a thousand of *your* dollars. If I lose, which is unlikely, you'll get two thousand."

Jewel clenched her teeth. "Sweeeeet!"

Dee waved her off. "That is . . . unless you want to save your money and just give us the clue."

Fairfeather first looked at Fats, who smiled, revealing two diamond-studded gold teeth. Then he turned back to Dee and declared, "Nobody could be that bad a player. Are you trying to hustle me, girl?"

"Let's put it this way," she cooed, "you might just want to hand over the clue and the money."

"And you," countered Fairfeather, "might just want to hand over *my* money . . . the money that Fats just won . . . and be on your way."

"What's the matter? Chicken?"

Fairfeather raised his brows in appreciation of Dee's balls and, after a minute or two of narrow-eyed contemplation, nodded to Fats, who once again demanded that someone "Rack 'em."

If possible, Deanna was worse. This time, homegirl put a tiny tear in the table's green felt and also showed tremendous dexterity by scratching in every pocket. Jewel wiped sweat from her brow and neck with each missed shot, not so much from nervousness, but from the room's blasted heat. When the debacle ended, she was left a trifle homicidal.

"Three out of five, double or nothing, girls?" cracked Fairfeather as Jewel marched a surprisingly cheery Dee to a corner.

"What the hell are you doing? I thought you were hustling them," she shouted . . . very quietly. "I hope you're prepared to pay him the money. Did you happen to notice they have guns, huh? Do you think we're just going to walk out of here?"

Dee smiled, radiating a fervent glow. "Sorry."

"I thought you said you could play?"

"Naaah, I was just bluffing."

"Bluffing?"

"I was hoping he'd back off and give us the clue if he thought he'd lose money."

"Well, guess what, Sweet?"

"What?"

"You guessed wrong, you bonehead."

"It appears that way." Dee turned to eye the men, who quickly pretended they weren't eavesdropping. Turning back to Jewel, she couldn't contain the bounce in her voice. "Did you see me, Jewel? I had them going there for a minute. I've never been so excited in my life. God, I've always fantasized about playing a slick hustler in a smoke-filled pool hall. And now I have . . . only thing missing was the sexy, low-cut dress . . . but who cares, right? . . . I mean, I did it! This has been great!"

Jewel shook her head as if she hadn't heard correctly, while her hand formed a tight fist at her side. Taking a deep, steadying breath, she whispered, "Okay, if you're through playing out your fantasies, what are we going to do about the clue?"

"Double or nothing?" giggled Dee.

Jewel was about to cream her, when a thought crossed her mind. *What am I, nuts? Sweet just distracted me with her professed pool prowess. I can do this. Piece of cake.* "Okay, Sweet, we'll go double or nothing. But this time let me do the talking *and* playing." She turned to the men and smiled. "I have a proposition for you gentlemen . . ."

Fifteen minutes later, Jewel and four others, including Fairfeather, were seated around the poker table divvying up chips and cards. The deal was: If she won, she'd get the clue and two thousand dollars. If she lost to any of the four men, she and Dee owed Fairfeather four grand. They would play with ten-, twenty-, and hundred-dollar chips. If Jewel won more than two grand, she could keep it. If she lost, she'd have to add to whatever amount she had in the pot to make up four thousand.

"What's it going to be?" she asked, swiping off the degrading sweat droplets gathered on her nose. "High-low Stud? Mexican Flip? Lowball? Cincinnati? Spit in the Ocean? . . ."

"Uh-oh, fellas, we got ourselves a player. I'll be watching you, Mrs. Averick."

"Likewise, Mr. Fairfeather."

"Draw? Deuces wild?"

"Fine."

"Would the lady care to deal?"

"Thank you."

Dee was duly impressed with Jewel's quick and graceful

hands as she cut and shuffled the cards. It was obvious she was no stranger to cards.

They started with a minimum bet of two hundred dollars. And the stakes grew rapidly as the players called and raised—raised and called. Eventually, Fats and Big Ralph dropped out, leaving Jewel, Fairfeather, and Frank—a slick little man with enough conk in his hair to grease lightning *and* thunder.

While Jewel was attempting to do the poker-face thing, she was nervously wiping her brow and around her neck. Her eyes held a desperate look Dee hadn't seen before, causing the "pool shark" to sober up a bit. *Lord, if we don't win, we don't get the clue that Graves and Snow already have. We'll be done.* And in Jewel's unique mind, that meant she wouldn't be able to save her marriage. *For your sake, Jewel, I hope you have one more trick up your sleeve.* Dee let out a little sigh as she focused on Jewel's sleeveless denim, button-down shirt. Perhaps their luck had run out.

But Jewel kept raising the stakes. When the combined Fairfeather contribution reached three thousand, the chief dropped out, leaving Jewel and Frank, who raised each other to dizzying heights until Fairfeather coughed theatrically—a clear signal to Frank. It was time to read the cards. Jewel promptly called Frank's last bet, making the pot a little over five grand. He paused (while everyone inhaled) and showed his hand. "Three ladies," he said with the slightest hint of childlike smugness.

Dee whimpered.

Jewel's face remained unmoved as she released the tiniest sigh, showed her cards, and let them speak for themselves. Fairfeather whistled (on purpose) as he stared in disbelief at her two aces and a deuce. "I can't believe it."

"Luck of the draw, Mr. Fairfeather. Luck of the draw," she said, throwing a wink to Dee. "Mr. Fairfeather, I believe you-all owe me thirty-two hundred dollars. And I *don't* take checks. Oh yeah, and I'll take that clue you promised me."

Harv Fairfeather sat back in his chair and eyed the young woman carefully. "I have to hand it to you . . . and admire you, Jewel Averick. You're as slick as they come. And pretty, too. A deadly combination."

"Oh, I bet you say that to all the girls. Now how 'bout that cashola?"

Finally, after the chips had been counted, Fairfeather excused himself and returned with a stack of bills and a piece of paper. "Here, this is Two-Mile's clue." When Jewel reached out for her booty, he captured her hand and squeezed it. "It was a pleasure playing with you, Jewel Averick. Come back anytime." She attempted to pull out of his grasp, but he held firm, causing her to meet his bemused stare. "And next time . . . I'll deal."

She raised her eyebrows in a silent salute and called for Dee, who was taking a few more cracks at the billiards table.

When they were halfway down the old wooden stairs, Fairfeather stopped them from the above landing. "Oh—and, girls, since you cooperated, you got the *right* clue," he whistled, displaying his buckteeth in a wide grin.

"What are you saying? Graves and Snow didn't?" They held their breath in hopeful anticipation.

"I'm afraid they'll be fucking . . . 'scuse my French . . . around in Kansas City."

Jewel wanted to run up and kiss the old man. "You're kidding! And where will we be?" she asked nonchalantly.

"Ah, ah, ah, Jewel Averick. That's for you to figure out."

"And we will!" she cried as she and Dee headed out of the store.

"No doubt about that—none whatsoever," said Harv Fairfeather long after the women had disappeared.

"I can't believe how lucky you were," said Dee for the hundredth time as the pair winged it from Pittsburgh to Washington.

"I *can't* believe you couldn't play pool worth a dime, especially after you talked such a good talk." Jewel allowed herself a small chuckle, realizing—with a shock—she had come to like Dee Sweet.

"Guess I couldn't walk the walk," Dee admitted, a rush of blood flooding her face. "But damn, that was fun. I don't know what's come over me lately." She paused. "*You*, however, not only walked, but walked away with the cash! I just can't believe it. We were so lucky."

Jewel twisted her delicate features before clearing her throat.

"Something wrong, Jewel?"

Jewel met Dee's inquisitive stare. "Well, I really wasn't all that lucky."

"What are you saying?"

"I'm saying I may have helped myself win." Jewel was unable to meet Dee's eyes.

"What? You cheated?"

"Shhh! Keep it down."

"I don't believe you. How?"

"I'm pretty good with sleight-of-hand stuff."

"Pretty good? You must be great! I didn't see a thing."

"That's the point, my dear," said the suave confidence woman while examining her fingernails, relieved that Dee hadn't immediately condemned her. Russell would have had a fit.

"How? What?"

Jewel lowered her voice and mumbled, "I palmed a deuce, and while I pretended to be wiping the perspiration off my neck, I tucked it under my bra strap . . ."

"You didn't! Did you? I saw you, but never guessed. You couldn't! Could you?"

Jewel Averick Cheshire-catted her companion. "And when it was time to show my cards, I simply reached in and traded up, if you will."

"You're unbelievable. I can't believe you cheated. How'd you get a deuce—and *two* aces, for that matter?"

Jewel looked around, then turned back to Dee. "Wait here."

"Where am I going to go?" The question hung in the air unanswered because Jewel had already disappeared behind the first-class curtain and into coach. Several minutes later she returned minus the rainbow-colored headband that had been holding back her black mane. And her denim shirt sported a dark stain the size of a grapefruit. "What happened to you?"

Jewel flopped heavily into her faux leather seat. "Told you all kids were brats—kid insisted on a trade for these." She held out what looked like a pack of children's playing cards. "The precious punk snatched off my headband when I leaned over to grab this deck of cards out of her fat little hands. Then her baby brother, who apparently didn't want his sister to fork over the goods, threw his apple juice on me! Can you believe that?"

"Did you ask nicely?"

"I said, 'Hey, kid, let me have those cards.' . . . I might even have smiled."

Dee stifled a laugh as she took in the flustered, disheveled, and juice-stained Jewel. The same woman who had conned an aged hood out of thousands became discombobulated after an encounter with a couple of tots.

"Anyway," continued Jewel, inhaling deeply and setting up her tray table, "let's play a little Old Maid, shall we?" She flashed Dee the card with the cheery-looking, gray-haired, pink-frocked main character. "Shuffle the deck." Dee flipped the cards to the best of her ability, which was only slightly better than her pool playing. With an apologetic smirk, she gave the deck back to Jewel, who grinned and declared, "Now it's my turn."

What followed next left Dee stunned and bug-eyed. Jewel Averick was a cardsharp. She shuffled and fanned, fanned and shuffled, finding the Old Maid at will. Once she even pulled the card out of Dee's blouse pocket. And while her graceful hands moved fast, they never moved fast enough to raise suspicion.

"Place her in the middle of the deck," she ordered. Dee did. Jewel then proceeded to pull the card off the top of the stack.

"That's amazing," said Dee, twisting her mouth in delighted amusement. "Where'd you learn this stuff?"

"Taught myself. Practiced. Practiced. Practiced."

"No, sir!"

"Yes, ma'am. It all started on a family trip to Manhattan when I was younger. I somehow got separated from my parents and brothers and had quite a day, as you can imagine. Anyhow, I stumbled upon a three-card-monte operation and was fascinated. I mean, here was this man with fast hands taking people's money. They were actually *giving* him their money! Needless to say, I was enthralled. So I tracked down my parents at the Empire State Building, went home with them, and began to practice, practice, practice."

"Wow. What were you, like sixteen?"

"Six."

"Stop it!"

"I swear. I had lots of time to practice after school because I really didn't have any friends to play with. Therefore I got good at it," Jewel said without the slightest touch of remorse or self-pity over her friendless past.

"Well, I guess it would be hard being friends with someone who swindled you out of your lunch money."

"I got suspended a total of seven times during the early years."

"Get out of here!"

"Honest to God."

"Jewel Averick . . ."

"Hmmm?"

"You are the most unusual . . . the most determined . . . the most . . . I don't know . . . You're the 'mostest' person I've ever met."

Jewel calmly refitted her tray table, relaxed back in her seat, and closed her eyes. "Is that a good thing, Sweet?" she asked quietly.

After several thoughtful moments, Dee concluded, "I'm not sure."

#6

YOU BEAT OLD HARV! YOU MUST BE SMARTER
THAN I THINK.
MAKE YOUR WAY TO OUR BIGGEST CITY FOR THE
NEXT LINK.
THERE YOU MUST GO TO THE TEMPLE OF HIM OF
MUCH DOUBT
ON THE MAIN DRAG 'TWEEN 50 AND 60 OR
THERE'BOUT.
THE NAMESAKE OF KING HENRY'S BROTHER . . .
AND MINE TOO.
BEHIND THE RIGHT ALTAR, YOU'LL FIND THE
SEVENTH CLUE.

Jewel refolded the latest piece of the puzzle and slipped it under her pillow as she snuggled deeper beneath her fluffy comforter. It was Wednesday, 11 A.M., and she was in no hurry to get up. Jacinta had brought up breakfast an hour ago and promised lunch at one—just in time for "All My Children."

She rolled over on her back, stretched out to put her hands behind her head, and smiled at the ceiling. She and Dee had figured out number 6—without any help—on their way home. Tomorrow, they were heading to New York City. Saint Thomas' Church, Fifth Avenue. *It all makes sense, yet none of it makes any sense.* Jewel giggled at the irony of her thoughts before dozing off again.

As he strolled up the concrete walkway, Xavier Lawrence eyed the Avericks' large Colonial house and tried to keep from being bitter. He rang the doorbell. Jacinta recognized him immediately.

"Mr. Lawrence, what a surprise. Haven't seen you in a while. Come in."

As Xavier took a seat in the living room, Jacinta informed him that Jewel was still napping but she would wake her. "Ah, no, no, Mrs. O'Hara. That won't be necessary. I'm content to wait until she's up . . . if you don't mind."

Jacinta O'Hara shrugged and ambled off to the kitchen, mumbling to herself. Xavier waited, making sure Jacinta was occupied with her chores at the back of the house, before he tiptoed up the stairs into Jewel's room.

If Jewel was at peace when she began her little siesta, she was rocked with a riotous emotional charge when she woke up half an hour later to find Xavier Lawrence staring down at her.

She bolted upright. "Wha—what are *you* doing here? How'd you get in?"

Xavier gave her a beautiful smile. "Mrs. O'Hara, of course."

"Into my bedroom?"

He didn't answer right away but took in her skimpy nightgown, forcing Jewel to grab her comforter and cover herself. "No," he said, boldly sitting on the side of the bed, "she let me in the house. I waited until her back was turned to come up here."

Jewel clutched her bedding tighter to her tingling form. "Get out of here, Zavie! You shouldn't be here!"

"Now, is that any way to treat a guest? If you really meant it, you'd be screaming the place down. I've witnessed too many of your tantrums to believe otherwise."

"I didn't invite you. Besides, I'm mad at you. In fact, you better leave right this minute, before I kick your butt!"

He chuckled. He stood. And before she could guess his intent, he snatched the comforter out of her hands and threw it back, exposing her short nightie and long legs. "You and what army?"

"STOP THAT! WHAT THE HELL . . . ARRrrrghhh!" she yelled as the would-be paramour dived onto the bed, capturing her and rolling over with her. Locked in his arms, Jewel felt as if her heart was about to burst from her chest, and her already ragged breath became painfully irregular. But she wasn't about to give in to her traitorous body. Her mind had to take over—soon! "How dare you? Get off of me right now, Xavier Lawrence! You've got a lot of nerve coming in here like this, after you deliberately left that misleading message on my machine. For your information, Russell heard it and was—was—" She stopped as her onetime boyfriend began to nibble her neck. "Quit it," she moaned.

Without meaning to, Jewel moved her head so that her mouth brushed against the side of his face. This was all the encouragement Mr. Lawrence needed; he clamped his lips on hers.

Jewel instinctively responded with eager, openmouthed shamelessness. But then, inner alarms set off a cacophony in her muddled mind. *Oh my God! This is wrong! Think about Russell, you slut!* "Xavier!" She twisted away from his lips. "Stop it! I'm serious! Get off me!"

This time, he knew she meant it. Xavier rolled off and didn't try to stop her as she scrambled to her feet. "Get up! Get up! This is Russell's bed!" she screeched, close to hysterics. When he just gave her a lazy grin, she grabbed her pillow and began pummeling him on his perfectly round head.

Laughing as he tried to evade her blows, Xavier pushed himself into a sitting position. His hand landed on clue number 6, left exposed when Jewel swiped her pillow. "What's this? Love notes from another?"

"Hardly," she muttered, walking over to get her robe.

"Oh, oh, oh—so you're still at this Two-Mile McLemore caper, are you, Jewely-girl?" Xavier stood and followed her into the bathroom.

"Uh-huh. We're getting close, too." She proceeded to wash her face, brush her teeth, and take a swig of mouthwash. *"Now* kiss me, you fool," she said sarcastically, slapping him with her hand towel. "Honestly, Zavie. You have got more nerve than most. How dare you come up here and try to seduce me after purposefully causing a rift in my marriage?"

"You know you're unseducible. So I caused a rift, did I?"

"Yes, you pig."

He returned his attention back to the piece of paper in his hand.

"Look, I'm going to take a shower. Go downstairs and have Cindy feed you something. I'll be down in a minute."

She thought he'd ask to join her for a little water sport, but he didn't. He seemed immersed in the clue. "Yeah . . . okay, Jewel, fine. Can I take this with me?"

She shrugged. "Sure, but we already know what it means."

"What?"

"I'll tell you after I shower."

Xavier seemed lost in thought when Jewel joined him in the breakfast nook. Jacinta was nowhere in sight. "Figure it out?" she asked, taking a peach from a bowl of fruit.

"No, not really."

She bit into the peach. "Weumph did. It's allurp reaoully sumfle."

"Would you please wait until your mouth is empty."

Jewel gulped down another chunk of juicy fruit. "Okay, we figured this clue must have some kind of baseball reference, so we started with 'King Henry.' The only one we could think of was Henry Aaron, the home-run king. His brother was named Tommie—and don't ask me how I knew that, must have read it somewhere."

Xavier frowned but seemed to be following.

"And who in history was a man of much doubt?" Jewel gave Xavier a wide-eyed nod as he released an awe-filled "Thomas?"

"Exactly! Doubting Thomas! So, apparently, we're to go to a 'temple' in New York between Fiftieth and Sixtieth Streets. And get this . . .'"

"What?"

"There just happens to be a Saint Thomas' Church on Fifty-third and Fifth Avenue—the main drag, as you know from our shopping expedition in 1984."

"Aren't you ladies clever . . . uh, Russell still doesn't know, right?"

Jewel shook her head. "Nope. And it's going to stay that way. I want to surprise him."

"Well, what's this about 'and mine too'?"

"Don't know. I suppose Two-Mile had a brother named Thomas . . . he just needed a rhyme, that's all that is."

Their eyes met over the bowl of peaches and plums—both momentarily thinking of some other, rather forbidden, fruit. But Jewel knew she had somehow passed safely through the danger zone. A voice from deep inside told her whatever temptation Xavier Lawrence presented was buried and behind her. "What brings you here, Zavie?"

"You, of course."

"What do you want?"

"You, of course."

"Can't have me."

"Please."

"Absolutely not. Besides, you had your chance, my good man."

Xavier groaned. "God! When are you going to stop torturing me with my mistake-filled past?"

Jewel looked at him for several minutes before dropping her half-eaten peach and grabbing one of his hands. "You know, Zavie, I've been thinking. You didn't make a mistake. I wouldn't give you something and you got it elsewhere. I don't blame you anymore. I'd probably have done the same thing if faced with similar circumstances."

"How can you say I didn't make a mistake? The most beautiful girl in the world was in love with me . . ."

"I wouldn't go so far as to say 'love' . . ."

"You *loved* me, Jewel. And I think you still do."

"Get over yourself!"

"Anyway, I let you go for sex."

"And with a slut like Rita Farr."

"Biggest mistake of my life."

". . . shoulda waited for me, Zavie."

"But you kept saying no! I was a goddamn twenty-three-year-old virgin! How long did you think I could wait?"

"Till we got married—but, no. As I recall, you said I was 'retardedly old-fashioned and not worth the wait.' "

"You know I didn't mean it."

"You most certainly did. Then you went behind my back and knocked up Darlene Olden." Jewel paused to let a soft smile grace her face. "Little Tanya is kind of cute. You must be very proud."

"Yeah, she is. Did I show you this picture when you were at the house?" Xavier pulled out his wallet and showed Jewel a school picture of his front-tooth-less kid."

"See, Zavie, everything worked out for both of us."

"The devil it did! You dumped me. My marriage to Darlene lasted a hot minute. And you're stuck in a loveless marriage . . ."

"How's that?"

"Don't deny it." Now it was Xavier who reached out to Jewel. "You and I are meant for each other. Leave him."

Jewel laughed. Not a little giggle, but a hearty, from-the-gut guffaw. "Oh, I'm sorry, Zavie. But you really are crazy . . . absolutely out of your skull. I'm married to Russell and I intend to stay married to Russell. Why on earth do you think I've gone through hell and high water these last two weeks?"

Xavier flopped back in his chair, a hard look crossing his face, a look that surprised Jewel with its intensity. "It's because I'm not rich, isn't it?"

"Of course not."

"Don't lie, Jewel. That's the reason, and you know it. Darlene only married me—got involved with me, for that matter—because she thought I'd inherit Dad's shoe business. If he'd helped me out when I went to him for a little cash, she wouldn't have left me. When he cut me off, so did she. God! You women are so mercenary."

The rancor in his voice and the far-off look in his eyes made Jewel uneasy. For the first time she felt uncomfortable with Xavier, as if he were a stranger. "Don't say things like that, Zavie. You know why I didn't marry you, and it had nothing to do with your lack of money."

He didn't seem to hear her. "My bastard father—I'll show him. One of these days, he'll come crawling to me . . . asking *me* for money!"

"Social work pay big these days?" she asked with her usual frank insensitivity.

"Social work? What are you talking about? I'm a CPA."

"You are?" She was genuinely surprised. "Well, what do you know about that."

Xavier couldn't contain his resigned chuckle. "You'll never change. You really couldn't be bothered caring about others. Anything that doesn't pay millions is social work to you." He brought the back of her hand to his lips and planted a soft kiss. "So there's not to be a you-and-me, Mrs. Averick?"

"I don't love you, Zavie. I might lust after you for some odd reason, but I don't love you. And if you take the time to be honest with yourself, you'll admit you don't love me either."

"I do!"

"No, you don't. You love my looks. But you don't love *me.*"

They were silent for a while, until Xavier finally smiled ruefully. "You may have a point. But, Jewel?"

"Hmmm?"

"How am I different from Averick?"

The validity of his question stabbed at her heart. "You're not. However, the difference is I'm married to Russ and determined to make this goddamn thing work . . . or at least be the one to do the dumping."

Xavier laughed out loud at her resolute statement. "Which, I guess, brings us back to your Two-Mile hunt. So tell me, what's brought you up to this point?"

Jewel filled him in on their trips to Baltimore and Pittsburgh, pausing only when Jacinta walked through on her way to the laundry room. "So we're heading to Manhattan tomorrow because Dee wanted to spend today with her kids." *And there's no great rush, since Lipless and Snow are somewhere in the heartland scratching their imbecilic heads.*

Xavier reread the clue. "Jewel? I thought you said Two-Mile left these in the fifties?"

"Actually, it may have been the late thirties. Remember, we found out he died in '39."

"Well, then, can I ask you something?"

"Sure."

"How'd he know Hank Aaron was the home-run king? For that matter, what about the Forbes Field wall? And, sweetheart, I never heard of anybody making out their tombstone inscription *after* they died."

Jewel's eyes began to ache from the strain of staring at microfilm for three solid hours. Her right hand was beginning to cramp from constantly turning the light machine's crank. And a feeling of futility had invaded her.

But she was determined to get to the bottom of the Two-Mile mystery as she and Xavier sat at side-by-side machines in the Library of Congress's Madison Building, poring over *Washington Post* issues from the summer of 1939. She was convinced there had to be *something* about Two-Mile's death in the paper. She was wrong. They found nada. Zilch. Zippo.

Nothing, that is, about Two-Mile.

Jewel was just about to finish up with the last of the August batch when she found a *giant* gem. Even a microfilm copy of an old newspaper photo couldn't contain its magnificence. Its brilliance. Its enormity.

The article's headline was even more spellbinding: "Star Diamond Stolen."

"What? What is it?" asked Xavier, pulling his chair over to get a better look at her screen.

"Zavie!" she squeaked. "This Star Diamond and a bunch of other jewels were stolen from the Smithsonian!" When he returned a blank stare, she continued lowering her voice conspiratorially. "Star Diamond! Sound familiar? '. . . to find D.C.'s Star Diamond . . .'?" Her heart literally stopped, then began to beat at a mercurial clip, while her eyes continued their frantic speed-reading. "Oh my God. Sweet Jesus. I wonder . . ."

"What? What are you thinking?"

Jewel gulped, trying to force her heart out of her larynx and back to its rightful place. "It says the Star Diamond weighed four hundred nineteen carats! Apparently, it came from the Transvaal Province. Four . . . hundred . . . and . . . nineteen carats, Zavie!"

She paused due to a sudden sensation of dizziness, then continued in a breathless whisper, "Seems King George the Sixth presented the Star to F.D.R. . . . It was stolen in transit from the White House to its permanent home in the Smithsonian . . . The police brought in Duke Crammer for questioning."

Jewel's eyes became so large, they seemed to obliterate the rest of her face, making her look like some cartoonist's deranged joke. There was not a doubt in her mind. Everything was becoming clearer. She somehow knew the deal.

"OH MY GOD!"

"What is it, Jewel? And stop looking like that; you're scaring me."

"Zavie! Don't you get it? Duke Crammer . . . D.C. . . . 'to find D.C.'s Star Diamond . . .' Two-Mile's clue? . . ."

"What are you saying?" Xavier was on the edge of his chair, charged with a tingling thrill that quickened his own breath.

"I'm saying that Duke Crammer stole the Star, and somehow Two-Mile McLemore swiped it from him. That's what Crammer's men, Graves and Snow, are after. That's what *we're* after. We're not hunting Two-Mile McLemore; we're hunting the Star Diamond . . ." Jewel's voice trailed off to an inaudible pitch. "A four-hundred-nineteen-carat diamond."

The thought caused a blackness to roll into Jewel's temporary clairvoyance. Her hands began to tremble. The possibility of coming into contact with such a rock was just too much. Thus, for the second time in as many weeks, she fainted dead away.

7TH INNING:
Hit and Run

Jewel Elizabeth Howard Averick remained in a state of semi-consciousness for the rest of the day. Her thoughts couldn't seem to wade through the quagmire that used to be her brain. Straight thinking was out of the question. Every time her mind even broached the subject of the Star Diamond, a gray haze turned her speech to babble.

"What was that?" asked Xavier, sitting across from her at the Occidental restaurant in D.C.'s posh Willard Hotel. She hadn't touched a bite. "Jewel? Are you okay, sweetheart?"

"Zavie! I've got to go to New York. Right now! I've got to get the next clue!"

"No way. We've already decided to wait until Saturday, when I can go with you."

"Come with me now!"

"I can't. Tanya's with me most of this summer. But this weekend she'll be with Darlene's mother. We're not all as carefree and responsibility-free as you are," he said, a slight edge in his voice. "Tell me you'll wait, please."

"Zaaavie," whined Jewel, picking at her soft-shell crab with her fork.

"Wait for me, please."

The irony of his words wasn't lost on either party. How many times had Jewel asked that of Xavier? He had not waited.

Now the once-impatient man grabbed Jewel's hand and brought it to his lips. "Jewely-girl, we can do this together. You know we make a great team."

She quickly lost the desire to bite into the Big Apple as she stared into his large round eyes. "Oh, all right. But we leave *first* thing Saturday morning. I'll be at your house at seven."

He grinned, exposing his blinding-white teeth, before turning her hand over and kissing her palm. "I knew you wouldn't leave me."

While Xavier headed back to Philadelphia, Jewel returned home still reeling in shock. Her only clear thoughts came when they turned to Deanna Duffy Sweet. *I shouldn't tell her. Why should I? I don't owe her anything. The Star could be mine, mine, mine, mine! After all, it's a dog-eat-dog world, right? Every man for himself. Certainly that goes for women, too, right? . . . Wrong. No, Jewel. You began this thing with Dee and you should end it with Dee. Remember, she saved your butt in Philly. If ever there's a chance to prove you're not all that bad, it's now. I won't leave her out; we'll split it. Cut the Star in two . . .* "Three hundred carats for me; one-nineteen for Dee. And they call me heartless." She giggled to herself.

It took all of ten minutes for Jewel to forget her resolve to wait until Saturday. The idea of a humongous diamond hidden away in some tree trunk or cave was too disturbing. *It's there for the taking! It's there for me to take!* She bolted out of Russ's favorite chair in the den—the old, beat-up chair that once used to repulse her now seemed to be the only comfortable seat in the house—and snatched the telephone to call Dee. "A woman's got to do what a woman's got to do—and all that," she muttered.

"Ain't that the truth," whispered Jacinta O'Hara as she tiptoed down the hallway to the kitchen phone for a little eavesdropping. After listening to Jewel's hyper blathering to Dee Sweet, Jacinta quietly hung up, then made a call of her own. "Mr. Crammer, please . . . Hello, this is Jacinta O'Hara . . . fine, thank you, sir . . . I've got some news . . . It seems like Jewel and Mrs. Sweet are on their way to New York tomorrow . . . No, sir, Kansas City wasn't mentioned . . . Huh? . . . as a matter of fact, she did say something about a star . . . That's very kind of you, sir, thank you . . . as always, cash is appreciated."

Duke "Quiet" Crammer's quivering bone of a hand softly hung up the phone. But there was no tremor in his voice as he barked to his elderly vapid-looking assistant. "Get Anthony on the phone. Now! And tell him to get his stupid ass out of goddamn Kansas!"

"I think they're in Missouri, boss."

"Missouri . . . Kansas, who gives a rat's ass . . . get those idiots back here tonight!"

Jewel was too pumped to sleep. She just *had* to tell someone the real reason behind Two-Mile's disappearance. Someone who would care. Someone who wouldn't laugh and say she was crazy. Someone like Russell.

The digital clock by her bed read 1 A.M. That meant it was midnight in Chicago. Russell should be back at his hotel by now, she reasoned, reaching to find the hotel's number in the team's official directory. She was so happy, she actually hummed as she waited for her husband to pick up.

Russell sat moodily at the hotel bar and threw back shot after shot of whiskey in an attempt to chase away a gnawing depression he couldn't seem to shake.

Then, with an uncharacteristic stumbling gait, he led an attractive, and blatantly wanton, groupie back to his hotel room, where the pretty stranger's mouth drove him to carnal distraction.

The phone was on its fourth persistent ring before Russell realized the sound wasn't coming from inside his head. "Mmm . . . I better get that." His hand flew toward the phone and slammed down on it, knocking the receiver to the floor. "Oops . . ." Rolling onto his washboard stomach, he leaned over the bed to pick up the willful phone, while his companion snickered and tugged at his boxers, exposing his buttocks like the Coppertone pixie.

"Yeah . . . ?" he muttered absently.

"Russell?"

"Jewel . . . what do you want?"

Jewel was instantly concerned and began to twist her bed-sheets nervously. While his speech wasn't slurred, it was abundantly clear her husband had been in the sauce. "Russ, have you been drinking?"

"Maybe a little."

"Sounds like a lot."

"So what? What do you care?" His new friend chose the next moment to grab his most private of parts. His lusty "Yoo . . . whoaaah" caused both the grabber and the grabbee to giggle.

"Russ? What's going on? Who's in there with you?" Now Jewel's fidgeting hands became two tight fists of fury.

"Oh, I dunno. Hold up a sec." He passed the receiver to the young woman who had crawled up to lie on his back. "Sweet-heart, tell my wife who you are."

"Hi, I'm Pam," she laughed into the phone, before returning to her task at hand.

"I'm with Pam, dear," Russell mumbled into the wrong end of the receiver. It didn't matter. Jewel had already hung up with a slam.

The loud disconnection seemed to sober him out of his temporary insanity. He quickly hustled the frustrated Pam out of his room, with a rebuke about the dangers of sleeping with strangers. "Next time you might not be so lucky," he warned as he began to shut the door on Pam's pouting puss.

"I could say the same thing to you . . . I'm a hooker," she informed him smugly.

"Jesus Christ!" Russell made sure the door was locked and dragged himself back to his bed, where he sat down and placed his swimming head in his hands. He picked up the phone and then hung up again. "Damn!"

From day one, he'd always been sure of himself, of what he

wanted and where he was going. Now he sat in a hotel room staring into space, confused and completely lost. He wasn't sure about anything—not one damn thing.

Dee was in Sweet Shangri-La as she powered Russell Averick's slick Ferrari 456GT along the New Jersey Turnpike, pushing the magnificent machine past eighty-five miles per hour and thinking it was all a dream.

At precisely 9 A.M., Jewel had bunny-hopped, screeched, and lurched the fabulous silver-colored supercar up her driveway, making it painfully apparent she knew very little about driving a stick.

"Jewel!" cried Dee, running her hands along the hood. "We're taking the Ferrari?"

Jewel just nodded and crossed her arms over her chest. Dee was so excited about the prospect of taking the car for a spin, she hardly noticed Jewel's less than perfect appearance. Her eyes were red and baggy; her black-and-orange Princeton rugby shirt was startlingly wrinkled; and, the most shocking thing of all: her pink jeans matched absolutely nothing, certainly not her red-and-blue-plaid Keds.

"Russ doesn't mind our taking it?"

Jewel shrugged and offered a bored "He might, but that's too bad."

"Oh, no, Jewel, we can't—"

"You can drive."

"What are we waiting for?"

Deanna Duffy Sweet was thoroughly entranced with the automotive excellence under her sure-handed guidance (and the rhythmic beats of Seduction blaring from the radio—a tape Jewel insisted on playing). It wasn't until they had flown past exit 4 on the New Jersey Turnpike on their way to New York that she noticed Jewel hadn't said a single word. "You're sure quiet."

Jewel only shifted in her seat to show Dee more of her wrinkled rugby back, resting her forehead against the window.

"Jewel, what's wrong? Yesterday, you were absolutely delirious with the thought of capturing the Star Diamond. What's going on? Lipless and Snow are in Kansas City, right?"

"Nothing's wrong," mumbled the uncharacteristically melancholy Jewel, as she watched the Ferrari overtake car after car.

Dee was silent while Seduction hip-hopped and sang that it takes "two to make a thing go right." She'd gone through too much with Mark not to recognize the signs. There was trouble in an already troubled Averick paradise. Dee decided to take a roundabout approach. "How'd you meet Russell?"

Jewel straightened in her seat and focused her gaze on the highway, not seeing a thing. "We met when he was with the Yankees," she began in a soft voice. "My father's company was a corporate sponsor and we were invited to a pre-season party. They made several of the players go schmooze with the guests. Anyway, Dad introduced me to Russ, who seemed to take an instant liking to me."

Dee rolled her eyes at Jewel's honest vanity. "What about you? Did you instantly like him?"

"He was well-mannered, articulate, intelligent, had a terrific body, and didn't talk with food in his mouth—"

"And a millionaire?"

"*And* a millionaire, so when he asked me out to dinner, I said yes. The rest is history."

"You went out on a date and then married him? I don't think so. There has to be more than that. How long did you date?"

" 'Bout a year."

"So you grew to love him?"

Jewel appeared to think long and hard before she answered. Dee guessed her partner had never really examined her true feelings for Russell, let alone put them into words.

"I don't know, Sweet. I think everybody loves differently. When we married, I didn't feel for him what I felt for Xavier . . ."

"That, I just *can't* believe."

"So you've said . . . several times," Jewel said dryly. "Anyway, after he met me, Russell unceremoniously dumped his girl-friend, Carla Hunter, like the proverbial hot potato, which was just as well because it was clear to me they weren't suited for each other. She was just a pro-athlete hanger-on. I knew she'd just latch on to another jock, probably a football player."

Jewel attempted a blasé tone, but Dee detected the soft sound of a silent fear. Was Jewel afraid Russell would dump her when the next hot thing came along?

"So one day," continued Mrs. Averick, "I woke up and said, 'What more could you possibly want?' The next month we were married. All three of us—Russell, me, and baseball."

Dee shot Jewel a curious look. "I know what you mean. It's very hard having to share your husband with the world; everybody demanding his attention, his time. It's like we're on the periphery of their lives." She paused and dropped her voice for meaningful emphasis. "It can make the most confident of us jealous."

Jewel's mouth twitched as she nodded. "So jealous," she whispered, "we'd do mean things, like sell his stuff . . . I *am* jealous of the time Russell spends away from me. And when he opted to attend the auction instead of spending the day with me, I guess I lost it."

After a long silence, Jewel swiveled toward Dee, clearing her throat. "You know, Sweet, sometimes it takes an outsider to help you see how things really are." She stopped to study Dee's profile. "Jealousy is a powerful emotion. I suppose it takes on different forms with different folks. I, for instance, am very proactive. Others may be a little more passive. You know, people who may withdraw into a shell."

"Is that what you think I did?"

Jewel shrugged. "I don't know. All I know is I just want another chance with Russell."

"So you do love him?"

"If you'd asked me that a month ago, my honest answer would have been, 'Kind of,' but the funny thing is, *now,* I'm certain I love Russell. And I believe I've always loved him. I even told him so the other day," she said, oblivious to the fact that many people say the words on a regular basis. "My feelings for Xavier don't even compare. We were, and still are, nothing more than good friends who have the hots for each other."

"What about Russell? Umm . . . you know . . . sex?" Dee blushed at her boldness.

Jewel didn't appear to take umbrage at her frank question. "Yes, there's some of that."

"Well, is it . . . is it . . ." This time, Dee couldn't push the intrusive words off the tip of her tongue.

"Is it great sex?"

Heaving a sigh of relief, Dee precariously cut off a Corvette that had the nerve to try to pass the 456GT.

"Well, I can't say I get all out of control like they do in the movies, or always have these mind-shattering orgasms," she confided matter-of-factly. "It's all right—often it's quite enjoyable. But, for all I know, I could be married to the world's greatest or lousiest lover; I don't have anyone to compare him to."

Dee swerved the car in disbelieving shock, causing the Corvette to honk petulantly. "Russ is the only one?"

"Waited till marriage, Sweet. Didn't want to get all mussy unless I had to."

"You're kidding!"

"Why would I joke about a thing like that? I take it you weren't a virgin on your wedding night."

Suddenly Dee was inexplicably ashamed standing in the bright light of Jewel's virtue. "Well . . . no . . . I wasn't."

"Tramp."

The slight upward curve of Jewel's mouth told Dee she was being teased.

"No, not a tramp. Just a couple of guys."

"Hussy! Haven't you been dating Mark since the womb?"

"We had some breaks in the relationship."

"But you always came back to him. Did you ever fool around when you were married?"

"No! Absolutely not! That's Mark's department, the cretin."

Feeling slightly better somehow, Jewel turned in her contoured seat toward Dee. "Last night," she began softly, "I called Russell at the hotel, and he was there with a woman."

Dee felt the pain as if it were her own. "Are you sure?"

"Positive. The bastard put her on the phone. He was drunk."

"Oh, Jewel, I'm sorry. Men can be such jag-offs! But I'm sure Russell wouldn't cheat on you; he's a good man."

"He thinks I'm fooling around with Xavier. I'm sure he was trying to get back at me."

"And you snatched his Ferrari to get back at him, is that right?"

An uncomfortable scowl ran across Jewel's face. "Yeah, but now I'm not so sure that was such a hot idea. He'd kill me if something happened to it. He loves this thing . . . probably more than those damn jock straps, caps, and jerseys. He doesn't even know I had a set of keys made. So, slow down, will ya?"

Dee dropped to a turtle-slow sixty-five miles per hour. The car seemed to be crawling.

"In fact," continued Jewel, "we better not take this baby into the city. We'll park at my grandparents' house in Teaneck and cab it."

They were silent again for several miles until Jewel asked, "Sweet? How could you live with Mark after he slept with other women?"

The simple, straightforward question hit Dee like a slap and brought the sting of tears to her eyes. She hadn't realized how pathetic she must look. Jewel certainly wouldn't stand for such blatant infidelity. Several more miles passed before she could even begin to formulate an answer.

"Somewhere along the way, I lost my self-esteem, Jewel. I convinced myself that being Mrs. Mark Sweet was a great thing and, no matter what, it was better than being plain old Dee Duffy. I forgave him and told myself I was partly to blame for his straying. I thought *I* should be a better wife, a better lover, a better friend. I told myself I wasn't doing my job properly; wasn't living up to my end of the bargain. So I got pregnant with Jessica, thinking everything would be fine with a kid. We'd be a real family. I was wrong, I caught him messing around again. This was"—Dee paused to gulp back the painful memories—"let's see . . . this was about four years ago. Mark was really sorry. He swore he was through and begged me not to leave him; I mean, he was bawling and everything. I forgave him again and quickly had Eric and Nina . . . God! I'm the biggest fool on earth!"

"No, you're not," said Jewel; but Dee could tell she only half meant it.

"Yes, I am!" A renewed Dee slammed her fist on the steering wheel's insignia horse. "Well, guess what? These last two weeks have been a rebirth for me. They've made me realize I *don't* need Mark to live, to have a life! While the kids have been at Mom's, I've had a lot of time to think. I'm going to divorce Mark."

"WHAT?"

"As soon as we find this diamond thingy or whatever, I'm contacting my lawyer."

"You don't want to do that!"

"Why not?"

"Since the time Mark swore off screwing around, which was *years* ago, when he was young and dumb, have you caught him?"

"He's at it again. I know it; the signs are there."

"But you don't know that for sure. I think you should have it out with him before you do anything you might regret. And, more importantly, before Russell blames me for the breakup of his teammate's marriage. I can hear him now: 'If you hadn't dragged Dee Sweet into your scheming adventure, she'd still be married. Her kids wouldn't have to split their time between mommy and daddy. Mark hasn't hit a home run since she walked out on him. I hope you're satisfied.'

"Why don't you just get that pool and see how that goes first. That's one way of exerting your independence."

"Mark would absolutely die. When I said he's afraid of water, I wasn't kidding. One time, when he was in high school, two of his older brothers were mad at him for some reason and slammed him in a bathtub full of water, holding his head under for several seconds. And, honest to God, he had to be temporarily hospitalized in a psych ward from the trauma it caused. To this day, Greg and Sammy still apologize!"

"Huh? Those Sweet boys ain't so sweet. How many brothers are there?"

"Five."

Attempting to keep the conversation off divorce, Jewel asked, "Are any of them—you know—literally sweet?" She wiggled her hand back and forth for emphasis.

"Naaaaww . . . don't think so."

"How do you know?"

Dee turned a wickedly playful eye on her crony. "Because, my virginal friend, I've had them all."

Jewel burst out laughing, before screaming "Slut!"

Dee liked Jewel's grandparents, Beata and Beau Brooks. They were, quite frankly, the cutest people she had ever met. Twin balls of chocolate topped with thick gray hair. Mr. Brooks was hard-of-hearing, which made for interesting and amusing conversation. When he asked what brought them to his neck of the woods, Dee said, "We're going to New York to check out big-city life."

"YES!" yelled the dapper old man, "MY WIFE IS AN OLD BIDDY! BUT WE LOVE HER JUST THE SAME!"

"KNOCK IT OFF, POP-POP!" hollered Jewel. "PUT IN YOUR HEAR-ING AID!"

When first eyeing Jewel's outfit, Mrs. Beata Brooks cried, "Good God, Jewel, have you joined a cut-rate carnival?"

Then, upon being introduced to Dee, Mrs. Brooks fussed and cooed over her like she was a long-lost friend. "It's a pleasure meeting you, sweetie. Jewel's never brought home a white person I didn't like," she enthused, the twinkle in her eyes practically doing a jig. "Of course, you're the first white person she's ever brought here. Actually, you're the first person, period—other than that fine husband of hers."

The Brookses wanted them to stay for lunch, but Jewel insisted they were just using the large Tudor home as a pit stop. "We're on an adventure, Nana."

"Oh, how splendid! May I be of assistance?"

Jewel let out a large laugh. "That, my dear old lady, is the absolute *last* thing we need. No, you stay here—out of trouble."

"Suit yourself, sweetie."

Anthony Graves squinted as he watched Jewel Averick kiss two old people at the front door before she and Deanna Sweet climbed into a cab. "The way I figure it, Snow," he said, chomping on a straw, "they gotta come back to pick up the Ferrari. So why should we tag after them into the city?"

Sitting in the cramped passenger seat of the car du jour—a 240SX—Mr. Snow heaved his giant shoulders. "We goin' to sit here and wait?"

"Not exactly, my friend. I propose we pay a visit to the old folks. When Averick and Sweet get back from doing all the leg-work, we'll persuade them to hand over the next clue or else Granny and Grandpa will meet their maker a little ahead of schedule. Get my drift?"

Mr. Snow didn't, but he nodded anyway.

❖ ❖ ❖

"This is it," announced the cab driver as he pulled up in front of the Episcopal Saint Thomas' Church at Fifty-third and Fifth.

"Could you please wait? We won't be long," Jewel requested. He insisted they pay for the inbound trip first. She grunted and forked over fifty bucks. "Will you wait?"

He grinned, revealing a serious lack of teeth, and nodded.

Climbing the stairs of the historic religious edifice, Dee smiled and mumbled a thank-you to the broad-shouldered, caramel-skinned, curly-headed man who held the door open for them on his way out. She stopped dead in her tracks once inside.

"What is it?" whispered Jewel.

"Nothing, really. It's just . . . I could have sworn I've seen that man before."

"What man?"

"The one who just held the door open for us. It seems like I've seen him before . . . maybe in Baltimore . . . maybe Pittsburgh . . . maybe D.C. I just can't say exactly where."

"You think he's working for Crammer?"

"Maybe."

"Well, we better put a move on."

"Shouldn't we be genuflecting or something?" Dee murmured as she and Jewel walked up (much faster than is customary in a house of worship) the long center aisle toward the massive altar.

"If the spirits in this place move you, I think you should," said Jewel, taking in the dark, colossal church. Its ceilings had to be at least eighty feet high. At the main altar, which was roped off, Jewel stared dumbfounded at the organ pipes that stretched eerily to the heavens.

Dee couldn't take her eyes off the high altar's reredos, an ornamental wall depicting the statues of about sixty saints. It was huge. "I've never seen anything like this," she said in a hushed voice. "Is it wrong to say this place is kind of creepy?"

"If a bolt of lightning strikes you down, you'll know it wasn't kosher. Anyway, all this place needs is a little more sunshine . . . Hey, check it out!" Jewel elbowed Dee and pointed to a nine-teenth-century painting of Mary and Baby Jesus. "They look black."

Dee had to agree. The golden paint made the holy duo appear quite ethnic. "Is that the side altar we want?" she asked, walking to her left and tripping over a piously placed prie-dieu.

"Watch where you're going," snapped Jewel, eyeing the dozen or so tourists and worshipers who milled about. "We don't want to draw too much attention. Besides, this altar is to the left. Two-Mile said 'behind the *right* altar.' " She paused to smile at a cler-gyman and a woman wearing a business suit as they walked past and out of sight.

The innocuous-looking fortune hunters meandered to the right of the church, where they found a half dozen steps or more leading to the funeral altar. Unfortunately, there also was a locked iron gate blocking their entrance. "I bet the clue is behind that white cloth draping the altar," whispered Jewel.

"I bet you're right. But how are we going to get back there?" Dee pulled on the gate; it didn't budge. She looked up and noticed the arched gate had pointy, spearlike protrusions along the top.

"Can't you hop over? You're athletic."

"ME!"

"Shhhh!"

Dee noted a curved railing running along the stairs. She knew she could do it, but wasn't about to. "Look, why don't I find that minister and get him to open this gate. I'm sure he will, if we explain."

Jewel pursed her lips and shrugged as a silent sign of indiffer-ent agreement. "I don't care how we get the clue, so long as we get it."

Dee hadn't walked five feet from the funeral altar when she spotted the good-looking black man, who'd held the door open for them, strolling up the center aisle. And, to her dismay, he was staring right at her with a knowing smile!

Dee literally sprang into action.

Jewel's mouth fell open. Her heart skipped a beat as she watched Dee hop on the stair railing and grab on to the top of the gate with both hands. Then, with the ability only Spiderman could rival, she leaped off the railing with one mighty push and flipped over the gate like a gymnast on a high bar. She completed her incredible vault with a solid two-foot landing.

"wow!" said Jewel quite loudly, considering her don't-draw-attention directive.

She drew attention.

"Hey!" yelled a praying patron.

"Hurry, Sweet!"

Dee ran over to the altar, which couldn't have been more than twenty feet away, but it seemed like a quarter of a mile. "Forgive me, God," she whispered, throwing up the altar's cloth covering and peering around for a clue. There, in the cross section of wood, she saw a yellowing piece of paper. "Thank you, God!" she added, yanking away the note.

"Come on! Come on! Come on!" urged Jewel, who could barely be heard above a high-pitched, Spanish-accented "Thief! Thief!" and the ensuing commotion such a proclamation brings.

The way out of the altar wasn't nearly as easy for Dee because there was no rail to use as a vault. "Put your hands through the gate to boost me up," she ordered.

Jewel grumbled, but did it. Being a weakling, she wasn't able to give her accomplice the big boost she needed. Dee was forced to perform a slipshod straddling maneuver, nearly impaling herself on one of the spears. And though she managed to clear the dangerous ornaments, one of the pointed posts snagged her belt during her harried descent.

She quite literally was left hanging.

"What are you doing?"

"I'm stuck!"

Jewel grabbed Dee's dangling legs and began to tug as a small crowd began to gather.

"Don't pull! Don't pull! Push me up! Push!"

Jewel did as instructed, allowing Dee to untangle herself before crashing on, and tumbling down, the stairs below.

Lying flat on her back, Dee opened her eyes. "You okay?" asked Jewel, looking to Dee as if she were staring down from heaven, with all the saints peering over her shoulders.

"Yeah, I think so."

Jewel helped Dee to her feet. "Did you get it?"

"Yeah, I think so."

"Shall we go?"

"Yeah, I think so."

They did not discuss the matter further as the pesky voice reached their ears. "This way, Father; they're right over there. She climbed the fence and stole something from the altar . . ."

As they barreled out of the church, Deanna Sweet stopped at the threshold of freedom, turned, genuflected, and crossed herself furiously.

"I'm going to shoot you."

Anthony Graves had threatened Beau and Beata Brooks every other minute for a solid hour—ever since he had knocked on their door.

Rather than being alarmed that two gun-wielding men had forced themselves into their home, the couple welcomed them and treated the whole affair as if it were a wonderful game.

"So, you say you're a friend of Jewel's?" asked the old woman in a lilting, dulcet voice. "She said she was on an adventure, but I didn't realize she was being *chased!*"

"We're your hostages, right, young man?" enthused Mr. Brooks. "I bet Jewely will be surprised. But, if I were you, I wouldn't count on winning—you don't know my granddaughter."

"Shut up!" snapped Graves. Unfortunately, he did know the granddaughter and was concerned there might be some truth to the old man's boasting.

"Would you like something to eat?" offered Mrs. Brooks.

"Yes, please, that would be—" piped up Mr. Snow.

"NO!" Graves cried, cutting him off not only with words, but with an angry glare. "We don't want to eat; we don't want to talk; we just want you to sit here and keep your traps shut. Ya hear me?"

Mr. Brooks ignored him and turned to his wife. "See, dear, if you hadn't banished Fog Horn and Leg Horn to the garage, they'd have already torn these young men from limb to limb."

His wife flopped back on her pillow-covered sofa and released a pouty puff of air. "Yes! Like I *knew* we were going to be held hostage today!" She sweetened her demeanor and turned to Graves. "Fog Horn and Leg Horn are our Great Danes. They're really precious, but one word from my husband and they'd have you for lunch," she explained pleasantly.

Graves smirked. "Well, maybe I should send Mr. Snow out to shoot them. They won't put up much of a fuss after that, now would they?"

The couple looked at each other and giggled before Mr. Brooks turned a gleaming eye back to Graves. "You can try, boy. But I wouldn't risk it, if I were you."

An uncomfortable feeling crept through Mr. Snow as he squirmed in a delicate love seat.

"So you say my granddaughter has something you want?" asked Mrs. Brooks. "What is it? You never know, we may have one here, which would save you a lot of trouble."

Graves let out a chuckle. "I doubt that, lady."

"Does this thing belong to you or Jewel?"

"Well, it for sure don't belong to Jewel."

"Is it yours?"

"Yeah."

"Is it bigger than a bread box?"

"Look, lady! I ain't here to play goddamn Twenty Questions, okay! Now shut your yap . . . Where are *you* going?"

"I've got to go to the bathroom," stated Mr. Brooks as he made his way to the foyer.

"I didn't say you could move. Do you want me to riddle your body with bullets?"

"Because I have to go to the bathroom? Honestly, you white folks are a goofy lot." Mr. Brooks continued his trek.

"Sit down!"

"Look, boy, I've got to go to the john. I got one foot in the grave anyway, so it makes me no never mind. But I can tell you one thing: If Jewely comes in here and sees me dead, she most certainly won't cooperate."

Graves turned red. "Go with him, Snow," he ordered.

"While you're at it, dear, turn up the air conditioner," Mrs. Brooks shouted after her husband. "It's getting hot in here. Are you hot, Anthony?"

"I'm fine."

"Good. Who knows how long we have to wait. I don't want you to be uncomfortable. Knowing Jewel, she could be shopping till the stores close."

Graves grunted. "She better not."

"Is it something old or something new?"

"Huh . . . what?"

"Whatever Jewel has of yours."

"Lady?"

"Yes?"

"Shut up."

"Fine. All you had to do was ask. No need to be cranky."

"I'm going to shoot you."

✿   ✿   ✿

"Uh-oh," said Jewel as the cab slowly turned onto her grandparents' street.

"What 'uh-oh'?" Dee smelled trouble in the air; remarkably, it smelled a lot like Old Spice.

"Stop here. Stop here!" Jewel ordered, handing the driver three twenty-dollar bills.

"Why are we getting out here?"

"See that red light over my grandparents' door?"

Dee squinted and saw the portico light was indeed pinkish. However, it was still too light outside to be a blazing red. "Yeah, I guess."

"That's a sign that everything isn't copacetic in the Brooks household."

Dee frowned as she bent at the waist and followed Jewel into a neighbor's backyard. "What do you mean, everything isn't copacetic?" she asked, hopping over a bed of flowers.

"My grandparents have a fake thermostat that's really a distress signal. It's a personal SOS to family members. It means there's trouble in the house."

"They're such sweeties; I can't believe they run into so much trouble that they need such an elaborate system."

"You don't know my grandparents. The police have a special hot line with their name on it. Anyway, they hit the light to let me know there's a problem inside, which means they can't get to the phone. Pop-Pop probably said he needed to adjust the AC," Jewel explained, quietly hopping a chain-link fence into the Brookses' backyard as she used to do when she was nine years old. "Foggie and Leggie must be locked up in the garage. There's never any trouble if they're in the house."

"Foggie? Leggie? What kind of trouble?"

Jewel stopped as she reached the detached three-car garage. "Dee Sweet—I *know* you're not asking me that? Ever since we've started this hunt, there's been nothing but trouble. I'm guessing Crammer's men are inside."

"Holding your grandparents hostage?"

"Exactly."

"Oh, those poor darlings! They're probably scared to death."

"I doubt that," Jewel said dryly as she slowly rolled up the garage door. Before she had even cleared six inches, four oversized doggie paws pushed toward the outside. "Hey, boys," she whispered, "you're going to have to be quiet for Jewel, okay? Shhhhh . . . arrrggghh!" As soon as they had enough room to scoot underneath the door, the two Great Danes, Fog Horn and Leg Horn, pounced on Jewel, sending her to the ground and licking her face like highly possessed puppies. Their eager, pendulous tails painfully wrapped Dee's thighs. Then, realizing that someone else was present, the dogs turned their crazed canine attention on her, leaving Jewel to brush herself off as she struggled to her feet. "Oh my God!"

"What is it?"

"What the hell am I wearing?"

"We can discuss your sense of fashion later; what are we going to do now?"

Jewel wrangled the dogs by their stylish rhinestone collars. "You go start up the Ferrari and be ready to roll. I'll go save the day."

"These aren't exactly attack dogs."

"No, but what they lack in courage, they make up for with enthusiasm and sheer size."

Fog Horn and Leg Horn practically dragged Jewel to the back door. She yanked as hard as she could to keep them from rumbling through their large swinging doggie door. "Me first," she ordered, dropping to her knees and pushing her head, arms, and torso into the house. An eager Fog Horn attempted to enter at the same time, causing both dog and infuriated human to get stuck. "Back off, Foggie," she whispered, bringing her left hand up and across her body to push the excited dog's mammoth head back outside.

"What's that?" asked Anthony Graves. "I heard a dog."

"Oh, that's probably Foggie and Leggie. You remember us telling you about them—"

Before Mrs. Brooks could continue, the Horn brothers were airborne. Their targets: Anthony Graves and Mr. Snow. Taken unawares, both men were knocked flat.

"Sit on them, boys!" Mr. Brooks commanded. The dogs immediately dropped down and continued their frantic licking. The lord of the manor then made himself busy collecting the guns, which, upon full-canine contact, had flown hither and yon.

"You better get going now, sweetie," suggested Mrs. Brooks. "Next time, I hope you can stay longer."

"Amen," said Pop-Pop Brooks.

Jewel hugged and kissed her grandparents as if Graves and Mr. Snow, who were struggling to push off the Great Danes, weren't even in the room. "I hope they didn't cause you too much inconvenience."

"Oh, please," said Mrs. Brooks with a dismissive wave of her hand. "Call me and tell me how this all works out, dear heart!" Then she watched Jewel and Dee rev the Ferrari down the driveway, while Graves and Snow pushed and cursed the old woman out of their way.

"Bye-bye to you, too, Mr. Graves and Mr. Snow," she called after them, before turning to her husband and giggling at the flustered men. "They don't stand a chance."

"Amateurs, pure amateurs," agreed her husband. "But they certainly made for a fun afternoon."

Dee was confident she could lose Graves and Mr. Snow once she got onto the open highway. But as they crept through the car-filled and stoplight-rich streets of northern New Jersey, the villains practically rode the Ferrari's bumper.

When Jewel yelled, "Here! Here! Turn onto the parkway!" a

rush of exhilaration poured through Dee's blood. "Hold on; it's time to shake the bad guys."

Dee was thankful for the maneuverability afforded her as she went from twenty to ninety miles per hour in five seconds flat. To her surprise, the Nissan 240SX soon caught up. She pushed it to a hundred.

"ARE YOU CRAZY?! SLOW DOWN!" screamed Jewel, fidgeting fretfully as she sat helpless in the passenger seat.

"I'm trying to lose them," Dee calmly explained, changing lanes and swerving in and out of traffic with the skill of a professional race driver.

"YOU'RE TRYING TO KILL US!"

The speed was an elixir to Dee's daredevil spirit. With each added mile per hour she felt rejuvenated. She left the hurt, the anger, and the humiliation of her marriage in her rubber-burning wake. For good.

"SWEEEET! SLOW DOWN! WE'RE COMING TO A TOLL!"

Dee's sharp eyes sized up the situation, "Gimme thirty-five cents," she said, not letting up on the gas.

"Wwwhat?"

"GIMME THIRTY-FIVE FREAKIN' CENTS!"

Jewel dug through her pink jeans pockets and fanny pack. "All I have is a dollar."

"Damn, now I'll have to stop," grumbled Dee before slowing to get in a lane that took bills, silently cursing the Garden State Parkway's frequent and infamous tolls. "Come on! Move it!" She laid on the horn as the driver in front of her apparently had the gall to ask for directions. Looking in the rearview mirror, she saw Graves and Snow pulling up behind them. "Come on, for Christ's sake!"

"You gotta problem, lady?" asked the toll attendant, checking out the car with appreciation. Dee didn't respond; she didn't wait for change. She floored it.

Covered with unladylike sweat, Jewel was sure she was having a heart attack as Dee pushed her husband's two-hundred-thousand-dollar toy to 125 miles per hour. Her heart thumped frantically in her throat, preventing her from making even the tiniest protest. Dee misread this as a sign of countenance. She thought Jewel trusted her driving and was on the same page in the playbook.

The next toll came up almost immediately. There was an empty lane, which Dee flew through, resembling a silver streak of lightning. "Already paid for it at the last one," she explained in a breathy voice, rocketing the Ferrari past everything in its path, and soon realizing she had truly lost Graves and Mr. Snow. They were nowhere in sight. She was about to mention this to Jewel, when the far-off distinctive shrill of police sirens reached her ears. Her heart—which had been all for the speed and as calm as a light summer breeze—dived to the pit of her stomach. "Uh-oh."

Jewel hadn't uttered a sound since the first toll; but she now cleared her throat and, and in a much steadier voice than she felt capable of, said, "You better pull over, Sweet."

Relieved that her passenger wasn't making a fuss, Dee slowed and moved from the center lane to the right-hand shoulder before gracefully purring to a stop atop a steep knoll where the parkway curved to the left. She was just about to blurt an excuse for her blatant disregard for the posted speed limit when Jewel's hand crashed into her face. Quite painfully. "OW!"

"YOU COULD HAVE KILLED US!"

"YOU BITCH!" cried Dee, reaching out to put her hands around Jewel's neck.

While she was being choked, Jewel slammed an open palm on Dee's face, in an attempt to push Maria Andretti's head off her shoulders.

Dee made a fist and punched her irate partner in her kisser. Not surprisingly, that bit of violence shocked Jewel. Nobody had ever laid a hand on her. She swung her left leg over the gearshift and kicked Dee right in the gut, temporarily knocking her worthy opponent breathless. When Dee looked up, she didn't need to gasp, "NOW I'M GOING TO KILL YOU!" It was clearly written on her face.

Who said, "He who fights and runs away may live to fight another day"? With that question burning a hole in her brain, Jewel opened the door, scrambling to make a hasty departure. She would have made it, too, if Dee hadn't lunged sideways to catch her by the ankle. "Let me go!" Jewel demanded, while twisting and turning to free her foot. Dee stomped wildly like a spoiled child, then crawled across the seat in hot pursuit—inadvertently throwing the car into neutral.

The two combatants continued the fierce battle, rolling completely away from the car, which had begun to do a bit of rolling itself. Jewel slammed her forearm against Dee's shoulder. "THE CAR! GET OFF ME! THE CAR!"

Both women shot to their feet and ran to grab on to the Ferrari's open passenger door, but neither was strong enough to keep it from drifting down the hill, nor stupid enough to jump in front of it. Seeing that they couldn't stop the inevitable, Dee let go. But Jewel hung on for dear life, running a good fifty feet down the hill until the Ferrari pulled ahead and careened down, down, down . . . stopping only after it had crashed into a couple of rigidly defiant trees with a sickening thud.

Jewel whirled to focus on Dee, ignoring the two police officers who stood on either side of the Sweet woman. She charged up the incline, swinging a mighty this-is-all-your-fault arm at Dee, who ducked. The blow caught one officer precisely upside his ill-humored head.

"Hope you're satisfied," Dee hissed as she and Jewel sat handcuffed in the squad car.

"Don't talk to me. Ever again!"

❖ ❖ ❖

It was hard to describe the mug shots.

Jewel's eyes twitched maniacally with indignation. *Booked and fingerprinted! Me? How dare Russell report the car stolen! And if that cop's head hadn't been so big, I would have missed him altogether.*

Dee, on the other hand, took it all with a good bit of humor. She'd never heard the word "reckless" used so many times in reference to her. "Can I get a dozen wallet size?" she asked playfully before posing for her police-file portrait.

"I'm glad you think this is funny," said Jewel in a low voice. "I also hope you're willing to say I had nothing to do with this. I was just an innocent party."

"Who took the car? Who hit the cop?"

Jewel huffed. "All right, never mind all that. What are we going to do?"

"I'm sure we each get a phone call."

"Who you gonna call?"

Dee's eyes twinkled.

"Don't you even say it, Sweet. I'm serious. I'd rather die than have anyone find out about all of this."

Dee sobered. How would a police record look in a child-custody case? "Yeah, come to think of it, me too."

"I'll call Xavier! He only lives about an hour from here. He can bail us out. Then I'll have Russell drop the auto-theft charges. We'll be free and clear. No problem."

"Sounds like a plan."

Xavier listened patiently to Jewel's incredible story and assured her he'd be there. "This is what you get, you know."

"For what?" she asked impatiently.

"For not sticking to our deal; for not waiting for me."

"Sorry, Zavie. But I couldn't wait. I just couldn't."

"Of course you couldn't, my sweet, greedy girl, but if you

exclude me again, I'll blow the whistle on this whole thing. Do I make myself clear?"

"Crystal. Honest. Now please come right away. I'm allergic to jails."

"I'll be right there, sweetheart," he assured her before hanging up and adding, "tomorrow." He laughed and made himself comfortable in front of his television. "Looks like you'll be waiting for me now, Jewely-girl. A night in the slammer might do you some good."

"That was nice of them, to give us our own cell, wasn't it, Jewel?" Dee bounced up and down on the hard prison cot, as if she were claiming the best bunk in overnight camp.

"Just great," mumbled Jewel.

"What do you think is keeping Xavier?"

"I have no idea, but I'm going to choke him when he finally shows up."

"What if he doesn't show up?"

"He'll show up." Jewel didn't dare think otherwise.

"This is some mess, huh?"

Jewel let out a hollow laugh.

"Well, at least we got the clue . . . Oh no, the clue! It's with our belongings! What if someone else . . ."

Jewel raised a calming hand from her bunk across the tiny cell. She then reached in her pants pocket and retrieved the yellowing piece of paper Dee had swiped from Saint Thomas' Church.

"Whaaa? How? . . . Oh, right . . . I forgot about your sleight-of-hand talents. Well, let's have a look; we've got nothing else to do."

#7

*MOVE TO ANOTHER SAINTLY THOMAS, WHO BY
    NAME IS PURE,
THEN TO THE CATHEDRAL OF CHAPEAU-K TO
    END YOUR LONG TOUR.*

*THERE FIND MY FRIEND MANNY-K WHO HAS
   D.C.'S DIAMOND CURE.
THAT'S IT . . . THAT'S ALL . . . YOU'LL BE THROUGH
   . . . FROM TWO-MILE YOU'LL HEAR NO MORE.
A WORD OF WARNING BEFORE I GO . . . THE STAR
   IS A DANGEROUS LURE,
IT CANNOT REPLACE A LOVED ONE LOST . . . OF
   THIS YOU CAN BE SURE.*

Dee and Jewel sat side-by-side quietly on a cell cot, reading and rereading this seventh, and apparently final, clue.

"Got anything?" asked Dee.

Jewel shrugged. "Not a thing. Although it sounds like maybe we're to go to France."

"France?"

"Chapeau? . . . Perhaps there's a Saint Thomas church in France. Get it? Cathedral?"

"What's that have to do with baseball?"

"Beats me. But if you stole a four-hundred-nineteen-carat diamond, plus some other little baubles, would you hang around here?"

"I see your point. Maybe we should let Gibby take a look at this one." Dee sighed. "This is all so confusing. I mean, who in the world is writing these clues anyway? We've already established that Two-Mile died before these were written."

"That's an excellent question, Sweet. And one we won't be able to answer unless we see this whole thing through." Jewel pointed to the last line of the clue. "What do you think he means by this: 'loved one lost'?" Her thoughts turned to Russell and his wounded Ferrari. "Russ is going to hit the roof when he finds out who took his car. He'd probably be less upset if a stranger had nabbed it. Damn! Why didn't I remember he'd be home today?" Jewel refolded the precious piece of paper and placed it back in her pocket. "He's a morning person. He probably got home right after I left, saw the car was gone, and freaked."

"I sure hope he drops the charges."

"He will." *He has to!*

They were quiet again, consumed with thoughts of French chapels and lost loves. Finally, Jewel chuckled. "Will you look at us, Sweet," she said, raising her arms to take in their accommodations. "It all sounded like a good idea at the start. Now, here we are in some godforsaken Jersey burg's jail."

"Go figure." Dee rubbed her gut. "Man, did that kick hurt."

"Yeah, well, you punch pretty hard, too, sis. If I'm scarred in any way, I'll sue you." Jewel paused to shake her head in wonder. "I don't know what came over me. I'm usually not such a violent person."

"Tell that to Barney Fife." Dee laughed. "Did you get a load of his face after you creamed him?"

"It was classic."

"Well, how are we going to bust out of this joint?" asked Dee, noticing the cell had not even a sliver of a window.

"I think we've done enough living on the edge for one day, don't you?"

"Right. Well, then, how about a Negro spiritual to see us through this dark time? You must know one."

Jewel laughed along with Dee. "Do you know what the most depressing thing about this whole day is, Sweet?"

"What's that?"

"I was arrested *and* photographed in this getup."

By the time the treasure seekers were dropped off at Dee's, it was late in the afternoon on Friday. And it was pouring in Washington. An absolute deluge. Xavier, who had been duly blessed out for taking his time, had been reimbursed for his bondsman services and was on his way back to Philadelphia.

"It's official," said Dee, snapping off the television. "The game's been called. That means our 'sweeties' should be home shortly."

Jewel's stomach knotted. She was in no hurry to meet up with Russell, who, she figured, must know everything by now. Thus hanging around with Dee for the afternoon held much appeal. The first order of business was getting out of those "horrid, dirty clothes." So she shopped. Buying things always picked up Jewel's spirits. She ran down to Saks to purchase a sexy red romper that clung to her curves and dipped in the front. That little number should sweeten Russell's disposition, she thought later when showering in Dee's guest bathroom. *God, I hope so.*

While Jewel scrubbed down, Dee called Gibson Sager—who had been relieved of his batboy duties due to the rain—and read the seventh clue to him over the phone. The child wrote it down. "I'll check into it, Mrs. Sweet, but I gotta tell you, none of this is ringing any bells."

"I know. Well, do the best you can, Gibby."

"No problem. Hey, are those two assho——ah . . . I mean . . . jerks bothering you?"

"Just a little."

"Need me to crack 'em over the head again?"

Dee chuckled. "Not right now, but I'll keep you in mind . . . Say, Gibby?"

"Yes?"

"Did Mark leave the stadium before you?"

"Yeah, Dad and I were the last to leave. Dad's always the last to leave."

"Are you sure?"

"Sure I'm sure; he's my ride home."

"No, I mean are you sure Mark left before you? He wasn't getting his knee worked on or anything like that?"

"Nope. Actually, he was one of the first to adios after the game was called."

"Thanks, Gibby." Dee hung up, looked at her watch. It was going on five o'clock. Mark should have been home.

"How do I look?" asked Jewel, bounding down the stairs, twirling around when she reached the bottom.

"Definitely more like yourself." Dee smiled, trying to insert a bright note in her voice. "I called Gibby and read him the clue. He said he'll think it over, but it doesn't look good."

"Rats. I was afraid of that. So, what do we do now, Sweet?"

"Well, I'd go to Annapolis, but the rain is so awful and I'm just too tired to drive. I didn't get much sleep in the old hoosegow last night."

"You miss your kids?"

"Somewhat . . . Is that a horrible thing to say? As crazy as this may sound, this has been like a vacation. Since Jessica was born, I've never really been separated from them. This is the first time in six years I haven't had to change a diaper for days at a time. It's actually quite wonderful. I suppose I'm the worst mother on earth for saying that. But I know they're in good hands."

"Sure they are. Your mom raised you, didn't she?"

Dee tilted her head in surprise and turned up the corners of her mouth as she stared at Jewel. "Is that a compliment, Mrs. Averick?"

"It's whatever you want to make it, Sweet."

"How about some dinner?"

"If you cook it; I'm all for it."

Jewel dreaded going home. But with each minute that passed sans any sign of Mark Sweet, his wife became more tense. Jewel decided it was time to face the music—no matter how sick the song.

Dee was concerned about Jewel, who hadn't said two words during the drive to her home. Her face was a drawn line of anxiety, and she gulped when she saw Russell's Jeep in the driveway.

"Do you want me to come in with you?" Dee asked softly. "I can tell him it was all my fault."

Jewel stiffened in her seat. *Yes. Yes, please. Keep Russell from strangling me.* "Gimme a break, Sweet. I can handle any little tantrum Russell might throw. You just worry about solving that seventh clue."

"Are you sure?" Jewel's answer was to get out and slam the car door shut. "Good luck, Jewel," Dee whispered.

As soon as Jewel walked through the front door she could tell Russell was struggling to control his temper.

"Hello, Russ," she said with a practiced coolness. "Rained out today?"

"I'm going to give you one chance to explain yourself. *One* chance." The steel in his voice gave each of his words a cold, unyielding edge that left Jewel paralyzed in the entry foyer, speechless. "Well?" he prompted, taking a step toward her. "I'm waiting."

Jewel swallowed hard, twisting her keys nervously in her hands. *Pull yourself together, old girl. You can handle this.* Stepping tentatively around her stone wall of a husband, she walked into the living room and casually threw her things on a chair, before turning back to Russell and taking a deep breath. She shrugged. "I took the Ferrari, what can I say? I certainly didn't *steal* it."

Following her into the living room, he ground his teeth at her cavalier attitude. "And how, may I ask, did you get a set of keys?"

"Had them made." Unable to make direct eye contact, she focused her gaze on an area just above his right shoulder.

"Behind my back?"

"I did it in case of an emergency."

"An emergency that would warrant you driving my car? Yeah, right," he spat. "Why didn't you tell me you had a key?"

"Slipped my mind."

Russell erupted. "GOD! I'D LIKE TO KICK YOUR ASS!"

Somewhat relieved that he'd let go of the icy, impersonal

facade, Jewel allowed her own temper to match his. "How dare you talk to me like that!"

"HOW DARE I? HOW DARE I? How dare YOU take my car without my permission and wreck it? A car that meant everything to me!"

"Your car! Your stupid old glove! Your goddamn trophies! They all mean more to you than I do! Isn't that right, Russell?! You thought I'd be another ornament for your collection, didn't you? Didn't you?! Well, guess what? I walk, I talk, and I make mistakes like every other human being. I'm sorry you can't just put me in a case with your other precious possessions."

Russell's jaw jerked. Jewel knew she'd hit a sensitive spot . . . the truth. She took advantage of his momentary silence to hurry toward the kitchen.

He was close behind her. "Don't you turn this around on me. Everything I have and everything I do is 'stupid' to you, isn't it? Even so, you shouldn't have taken my car. Just like you shouldn't have sold Cool Papa Bell's glove. But you don't give a shit about me, my things, or my feelings. You do whatever the hell pleases you. *Now* who's right?"

She didn't answer, just slammed cabinets and drawers as she went about making a cup of coffee.

Russell continued in a calmer voice, "Just tell me: Why'd you do it?"

Now it was Jewel's turn to catch the fire of anger. She whirled around and marched up to stand within an inch of her husband. "I'll tell you why I took your damn car. I'll tell you! I wanted to wreck it! I *wanted* to hurt you for sleeping with that Pam girl in Chicago! So there!"

Russell's face became a contorted mask of confusion. He blinked at Jewel as if he didn't recognize her. "What the hell are you talking about?"

"Oh, spare me the innocent crap! You put her on the phone, remember?"

"You're crazy. I wouldn't—"

"Oh yes, you would . . . you . . . you . . . you . . ." Jewel couldn't quite bring herself to scream "bastard!" "But, of course, you were drunk as a skunk. You probably don't even remember. Well, I certainly do!"

Russell seemed to give his brain a good racking. "Look, Jewel, I *was* drunk, but nothing happened."

"Could have fooled me."

"Oh, what the hell are you worried about? After all, you've been running around telling people I'm impotent! . . . Don't look like that—Pete told me!"

That big mouth . . . I'm going to kill him. "I can explain . . ."

Russell cut her off with a weary, mirthless laugh. "You always have an explanation. Besides, even if I did sleep with her, which I *didn't* . . . how would that be different from you and Lawrence?"

"WHAT?"

"Now who's playing innocent?" he mocked, crossing his arms over his chest.

"Xavier and I never—"

"Shut up! Just shut up! I don't want to hear any more of your lies! Mrs. O'Hara told me he was here the other day—and in our bedroom! Do you deny that?"

She's dead, too. "No, but—"

Russell reached out and painfully seized her by the arms. "I ought to—how could you?"

Having had just about all the physical abuse she could stomach, Jewel kicked him in the shin with every ounce of her strength, then grabbed a nearby bag of whole-bean gourmet coffee and slammed it over his head. They were silent as hundreds of arabica beans landed all over the large kitchen.

"We're through," he said softly.

She staggered back from him. "What did you say?" It came out choked and barely audible.

Russell kept his gaze level. "I want a divorce; we're through."

Jewel stared at him long and hard, looking for any sign of a weakening stance. She detected none. Panic made her dizzy and a little faint. "You can't mean that," she whispered.

"I do mean it."

"Why?"

Her plaintive question caused Russell to spew a harsh laugh. "Why? The question is, 'Why have I waited so long?' "

That stung. Jewel had never seen this side of her husband of four years. The hard, scornful side. A side, she silently admitted, she'd brought about with her careless and unfeeling behavior. A feeling swept through her that was so foreign, it weakened her knees and brought tears to her eyes. For the first time in her life, Jewel Elizabeth Howard Averick was truly sorry.

It was time to explain about Two-Mile. She prayed it wasn't too late.

"You won't want to divorce me when you hear what I've been up to. What I've been doing for you."

Russell shook his head sadly and began to walk out of the kitchen.

She followed, slipping on a renegade pack of fleeing beans. "No, listen! It's true. Dee Sweet and I have been on the trail of Two-Mile McLemore."

He stopped in the corridor and turned halfway back to her. She knew she had his attention. "A clue was in that old glove you brought home. And it promised we'd find Two-Mile McLemore. We followed it to Philadelphia. Only Two-Mile wasn't in Philly; just a sweet old man named Harry, who gave us another clue. So, we followed that to the stadium—"

"Stop it! Stop it! I don't want to hear your bull," Russell interrupted with two raised hands.

"I know it sounds crazy, but it's true."

"Oh yeah? What would make you run all over God's green earth for a man you couldn't care less about? Don't you remember throwing a shoe at me when you found out I bought his glove?"

"Yes, and I was wrong. That's why I tried to find him, to make it up to you. Don't you see that?"

"No, I don't. But I *do* see a cracked-up Ferrari. I *do* see you and that idiot Lawrence rolling around in my bed. I *do* see you selling my personal belongings to strangers . . . Shall I go on?"

"Why won't you listen to me? Why won't you let me explain?"

"I'm through listening, Jewel. I don't want to hear it anymore. We're done. End of story."

There was no mistaking the finality in his voice. He meant it. It was over. Jewel knew that if she let him walk out the door, the next time she'd see him would be in a courtroom with their respective lawyers. *How can I stop him? What can I say to make him stay? Dear Lord, what can I say?*

"You can't leave me, Russell," she said in an iron-nerved voice that belied her internal upheaval. "I'm pregnant."

He pivoted around to her and gave her a wide-eyed, open-mouthed stare. "What . . . did . . . you . . . say?"

Hang tough, Jewel. "I'm pregnant."

"You're lying."

"I'm very serious."

"You can't be."

"I am."

Russell's breathing became uneven with a wary excitement. "Jewel—I swear, if this isn't the truth—"

"I'm pregnant."

He closed the distance between them and jerked her face up to meet his. "How far along?"

"Eight weeks."

He hesitated, then began sputtering nonsensical sounds as an incredulous gleam lit his face, chipping away at his hardened mask. "Y-yo-you went to the doctor and everything?"

Jewel just nodded, a sickening feeling creeping through her.

She knew she hadn't stepped over the line—she'd plunged off the cliff.

"This is no joke?"

She shook her head. They were silent as they stood underneath the overhead hall light, just looking at each other, uncertain of their next step, uncertain of anything. Then, similar to the Grinch about to give Christmas back to Whoville, Russell's entire face changed. It was like watching a time-lapse metamorphosis. The tired facial lines that had aged him beyond his thirty years changed into crinkling lines of joy. His mouth, which had seemed permanently grim, turned up to touch the outside corners of his suddenly sparkling eyes. He was ecstatic. Jewel shrieked with surprise when he lunged forward, gathered her in his arms, and began spinning her around. His delighted laughter tore at her wretched heart. *How can I do this to him? Because I have to. I can't back down now! How can I get away with it? I can say I fell down the stairs or something like that, and lost the baby. Yes, that'll work! He'll be crushed, but at least I'll keep him. It'll work. It has to!*

Russell gently placed her on her feet and drew her into a comforting bear hug, kissing her forehead tenderly. She could hear his heart beating wildly. A joyous beat that spoke directly to her conscience. *I can't do it. I just can't do it.*

He drew her away from him, but kept a wonderfully warm touch on her arms. "I know you probably don't think you're ready for this, Jewel. But you'll be fine; you'll see. We'll be a happy family—Lord, I hope the kid looks like you!"

"I'm not pregnant." Her voice sounded as if it came from miles away, even to her own ears.

Russell dropped his hands. She suddenly felt ice-cold. "What?"

Jewel couldn't look at him. She couldn't face his hurt, his rage, his disdain. "I'm not pregnant. I'm sorry, Russ. I don't know why I said it. I just didn't want to lose you."

He didn't yell. He didn't scream. He simply walked to the

front door, pausing on his way out to turn and say, "Good-bye, Jewel."

Guilt was having its way with Dee, as she paced back and forth in her family room, wondering what was taking place at the Averick household. "It's not Jewel's fault," she informed the walls. "I was driving too fast. I'm the reason the car rammed into the trees." After a moment's hesitation, she grabbed the nearest phone to call and explain to Russell.

Frozen in time, Jewel hadn't moved from the spot where her husband had left her in the hallway. Her mind could not fathom what went down . . . only seconds ago? Minutes? Hours? She had no idea how long she'd been standing rooted to the floor, staring at the door he'd walked out of—waiting for him to return. *Russ would never really leave me. He's got to come back.*

When the phone rang in the still silence of her house, Jewel jumped. *It's Russell!* She ran to the phone in the den. "Hello?"

"Jewel, it's me, Dee."

Jewel closed her eyes, feeling an acute disappointment, and dropped the receiver to her side.

"Jewel? Jewel? Are you there?"

The muffled voice finally registered in her hazy mind. She brought the phone up to her mouth. "Yeah, I'm here," she whispered.

"Is everything all right?"

"Russell left me, Sweet. He's gone. I . . . um . . . I don't know what to do."

Deanna Duffy Sweet knew what to do. "I'm coming right over." She hung up, threw on a rain slicker from the front closet, and headed out the door—just as Mark was coming in.

Being a second baseman, he was trained to keep things from rolling past him, even if it was his five-foot-six-inch wife doing a damn good impression of a speeding freight train. "Hey, hey, hey, where are you off to?"

Dee jerked out of his grip. "I've got to go over to Jewel's."

"What did I tell you about her?"

"I don't have time for this."

"You don't have time for much of anything anymore, do you? No time for your kids. No time for me . . ."

"HA! *I* was here for hours, where were you? Out with your bimbettes, no doubt."

"I was with our kids! I called you from the stadium to see if you wanted to go, but *you* weren't around. Getting into trouble with Jewel Averick, no doubt," he said, mimicking her tone to perfection.

Dee narrowed her eyes. He wouldn't lie about visiting the kids because she could easily check up on that alibi. But she knew that wasn't the whole story, just a cover-up. She leaned in and gave him a hug. Although surprised, Mark gladly accepted the embrace. Dee pulled back with a smirk. "Since when did Nina start wearing Obsession?" She reached out and plucked a long dark hair from his collar. "And the last time I checked, my mother had gray hair."

"Duffy, listen to me—"

She didn't. She jogged through the heavy rain to her beat-up Volvo. But before hopping in, she shouted, "I want a divorce!"

"Duffy! Don't do this! Duffy . . . Come back! Duffy . . ."

The front door of the Averick house was open. "Jewel?" called Dee, entering the house. There was no answer, so she moved toward the kitchen where she, too, slipped on a few coffee beans before stepping out onto the screened-in back porch. There, she found Jewel in the yard, getting drenched. She was just standing there, with her face to the sky.

Dee ran to her. "Jewel! Are you okay? What are you doing out in the rain? You're ruining your new outfit. Let's go inside."

Jewel stared straight through Dee. "All those songs about letting the rain hide your tears. That's what I'm doing, Sweet." Her voice was so distant and detached, Dee thought she might have snapped or something. Jewel didn't protest as Dee steered her onto the porch and gently pushed her down on a cushion-covered wrought-iron settee. "You want to catch pneumonia?"

"My husband left me. By comparison, a nasty cold doesn't seem all that bad." Dee wrapped an arm around her sopping partner's trembling shoulder; she knew the floodgates were about to open. Jewel proceeded to howl, cry, laugh, and hiccup uncontrollably. If there was an emotion left to purge, she'd purged it. "I—I—ah—told him I was pregnant."

Shocked, Dee pulled back to look at Jewel's anguished face. "What? Are you?"

"No . . . I lied," she sobbed.

"Oh dear. He'll be really mad when he finds out about that."

"He already knows. I told him I made it up. That's what sent him packing." Jewel suddenly straightened and stopped bawling, furiously wiping away her tears. She sniffed and pulled herself together so that when she spoke, her voice was strong.

"It's over, Sweet. He wants a divorce. Russell hates me. The thing is—now I'm sure he never loved me. He just tolerated me." Her words were forged with such a depth of realization, it was hard for Dee to argue—even halfheartedly.

"He's just upset."

"No," she sniffed, "that's not it. Sure, he's mad; and, yes, I screwed up royally and deserve his scorn. But it goes deeper than that. He loves playing baseball. He loves his family. He loves his collectible trinkets. He loves that car. And you want to hear the real kicker? He loved my make-believe kid. You should have seen his face. He's never looked at me with such rapture."

"That can't be true . . ."

"I'm afraid it is. He even said, 'I hope the kid looks like you.' Don't you get it, Sweet? He's only seen me as some sort of trophy. A pretty piece of property. He didn't say, 'I hope the kid is healthy. I hope the kid is smart. I hope the kid can play baseball.' Nope, his first wish was that junior look like me."

"Jewel, I'm sure he meant it as a compliment. I think you're reading way too much into it."

"Am I?"

Dee sighed before she let out a soft chuckle.

"What?" asked Jewel, wiping the last tear from her eye. She knew there'd be more, but for now, she was all out.

"We're quite a pair, you and me. Before I came over here, I told Mark *I* wanted a divorce."

"You didn't!"

"Yup, I did."

"What did he say?"

"I didn't stick around to listen."

"How do you feel?"

"I'm not really sure. But I know it felt damn good to say it, even if—"

"You didn't mean it?"

Dee batted back a few of her own tears as her bottom lip quivered. "God! I'm so stupid! I can't believe I still care for that asshole. He came home smelling like perfume and I still can't hate him like I know I should."

Now it was Jewel who slung an arm around Dee's shoulders in a show of camaraderie. "Let's consider this the beginning of the rest of our lives, Sweet. Who knows where we'll go from here, or where we'll end up? But we won't shed any more tears for those overgrown jocks of ours—at least not for the next fifteen minutes." She sniveled. *"If* we're going to be unattached, we should live it up."

Dee gave her a brave smile and wiped her runny nose. "Hey, Jewel, maybe now you can have your way with Xavier and see if Russell was a great or lousy lover, as you put it. I still can't believe you were a virgin when you got married."

"It happens, Sweet. Some of us remain pure until the last minute, until the wedding night . . . until you know you can't put it off any longer," mumbled Jewel dryly. "Besides, I was thinking of something more exotic, like kicking back on a tropical paradise's beach and sipping potent drinks out of coconuts."

Neither said a word as they stared out into the darkness and listened to the rain fall. Then, without warning, Jewel shot to her feet. "That's it!" she cried, before running out into the rain to try a cartwheel.

Dee followed, fearing Jewel had truly gone round the bend. "What is it?" she asked, laughing in spite of herself.

"Sweet! I figured it out! 'Another saintly Thomas'—as in Saint Thomas."

"Yeah?"

" 'Who by name is pure' . . . as in virgin."

"Yeah?"

"Saint Thomas, Virgin Islands!"

"JEWEL!" Being more athletically inclined, Dee put Jewel's cartwheel to shame with a combination round-off back flip. When she was through showing off, she ran up and grabbed her sister-friend by the hands. "Do you know what this means?"

"We're one step away from placing our greedy little hands on a four-hundred-carat-diamond," Jewel whispered gleefully.

"Now *that's* the Jewel Averick I've come to know and love."

8TH INNING:
Runners in Scoring Position

Jacinta O'Hara showed up at the Avericks' bright and early Saturday morning, just as Jewel was struggling down the main staircase with two heavy-duty canvas suitcases.

"Oh, hello, Cindy," Jewel said, squeezing the straps of her hastily packed bags as if they were the woman's neck.

"Jewel? Where you off to?"

"To a tropical paradise, not that it's any of your business. By the way, you're fired."

"What?"

"You heard me."

"What for?"

"For deliberately telling tales out of school and stirring up trouble between Russ and me."

"Russell hired me, and he'll be the one to fire me, not you. So I ain't leaving until he tells me to."

"Do you want me to call the police and have them drag you out?"

"You wouldn't dare—"

"Oh, wouldn't I?" Jewel grabbed a pudgy arm and was leading the outraged housekeeper to the front exit when the doorbell rang. She released her hold on Jacinta to answer it. Framed by a steady downpour, Gibson Sager stood on the other side. He was holding one of Russell's trophies—some sort of glove. Jewel looked past the youngster and waved to Pete, who was sitting behind the wheel of his Cadillac in her driveway, apparently performing chauffeuring duties.

"Gibson? What brings you to my house at"—she checked her watch—"eight-thirty on a Saturday morning?"

"Good morning, Mrs. Averick." Gibby stared at her in awe, taking in her yellow shirt and denim shorts. Her hair was falling around her face in delicious disarray.

"Gibson?"

"Oh, right." He cleared his throat to give his mind time to remember why he'd come. "Mom made me clean out my room, 'cause we found a cat who'd been living in it for who knows how long. Didn't even know it was there. But that, at least, explains why the goldfish kept disappearing."

"Excuse me?"

"Psych. Just joking. Anyway, I'm returning Russ's Gold Glove from 1990. He lent it to me two years ago. Sorry I kept it so long."

"You should have sold it, kid."

"Excuse me?"

"Psych. Just joking." Jewel reached out and grabbed the object. "Thanks, Gib. I'm sure he'll be happy to have it back."

Gibby looked at her colorful pieces of luggage. "Goin' somewhere?"

"As a matter of fact," she said with a wink, "Dee Sweet and I are heading to the Virgin Islands, Saint Thomas. We're coming to the end of our Two-Mile hunt."

"Get outta here! Man! I wish I could go with you. What do you think you'll find—I mean, since Two-Mile is dead and everything?"

Jewel shrugged and affected an innocent expression. "Don't know."

Jacinta stirred in the background, which reminded Jewel she had trash to dispose of. "Ah . . . Cindy, I think you were leaving?"

Walking past Jewel with her chin to the ceiling, the older

woman huffed as she made a vain attempt to fasten the buttons on her too-small trench coat. She opened her umbrella with dramatic flair on the front porch, spraying Gibby with remnant raindrops. "Good-bye, young man," she said, mustering a digni-fied air like the butler in "Upstairs, Downstairs," before turning back to the mistress. "Jewel Averick, you'll be sorry one of these days," she promised like a vindictive vixen on "Days of Our Lives."

"Yeah, yeah . . . whatever," Jewel said, waving her on her way.

Gibby twisted his mouth. "Isn't she a charmer?"

Jewel spent the next couple of minutes rushing about. She deposited Russell's Gold Glove next to all the others in one of his showcases and secured the house while filling Gibby in on her adventure—diligently forgetting to mention a long-lost gigantic diamond. The young man helped put her bags in the Lexus's trunk. "Is this all still a surprise to Russell?"

Jewel paused to let a sad grimace cross her face. "I'm afraid so."

"I'm still sworn to secrecy? 'Cause I'd love to tell Dad."

"When it's all over, Gibson. When it's all over . . . okay?"

"Okay."

Jewel leaned over and planted a soft kiss on the man-child's cheek. She'd come to realize that, when they're not brats, kids can be all right—even pleasant. "You better go now; your dad's waited long enough."

Several blocks from the Averick homestead, Gibson was still delighting in the feel of Jewel's lips on his baby-soft skin, when he caught sight of something that made him sit straight up in his dad's car and lose the silly grin. There, on a busy corner not three blocks from the Avericks', he spotted their housekeeper, Mrs. O'Hara, talking with one of the guys he'd clobbered at the stadium—the dark-haired man who had held them at gunpoint, the one they called Lipless, the one who was also after Two-

Mile's clues. He blinked to make sure he was seeing correctly. When Mrs. O'Hara hopped into the man's car, he let out a disbelieving "Oh, shit!"

"What?" asked his oblivious father. "You forget something?"

Gibby slumped in his seat with eyes the size of medium pizzas. His mind raced.

"Son?" prompted his pop.

"Ah—it's nothing, Dad," he murmured.

"I've got to hand it to you, Jewel, you know how to travel in style." Xavier Lawrence clinked his cocktail glass against Jewel's orange juice and reclined his spacious first-class seat as they flew to their Caribbean destination. "I can't believe you can't fly coach."

"I *can* fly coach, Zavie," she sighed, trying very hard not to think about Russell, which she found nearly impossible. "I just didn't *want* to fly coach."

"But to pay off the people who had these seats—"

"Hey, they're going to get to Saint Thomas just like you and me, only now they'll have walking-around money. It all worked out; everything's copacetic. So relax, will you? Look at Sweet." Jewel motioned toward Deanna Sweet, who sat in the opposite aisle seat. She was completely conked out and snoring softly.

Xavier lowered his voice. "That senator's wife didn't take too kindly to your offer for her and her daughter's seat . . ."

Jewel rolled her eyes at the thought of the sixty-something woman and her late-thirties daughter sitting in the row behind them. "Yeah," she whispered, "bet her husband—what's his name? Horndae?—I bet Senator Horndae would have taken the money. Did you see her face, Zavie?" Jewel manufactured an outraged, snobbish expression. "'Why, I've never . . . a lowly black person offering *me* money for my seat! What's the world coming to?'"

Xavier laughed at the theatrics and stopped short as the lady in question spoke up in her affected voice. "This coffee is cold," she complained to the heavily made-up, but attractive, flight attendant, who was black. "And my daughter needs another blanket. I asked you half an hour ago for one. Can't you turn down the air-conditioning? It's freezing on this plane."

"She didn't ask for another blanket, because when she got on, she was bitching about how hot it was in here," Jewel whispered to Xavier.

"Honestly," said the younger Horndae, as the flight attendant went to get her mother some hot java, "this must be her first day on the job."

"Well," said Mommy Dearest, "at least she's not on welfare."

Jewel gasped at the woman's ignorance, while Xavier shook his head. Soon after Mrs. Horndae finished her coffee, she thumped the back of Jewel's seat with her foot about ten times, which was about eight times too many. So the Averick woman unbuckled herself, stood in the aisle, and focused a hoity-toity stare on the senator's wife. "Would you *please* stop banging on the back of my chair?" she said in a loud voice, mocking the Horndae tone. "Honestly! Where, in heaven's name, are your manners? You must have left them in the barn in which you so obviously were raised." That said, she reclaimed her seat, leaving a flabbergasted Horndae duo.

Not one to be put in her place by the likes of a young black woman, Mrs. Horndae attempted to regain the superiority edge and began talking with a trumpet-tongue to the ritzy-looking couple sitting across from her. She didn't want Jewel to miss a word.

"Are you staying in Saint Thomas?" she asked.

"Yes," answered the couple's female component pleasantly.

"Where are you staying?"

"Bolongo something-or-other. I can't think of the name right now. Where are we staying, dear?"

"I don't know; you made the arrangements."

Mrs. Horndae didn't care if they ever remembered. "Oh,

we're staying at the Redbeard Cottages. They overlook Magens Bay. You need to make reservations a year in advance."

"Oh?" said the obviously disinterested, but polite, woman across the aisle.

"They have everything at the Redbeard—they're really wonderful little two- and three-bedroom cottages. Each one has a hot tub, and a phone and television in every room—even the bathrooms. They positively spoil you to death and have one of the best restaurants in the Caribbean. And the views! Absolutely marvelous! I tell you, it's quite exquisite. Of course, it would have to be; we only stay at the *best* places when we travel . . ."

"Probably at the expense of taxpayers," Jewel grumbled.

"It's very exclusive. And, I can assure you, we won't have to *pay* people to let us stay there," she concluded, taking a well-aimed shot at Jewel.

Not having a place to call home when they reached the island, Jewel decided the Redbeard Cottages sounded as if they just might do. Rather than using the phone at her seat, she popped up and excused herself.

"Going to the bathroom?" Xavier asked.

"Nope, going to get us a room at the inn," she mouthed without uttering a sound.

Jewel ran her credit card through the communal phone in the rear of the aircraft and patiently waited for the operator to give her the number for the Redbeard Cottages in Saint Thomas. It didn't take long to discover that the place was booked solid for the next eighteen months. The reservationist even chuckled at Jewel's request for "Three? . . . Two? . . . Okay, do you have one cottage with a non-ocean view?"

"I'm sorry, ma'am, I can't help you."

Wanting to make sure the place was all the Horndae lady made it out to be, she asked, "Well, can you at least tell me what you have to offer, in case I want to stay there in the future?"

After hearing a litany of amenities, she hung up and decided it was indeed the place where she'd rest her head that evening.

"Any luck?" Xavier asked.

"Booked till the end of the century."

He sighed. "Oh, well, we'll find something."

"I already found where we're staying."

"Where?"

"The Redbeard Cottages."

"How?"

Jewel made a patting motion with her hands, telling him to keep it down. "It's easy. Now, here's what we'll do . . ." She then mapped out her plan—very quietly.

When she woke, Dee was clueless as to what Jewel was up to. But she knew she'd find out sooner or later. So she closed her eyes, deciding that later was, more than likely, the best choice.

Xavier Lawrence committed a cardinal sin of air travel—he got up before the plane had come to a complete stop at the gate. But he was anxious to get on with Jewel's plan. He was even more anxious to find the Star Diamond. After a public-address scolding from the head flight attendant, he took his seat once more, only to pop up again when the "ding" told them they'd arrived at the Cyril E. King Airport in Saint Thomas, U.S.V.I. He was the first one off the plane.

"What's his hurry?" asked Dee, as they meandered through the airport. "And, by the way, I saw you 'accidentally' knock your bag into the backside of that senator's wife. You ought to be ashamed of yourself."

"It was a love tap."

"Whatever you say." Dee squinted when they walked out into the beautiful sunshine. While digging in a bag for her sunglasses, she continued, "So where're we going to stay?"

"At the Redbeard Cottages," Jewel said, letting an eager cabbie throw their things in the back of a van.

"Shouldn't we wait for Xavier?"

"We're going to meet him later at the hotel."

Dee and Jewel couldn't help but smile at the beauty surrounding them as they sped along in the taxi-van. There were no muted colors on the island. The landscape was painted in bright greens, blues, reds, and yellows, with tropical breezes lazily ruffling gauzy skirts and palm trees. "I forgot how lovely it is down here," said Dee. "Every time I come, I say, 'I could get used to this. I could live here.'"

"I know what you mean," mumbled Jewel. "Oh! I forgot to tell you."

"Tell me what?"

"How we're going to get a cottage."

"How?"

"Okay, now listen closely . . ."

Mrs. Horndae and her daughter were becoming a little concerned. They'd been bumping along the roads of Saint Thomas for forty-five minutes in the shuttle van with "Redbeard Cottages" emblazoned on both sides. The hotel staff had said the ride was no longer than twenty minutes.

Everything had gone smoothly enough when they arrived at the airport. They first were greeted by a driver, holding a card in front of his face with their name on it; then they climbed in the van while he loaded their bags in the back. "You ready for a wonderful time on da island?" he asked, hopping behind the wheel.

"That's why we're here," Mrs. Horndae responded in a terribly bored, just-drive-the-van manner.

"First, I'll need your confirmation number for the cottage and some identification."

"We are who we say we are, and I can assure you we have a cottage reserved," was her hot retort. When he just held out his hand, she mumbled a euphemistic curse and gave him the information. Soon they were on their way.

Forty-five minutes later, they were still on their way. "Are we almost there?" asked Mrs. Horndae from her position right behind the driver, who only nodded his straw-hatted head. "I was told it would take twenty minutes. It's going on fifty."

"We almost dare, mom. Deez tings take time," he assured her, turning onto a remote dirt road and beginning a steep climb up one of the island's many hills.

"Are you sure you know where you're going?"

He nodded again.

"I don't think this boy knows, Mother," stage-whispered the junior Mrs. Horndae.

Shortly thereafter, the driver found the place *he* was seeking. He swerved the van roughly, landing in a shallow ditch, six inches deep in mud.

"Yoooww! What the devil are you doing?" screamed the passengers.

"Eees a problem wit da steerin', mom. I got to go git help."

"You're *not* leaving us here!"

"You wanna come? Dat's a lot of luggage for you to carry. Look, ladies, town is just a short deestance. We'll have you to da cottages in no time. I'll be bok."

"No! Don't go! Don't loave us here!" cried Mrs. Horndae, bravely stepping into the mud and watching her three-hundred-dollar sandal disappear beneath the mire. She pulled up a blackened foot and ankle. "Uuuuggghh! You better hurry back! Wait until I tell my husband! He's a senator with the United States Congress! This will be your last job, you dumb lummox! I'm going to report you! I never—"

She continued to yell as the driver started to jog down to the main road. However, before stepping onto the much busier street, he ducked behind a leafy tree and peeled off his official tan-colored Redbeard Cottages safari shirt and straw hat, revealing a Princeton T-shirt and a perfectly round head. He walked onto the road and waved at a waiting blue Dodge. Up rolled the car; in he jumped.

"How'd it go, mon?" asked the young black man driving the old Dodge Swinger.

"Perfectly. They should be sitting up there awhile." Xavier Lawrence laughed. "Here ya go." He handed over the shirt and hat. "Thanks a lot, Rudy."

The man smiled broadly, shaking a fistful of big bills at Xavier. "No, thank *you!*" Xavier worked his face into one of great contemplation. "Say, my friend," he asked, "would you happen to know where I can get my hands on a . . . a . . . well, a gun?"

"A real one, mon?"

"Of course, a real one."

"Watchoo want wit a gun, mon?"

"I'm in town on business—might be some trouble, that's all."

After a quiet moment of consideration, Rudy said, "It'll cost you some."

"No problem."

"All right, then," Rudy acquiesced, slapping the dashboard, "we'll make a little pit stop before we go to Redbeard."

"Excellent. I believe there's a room waiting with my name on it."

With a loose-fitting scarf tied around her head and sleek sunglasses, Jewel strutted into the Redbeard Cottages reception area with the look of a movie star and a purposeful stride.

"Can I help you?" asked the pie-faced younger woman at the front desk.

"Yes, I have a reservation for Aver-*rich,* spelled A-v-e-r-i-c-k," she said, taking a few liberties with the pronunciation of her last name.

The woman pounded her computer's keyboard. "Huh? I'm not finding anything for Averick."

"Well, check again; I'm sure we made one."

The woman did and reported there was nothing for Jewel. "Are you sure you have the right date?"

"I could ask you the same thing, Miss . . . ah"—she read the girl's tag—"Linda."

"I'm sorry, ma'am, but we have nothing under your name."

Jewel released a world-weary sigh that told Linda she wasn't going away easily. "Well, just put me in the best cottage you have available."

"I'm afraid we're all booked."

"I'm afraid you'll have to unbook."

"I can't do that, ma'am."

"I made reservations a year ago."

Linda shook her from-a-bottle towhead and pounded on her keyboard again for effect, to make Jewel think she was actually trying to help. "I'm sorry, Mrs. Averick, there's nothing available. We'd be happy to find a room for you at one of the other hotels."

"I don't want to stay at another hotel. I want to stay here. Where's the manager?"

While Linda gladly went in search of her boss, Jewel looked at her watch. She had exactly ten minutes to make a first-class fuss. And she did it with flawless virtuosity. She demanded. She rapped the desk in anger. She lamented. She threatened. She even montioned her friend "the sheikh."

"Sheikh?" asked the manager, Brandon Bradley, his eyes suddenly very attentive, practically glowing with the color of money.

"Yes, Sheikh Abilaba. He was to join—ah, well, you just never mind about that."

Mr. Bradley chewed on his knuckle and appeared to be praying for a miracle. Jewel looked at her watch. His prayer was about to be answered.

Dee was nervous. But she dialed the number just the same, her hands shaking with antsy excitement. *Here goes nothing.*

"Redbeard Cottages; how may I direct your call?" came a pleasant voice through the pay phone outside the cottages.

Dee hoped the operator couldn't hear the laugh-filled splashing of the swimming-pool festivities taking place behind her. "Reservations, please."

"How may I help you?"

"Yes, I'm the administrative assistant for Mrs. Horndae, Senator Horndae's wife here in the States. And I'm calling on her behalf. I believe she and her daughter have a cottage reserved for today . . ."

There was a moment of silence as the operator tapped her computer. "Yes, I have it here."

"Well, unfortunately, Mrs. Horndae has to cancel those reservations due to an unexpected emergency."

"Oh, okay. I just need the confirmation number."

Dee nodded to Xavier, who was standing by with the number; she read it off a tiny piece of paper.

"We usually charge for one night when a reservation is canceled this late."

"She understands."

"But because we would love to have the Senator and Mrs. Horndae stay with us at a later date, we will be happy to waive that charge."

"Oh, no! That's quite all right. Unlike other Washington residents, we don't want any special treatment; we play by the rules."

The reservationist chuckled before saying, "Okay. Shall I leave it on the American Express? I'll give you a cancellation number."

"Absolutely."

Back inside, Jewel was in full rant, but stopped abruptly when Linda poked her head out of a door behind the front desk and signaled to Brandon Bradley. "Will you excuse me for a minute, Ms. Averick?" he said. A minute later he came back beaming. "Today must be your lucky day! I've got great news for you."

Twenty minutes later, Jewel, Dee, and Xavier were popping the cork of a complimentary bottle of champagne in their very own, very secluded Redbeard Cottage. The threesome stepped onto the terrace to take in the breathtaking panoramic views of the lush green mountains and vivid blue-green sea. "To Mrs. Horndae, wherever she is," toasted Jewel.

"Here, here," laughed Dee. "That'll teach that show-off to brag her business to strangers." A frown came over her face. "I hope that driver isn't fired."

"Naaa," said Xavier, "I told him to say some man came up to him—wearing the proper uniform and carrying what looked like legitimate hotel identification—and claimed he was a special driver for the very special Horndaes."

"Don't worry about it, Sweet. By the time they straighten out the whole thing, we'll be back in the States. With any luck, that'll be tomorrow," said Jewel, emptying her champagne flute. "Now, let's grab a phone book and a map and find this Chapeau-K, shall we?"

"Chapeau—shit!" cried Jewel, slamming shut the last of the tour books. "I can't find anything."

Dee had long ago stopped looking and was polishing off a tropical rum punch with loud slurping noises. "Why don't we call down to the front desk and ask them?" she suggested, flopping over on the living area's pink-and-green couch.

"That's a good idea," agreed Xavier.

Dee called the concierge. "Hello, I was wondering if you could tell me where I may find Chateau-K?"

"Cha-*peau*-K," corrected Jewel, frowning at Dee's empty cocktail glass.

"I mean Cha*peau*-K . . . No? We think it's a church of some sort with a cathedral . . . No? Right, Chapeau-K . . . No . . . No . . . No, that's not it either . . . No . . . What was that one? . . . No . . . Any more? . . . No . . . No . . . Say that again? . . . No . . . Okay, well, thanks for your help." She hung up and was greeted with curious stares.

"What was that all about?" asked Jewel.

Dee snuggled in the sofa and mumbled, "I don't know, the concierge started naming all these *K*s."

"Any named Manny?"

"Nope. But there was a Patricia-K and stuff like Thatch-K, Grass-K, Green—"

"Wait a second," Jewel said, sifting through all the literature on the floor until she found a map of the Virgin Islands. "Did you say 'Thatch'?"

"Thatch correct," said Dee.

"As in Thatch Cay?"

"Uh-huh."

"Sweet! Zavie! It's not *K* like the letter, it's 'cay' like . . . well, like whatever a cay is! See! Right here on this map, there's a Patricia Cay, and a Thatch Cay, a Grass Cay, a Green Cay, Rotto Cay, Cas Cay . . ."

"Hello? He mentioned all of those," Dee said with a hiccup.

"So we should be looking for a Chapeau Cay?" reasoned Xavier, taking a seat by Jewel on the floor to help her look.

There wasn't a Chapeau Cay to be found. "Wait, Zavie, how about this—see, Frenchman's Bay? Chapeau is a French word."

"Yeah, you could be right."

They knew they were close as they continued to scour the map of Saint Thomas. Their eyes searched east, then south— bingo!

"FRENCHCAP CAY!"

They yelled so loud, it roused a semi-snoozing Deanna Sweet. "Whaa—what? What?! We find the diamond?"

Jewel kissed the map right on the tiny little cay. "Oh, Two-Mile, you are a playful one . . ."

Russell took a deep breath and straightened his navy-blue sports jacket before ringing the doorbell. Although it felt like an eternity, it took exactly fifteen seconds for Carla Hunter, his old girl-friend, to answer her door.

She looked great, he thought, checking out her tight jeans and clinging red-and-white-striped top that showed off her curves. After five years, she still kept her hair pulled back in a tight bun to highlight her plump brown cheeks and the saucer-sized eyes of her doll-like face. There was no getting around the fact—Carla was a cutie.

Carla seemed quite shocked to see him at her door. "Russell!" she squealed before adding a cool "What an unexpected and pleasant surprise."

Feeling like an embarrassed sixteen-year-old picking up his Homecoming date, he just stood and grinned stupidly.

"It's Saturday afternoon; don't you have a game or something?"

"Ah—no, postponed." He waved his large golf umbrella to show Carla the teeming rain, as if she couldn't feel the rebel, windswept drops pelting her face.

"Oh yes, I see." The most awkward silence fell upon them, before the young woman remembered her manners. "Come in! Come in!"

His sigh of relief was overt as he dropped the umbrella on her small covered porch and crossed the threshold of her Cherry Hill, New Jersey, town house. "So, what brings you to my humble home, Russ?" she asked, showing him to her sofa.

He didn't answer. Instead, he grabbed her hands in his as she sat next to him. "You look great, Carla."

She smiled. "Thanks, so do you!" This was followed by another awkward minute of quiet. "Can I get you something to drink?" He shook his head. "You're doing so well with the Diamonds, Russ. I've been following your progress. You ought to be very proud of yourself."

"Thanks, Carla," he said softly, looking into her big baby-browns. He gripped her small hands harder.

"Russell, is everything all right?"

"Well, no. I mean yes. Everything is fine . . . really," he stammered, before letting out a sigh. "Actually, nothing's right. I—I—"

"Russ?"

"Carla, I made a big mistake. I never should have dumped— ah, broken it off with you. You and I got along; we wanted the same things. You were good to me; you were good *for* me. I never should have married—" He stopped, still unable to say "that woman's" name.

"Jewel?" finished Carla. She cleared her throat delicately.

"Carla . . . I've missed you."

"I've missed you, too. We had some good times."

They fell silent again, not sure what should be said next. Then Russell slapped his thighs and bolted to his feet. "Damn!" he muttered, pacing back and forth.

"What is it, Russell? What can I do for you?" she asked, hitting just the right come-hither, sex-kitten voice and leaning forward to give him an enticing cleavage shot.

He groaned her name. Before he could stop himself, he'd drawn her to her feet and planted a long, demanding kiss on her upturned lips. But she wasn't responding with the proper amount of ardor. In fact, she was barely responding at all. Russell stepped away from her, feeling uncomfortably foolish. "Uh . . . I'm sorry, Carla. I don't know what's come over me." He flopped down in a chair, wishing it would transport him out of this macho, man-made humiliation.

"Russell, what are you doing? Have you forgotten you're married?"

His sagging spirits buoyed a bit. "I've asked her for a divorce."

"Russell," she began, "I'm engaged. I'm going to be married next month."

Duly chagrined, he looked at the rock on her finger, silently chiding himself for not noticing it right off the bat. He could have saved himself a good deal of face and the full ache in his head and heart. "Is that so?"

"I'm marrying Johnny Camp," she announced with no small amount of pride.

"The football player?"

"Right. He plays for the Eagles . . ."

"Yeah, yeah, I know who he is." *That thick-neck punk* . . . "I can't believe it, Carla! A football player?"

"What? Was I supposed to just shrivel up and die?"

"Of course not, but—but—"

"But what, Russell?"

"But what about me? I thought you loved me?"

"I don't believe you, Russell Averick! You have a lot of nerve, coming to my house five *years* after we broke up, questioning who I'm marrying and who I love!"

"I apologize, Carla. But I thought you cared for me."

"Russell! Get a grip! Being drop-kicked for another woman tends to sour a girl on a guy, if you know what I mean!" Carla stopped to take the conversation down a notch. "Look, Russ, you're obviously going through something heavy with Jewel, and instead of moving forward, you want to turn back. Well, it can't be done. I'm not the same girl you dumped. I found someone I truly love. And he loves me. What we had wasn't love. We were just convenient for each other. You knew it way back then. And I know it now."

Russell shook his head. "Jewel said you'd marry a football player."

"Is that right? She's smarter than she looks."

Russell allowed himself a small chuckle before capturing one of Carla's hands and forcing her to meet his pained gaze. "Are you sure, Carla?"

She planted the softest of kisses on his lips before pulling back and placing her palm on the side of his face. "I can't, Russell," she whispered. "It's too late. We've both come too far to turn back. Deep down, you know that."

In this month of "new lows," Russell felt like he'd somehow dropped even lower. Being with Carla again had made him yearn for a kind and sensitive woman. A woman who would understand him and stand by him. A woman who wouldn't deceive him. The antithesis of Jewel.

"I feel so stupid," he said.

Carla smiled at his downturned head. "You wanna stay for lunch?"

He straightened and shook his head. "Ah—no, thank you. I'd better be going."

"You sure?"

He stood and nodded.

At her door, Carla gave Russell a hug. "I'm glad you came, Russell. It's every dumped girl's dream to have the man who broke off their relationship come—I think the word is 'crawling'—back. It's been terrific for my ego. I hope we can be friends."

He looked down at her glowing visage and kissed her forehead. "I *am* happy for you, Carla. I'm glad you've met the man of your dreams. I'm just feeling a little sorry for myself right now." He paused to give her one more heartfelt hug. "And, of course, we can be friends. I'd like that a lot."

She watched him walk through the rain, his umbrella dangling useless behind his back, his head hung low.

Carla Hunter closed the door, leaned her back against it, and raised her hands to the heavens. "THANK YOU, GOD!" she cried, before clicking her heels and running off to call the florist about the status of her wedding bouquets.

The raven-haired woman leaned over and patted Mark Sweet on his knee. "Somehow I get the feeling you're not into this tonight."

"Huh? I'm sorry," he mumbled, trying to focus on the task at hand. "Where were we?"

"Where were *you*? You haven't been paying attention since you stepped in here," she said, smiling kindly. "Do you want to talk about it?"

"My wife, Duffy . . . Deanna; she wants a divorce."

"I see. Well, we can always do this another time, if you're not up to it."

As he drove home that Saturday evening, Mark was determined to set the record straight with Dee. He'd tie her up if he had to. He had to make her listen. He'd made many mistakes—huge mistakes—in his life and he regretted each one, but the biggest mistake would be to stand aside while Dee divorced him. He just couldn't let her and the kids walk out of his life. *That's not going to happen, Duffy. Over my dead body.*

His heart sank when the only sign of Dee was a cryptic note left on the refrigerator.

Mark, went to St. Thomas, USVI
for a day or two with Jewel.
Will be back to discuss things.
Duffy

"Damn!" He crumpled the paper and violently threw it across the kitchen. Dissatisfied with that gesture, he grabbed a sturdy wooden dinette chair and slammed it over the counter, breaking it into several pieces. Then he kicked aside an amputated chair leg and stormed out of the house into the dark, rain-filled night.

It was four in the morning when he staggered home, having closed down two bars in remote D.C. areas. He forgot about the broken chair and tripped over it. "What the—?" he cursed, fumbling for a light switch. When the lights came on, Mark thought he'd stumbled into the wrong house, because there were three men in his kitchen. Three men he didn't know. Three men holding guns. Three men holding guns on him!

"We were beginning to wonder if you planned on showing up, Mr. Sweet; you look like you've had quite the night," said Duke "Quiet" Crammer, flanked by his goons, Anthony Graves and Mr. Snow. "Oh yes, and thanks ever so much for conveniently leaving the door open. That kind of courtesy makes our job so much easier."

Mark's alcohol-laden brain was spinning like a hamster on an exercise wheel in slow motion. He couldn't comprehend. He didn't know what to think, but was positive this was the biggest kind of trouble. "Duffy!" he finally blurted, pitching forward and catching himself on the counter, as he tried to fight a growing sense of hysteria. "Where's my wife?"

"She's not here; but we're going to take you to her," said Crammer in a patient, fatherly tone.

"Who are you?" Mark pushed himself away from the counter and stomped clumsily over to the phone. "I'm calling the police!"

Crammer sighed and gave a weary signal to Mr. Snow, who promptly pistol-whipped Mark into unconscious submission.

"Now what?" Duke Crammer said when he and his men pulled up to the entrance of a private airport where they planned to be whisked away to the Caribbean. There, in the pale early dawn, stood Jacinta O'Hara. Crammer rolled down a backseat window and watched her trot quickly to his Lincoln. "Mrs. O'Hara," he began with a hard edge in his voice, "what brings you here so early in the morning?"

"Your assistant told me you'd be here. I've been waiting forever."

"What can I do for you?"

"I've been fired, Mr. Crammer."

"Is that right?" He scratched his chin. "I'm sorry to hear that."

"So I was wondering if you could pay me for that last tip I gave you?"

"You'll get your money, Mrs. O'Hara. All in good time. I'm in a hurry right now, but I'll be back in a few days and we'll settle up then, providing I get what I'm after."

Jacinta narrowed her eyes at the man with the face like a basset hound. "You owe me two thousand dollars, Mr. Crammer; and I want my money—now."

Not about to stand around and be bossed by someone no longer of service to him, Crammer swung open his door, effectively pushing Jacinta to the side, and climbed out. "I *said* I'll give you the cash in a few days. Now don't push me."

Jacinta simmered as Mr. Snow and Anthony Graves emerged from the car. They were propping up a third man, who appeared to be in some sort of stupor. When they dragged the limp body around the back of the car, she thought he actually might be dead, but a tiny moan escaped from his ashen face. "That's Mark Sweet!" she cried, throwing a hand over her open mouth. "What have you done to him?"

"Now, now, Mrs. O'Hara. No need for alarm," said Crammer, "he's just drunk, that's all." He then pointed to a small jet behind the tiny airport's fence. "Get him on the plane, the one with the red stripe."

"Where you taking him?"

"To see his wife."

"In Saint Thomas?"

"That's where you said they'd be, correct?"

"Well—yes, but . . . he don't look like he's going willingly."

"You mind your own business, Mrs. O'Hara. Remember, you're involved in this, too."

Jacinta looked nauseous. "I am not. All I did was pass along some information—in fact, did I say Saint Thomas? I think it might be Bermuda, or was it Antigua? Or maybe it—" The very next second, Jacinta felt the cold steel of a gun on her forehead. She gulped. ". . . no, no—I was right the first time—it *was* Saint Thomas!"

"Now, if you'll excuse me, my pilot has been waiting too damn long as it is." He began to walk away, then read Jacinta's mind and turned back to her. "Oh, and don't even think about going to the cops. I know where you live. I'm sure you don't want anything *unfortunate* to happen to you or your children . . ."

Jacinta stood motionless as she watched the jet take off with the rising sun as a perfect backdrop. "What should I do? What *can* I do? I *have* to tell someone."

"This looks like the kind of place Two-Mile would send us to," complained Dee, who, along with Jewel and Xavier, took in the block-letter faded pink sign that read "Manny's." It was attached to what could only be described as a run-down thatched-roof contraption of some kind.

Finding the place wasn't as hard as they had feared, because several members of the Redbeard staff knew of Manny Kimbro, who ran a boating operation from a tiny island in Saint Thomas's Jersey Bay. Stepping off a speedboat shuttle, Dee wondered if Manny's hut was the only unnatural element on the unnamed island, which had a jungly, overgrown feeling. She doubted it was habitable for humans accustomed to basic necessities, like indoor plumbing. Dee glanced at Jewel, whose facial expression was hard to read behind her sunglasses and floppy straw hat. It didn't matter. Dee knew Jewel wasn't going to turn her nose up at the hutch's disrepair. In fact, that was the quality she admired most about Mrs. Averick: Although used to the finer things, Jewel never seemed to look down on those who had less.

However, as she stood in front of Manny's, Jewel's breathing appeared to be an uneven pant. Dee smiled, knowing her partner was daydreaming of starry diamonds.

The trio carefully climbed what should have been six steps (but numbered only four) to the porch of "Manny's." Jewel knocked on the swinging door that said "In." Even though its "Out" twin was missing, leaving a grand hole for an entrance, she stuck to the proper protocol, not sure what was waiting inside.

" 'Ello? Who dare?" sang out a thin West Indian voice.

The treasure seekers exchanged raised-eyebrow stares and shrugs before stepping into Manny's hutch. "Hello?" hedged Jewel, taking off her sunglasses to look around a wide-open room, searching through sun-streaked shadows for the voice. She saw what looked like remnants of boats and paddles of all shapes and sizes leaning against the wall. There was also a decent smattering of life buoys, snorkeling equipment, and sketchy-looking scuba gear only a suicidal diver would dare strap on. "Hello?" she called again.

A head popped out from behind a curtain of beads leading to a back room. " 'Ello dare!" said a dark brown man sporting a gray Mohawk hairdo, startling green eyes, and a beautiful, white-toothed smile. Jewel could only stare at this unique creature as he emerged from behind the beads to show about a hundred and six pounds on a six-foot frame. He looked to be about sixty years in age. His rail-thin body was clad in low-hung boxers adorned with retro, yellow smiley-faces, and he wore black wrist- and ankle bands. He floated over to his visitors in very worn flip-flops, his toes were so long, they scraped the floor. "I'm Manny. And who might you be?"

"Uh . . . I'm Jewel Averick, and this is . . . uhm . . ." She just couldn't stop staring. The man had three emeraldlike studs in one earlobe.

"I'm Deanna Sweet and this is Xavier Lawrence," said Dee, reaching out to shake his bony hand.

The man grinned. "Well, den, it's nice to meet you, Jewel Averick, Deanna Sweet, and Xavier Lawrence."

Never had the girls heard their names pronounced so beautifully.

"What brings you to Manny?"

"Two-Mile McLemore," said Xavier.

Manny Kimbro narrowed his eyes to slits. "Watchoo talkin' 'bout, mon? Watchoo know 'bout Two-Mile McLemore?"

245

"Show him the note, Jewel."

"Oh yes, right." She dug around in her pants pocket and forked over clue number 7.

Manny read it and let out a long, low whistle. "I can't believe it. It actually worked!"

"What?" asked Jewel, goose bumps gathering along her skin.

"Somebody come looking for da Diamond."

She grinned idiotically. "You better believe it. Where is it?"

Manny just laughed softly. "Aren't you the anxious one, my beautiful sister?"

"You *do* know where it is?"

"I do."

"And you'll take us to it?"

"I will, in good time. I will."

A thought crossed Jewel's mind. "Wait a minute. Wait a minute." She lowered her voice barely above a whisper. "You mean to tell me you know where there's a four-hundred-nineteen-carat diamond, and you'll take us to it?"

He nodded.

"Why don't you keep it for yourself?"

"What I gonna do wit someteen' like dat? I con't wear it. I con't sell it. It's no good to me."

"B-b-but it's beautiful!" *The man is insane.*

"Baaahh! It's a rock. Come wit me." Manny led them back to his porch and waved his outstretched arms to the gorgeous landscape sprinkled with bright red and yellow hibiscuses, and the breathtaking sparkling blue water and white sand. "Dis here is beautiful. Not'ing can compare. A rock is not'ing, you remember dat, young lady. Material t'ings arc not'ing—not'ing at all. Milton say: 'In dos vernal seasons of da year, when da air is calm and pleasant, it were an injury and sullenness against Nature not to go out, and see her riches, and partake in her rejoicing with Heaven and Earth.'"

Jewel was more impressed with his quoting Milton than with

the message he so elegantly conveyed. *You got your beauty; I got mine, pal.* "So, are we the first to come looking for the Star?" she asked in a hushed tone.

"No need to whisper, we da only ones on my island."

"Are we the first ones to come in search of the Star?" she asked in a normal voice.

"Yes."

"How long have you known its whereabouts?"

"All my life."

"Who told you about it?"

"Two-Mile McLemore, of course."

"When? Why? How?"

"Pull up a chair, my child; I'll tell you da whole story," offered Manny, waving a bony arm at some folded deck chairs that were leaning against a railing.

Jewel chose a pink one and sat down with an easy grace. Dee took a slightly ripped teal one and sat down daintily. Manny unfolded a yellow chair and took a seat with skilled aplomb, Xavier chose a blue one and flopped heavily into it, sending himself and the chair crashing through an unidentified weak spot on the porch.

"Sorry 'bout dat, mon," said Manny, who, along with Dee, struggled to lift Xavier out of the newly created hole. "I'm having a bit of a dry-rot problem."

Jewel remained in her chair and howled. When Xavier's big buttocks were finally extracted from the gaping abyss, he turned a dour look on her. "Thanks for your help," he said with a hiss.

"Hey, don't look at me," she giggled. "It's all I can do not to wet my pants. You should have seen your face!"

When everyone was safely seated, Manny cleared his throat and began to weave his tale. "As you must already know, Two-Mile McLemore was probably the greatest bossball player ever known. He could hit a ball so far—"

"Yeah, yeah, it traveled two miles . . . we've heard all this, Mr.

Kimbro," Jewel said, circling her forearms in a speed-it-up motion.

"My, we are in a hurry, aren't we?" Manny allowed a light to twinkle in his sea-green eyes. "Well, den, I won't bore you wit embellishments. He had a brother named Robert."

Jewel and Dee swapped frowns. "Ah, excuse me, Mr. Kimbro, don't you mean Two-Mile's name was Robert? We saw his grave in Baltimore," said Dee.

"I guess you're right. His name was Robert. But the *real* Two-Mile, the one legends were made of, was named Thomas."

Dee rubbed her temples. Xavier just nodded blankly. And Jewel opened and shut her mouth, not sure what her next comment should be.

"You see, ladies and gentlemon," said Manny Kimbro, "dare was two Two-Miles."

"We figured it had to be something like that because Harry B. and Clare Christie gave us distinctively different descriptions!" said Jewel. "So there *were* two, huh?"

"Yes, two." Manny held up two incredibly long fingers to assist his story. "There was Thomas McLemore and Robert McLemore. Dey was brothers."

Jewel remembered the one clue about Hank Aaron's brother's namesake . . . 'and mine, too.' Then she thought out loud. "Thomas! He was talking about his own name!"

Everyone looked at her as if she were insane, before Manny continued. "Thomas was the real Two-Mile; he barnstormed around the East Coast and Midwest. He was a huge man. Robert was short and stocky and could only hit balls—I dunno, maybe a mile. He played all the Diamonds' home games."

Dee continued her temple massage, while Jewel took to scratching her head under her straw hat.

"So what does all this mean, Manny?" Xavier asked. It was obvious he really wanted to say: "So where the hell's the diamond?"

"In Washington, D.C., one August day in 1939, Robert was

walking along an alley on Georgia Avenue, up around U Street, near the old stadium. He bent to tie his shoe. As luck would have it, or not have it, he was behind some grain barrels, out of view of two men leaving a local pub after the game. Dey deedn't see him. Deedn't know da mon was dare. And dey was talking 'bout a bunch of jewels coming in from England for President Roosevelt to da Navy Yard on Anacostia River."

Jewel sat straight up and leaned forward, as did her compatriots.

"Dees blabbermouts said dey had an inside man who could get da jewels, while dey was beein' transported to the Smithsonian."

"I KNEW IT! I KNEW IT!" cried Jewel.

"Da inside man was to meet dem in dat very alley in two days at midnight, after he got da jewels. Dey was to split dem. Now, one of deez men called da other one 'Quiet Crammer.' Well, Robert recognized the name belonging to Duke Crammer, a fairly well-known hood back in dem days. Everyt'ing went according to Crammer's plan, 'cept dat Robert was waiting for dem in da alley and held dem up."

"With a gun?" asked Dee, wide-eyed.

"No, with a toothbrush." That, of course, came from Jewel.

"Yes, with a gun, young lady." Manny flashed that gorgeous grin of his. "Robert, like Two-Mile—and, I imagine, a lot like you three—was one for adventure. He got the greed bug and saw an easy way to a small fortune. So he robbed da bad guys. Only Crammer recognized him as the D.C. Diamonds' player, Two-Mile McLemore. And, of course, was determined to retrieve his stolen stolen jewels.

"Robert got word to his brother, Thomas, that he was in serious need of some assistance, and Thomas beat it for D.C. and met Robert in dat park dare in the city . . . what's it called?"

"Rock Creek?"

"Could be. Anyhow, dey met dare and Robert explained da

whole story. Thomas was mad and told his brother he shouldn't have done it. He wanted no part of it. Robert ignored him and told Thomas he sewed da jewels in his ball glove."

Jewel gasped.

"Later, dey was walking to Robert's house in da northeast section of town to discuss what dey should do, when dey was intercepted by Crammer and a couple of his boys. Of course, da brothers ran like hell, splitting up to confuse Crammer. Dey was gettin' away, too; only Robert ran blindly out into a busy street and got runned over. He died shortly thereafter."

"No," whispered Dee.

"It's true, I'm afraid. Well, Crammer was furious because, as far as he knew, Robert was da only one who for sure knew where da jewels was hidden. And, as you know, dead men tell no tales. He tore up Robert's place, threatened his teammates, threatened everyone Robert knew. In da meantime, Crammer was da feds' number-one suspect. So he was takin' da heat without da hot rocks, if you know what I mean."

"What about Thomas?" demanded Jewel, on the edge of her seat.

"He was broken up about his brother's death. Such a senseless loss of life, he thought. But he wasn't going to let him die in vain. He found dat old glove in Robert's ransacked apartment, fenced what he could, and moved down here to da islands."

"So that's what he meant by the Star can't replace a loved one lost. And that must be why he just disappeared."

Manny nodded his Mohawk head.

"He kept the Star?"

"If he tried to get rid of it, he'd have been arrested."

"I see. So, let me get this straight. *Thomas* 'Two-Mile' McLemore is the one who brought us here?"

"Correct."

"And he wants us to find the Star Diamond?"

"Well, he actually wanted to have a little fun with Duke Crammer, who was instructed to buy da glove to begin da journey. You, apparently, got in the way."

"My husband purchased the glove at an auction. I found the first clue inside."

"So it seems, so it seems," chuckled Manny.

"Is Thomas still living?" Jewel couldn't believe she was actually holding her breath and praying, *really praying,* that the answer was yes!

"No."

She shrank in her chair. *Now, there's no hope of getting Russell back. None whatsoever.*

"Well, Mr. Kimbro, if Thomas is dead, who left all these clues? We know they were left relatively recently," Dee asked.

"Oh, he left them, all right. He only died some three weeks ago."

Jewel groaned at the injustice of her poor timing. "I'm going to vomit," she gulped, taking a deep breath to calm her sudden queasiness. "How do you know all of this?"

"He was my stepfather. He told me everything."

"Is your mom still living?"

"No, she, too, is gone."

They were silent, until Xavier finally slapped his thighs and rubbed his hands together. "So! Nobody else has come for the diamond?"

Manny shook his head.

"I can't believe you never went for it yourself."

Manny held out his hands to take in his kingdom. "Brotherton said: 'My riches consist not in the extent of my possessions but in the fewness of my wants.' "

Three pairs of curious eyes focused on this strange man named Manny Kimbro. "Yeah, whatever," muttered Xavier. "Where exactly is it? We figured out something about Frenchcap Cay . . ."

"Very good. It's hidden in Frenchcap Cay's Cathedral, which is an underwater cave."

"How much underwater?" asked Jewel with a generous helping of reservations.

"I dunno, maybe ninety feet."

"WHAT?"

Dee began to do the same little jig she had danced at Harv Fairfeather's after making like a pool hustler. "You mean you have to dive there?"

"That's right. Do you dive?"

"Absolutely."

"You have equipment?"

"Yes. But I'll need a tank."

"No problem. Okay, you go back to your hotel and get your gear, and I'll get t'ings ready on dis end. Let's say we meet back here at noon?"

"Sounds like a plan," said Jewel, turning to Dee. "I can't believe you packed your scuba stuff."

Dee shrugged. "You know I like to be prepared."

Jewel threw an arm around Dee's shoulder. "Sweet, you never cease to amaze me."

9TH INNING:
Suicide Squeeze

Russell Averick was ready to lose it. He tried to focus on the four people in his living room who were simultaneously hollering at him in highly agitated states. "WILL YOU ALL JUST SHUT UP, PLEASE?!"

Russell had returned home to pick up a few things before Sunday afternoon's game. Just as he was ready to leave, Yvonne, Pete, and Gibby Sager arrived in a state of clear agitation. Then, before he could even usher them into the house, Jacinta O'Hara flew in like a madwoman, mouth flapping.

"Okay, okay," said Russell, raising his arms to instill some sense of calm. "Yvonne, you first."

Yvonne took a deep breath. "All right. A few weeks ago, Jewel came over and showed me a riddle she thought Two-Mile McLemore had written. She decided to follow this clue to find him—"

"Yeah, that's right!" interrupted Gibby. "I was there. And Mrs Sweet was going along for the ride."

"It all seemed so harmless; it was kind of fun, solving these clues," said Yvonne.

"Only Jewel and Dee wasn't the only ones interested in finding Two-Mile," Jacinta said. "There was a man named Duke Crammer that wanted me to tell him where the girls was going."

"And you told him, Jacinta?" demanded Yvonne.

Jacinta gazed at her feet and nodded sadly. "I'm sorry now, but he offered me a thousand dollars for each tip."

There was a moment of silence as everyone in the room began

to realize the significance of Jacinta's confession. Then Gibby continued the convoluted saga. "Those weren't just random robbers at the stadium, Russ. Those were the men after Mrs. Averick and Mrs. Sweet. They were trying to get Two-Mile's clues . . . but *I* stopped them." Gibby's chest swelled like a bullfrog's. "And when I saw Mrs. O'Hara talking to one of them yesterday, I knew something was fishy." The teenager glared at the ex-housekeeper.

Yvonne gave her son a hard whack on the shoulder. "You are in big trouble, mister, for not telling us the truth sooner. If we'd known how serious this whole thing was, we would have tried to stop Jewel and Dee."

"Hey! What about her?" cried a defensive Gibby, pointing to Jacinta.

"I'm so ashamed," said Jacinta. "I don't know what to do. They said if I went to the police, they'd come after me and my kids."

"Mrs. O'Hara," said Russell, "you said something about them having Mark Sweet?"

"Yes, I seen them drag him to a plane on their way to Saint Thomas, where Jewel and Dee is. He was out cold; they said he was drunk, but I think they drugged him or banged him on his head or something."

"Good Lord!" cried Pete Sager. "We need him for this afternoon's game." He flew off in the direction of a phone.

Russell ran his hands slowly down the front of his face. "Let me get this straight: Jewel and Dee are *actually* trying to find Two-Mile McLemore?"

"That's right; they want to find him or proof that he existed," said Yvonne. "Except, they found out he died back in 1939; he's buried in Baltimore. Heaven knows what they're after now. My guess is some proof that he actually existed, like an old home movie."

"And there are some shady characters who also want to find the same thing? Perhaps because it's worth a lot of money?"

"That's how I see it."

"And these men bopped Mark Sweet on his head and carted him off to the Virgin Islands?"

"Seems that way. Don't you see, Russell? Jewel, Dee, and Mark are, more than likely, in grave danger."

Russell fell into a nearby chair. His head was pounding. He said nothing as Gibby, Yvonne, and his maid hovered, obviously waiting for him to spring into action. Pete Sager returned from his phone call. "There's no sign of Sweet. He's not at home and he's not at the stadium, and I can't reach him on his car phone."

"I told you," said Jacinta, "he been kidnapped. He's in Saint Thomas. Why won't you people listen to me?"

"I say we call the police," said Yvonne.

"And tell them *this* story?" Pete asked.

"Yeah, plus Crammer threatened me and he knows where all of you live, too, don't forget . . ." said Jacinta.

Yvonne saw their points. "Okay, then there's really only one thing we can do."

"What's that?"

"We go to Saint Thomas and find out what's really going on."

"Yvonne's right," Pete said. "What choice do we have?"

"What choice do we have? WHAT CHOICE DO WE HAVE?" Russell yelled, vaulting to his feet. "Are you people crazy? Do you know who we're talking about here? Jewel. Helloooo? Jewel . . ."

"Russell, surely you're not going to sit back and do nothing," said Yvonne.

"That's exactly what I intend to do. You guys can go and do what you want, but leave me out of it. Believe me, Jewel can handle any situation; she's in no danger. And if Mark and Dee Sweet are up to their necks in it, they were sufficiently warned. That's all I have to say. Now, if you'll excuse me," he spat, making his way out of the living room and into his den, leaving four mouths hanging open in disbelief.

Yvonne waited about a minute before following him into his sanctuary. She found him resting his head and forearms on the fireplace mantel, moodily kicking at an old log that had been temporarily spared a torching due to the arrival of summer. "Russell?" she said softly.

He jerked upright. "What is it, Yvonne? My mind is made up. Jewel is always up to something and no matter how great the fall, she'll always land on her feet. This whole crazy story could be one big lie. You're foolish to go chasing around the world to save her. She doesn't need saving."

"*I* may be, but you'd be foolish not to." Yvonne walked softly over to where he stood and rubbed his shoulder. Through his polo shirt, she could feel his big, sinewy muscles bunching with tension.

"You think so?" She nodded. "Well, that just shows you how much you know, Yvonne. I don't suppose you've heard, but Jewel and I are through."

"No! Russell? Because of this?"

"This and everything else. You don't understand. And I'm not about to go into it now. You'll have to trust me on this one," he said wearily.

"May I ask you something, Russell Averick?"

"Hmm?"

"Why did you marry Jewel in the first place?"

Russell looked at Yvonne, not sure where she was going. "Why?"

"Just answer the question, please. Was she nice?"

"Ha!"

"Was she thoughtful and truthful?"

"Ha!"

"Was she giving and caring? Was she kind to children and all God's creatures?"

"Ha! Ha!"

"A great lover?"

"Ha! Ha! Ha!"

"Was she smart?"

Russell moved his head in a "yeah, maybe" manner.

"Was she rich?"

He shrugged. "Her family had some money. But she had no money of her own. Believe me, Yvonne, I didn't marry Jewel for her money. If anything, she married me for mine."

"Then what was it? She was smart? Surely, smart black women are not hard to come by. What was it about *Jewel?*"

"She was . . . she was . . . I dunno . . ."

"She was pretty? Beautiful, perhaps."

Russell realized he'd fallen into some sort of Sager trap. "What's your point, Yvonne?"

"My point is, Russell Averick, you chose to marry Jewel because she was pretty. You overlooked her shortcomings and vowed to be her dutiful husband. Then, at the first sign of trouble, you want to bail out."

"*First* sign? With all due respect, Yvonne, you don't know what the hell you're talking about. This thing has been snowballing from day one. Jewel doesn't give a flying fu . . . ah . . . fig about me."

"See, that's where you're wrong. She began this whole thing for you. She wanted to do something special for you. At least, that's what she told me, and I believe her."

Russell just shook his head.

"Did you ever stop to think that, in her own way, Jewel may love you? And that she just has trouble competing with your baseball career? That she may do seemingly thoughtless things to get your attention?"

"No, absolutely not."

"You think she only married you for your money?"

"There's no doubt about that."

"Well, I happen to know that Chris Stanton, the network sportscaster, was hot after Jewel while she was dating you."

"What?"

"That's right. And at the time, I'm sure he was making much more than you were. But Jewel wouldn't give him the time of day. In fact, rumor has it there were several upper-income types after her."

Russell couldn't deny it. During their year-long courtship—and even during their marriage—many a man had made a bid for Jewel's affection. But she always seemed to be disinterested. *The only one of any concern has been that ass of a college boyfriend of hers, Xavier Lawrence. And he doesn't come near the money I'm making.*

Yvonne knew she'd hit an emotional home run. "I believe that young woman has loved you all along, even if she has a peculiar way of showing it. But you only viewed her as a trophy you could trot out to impress family and friends. Now, however, your feelings have changed, haven't they?" She paused. "So, are you going to let foolish pride stand in your way? Are you going to let something bad happen to Jewel, because you won't allow yourself to admit that you've grown to love her, too?"

Russell's entire body seemed to collapse, but Yvonne was right there to prop him up with a motherly hug. "It's okay, dear heart; everything will be fine, you'll see."

Fluctuating between semiconsciousness and death, Mark Sweet was one woozy man when he came to in what looked like a small private plane. "What? Where?" he mumbled in a daze.

"Hello, Mr. Sweet?" came a far-off voice that filtered through the sharp pains in his cranium.

Mark tried to focus his blurry eyesight, but the stranger's image faded in and out. "Who are you?"

"Let's say I'm a friend of your wife's."

"Duffy?" Because thinking was so excruciating, he was tempted to return to the blissful blackness. "What do you want with us?"

"I really don't want anything from you, Mr. Sweet. You're just a means to an end. You see, your wife and her friend, Mrs. Averick, have been looking for something that belongs to me. And

I'm afraid, if and when they find it, they won't give it back. So I'm hoping to use you to make sure they do as I desire. I'm sure your wife will see things my way."

"Oh," groaned Mark, trying to sit up and focus his distorted vision on the slight elderly man with an abundance of silver-gray hair and a great number of bags under his eyes. "I'm your hostage?"

"If it makes you feel better, you can consider yourself my 'guest,' Mr. Sweet."

Mark started to chuckle like a lunatic, causing Duke and the boys to exchange confused looks. "May I ask what's so funny?" Crammer inquired.

You dumb bastard, my wife hates me and won't give a shit if you kill me on the spot. You picked yourself a fine hostage. Mark quickly checked his histrionic laughing. "Who are you? And what does my wife have of yours?"

"Don't you worry about that."

"Hey, boss, we're coming close," said Mr. Snow.

"Where are we?" Mark peeked out a tiny window and saw the brilliant green sea and knew if they weren't landing in Saint Thomas, it was somewhere pretty damn close. The nausea that swelled inside him had less to do with his distaste of water than his concern for Doc. Seeing that he wasn't going to get any information from them in a fully conscious state, Mark opted for a game of cat and mouse. He clutched his head and groaned loudly before rolling his eyes to the back of his head and falling to the floor in a dead faint, only half acting.

"Looks like he's out again, boss."

"It's just as well, Snow. He'll be less trouble this way."

Mark feigned senselessness as they landed, and then again as they dragged him to a waiting limo. "He's out cold," noted Anthony Graves, speaking to the limo's driver. "What have you heard from Leo?"

"There's a man with them. They're staying at the Redbeard

Cottages. They've contacted a local character named Manny Kimbro, who's taking them on some shit-ass boat to Frenchcap Cay. Seems like Two-Mile hid it in the water. It also appears that the white chick is going scuba diving. But Leo has plans for her when she gets down among the fishies."

Mark thought he'd pass out for real. His heart was beating so fast, he was afraid they'd hear it. The thought of Dee coming to a tragic watery end, while he stood by and let it happen, was too much. He couldn't, *wouldn't,* let it happen! Not again! Not Duffy! He dared to open his eyes ever so slightly. As he suspected, he was in the limo's backseat, sandwiched between the two goons and across from the old man. He knew what had to be done; he had a chance.

Mark jerked upright from his slumped position and uttered an animal-like war cry, successfully startling the other passengers into a momentary paralysis. He immediately brought up two rocklike fists and slammed them into the unsuspecting faces of Anthony Graves on one side and Mr. Snow on the other. Simultaneously, he delivered a karate kick to Crammer's face. Having rumbled with four brothers for twenty-some years, he was well prepared for such a skirmish. Then, with the speed and agility of the professional athlete, he lunged across Graves, unlocked the door, and flung himself out, screaming "HELP! HELP!" before he even hit the pavement.

Mark Sweet missed feeling the tires of a Jeep on his back by inches. Scrambling to his feet, he banged his arms down on the Jeep's hood.

"You crazy?" asked the incensed driver.

Mark ignored him, and, with one mighty heave, ripped the antenna off the vehicle. Going on nothing but instinct, he whirled and slashed the antenna down on Mr. Snow's arm before whacking the giant's torso. He then swiveled to deliver similar blows to Anthony Graves. Using the antenna like a rapier, he backed up to the Jeep's passenger side. Daring to look at the stunned driver, he ordered, "Take me to the police! NOW!"

Dee was entranced. She was enthralled. She was captivated by the spectacular coral that surrounded her as she entered the Cathedral Cave at Frenchcap Cay. She watched the wrasses swim past pink hydrocoral. It had been a long time since she'd gone diving, what with Mark so adamant against water ventures of any kind. She was so absorbed in the undersea beauty that she'd almost forgotten that Jewel, wearing at least two life preservers, and Xavier were anxiously waiting for her in Manny's sorry excuse for a boat.

When she had first seen the battered cabin cruiser, Dee had thought Manny was joking. It was in bad need of a paint job and just about everything else. It hardly looked seaworthy.

But it managed to make it to Frenchcap, which was about five miles southeast of Saint Thomas. There were a few other scuba outfits in the area, but none had cast anchor where Manny stopped. She'd followed his descent line about fifty feet down and then was on her own. It was so peaceful, so colorful, so beautiful. For a split second, she didn't care if she ever resurfaced. She was born to be in the water; it was her own heaven. After a few happy, undulating dolphinesque turns, she consulted her compass and began swimming toward the west, following Manny's instructions.

Dee dived down to ninety feet, where she was almost immediately greeted with the wondrous sight of stingrays and barracuda. She continued to follow Manny's instructions, winding up in a short, narrow tunnel filled with coral. She turned on her flashlight. *This must be the place.* Thankful that she was wearing her diving gloves that matched her black-and-yellow custom-made wet suit, she began to sift through the ocean bottom, occasionally startling sea creatures that, at first, appeared to be rocks. She had covered about four feet when her hand struck upon something hard that didn't swim or scurry away. Dee dusted the sediment off the object and dug around it, exposing what looked like a rusted old metal box. Carefully, but quickly, she dug out the box and placed it in the net attached to her weight belt, before turning to leave the tunnel.

She had barely gotten out when another diver, a man, appeared at her side. Dee smiled and gave him a friendly "Hi" sign. He didn't reciprocate the gesture, only stared at her through his mask. Something about his eyes and the way he looked down at her treasure told Dee he wasn't an innocent midwestern tourist on a scuba-diving adventure. This man meant trouble.

Trying to remain calm, Dee mentally retraced her path, knowing she was going to have to make a hasty break for Manny's descent line. She kicked her fins harder, propelling herself ahead of the unwanted visitor. She hadn't gone four feet before she felt a tugging on her net. She whirled around and attempted to pull it out of his grasp. It was useless. He was too strong. She released the net from her belt.

His eyes behind the mask showed surprise; no doubt he was relieved that getting the box had been so easy. Dee swam as fast as she could up to the Cathedral Cave's entrance. The intruder took the time to check out the box in the net before extracting his razor-sharp diving knife.

Cutting through the water like the rays and barracuda, Dee swerved to a clumping of coral and stayed stationary behind it, out of view.

The man soon swam past. Dee attacked, yanking on his finned foot and grabbing for her net. It was clear he wasn't about to give in as easily as she had. He fought to keep her at arm's length as the two struggled in a whirling, spinning, floating mass of confusion. Then, all of a sudden, her air supply ceased. He had cut her air hose and ripped the regulator from her mouth. *Keep calm, exhale slowly.* She reached for her own diving knife as he swam away toward Manny's descent line. She caught up quickly and stabbed at his arm carrying the net. He furiously spun around. She stabbed at his ungloved hand, causing him to drop the box into her waiting clutches. She watched with wonder as a blue cloud of blood floated from his wounded hand.

Dee hadn't gone far up the line when he grabbed her from behind.

"Should this rope be jerking like that?" asked Jewel, leaning over the side of Manny's cabin cruiser, eagerly searching for any sign of Dee.

Manny and Xavier came to stand by her as the rope danced in the water with tremendous animation. "Somet'ing must be wrong," said Manny. "She bin down dare too long as it is."

"Well, DO something!" Jewel yelled. The last couple of weeks had truly changed her; she cared more for Dee's safety than the diamond's.

On board a police speedboat, Mark Sweet recognized Jewel Averick from a hundred yards. "There they are! That's them! Hurry!"

Jewel couldn't believe her eyes. Mark Sweet was rapidly approaching in a police boat! "What the hell . . . ?"

"Jewel!" he hollered. "Where is she?"

Jewel made a frantic motion, pointing to the water below. "She's in trouble!"

The sea had turned ugly on Dee. She must have jabbed at the man six times, before she was finally able to cut off his air supply in a perfect example of tit-for-tat. He was no match for the NCAA swimming champion, whose stamina and lung capacity tripled his. Exhaling the last of her breath—and clutching the metal box—Dee left her underwater nemesis floundering in her hasty ascension wake.

She surfaced gasping for air, knowing another second without oxygen could have been the end. As it was, she was disoriented and wondering if she was suffering from the bends. Her head felt as if it were floating off her shoulders, as she lifted her mask off her beet-red face and climbed up the boat's ladder. Weighed down by the heavy tank, she was too spent to lug herself up and over the side. But she found the strength to toss the much-sought-after box onto the deck.

Hanging on to the side of Manny's cabin cruiser, Dee was positive she was suffering from some sort of nitrogen narcosis, because when she tried to focus on Jewel and Xavier on the other side of the boat, she could have sworn she saw *Mark* jump into the water from an adjacent boat. The image was so ludicrously unbelievable, she began to laugh in a close-to-tears manner.

"SWEET!" Jewel cried, running over with the others to help hoist her into the cabin cruiser. "Oh my God! Sweet! Are you all right? Your face is cut! What happened?"

Dee giggled while they took off her tank and held her up on jelly legs. "I swear I saw Mark jump into the water; isn't that funny, Jewel?" she said in a slurred voice as if she were drunk.

Jewel frowned, placing Xavier's handkerchief on the ugly-looking cut on Dee's right cheek to stop the flow of blood. "He did. He thinks you're still down there. So much for his hydrophobia . . ."

Dee's head snapped away from Jewel's touch, not sure she was serious. "You're joking," she gasped. The idea of Mark jumping into *water*—of him even being in Saint Thomas—was too absurd, too ridiculous for her frazzled brain to comprehend. It was simply too much for her to handle at that particular moment. She swooned in Xavier's direction; but he was too busy bending to retrieve the metal box to catch her. Dee literally hit the deck.

She soon regained consciousness to find the police divers hauling Mark onto their speedboat. She immediately dived over the side of Manny's wreck, swam the short distance to the sleek official vehicle, and climbed on board. "Mark! Mark! Mark!" She knelt by him as his pale face coughed up water. "Mark Sweet! Why? . . . What? . . . When? . . . How'd you know I was here?"

He turned a dazed gaze on her with a shaky, but warm, smile that went right through her. "I thought . . . um . . . I thought you might have needed me. I was going to save you," he explained softly, grinning wryly.

Tears flowed down Dee's bloodstained cheeks. He had faced his greatest fear for her. "You can't even swim, you jag-off," she teased, moving aside as the police gave him a blanket.

"I forgot about that." He smiled. Then his face changed to one of great pain as he reached up and wiped away her bloody tears. "I was so scared, Duffy. I don't ever want to lose you. Please don't leave me. Please . . ." His already weak voice cracked with emotion. But Dee didn't want him to talk anymore. His actions said more than he could ever express with words. She leaned over and kissed him with all the love she had tried to deny.

They kissed so long and tenderly, the police had to clear their throats and turn away, then made themselves busy by heaving another soggy body on board. The newcomer was no stranger to the law officers. "Hello, Leo; why am I not surprised to see you da one causing trouble?"

Standing on the deck of Manny's cabin cruiser, Jewel witnessed the Sweet scene between Mark and Dee. She was happy for them.

Manny came to stand by her. " 'Many waters cannot quench love, neither can the floods drown it.' " Jewel looked at him. "Old Testament, Song of Solomon," he said.

Jewel couldn't help but think of Russell. "Solomon was a smart guy, Manny. A real smart guy."

Duke "Quiet" Crammer watched from a distance as the police pushed Leo—his best, and last, hope—into a squad car. Graves and Mr. Snow had already been taken off to jail due to that bothersome Mark Sweet and some surprisingly helpful citizens. If that idiot driver hadn't plowed onto a sidewalk in the heart of Charlotte Amalie, they might have gotten away. Some touristy types had become extra ornery after having a day's worth of shopping steamrolled by a runaway limo.

Crammer himself barely got away from the chaos, blending in with the disquieted rabble. Of course, the pop he delivered to Graves's head only added to his credibility. Nobody heard the "You fucking moron! You've messed up for the last time!" which accompanied the sock.

It was shaping up to be quite a day. First, there was a quick trip to the hospital for precautionary measures. While Dee's cheek was being bandaged, a sturdy, no-nonsense-looking policeman asked, "Ma'am, can I ask what happened down there?"

"I was simply scuba diving, Officer. Then that man, Leo, attacked me."

"And how did you know she was going to be attacked?" the officer asked Mark.

"Those guys you arrested—the ones who dragged me down here—said they sent Leo to take care of my wife."

The confused policeman turned back to Dee. "Leo said you found a huge diamond that was stolen from Washington a long time ago."

Dee looked at Jewel, Xavier, and Mark. There was a slight hesitation before they all burst out laughing in a forced manner. Dee dabbed at nonexistent tears of mirth. "Excuse me, Officer. I don't mean to laugh. But really! A diamond? I'm sure if there was any buried treasure left in the Caribbean, it's long been discovered."

The officer smiled. "Yes, I guess you're right. Leo's probably been at the ganja again." He started to leave, then turned back. "How long did you say you were visiting?"

"We're out of here this evening, Officer."

"I think that's just as well."

❖   ❖   ❖

"Oh, here, let me do it!" said Jewel, as the four gathered around a wicker and marble dinette table back at their cottage. She grabbed the screwdriver from Xavier's hand and whacked, poked, banged, and twisted the tiny lock on the rusty metal box.

"Wouldn't it be funny," said Mark quietly, "if there wasn't anything in there but a note that said 'Suckers!'" Three sets of annoyed eyes told him it wouldn't be the least bit humorous. "Hey," he said, backing up with his hands raised, "it was just a thought."

"You're not here to think, Mark," said Jewel, delivering a powerful blow to the lock, finally breaking it in two.

Jewel opened the box and, with quivering hands, extracted another box. This one was made of tanned leather and featured an insignia of some sort with what looked like a lion. She slowly opened this box to find another, smaller, heavy-duty safelike box. Jewel paused to look at Dee, who nodded encouragement. Finally, Jewel opened the smaller box's lid. It was lined in black velvet and contained a black velvet pouch. Her hands were shaking so violently, she had to pass the pouch to Dee.

Dee shook out a magnificent rock. A diamond among diamonds. The Star Diamond. "Dear God in heaven . . ." she breathed, placing the thick gem, which took up Dee's entire palm, back in the black velvet box.

They all stared at it in silence. Then came a terrible wheezing sound. All eyes turned to Jewel Averick, who apparently was having trouble breathing. "Oh, Jeez, not again," groaned Xavier. "Calm down, Jewely-girl; just calm down."

Jewel closed her eyes and took three deep, steadying breaths before daring to look at the Star again. "We did it, Sweet," she said in a choked voice.

"How much you think this puppy is worth?" asked Mark, picking it up and tossing it in the air like a baseball.

Jewel snatched it out of the air and hugged it to her. "Doesn't matter, we're going to keep it."

"Well, the way I figure, only one of you can keep it."

"Oh, right," said Jewel. "Well, I guess I could keep it at my house and you guys can come look at it anytime you want."

"Coming from you, that almost sounds fair," said Dee.

"Not to me, it doesn't!" said Xavier.

"Well, I guess we'll have to find an *extremely* discreet underground type to cut it up for us—surely, during this hunt, we've met a couple of people who fit that description. This way we *all* can get a piece. I just want the biggest," said Jewel.

"You guys are dreaming," said Mark with a smirk.

"So what? As long as no one wakes us up, we're all right," answered his wife.

"I still can't believe it." Dee snuggled deeper into her husband's arms as they lounged on the sofa in the spacious Redbeard Cottage.

"Yeah, that's some rock," he said, nuzzling her soft hair.

Dee pushed up on his chest in order to see his face. "I'm not talking about that. I'm talking about what you did." An involuntary shiver ran through her. "I can't even think about how you got here. When I picture those jag-offs hitting you like that, then dragging you onto the plane, I just get sick."

"Bastard didn't even let me pack my ditty bag."

Dee gave a little chuckle. "You took a big chance, Mark. What if they had shot you while you ran for the police?"

"It was a busy part of town. I doubt if even those clowns are that stupid. Besides, why would you give them the diamond if I was dead?"

Dee still felt the goose bumps. "Still, it was very brave."

"Brave? Ha! I'm nothing compared to you. I can't believe what you did today! And in Philly . . . and in New York. It takes wild craziness like this to find out who I'm married to. I love it! I love you." Mark gently touched the bandage on her face. "God,

Duffy, if anything had happened to you, I don't know what I would've done. I've been such an ass."

"I won't argue with that," she teased, planting a quick kiss on his mouth. "After all I've been through the last few weeks, you know what I'll remember the most?"

"What's that?"

"*You* jumping into the big blue sea! A man who won't even take a bath."

"I'm finding that hard to believe, too. But I swear, Duffy, all I could think of was you. That you needed me. I mean, I didn't drag up any old baggage about Mom's drowning. I *insisted* on going with the police in that boat. And when Jewel said you were down there, in trouble, I just jumped in. Can you believe that?"

Dee took his bottom lip in her mouth with loving nibbles. "My hero."

"I guess I've been wasting all that money."

"What money?"

Wearing a sheepish expression, Mark sat up, pushing Dee away from his warmth. "God, this is embarrassing . . ."

"What?"

Mark took a deep breath and grabbed his wife's hand. "For the last few months, I've been going to a shrink."

"What? For what?"

"Pete convinced me that I needed help to get over my phobia; and he recommended I seek out a psychiatrist."

"Pete knew?"

"Yeah, he's known from the very beginning, when I first joined the team; I went berserk on a fishing trip."

"Oh, I didn't know about that."

"That's because I didn't tell you, because it's all so damn humiliating. Anyway, I knew our marriage was on some pretty rocky ground and I wanted to prove to you I was serious about getting my act together. I wanted to do something special for you. I thought if I got over my phobia by going to a shrink, I could surprise you and take you on—well, a Caribbean vacation. I wanted to see your face when I took you and the kids to the beach and actually got my feet wet!"

"Why didn't you tell me?"

"I wanted it to be a surprise. Besides, I didn't want to get your hopes up in case the therapy didn't work. And up until this afternoon, it was a complete failure."

"Is your shrink a woman?"

He nodded with a penitent smile.

"She has dark hair and wears Obsession?"

"Yup."

"Oh, Mark!"

"She's been trying to get me in a pool. But of course, as soon as I'd see that water, I'd freak and she'd end up holding me to calm me down. But I swear, Duffy, that's it. There's been nothing else—*no one* else—with God as my witness."

"Then the nights you stayed late to get your 'knee worked on' were actually spent with a psychiatrist?" When he nodded, she punched his arm. "Do you know what you put me through?"

He gathered her in his arms and placed soft kisses along her neck and shoulders. "Who would have thought all it took was another person I loved to be in danger of drowning to reverse the problem? It's like on those TV sitcoms when a person bumps his head and gets amnesia; then they hit him again to get him back on the right track."

"Speaking of getting back on the right track," she giggled, before whispering Sweet-somethings in his ear.

"That's one way to keep me from lapsing into a coma." He laughed, rubbing the bump on his head, before quickly leading her to one of the cottage's bedrooms.

❖   ❖   ❖

"Are they still at it?" complained Jewel, handing Xavier a glass of iced tea. "If they keep it up, they'll be welcoming the fourth little Sweet."

"You sound jealous."

"Yeah, right." Jewel was sure of only one true feeling. Misery. They'd come to a successful conclusion to the adventure of a lifetime—of *a dozen* lifetimes—and she couldn't celebrate. Instead of getting tanked with her, Dee was in there making goo-goo eyes (and who knew what else) at her not long ago cursed husband. And although he had made an insincere offer to imitate the Sweets, Xavier was proving to be the worst kind of company. He just sat moodily in a chair, lost in his thoughts.

Dee and Mark finally emerged with sickeningly Sweet looks, before informing Jewel and Xavier that they were going to take a moonlight stroll along the beach.

Jewel sat down and sighed.

"What's the matter? You've found your diamond. Why aren't you delirious?" asked Xavier.

Jewel had asked herself the same question every minute since they returned from the hospital. The answer was always the same. Russell. After realizing he didn't love her, she had tried to kid herself into thinking she could stop caring about him. But that wasn't the case. She'd trade in every damn thing she owned, including the Star, if it meant another shot with Russell, another chance to prove herself.

Trying to soothe her bruised soul, Jewel took the Star out of its velvet home and walked onto the terrace. While the peaceful trade winds blew her hair off her shoulders, she tried to conjure up the feeling of contentedness she thought the trinket would bring. *Two-Mile was right. The diamond can't replace a loved one lost.* Nor would anything she owned.

Then her hair stood on the back of her neck, and not from any mystical powers of the Star, but from the distinctive sound she'd come to know so well—that of a gun being cocked. She froze. "Graves?" she whispered, not daring to turn around.

"Hand it over, Jewel."

Her heart jumped. She turned around very slowly. Xavier Lawrence was standing there with a gun pointed right at her. Jewel blinked rapidly, sure she was seeing things. She couldn't move. She couldn't respond in any way.

Keeping the gun level on her, he closed the distance between them and snatched the Star out of her petrified fingers. "Thanks," he said, before returning inside to grab his overnight bag, which evidently had been packed and waiting.

She somehow found the will to move inside the cottage, while he headed for the front door. "Xavier? Why?"

"Isn't it obvious?"

Sadly, she shook her head.

"This is my ticket, Jewely-girl. This is my ticket to get the respect I'm due. My father won't turn his nose down at his pathetic little accountant of a son. With money, Darlene will be all over me. Dare I say, I'll even look better to you with a little cash hanging out of my pockets. Maybe with this I'll be as good-looking and athletic and intelligent to you as your crummy husband."

"I thought we were friends."

"You don't even know the meaning of the word! You only see what others can do for you. Hell, are you forgetting you called me to bail you out *twice* in this little adventure? And let's not forget how I asked you to wait for me before you went to New York; but your greedy little heart just said, 'Fuck him . . . I'm going.' "

Jewel flinched. "I may not be the best kind of friend, but I wouldn't do what you're about to do. That's just plain low, Zavie. I wouldn't point a gun at you!"

"If it suited you, you sure as shit would. Remind yourself how this whole thing started. Did you, or did you not, sell something of Averick's behind his back? Your beloved husband?"

She opened her mouth to deny it, but knew he spoke the truth.

"Face it, Jewel; we're a lot more alike than you're willing to admit. I guess it turns out I'm just as greedy as you."

His words infuriated her. She charged at him and he raised the gun. "I swear to God, Jewely-girl, I'll shoot you. Don't make me prove it." In the next second, he was gone.

Yvonne Sager pointed to the large cottage on top of the hill. "There it is. Yes, that's the Seabright Cottage."

Russell ran ahead.

It had been a long day. There had been the initial fuss over whether Gibby should accompany his idol and parents on the journey. In the end, Pete had won out, saying, "The kid has proved his maturity. He deserves a chance to see this thing to an end."

Then there was Jacinta O'Hara, who had also wanted to go. But Russell had firmly sent her on her way, promising to give her a decent recommendation.

When they arrived on the island, finding Jewel and Dee wasn't as hard as they had feared. "All we have to do is locate the most luxurious hotel on the island," Russell said. He was right. There was an Averick registered at the Redbeard Cottages.

Russell's steps, as he jogged to the Seabright Cottage, were bouncy and jubilant, his face wore a mask of eager hope; his smile was broad. "Jewel," he whispered tenderly. Then his happy countenance turned murderous. "I'm going to kill you!"

A blinding white rage ripped through Russell as he watched Xavier Lawrence leave Jewel's cottage, after shoving an object in his jacket pocket.

Xavier, in turn, appeared shocked to see the brawny and obviously livid Russell Averick. "Oh, shit! I should have put bullets in this thing. Who am I kidding; I'm going to get my ass—" Russell slammed a powerful fist into his round face. Xavier went sprawling to the ground.

Ignoring Yvonne's plea to stop, Russell straddled Xavier's body and yanked him up by his collar, then he sent him down like a punching bag with another fierce, bone-crunching blow. Pete intervened. "Okay, okay, Russ, stop it! Stop! Right now!"

Russell pulled Xavier to his useless legs by the lapels of his lightweight cotton sports jacket. The Star fell to the ground. There was a collective gasping sound. "Tell me this is zirconium," Russell said, bending to pick up the fallen Star.

Xavier sneered. " 'Fraid not, Averick. That's the real thing. That's what your wife's been after. And I helped her get it. Did you come down here with some noble purpose? You think she was doing this for you? Ha! You're a bigger fool than I thought. Jewel is—"

Russell's lip-splitting slap sent Xavier back to the ground. "You stay the hell away from my wife."

Russell ran the rest of the way to the cottage.

Yvonne and Gibby stood by in wide-eyed silence, not knowing exactly what to do. Pete pulled Xavier to his feet and checked the inside pocket of his jacket, pulling out his return airline ticket. "Aha. Your flight leaves in an hour; you don't want to miss it, now do you, son?" Pete dragged Xavier all the way to the Redbeard's main entrance and threw him in a taxi-van. "Take him to the airport, and here's fifty bucks to make sure he gets on the plane."

"Russell!" Jewel's prayers had been answered.

She was running to throw her arms around him, when he stopped her by holding out the Star. "I could ram this right down your miserable throat."

"The Star! You got it back! That's wonderful!"

For half a second, Russell contemplated whether he should use his strong center-fielder arm and bean her with the rock right between her eyes. "I came all the way down here—and missed a game—for what? FOR WHAT?"

274

Jewel could see that Russell hadn't come in the same spirit as Mark Sweet and was at a dangerous breaking point; she decided to stand very, *very* still and not say a word.

"I let them convince me; hell, I convinced myself, that you really were trying to find Two-Mile McLemore to please me!" He stopped and tried to lower his voice a few decibels. "And what do I find? Huh? Xavier Lawrence coming out of your goddamn hotel room. And you know what he told me? He said you were after this friggin' rock! Is he right, Jewel? Is that what you were really hunting? IS IT?"

He waited for her to answer, but Jewel was struck dumb. She couldn't say anything. Her mind refused to formulate the necessary words to make him understand; because, she realized sadly, those words didn't exist. They had yet to be invented.

"Well," continued Russell in a much softer and almost tortured voice, "I'm not going to let you have your way this time, Jewel. *I'm* going to keep this diamond and do with it as I see fit. I may donate it to a poorhouse. Or, better yet, since I'm positive it's stolen, I may contact the feds and have them put your greedy, scheming butt in jail!"

Russell stormed out of the cottage with a ferocious slam of the door. The finality of the sound stirred Jewel into action.

Duke Crammer held his silencer-sporting gun on the Sagers with a perilously shaky hand. He'd already proved he meant business by shooting at Pete's foot when the manager tried to take the gun away. The trio was duly subdued.

Crammer looked up when he heard the sound of the cottage's front door slam shut. It was Russell Averick; and he was holding *his* diamond! The jewel he'd waited almost sixty years to get his hands on. Then, in the blink of an eye—and the snap of a brain—Crammer's feverishly decrepit mind transformed Russell's image into a young Robert McLemore in the late thirties.

"What's going on?" asked Russell.

"Just give me the Star, Two-Mile, and everything will be fine," Crammer ordered, as Russell approached carefully.

"Who are you?"

"I'm Duke Crammer, the man you stole that from back in '39. That wasn't very nice. You made me the joke of the syndicate. I could have gone to great heights, but because of you, I was stuck in D.C. doing piddle-shit, a go-between with no *real* status. Well, I'm here to take back what you took from me."

Perhaps because he was emotionally exhausted, Russell wasn't about to put up with any more crap, especially from a crazy old man who thought he was Two-Mile McLemore. "Come on, guys, we're outta here," he said casually, ignoring the gun, and unaware of Jewel standing behind him.

"GIMME THE STAR!" yelled Crammer, waving the gun.

Russell cocked a bored eyebrow. "Look, old man, I don't have time for this shi——"

Crammer fired.

"NO! RUSSELL!" Jewel screamed, moving to her left in an awkward motion and toppling her husband to the ground.

Pete slapped the gun away from Crammer and knocked the spindly man down. "Gibby! Go get help!" he ordered.

"Jewel? Russell? Are you all right?" Yvonne ran to help them to their feet.

"Yeah . . . um . . . I'm fine, Yvonne," answered a disoriented Russell, brushing off dirt and bits of bark.

As soon as Jewel stood, she lurched forward into his arms.

"Jewel?" Russell was unable to keep the concern out of his voice. There was something wrong with her eyes. "I think she's traumatized!"

Jewel knew she didn't have much time to talk; the pain was unbearable. She had to say something to him. She had to try to make him understand. "Russ," she gasped with a suddenly dry mouth, "it's not what you think. I love you. Please say you believe me, please . . ."

She sagged against him and he gripped her arms harder. His heart almost stopped as he felt something warm oozing over his left hand. "Oh God! Jewel!" He pulled his hand away to find it covered with blood. "Jewel?"

"I did it for you. Do you believe me?" she whispered almost inaudibly. But, to his heart, it was uttered at a deafening level.

"Yes! I do believe you! Sweetheart? . . . Jewel!"

She didn't hear him, she'd already succumbed to dark nothingness.

"Tell me again, Sweet."

Dee grinned down at Jewel, who was lying restlessly in her hospital bed after having a bullet removed from her arm.

"Come on, I've told you three times," said Dee. "Anyway, I've got to go soon. The doctor said you need your rest. You lost a lot of blood."

"Please," Jewel begged. "Russell really acted the fool?"

"Completely." Dee giggled. "But a fool obviously in love. It was quite the scene. He would have killed that scrawny old no-good Duke Crammer if Pete and Gibby hadn't stopped him. Russell was out of his mind; actually, it was kind of scary. Then, when we all got here to the hospital, he started crying. None of us knew what to do, except, of course, stay away from him. He was a wreck."

"Was it like a-few-tears crying? Or was it like heavy, dramatic sobs?"

"He was bawling. I mean, he was completely unglued."

When Jewel first opened her eyes after the operation, Russell had been there. His eyes were red and puffy. She could only manage a rocky smile and a whispered "Hi." He kissed her hand and smoothed her forehead with a tender touch, before instructing her to go back to sleep.

During the following twelve hours she saw a lot of him, but he wouldn't really talk about anything; he just kept telling her to rest and get better. So when Dee was allowed to spend some time with her, Jewel was anxious to chat. Dee told her Duke Crammer was finally behind bars and Jewel was considered the bravest of brave for throwing herself on top of Russell and taking a bullet meant for him. She also was considered a suspicious pain in the ass to the police, who wanted her to make a speedy recovery and vamoose.

Dee was just about to leave the hospital room when Jewel began giggling, throwing a hand over her face.

"What is it? What's so funny?"

"I was just thinking. I knew one of us was going to end up getting shot. It was inevitable; however, I had hoped it wouldn't be me."

Had Jewel made such a declaration three weeks ago, Dee would have rolled her eyes and called her an unflattering name under her breath. But since then she had come to know the real Jewel Averick. "I was thinking the same thing," she said, laughing. "I guess I got the better part of the deal this time." She paused and placed her hand on Jewel's. "Some friends we are, huh?"

Jewel's smile faded as if Dee had slapped her. "Is that what we are, Sweet? Friends?"

Dee frowned and gripped her hand harder. "Of course we're friends. How can you even ask? After what we've been through, I'd say we're best friends."

"Best friends . . ." Jewel said disbelievingly. She never thought she'd hear those words in reference to herself. "I've never really had any friends. I thought Xavier was my friend, and you see how that turned out. But a best friend . . . *me?*" She paused and then twisted her hand so their palms were pressed together in a sisterly grip. "Thanks for everything, Sweet. Most people wouldn't have hung in there with me."

"Thank you, Jewel Averick, for pulling me out of my cocoon and giving me back my life."

Jewel was silent for several seconds. Finally she took a deep breath. "Best friends share secrets, right?"

"Absolutely."

"Okay, here's one for the ages. You know how I fell on Russell and saved him from Crammer's bullet . . ."

"An unparalleled act of heroism, Mrs. Averick. I still can't believe it."

"Well, I tripped."

Dee's mouth fell open. "Get out of here!"

"It's true. Can you believe that? Don't get me wrong. Honest to God, my first reaction was to push him out of the way. But my feet got caught up on one of those stupid stepping-stones and I fell right on top of him. I swear, Sweet, I don't think I could have generated enough strength to do it any other way."

Dee started to chuckle softly and then burst into sidesplitting laughter. Jewel joined in. "And you said white people were goofy," gasped Dee.

"Well, sounds like somebody's recovering nicely" came a voice from the door. Jewel focused on her husband. He looked much better, much more composed. Still giggling, Dee kissed Russell on the cheek and departed.

"Hi, there," said Jewel, feeling inexplicably shy. She raised her slinged arm slightly. "Some mess, huh?"

Russell sat in the chair Dee had just vacated and reached out to bring Jewel's good hand up to his lips. "If you ever get in the way of a bullet aimed at me again, I swear I'll kill you."

"You'd do the same for me, right?" She actually held her breath as she waited for his response.

"You know the answer to that."

"No, I don't; I want to hear it."

"Yes, I'd take a bullet for you. I'd throw myself in front of a speeding train for you. I'd jump off a cliff for you. Why, I'd even go shopping with you for *ten* solid hours." He stopped to let the most wonderful smile spread across his face before leaning over to kiss her gently.

"Now, if that isn't love, I don't know what is, Russell Averick," she said, grabbing the back of his neck so he wouldn't be able to pull away.

His face grew serious again. "I do love you, Jewel. I've been an idiot. I'm so sorry."

Jewel brought his mouth down to hers. "And I love you," she whispered. "I'm the one who is sorry. I'm sorry for everything, Russ. For every stupid, insensitive thing I've done. But I was jealous of your career and afraid you'd find somebody else while you were away from me."

"We've been kind of dumb, haven't we?" he said. "I guess we have Two-Mile McLemore to thank for bringing us together."

"Yes, in a roundabout way, I guess he did."

"Oh, that reminds me. I have something for you from Two-Mile. Close your eyes." She laughed, hesitating before shutting her peepers. "Hold out your hand . . ."

Jewel opened her eyes when she felt him slip something cool and crinkly on her wrist. "RUSSELL!" It was the Star Diamond, in a crude, giant, aluminum-foil setting, which made it look like the world's largest ring. "You kept it?"

"Shhhh . . . your bad ways are beginning to rub off on me," he said before reclaiming her lips.

"Xavier will tell, you know. We'll probably have to give it up."

Russell pulled away. "Do you care?"

"Couldn't care less . . . I have you."

"They're beautiful," gasped Jewel as Mark, Dee, and the Sager clan brought in an unwieldy arrangement of colorful tropical plants. "You guys didn't have to do that."

"We didn't," said Dee, handing Jewel a sealed envelope. Pulling out the card, she read:

> *Congratulations, Jewel Averick and Dee Sweet, you two*
> *   make quite a pair!*

You found Crammer's Star Diamond, you beat him fair
    and square.
You've made friends in Harry, Manny, Harv Fairfeather,
    and dear Clare.
Two-Mile had fun and hope you did, too, until next time . . .
    if you dare . . .

                                                    T.M.M.

"SWEET! OH MY GOD!" cried Jewel, waving the note. A piercing
pain shot through her right side. "Ow!"

"Jesus, Jewel, take it easy," Russell ordered, gently pushing
her back down.

"What is it?" asked Dee, taking the note from her. After quickly
scanning its contents, Dee ran out of the room.

"What's this all about?" asked Pete. The Sagers took turns
reading the note, because Jewel's heart was beating so fast in her
throat, she couldn't speak.

"Dad! Don't you get it?!" said Gibby. "Two-Mile McLemore
must have written this!"

"I don't think so, son . . ."

Dee burst into the room. "I SAW HIM! I KNEW IT! I HAD A FEEL-
ING HE WAS INVOLVED! HE WAS RIGHT HERE, IN THE HOSPITAL, BUT
WHEN HE SAW ME COMING TOWARD HIM, HE RAN INTO A CLOSING
ELEVATOR!"

"WHO?!" asked Jewel.

"That man! Jewel, don't you remember? The man at the
church; the one I thought I'd seen before . . . in Baltimore . . . in
Pittsburgh . . ."

Jewel's heart sank. Dee was talking about the big caramel-
colored man and not some eighty-five-year-old Negro Leagues
star. Still, it was something. "Go after him! Now! All of you!
Catch him! Quick! . . . Why are you all still standing here staring
at me? Catch that man! . . . PLEASE!"

As her compatriots ran out of the room, Jewel realized that

only she and Dee could identify the man. She ripped off her IV and tumbled out of bed. She struggled to her feet, awkwardly hopped into her jeans, and threw her good arm in the Diamonds jacket Russell had left on the end of her bed. *Shoes? Shoes? Where are my shoes?* Once she had her untied plaid Keds on her feet, she was almost good to go. She scurried around to the nightstand, pulling out her purse and the Star Diamond. She dropped the latter into the purse and was ready to roll.

Jewel ignored the stabbing pain and rushed for the exit, disregarding the nurses' calls for her to get back in her bed. Not far from the hospital she saw the entire crew surrounding the man, who was brushing dirt and grass off his arms and legs. He seemed to be chatting pleasantly.

Yvonne was the first to spot her approaching. "Jewel!"

Russell ran up to hold on to her good arm. "Jewel, what the devil are you doing out here?" To her relief, he began to lead her to the circle of friends, explaining how young Gibby had tackled the man on a dead run.

"So, who is he?" she asked.

Russell turned gleaming eyes on her. "You're not going to believe this, but he says he's Two-Mile McLemore's grandson. His name is Jeffrey McLemore and he's apparently the one who set up this whole thing. He said he planted all those clues. He was following a game his grandfather had concocted years ago for Duke Crammer."

"At last we meet, Jewel Averick, it's a pleasure," said the handsome young man, bending to bring her hand to his lips. His brown eyes crinkled with lines of good humor and laughter.

Jewel smiled brightly at him. "So you're the one responsible for all of this, huh," she said, moving her sling in his direction. He looked chagrined.

"My sincere apologies. I never meant for anybody to get hurt."

"You hid the notes?"

"I could barely keep one step ahead of you."

"The paper seemed old."

"A simple antiquing process."

"And Harry, Harv, Clare—they were all in on it? The clues weren't left in the fifties?"

"Wonderful actors, aren't they?"

Something about the uncomfortable shuffling of his feet told Jewel he was in a hurry to be on his way. *What are you hiding, son?*

"Ladies and gentlemen, it's been delightful . . ." he began.

"Two-Mile was quite a character," Jewel said.

"Yes he was, Jewel. I wish you could have met him."

"We all would love to meet him, Jeffrey. But"—she sighed— "Manny Kimbro told us he died several years ago."

"Yes, that's true and we miss him very much."

Jewel narrowed her eyes. "I tell you what, Mr. Jeffrey McLemore, you can either take us to your grandfather right this minute, or I'll go to the feds with the Star and tell them exactly where and how I found it—"

Everyone gasped.

"Now, there's no need to do that, Jewel," began Jeffrey.

"I know, because you're going to take us to meet the infamous Thomas 'Two-Mile' McLemore. You see, Manny said your grandfather died three weeks ago. Now, I ask you, how could two seemingly smart men come up with such disparate answers? There's only one explanation. He didn't die. He's still living. And, I swear to God, if you don't take us to see him, whatever time he does have left on earth will be spent in a state penitentiary."

"I didn't think I could get away with it, Mrs. Averick. You're much too clever," said the man, who was seated on the sprawling porch of an impressive two-story white stucco building with cast-iron grillwork adorning the upstairs balconies.

At last, I'm face-to-face with Two-Mile McLemore, thought Jewel. She took in his smooth dark brown skin, his sharply chiseled face, and his incredibly fit body. Although he had to be in his early eighties, Two-Mile McLemore looked as if he'd have trouble getting any kind of a senior citizen discount. The only thing old about him was his ancient D.C. Diamonds baseball cap sitting skewed on his head. He still towered over six feet, with huge shoulders, strong upper arms, and such a flat stomach that Jewel could hear Russell and Pete sucking in their guts. It wasn't until he walked a few steps to shake their hands that Jewel noticed a glitch in his perfection. He walked with a slight limp.

Two-Mile kissed Jewel's extended hand and repeated the gesture with Dee. "Mrs. Sweet, I heard about your little adventure under the sea. You are a remarkable woman."

Dee blushed and wiped a nonchalant hand at the new scar of courage on her cheek.

The living legend proceeded to greet everyone with such glowing compliments that each was left grinning foolishly. Even Gibby, who got a pat on the back for his parking-garage heroics.

It was Jewel who finally found her voice. "Why?"

Two-Mile invited them to sit. "As you know, Mrs. Averick—"

"Please, call me Jewel."

"Well, Jewel . . . I think you've heard the story of how I came to be here and how I came to possess the Star Diamond. But now my days are numbered. I simply thought, since the Star was only a painful reminder of my brother Robert, I'd give it back to Duke Crammer. Or, at least, I'd give him an opportunity to get it back. I decided to send him on a little scavenger hunt to reclaim it. I just wanted to have a little fun with him. I had Jeffrey travel to Washington and donate my glove to the auction. He called Crammer anonymously and said the first clue to recovering the diamond was inside. Only, Russell surprised us and bought my glove instead."

Russell beamed with pride.

"When Harry Burrell called and said you two had come for the second clue, I knew something had gone wrong; but I also knew this was going to be a much better game than I had first anticipated. And I thank you ladies for that," he said, bowing at the waist. "Jeffrey kept me posted on the status of the two teams. And, I must say, ladies, from the very beginning, it looked like Team Crammer didn't have a chance."

"Well, I don't mind telling you, Mr. McLemore—"

"Two-Mile."

"I don't mind telling you, Two-Mile, things got hairy at times."

"But you weren't going to quit, were you?"

Jewel and Dee smiled at each other. "No," they said, laughing.

Two-Mile turned to Pete. "I like the Diamonds' chances to make the playoffs this year, Pete."

Pete straightened. "You think?"

"Sure I do. With players like Russell Averick and Mark Sweet here, poised to have career years, you can't lose. You're going to have to find a way to beat New York, however. Have you ever considered pitching Haversham on three days' rest?"

The men began a lively conversation of baseball strategy, with Gibby being the most eager contributor.

"So tell me, Two-Mile," said a bubbling Gibby, "could you really hit a baseball out of a ballpark?"

"Absolutely, son. My only regret is that I didn't stay around long enough to prove it."

"Is there really a home movie or film that shows you hitting?" asked Jewel.

"Not that I know of. But I still have proof. Why don't you all come around back; there's someone I want you to meet."

Russell put his arm around Jewel. "How do you feel, sweetheart? Are you okay?"

She rose on her tiptoes to plant a quick kiss on her husband's cheek. "I've never felt better."

Two-Mile had a regulation-size baseball diamond, complete with a few sideline bleachers, in his backyard. A dozen or so youngsters were hitting, running, pitching, and sliding around the field. "Robby!" called Two-Mile. "Come on over, son."

A strapping lad about Gibby's age trotted over with a giant black bat. "Yeah, Gramps?" he said, smiling politely at the visitors.

"Why don't you take a few swings for our guests."

"But you said you didn't want me losing any more balls . . ."

"Never mind that, these are special guests."

"Okay," said Robby McLemore, trotting off to the plate and calling for Jeffrey to pitch to him. Jeffrey jogged to the mound and stood next to a bucket of baseballs, while the other children sat down in the field.

"I don't mean any harm, Two-Mile," said Pete, "but you're not developing the best fielders down here, are you?"

Two-Mile just nodded toward the diamond. "Watch . . ."

Jeffrey wound up and threw a pitch way wide of the plate. The second pitch was right on target. Robby delivered a fierce blow. Not many present will ever forget the sound of the kid's bat hitting that helpless ball. Nor will they forget the sight of the ball traveling up, up, up—and away, away, away. They had no idea where it landed. Jewel's guess was about "two miles" from home plate. They wouldn't have believed their eyes if the kid hadn't sent pitched ball after pitched ball into the lush greenery far behind the field.

"Sweet Jesus," gasped Pete.

"He's going to need an agent. I could be his agent, couldn't I, Dad?" said Gibby.

"I'm glad I'll be retired when this kid's in his prime," said Mark.

"I'm going to get some batting tips." Russell laughed, leading the charge out to Robby as he sent the last ball to Saint Croix.

Yvonne turned back to Jewel and Dee. "Aren't you girls coming to meet the next Two-Mile McLemore?"

"In a minute, Yvonne," said Dee, who turned to Jewel. "How's your arm?"

"Sweet, at this moment, I'm feeling no pain. None whatsoever."

"I know what you mean. It's been some wild ride, hasn't it?"

Jewel watched as Russell caught her eye and blew her a kiss from home plate. "It's been a great ride, Sweet." Jewel Elizabeth Howard Averick threw a kiss back to her husband and patted her purse, feeling the Star through the soft leather. "A great ride."